Peter Watt has spent time as a soldier, articled clerk, prawn trawler deckhand, builder's labourer, pipe layer, real estate salesman, private investigator, police sergeant, and adviser to the Royal Papua New Guinea Constabulary. He has lived and worked with Aborigines, Islanders, Vietnamese and Papua New Guineans.

Good friends, fine food, fishing and the vast open spaces of outback Queensland are his main interests in life. *Shadow of the Osprey* is his second novel. The final novel in this historical trilogy, *Flight of the Eagle*, will be available in November 2001.

Peter Watt can be contacted at www.peterwatt.com

Also by Peter Watt

Cry of the Curlew

SHADOW
OF THE
OSPREY

PETER WATT

PAN
Pan Macmillan Australia

This work is purely fictional, although certain historical characters are mentioned. Otherwise, no reference is made to any persons living or dead. There are scenes in this work that may be considered disturbing and certain characters' language and attitudes may be considered racist. Any language or attitudes that may be considered racist are intended to be seen in the historical context of the novel and in no way reflect the personal views of the author.

First published 2000 in Macmillan by Pan Macmillan Australia Pty Limited
This Pan edition published 2001 by Pan Macmillan Australia Pty Limited
St Martins Tower, 31 Market Street, Sydney

Copyright © Peter Watt 2000

National Library of Australia
cataloguing-in-publication data:

Watt, Peter, 1949– .
Shadow of the osprey.

ISBN 0 330 36277 1.

1. Frontier and pioneer life – Australia – Queensland – Fiction.
2. Australia – History – 1851–1891 – Fiction.
3. Historical fiction. I. Title.

A823.3

Typeset in 11.5/13 pt Bembo by Post Pre-press Group, Brisbane
Printed in Australia by McPherson's Printing Group

For my uncle John Payne.

In war – a true hero of the sea.
In peace – always there for me.

ACKNOWLEDGEMENTS

The fictional Duffy and Macintosh families would not have existed except for the unstinting faith many people had in me. The size of the project appeared daunting at times but Duckie's daughters were there to encourage me. These remarkable women are my mother Leni Watt and my aunts Marjorie Leigh and Joan Payne.

Support also came from my sister Kerry and brother-in-law Tyrone McKee whilst I was struggling to get published.

Phil Murphy and his company Recognition Australasia in Cairns continued to supply me with invaluable facts on military and historical matters. Thanks mate!

In Sydney, my old *wantok* Robert Bozek from my days policing in Papua New Guinea has proved a wonderful support.

A special thank you to Gerry Bowen and Renata

from Tugun who, over the years, saw the potential of the project and backed it with their zeal.

My old mates from northern Queensland, Len Evans and Brian Simpson, have since married and settled down and I welcome to my circle of friends their respective spouses Shirley and Betty.

My old workmates from my days labouring on building sites in Cairns and Port Douglas whilst I worked on the novels always took it for granted that I would be published. Thanks for your faith Wayne Coleman, Benny Waters, Frank McCosky and Clive Whitton.

I would like to single out Rob and Beth Turner from Brisbane whose trust in me extends beyond friendship. And a special thank you to Mike and Patsy Cove who provided sound advice and encouragement at the birth of the trilogy.

At a professional level thanks go to my agent Tony Williams and his wonderful staff Ingrid, Sonja, Geoffrey and Helen for their years of support when things looked less than promising. Thanks also to Brian Cook who appraised the project and recognised its potential.

If people enjoy the books much credit must go to my wonderful publisher at Pan Macmillan Cate Paterson, editor Elspeth Menzies and Anna McFarlane. But the thanks do not stop with editors. A big thank you is extended to publicist Jane Novak who has looked after me from the very beginning of the project's release. My thanks to all at Pan Macmillan for their unstinting faith in me. And thank you also to Rea Francis from R.F. Media.

A special thank you to the great master of this genre Wilbur Smith for his kind words early in my time as a writer. To me he will always be the greatest storyteller of the twentieth century.

Finally a special thank you to Naomi Howard-Smith who has brought romance to my life.

Colony of Queensland
1874

Torres Strait
Islands
Somerset

CAPE
YORK

Princess
Charlotte
Bay

Gulf
of
Carpentaria

Normanby River

Cooktown

Palmer River
Goldfields

Endeavour River

Hell's Gate

Coral Sea

Burketown

BURKESLAND

Townsville

Port Denison

Queensland

Fitzroy River

Rockhampton

CHANNEL
COUNTRY

GLEN VIEW

Tambo

Brisbane
River

Toowoomba

Brisbane
Town

Kilometres

0   100   200   300   400   500

The wallaroos grope through the tufts of grass,
And turn to their coverts for fear;
But he sits in the ashes and lets them pass
Where the Boomerang sleeps with the spear:
With the nullah, the sling, and the spear.

'The Last of His Tribe', Henry Kendall

PROLOGUE
1868

The island was a green-shelled turtle floating on a turquoise sea . . .

At least that was David Macintosh's first impression of the distant island. The twenty–six–year–old heir to a financial empire stood at the bow of the blackbirding barque *Osprey* and watched the jungle clad island rise and fall on the horizon. Of medium height and clean shaven, he had the bearing of one born to wealth. But he also had an unpretentiousness that made him likeable.

Against the wishes of his mother Lady Enid Macintosh, David had sailed on one of the family's ships to observe village life in the South Pacific. Although she had informed him of her premonition of a terrible risk to his life, should he sail on the *Osprey*, he had gently chided her for her foolish and unfounded fears. But his mother had succumbed to the superstitions concerning an ancient and obscure Aboriginal curse on the family. He still vividly remembered the anguish in her normally serene face as he waved from the deck before the *Osprey* pulled away from the wharf in Sydney.

Now, standing at the bow and gazing at the island, her fears were far from his thoughts as he anticipated the chance to observe at first hand a culture older than Western civilisation itself. The arrival of the Europeans to the Pacific islands had brought more change in the past half century than the preceding thousands of years. Replaced by the newcomer called Jesus the island gods were dying. The old gods now hid in the jungles where the true believers still visited them with traditional offerings to appease their anger at being usurped.

Captain Morrison Mort, the taciturn skipper of the *Osprey*, had informed David that the island had little contact with the blackbirders. However, the inhabitants had proved to be more warlike than most of the other islanders in the Pacific. They had in past years massacred the crews of visiting sandalwood ships. But that was back in the fifties, he had quickly reassured David, adding nevertheless that Chief Tiwi, the ruler of the island, was one of the old-style warriors who resisted the missionaries and their teachings. The ferocious old chief was usually avoided; other island chiefs were more readily compliant with the aims of the Kanaka trade.

The warlike disposition of the islanders did not deter David. He was eager to meet and observe the people whom he suspected might still adhere to many of the ancient customs. For the quiet and scholarly young man, the accumulation of knowledge was far more important than the amassing of further material wealth for his family's already vast financial interests.

As David made his way along the deck to Mort he thought he glimpsed the faintest of smiles on the dour captain's face. But it was not a smile reflected in the man's pale blue eyes. Only a bestial madness lived there.

Captain Mort was not a happy man. Although Jack Horton, his first mate, had the *Osprey* on a tack to place her inside the coral reef which sheltered the beach from the rolling power of the Pacific Ocean, Mort trusted no-one except himself to bring his barque safely to anchor. In his mid-thirties, the captain was a handsome man, whose brooding nature attracted the attention of many a young lady. He had a dark mystique that women found intriguing and there were rumours of a troubled, even savage, past that added to his allure.

He watched with a dangerous resentment as David approached him at the bow. His employer's presence was a thorn in his side. But a thorn can be removed, he mused. He suspected that even now young Macintosh was planning to remove him from command of the *Osprey* – probably after the barque returned to Brisbane when Macintosh had completed his mission.

Mort was suspicious of everything and everyone. He knew Lady Enid's son had strong views on the

Kanaka trade. David had often espoused the opinion that he would close down that side of the family business if there was anything that could cause a scandal to the Macintosh name.

The year 1868 was proving to be a bad one for Mort. There had been the trouble with the damned Presbyterian missionary John Macalister back in Sydney. The tough Scot had attempted to use his influence to bring him before a court on charges of murder. Only the Devil's luck had kept him from the gallows.

And recruiting figures had been down. Too much competition coming from other ships in the trade. With his problems compounded, he had decided to search for recruits in islands normally avoided by blackbirders. He knew the natives would be less knowledgeable of their rights and he had heard that Chief Tiwi would cooperate for what he carried in the hold of the *Osprey* – muskets, powder and shot. The chief was intending to take heads and women from neighbouring islands. He needed the white man's technology and the white man needed recruits – a sensible trade.

The closest thing to love Mort had ever experienced in his violent life was that for the ship he now commanded. He had vowed that no-one, not even the owners of the *Osprey*, would ever part him from his ship. He would rather scuttle her than lose her to another captain.

No matter, he brooded. The problem of Mister David Macintosh being aboard the *Osprey* was not one of great concern for much longer. The carefully

4

coded telegram, veiled in the language of cargoes and sea routes, transmitted by Granville White in Sydney via Brisbane, authorised him to act in any manner he saw fit to retain the *Osprey* under *his* command. He conceded that Macintosh's cousin, who was also his brother-in-law, was a man as ruthless as himself.

Just after midday the *Osprey* sailed into the waters Chief Tiwi controlled and sleek outrigger canoes were launched from the beach. The muscled warriors rowed enthusiastically to meet the Macintosh barque as she glided into the sheltered lagoon behind the coral reef.

Mort and his crew watched warily as the canoeists paddled towards them. Mort had weapons stacked ready for use: rifles, iron axes, belaying pins and gaff hooks. But when the dugout canoes with their sweeping outrigger pontoons neared, the captain could see the rowers were not armed.

The outriggers circled the *Osprey* which now furled her sails while her anchors rattled into the calm waters of the lagoon. Cheap trinkets were tossed from the ship. Some of the brown-skinned men dived into the clear and placid waters to retrieve them while a ribald banter was exchanged between the *Osprey* crew and those islanders still in the canoes.

Satisfied that the natives did not offer an immediate threat, Mort issued his orders.

'Prepare the landing party Mister Horton,' he said quietly to his first mate.

'Mister Macintosh comin' ashore with us skipper?' Horton sneered.

'I'm afraid he will insist. Not much we can do to stop him. Though I have warned him, on many occasions, about the treachery of these people,' Mort replied with just the faintest of smiles. 'He is, after all, one of our employers Mister Horton, and can go where he pleases.'

Horton nodded and spat into the clear waters below. He disliked the young man as much as he had disliked anyone. He had no time for toffs and it would serve the bastard right if the darkies turned nasty.

Although David had refused the offer of a sidearm Mort and his crew carried rifles. Mort also wore the infantry sword that was rarely far from him. But there was little chance of old Tiwi turning nasty. He would be on his best behaviour because he wanted the muskets they carried as barter more than a confrontation with the blackbirders.

The villagers on the beach hurried to inform Chief Tiwi of the arrival of the *Osprey*. At first the Chief thought hopefully that it might be the ketch returning for the troublesome little Scot missionary staying on his island with his equally troublesome wife. At least, if nothing much else, the missionary ketch that had originally brought John Macalister to his island had also brought gifts of blankets. Chief Tiwi only put up with the fiery Scot, who ranted against the custom of strangling widows and the drinking of the intoxicating traditional drink kava, for this reason. He had also decided against killing the Presbyterian missionary because he respected the man's courage. But that was not a binding decision and it was the only respect that kept a thin line between life and death.

As soon as the longboats grounded on the beach of eroded and bleached coral, the landing party was met by a mixed crowd of semi-naked men, women and children who milled around the crewmen chattering excitedly. Regardless of the reception, Mort had left Horton in charge of the *Osprey* with orders to keep the stern cannon trained on the village at all times. Loaded with grapeshot, the gun was well within range of the palm thatch and coconut log houses. Chief Tiwi was acutely aware of the gun covering his village as his canoe crews had brought him the intelligence and he was aware of the power of the cannon from previous encounters with similar ships.

Chief Tiwi was on the beach with his people to meet Mort and his crew. So too was the Reverend John Macalister, although David did not see the missionary until he pushed his way through the crowd of handsome bare-breasted men and women.

'Ye come off the *Osprey*, I see,' Macalister stormed belligerently as he thrust himself to the front of the islanders and planted himself squarely in front of Mort. 'Ye can turn around and go back to your murderin' ship Captain Mort. We don't need your cursed evil kind here.'

Although Mort towered over the missionary, Macalister appeared not to be the slightest bit intimidated by him. Behind him was the imposing figure of Chief Tiwi, an obese man, who carried himself with an air of regal authority.

'Sir, you know who I am,' Mort said in a frosty tone as he stood inches from the missionary. 'But I have not had the pleasure of making your acquaintance.'

'The name is John Macalister, Captain Mort. And I'm surprised you do not know of me by now,' he replied angrily, quivering like a terrier dog. 'You and I almost met in Sydney. But fate was on your side, it seems.'

'Macalister! Ah, yes. The man who wanted to see me hang,' Mort sneered. 'Well, Mister Macalister, I would advise you to step aside and let me carry on my business which is as lawful as yours of bashing these poor niggers with your Bible. I'm sure Chief Tiwi has more use for what I have than he has for your sanctimonious words.'

It was obvious that Macalister had no intention of stepping aside to let the blackbirder advance another step on shore. Macalister was all hackles and spoiling for a fight. If martyrdom should come, then it was God's Will.

David sensed that he should allow Mort to go about his business or the missionary might come off second best in a confrontation. He respected the little Scot's courage but was also pragmatic enough to know a clash with the missionary would be eventually reported to Sydney. He tactfully worked towards avoiding any further scandal surrounding the

Macintosh barque and inserted himself between Mort and the island missionary. 'Sir, I am David Macintosh, one of the proprietors of the *Osprey*,' he said offering his hand. 'Do you think you and I could talk?'

John Macalister was still bristling when he turned his attention to David and saw before him a young man whose expression was frank and honest. 'I would rather not shake your hand, Mister Macintosh. Although I feel, God knows, that you might be an honourable man despite your connections with this evil face,' he replied. 'But if I should talk to you, I would tell you to return with your captain to your cursed ship and sail away from here immediately.'

David dropped his hand.

With some amusement Chief Tiwi watched the confrontation between the white men. But he was more eager to find out what the blackbirding captain had for him and spoke in his own tongue to the missionary. Although David did not understand the language he realised that the exchange of words was heated and, for a chilling moment, he feared for the missionary's life. But Macalister seemed to agree with the island chief, albeit reluctantly, which defused the situation between them.

Ignoring the old chief glaring angrily at him, Macalister turned to David. 'It seems, Mister Macintosh, that you and I have the opportunity to talk. Chief Tiwi has told me to leave while he discusses recruits with your captain,' he said, almost being polite. 'Tiwi says he will listen and then send him on his way. But the old devil is lying, as always. I know he intends to barter with Captain Mort. I have warned him that not one man or woman will leave this island except over my dead body. He says that can also be arranged.'

'Mister Macalister, I give you my word as a Macintosh,' David replied respectfully, 'that your wishes will be honoured. I have no intention of allowing a situation that would disrupt the fine work you are doing here to bring God to these poor people. For myself, I am only interested in their customs and would be honoured if you would allow me to make certain observations of their way of life. I will instruct Captain Mort that he is to only trade for fresh foods that we might use on the *Osprey*.'

David called to Mort who was supervising the removal of a wooden case from one of the longboats. 'Captain Mort. I have given my word that we will trade for fresh supplies of food and nothing else,' David said to him. 'I think it is best that we then leave these people and recruit elsewhere.'

'Mister Macintosh, it has cost a lot of money and time to get here,' Mort scowled. 'And with due respect for your position, I feel I should point out that I am also under instructions from Mister White. We are engaged in a lawfully sanctioned activity and do not have to bend to the whims of these blasted missionaries. Especially one who is trying to get me hanged.'

'With due respect to my position captain,' David replied firmly, 'you will carry out my orders, or I will ensure that you are disciplined.'

Both men stood toe to toe.

Mort struggled to contain his anger and for a brief moment David regretted standing up to him. He was a long way from home he realised, with a sick feeling. The authority of his position relied on the legalities of civilisation. On a lonely Pacific island such legalities held little practical meaning. 'If that is what you feel we should do Mister Macintosh,' Mort said quietly, 'then I will talk to the Chief about fresh supplies.' He turned and strode back to supervising the removal of the other crates from the longboats.

David felt uneasy. Mort had capitulated too quickly.

Macalister frowned. He was becoming aware that all was not well between the young owner of the *Osprey* and her captain. 'Mister Macintosh, I think you and I could talk over a cup of tea and some fresh scones,' he said cheerfully.

David was surprised at the hospitable invitation. Such a custom was so far divorced from anything he expected here. 'My wife was just making a batch when your boats landed,' the missionary continued brightly. 'She is a fine Christian woman. And a God-sent cook.'

As the two men walked together along the beach Macalister pondered on David Macintosh, concluding that the young man spoke with obvious sincerity. It was a queer situation to almost like the owner of a notorious blackbirding ship.

Anne Macalister was just a little flustered meeting the handsome young man her husband had unexpectedly brought to their hut. As for David, the years in the islands clearly had taken a toll on Missus Macalister's health, and he could see that she had a touch of the fever although she was cheerful and uncomplaining. She was near forty he guessed, and wore a neck-to-ankle dress that must have been uncomfortable in the tropical heat. Even shorter than her husband, David guessed that her quiet courage was equal to that of the little missionary himself.

'I must apologise for the scones Mister Macintosh,' Anne Macalister said, brushing away a spot of flour from her cheek. 'But we are away from our usual home on Aneityum and I am not used to this oven.'

David was quick to heap elaborate praise on the scones which he found not only delicious but a pleasant change from the monotonous fare aboard the *Osprey*. Many times he had regretted not taking his mother's advice to take his own hampers. But he had somewhat foolishly insisted that he should experience life aboard one of the Macintosh ships in the same style as the crew.

John Macalister poured the steaming tea into mugs and led David outside the hut. They perched themselves on a driftwood log, smooth and white, like the ghost of a long-dead tree.

'You know your ships bring death to the islands Mister Macintosh,' Macalister said, without any polite preamble. 'I suspect your captain will be trading muskets for recruits right now. I only hope that you will intervene and forbid the trade.'

'I promised you I would not take any of your

islanders away from here,' David replied sincerely. 'And that promise stands.'

The missionary had to be wrong, David thought naively. Mort would never dare put himself in a position to give him the excuse to have him relieved of his command of the *Osprey*.

A cloud of doubt fell across the missionary's face. He did not doubt David's sincerity – only his lack of perceptiveness about his captain. 'Tiwi intends to attack the other islands for heads,' he said quietly as he stared out to sea. 'He has this pagan idea that they are needed to appease his gods. They are children of Satan, Tiwi and his people. Missus Macalister and I have the mission to bring them into the light.'

'You are doing fine work bringing God's word to these poor people. But do you not feel that you might be disrupting a way of life that seems to have survived all these years without Christianity?' David asked politely.

'Survived, yes. But it has been a playground for Satan. Sir, I could tell you things about these people that you could never repeat in genteel company lest it caused embarrassment to good Christian men and women. They . . . ' The sight of a young islander hurrying along the beach distracted Macalister. 'Ahh! I see Josiah has something on his mind.'

David could see that Josiah was obviously one of Macalister's converts, the young islander wore European clothes. 'Mister Macintosh. This is Josiah,' Macalister said, turning to David with a note of pride in his voice. 'He is from Aneityum and is helping us spread the word of God among Chief Tiwi's people.'

13

Josiah smiled shyly and held out his hand. His grip was strong and forthright. A fine-looking man with white flashing teeth when he smiled, David guessed him to be in his mid-twenties. 'Mister Macintosh has promised us his ship will be leaving without any recruits,' Macalister said to Josiah. 'Or giving Tiwi any muskets.'

Josiah ceased smiling. He bent forward to whisper something in the Scot's ear. Macalister paled and sprang to his feet spilling his tea. 'Mister Macintosh, I fear I was right,' Macalister growled. 'Captain Mort has just traded nine muskets. But Josiah is mystified as to what your captain has traded them for as it appears that it is not for recruits as I would have presumed. I think you and I should get back to speak to your captain immediately.'

David followed Macalister along the beach at a fast pace but came to an abrupt halt when he saw the *Osprey*'s longboats being rowed away from the shore. Mort was visible in the stern of the last one to leave and waved to him with a sardonic smile.

It was at that moment that David realised he would never see Mort again. For that matter, he knew he would never see his family or friends again. The realisation numbed him with paralysing terror for he also knew – with the clarity that comes with the certainty of one's imminent death – that his evil cousin Granville White had most probably conspired with Mort to have him killed. He knew that, with his death, Granville would be one step closer to controlling the vast Macintosh empire. He remembered bitterly how he had laughed off his mother's intuition that his life might be in jeopardy. He should have known that Mort was capable of murder. His mother obviously had.

David turned to shout a warning to Macalister who was striding with a grim expression towards Chief Tiwi. He watched in horror as Tiwi casually raised a newly acquired musket and aimed at the missionary. The flash from the igniting powder in the pan of the musket was followed by a bang. The heavy lead ball flew high and struck Macalister in the jaw. The bones in his face shattered on impact and the stricken missionary flung his hands up to his smashed face as Tiwi's howling warriors fell on the Scot with blood-curdling cries. Stone axes and war clubs rained down on the missionary. As if praying, he fell to his knees as sprays of blood splashed the white coral sands turning them a dark red.

Macalister tried to pray for the souls of his attackers without attempting to ward off the savage blows. But a stone club smashed the life from the courageous Presbyterian missionary and he pitched forward, dead.

The howling warriors turned their attention to Josiah who tried to flee but they were on him as he waded into the lagoon. He screamed for mercy, useless sounds drowned by the savage war cries of the warriors spurred on by the cries of encouragement from their women on the beach.

Paralysed, David glanced out to sea. He could see that the longboats had almost reached the *Osprey*. 'You murdering bastard Mort! You and my cousin will burn in hell,' he roared in rage. But it was unlikely that Mort heard his cry. All that drifted to him on a gentle sea breeze was a faint and pathetic sigh above the creaking of the oars in the rowlocks and the splash of oars in the water.

Mort smiled grimly having witnessed the slaughter at the edge of the beach. He knew it was only a matter of time before Macintosh would share the same fate as the damned missionary. That was if he was fortunate to die quickly, he mused. It was rumoured that Tiwi enjoyed torturing his victims. He would have a fine time with Macalister's wife! It was with some regret that Mort realised he would not personally witness the pain she would most certainly suffer.

Momentarily David stood alone and still untouched while only a short distance away the frenzied villagers hacked at Josiah's body in the shallows of the lagoon. David searched desperately for somewhere to run and hide. But he knew with an increasingly fatalistic despair that his options were limited. His only rational thought was that he should flee.

He turned to run and suddenly felt a searing pain deep in his leg. An arrow shaft protruded from his thigh. He cried out in agony as his leg gave way. He fell to his hands and knees and attempted to scramble back onto his feet. But the pain refused to allow his leg to cooperate and David was still on all fours when he felt the same pain explode all over his body.

The pain was like fire as the vicious barbs of arrows punctured his flesh. However, mercifully, one soon pierced his throat, severing the carotid artery. Blood spurted onto the white sand. Just before the darkness came, David Macintosh had a vague thought about an avenging angel, images of a white warrior holding a spear above his head as if poised to strike.

David Macintosh, sole remaining male heir to the Macintosh fortune, died within sight of the crew of the *Osprey*.

The first mate had anticipated his captain's order to haul up anchor in preparation for sailing out of the lagoon when he observed the bloody events unfolding ashore. Mort prepared to scramble aboard the *Osprey* from the longboat when Horton came alongside. 'What in 'ell 'appened?' he screamed down at Mort in the longboat.

'Niggers got it into their heads to attack us,' Mort yelled back. 'Let 'em have a taste of the stern gun Mister Horton.'

Horton pushed aside the native gunner and took command of the gun himself. He had little trouble aligning his target with the gun as the barque floated on the calm waters of the lagoon. With a savage smile he touched the fuse with a match and the stern gun belched death. The lead shot sighed through Tiwi's people on the beach and they crumpled like a crop falling before the scythe of a farmer.

Any surviving islanders fled the beach for the jungle while the wounded screamed in pain and shock as they attempted to crawl away.

Chief Tiwi was amongst those who fled. Enraged and confused he could not understand why the blackbirding captain had fired on him. Had they not

17

struck a deal to kill the white man that the Captain had nominated in exchange for the guns?

He ranted curses upon all white men and quivered with impotent rage as the *Osprey's* small cannon raked his canoes lining the beach. Turned to shredded scrap the outriggers were now useless to retaliate against the ship floating arrogantly in the lagoon, mocking them with its devastating power.

The bloody, mutilated bodies of David Macintosh and John Macalister lay on the beach amongst the wounded islanders who cried pitifully for help.

Then the cannon was loaded a third time for a parting shot. Horton swung the brass barrel onto the village itself. He did not expect to cause much damage as he was not using explosive shells. This shot was intended merely as a demonstration of the power of the blackbirding ship. The small cannon let loose a booming blast of lethal lead balls which tore through the woven fibre sides of the huts. Satisfied at the damage Mort gave his orders. The *Osprey* unfurled her wings and fled the placid waters of the lagoon for the open sea.

Chief Tiwi did not get a chance to vent his rage on the one remaining live white person on the island. Anne Macalister had been struck down in the final hail of lead shot.

From the *Osprey* Mort surveyed the island disappearing on the horizon whilst Horton standing beside him wondered at the events that had occurred so explosively fast. His captain's explanation had not coincided with what he had witnessed from the deck of the ship. But there was little chance that he was going to say anything about what he had seen; he now feared Mort more than ever. The man was by far the most ruthless killer he had ever met, even more dangerous than himself, Horton grudgingly admitted.

'It was a terrible thing Mister Horton,' Mort said casually as they both stared at the island, now a wounded turtle in that turquoise sea. 'The way those niggers fell on Mister Macintosh and that poor brave missionary. I only regret that we were unable to punish them all for the cowardly murder of Mister Macintosh. But at least we were able to teach them a lesson for their treachery,' he added sardonically.

'That we did Cap'n,' Horton answered dutifully. 'I 'ope that will be a consolation to Mister Macintosh's family when you make your report to Sydney.'

Mort turned to his first mate. He knew that he would not have to kill him. There was just enough trace of fear in Horton to keep his mouth shut. 'I am sure you saw everything happen the way I will report it, Mister Horton,' he said, fixing his first mate with his pale and terrible blue eyes.

'That I will, Cap'n,' Horton replied without hesitation. The eyes that stared at him had that madness Horton had come to know so well. 'That I will.'

Mort smiled as he thrust his hands behind his back and turned to observe his crew going about their assigned duties. The death of one of his employers meant nothing to him other than that he had followed orders from Mister Granville White. But he also brooded that there would be many more he would have to kill to ensure that he kept his beloved *Osprey*.

RETURN OF THE SPIRIT WARRIOR

1874

ONE

At that time between day and night, the time before the curlews called with mournful and haunting cries from the depths of the brigalow scrub, the warrior came armed with spears and hardwood fighting clubs known as nullahs.

The tall, broad-shouldered young Aboriginal's black skin bore the scars of his tribal initiation – and the wound of a white man's bullet. His long beard touched his chest and he was naked except for the belt of human hair encircling his waist. Two lethal nullahs were tucked behind the belt. Balanced in his left hand were three long and deadly spears whose tips bore the distinctive barbs that white settlers on the Queensland frontier had come to recognise over the years as the spears of Wallarie.

Wallarie strode purposefully across the plain

towards the setting sun which was hovering low over the brigalow scrub. For countless generations the Nerambura clan of the Darambal people had lived out their lives on these plains. But that was before the white man came with his herds of cattle and flocks of sheep to tear forever the fragile fabric of the world the Nerambura knew.

The red earth was warm beneath the warrior's feet even as the sun cooled in the shadow of the range of low and broken hills that rose from the drought-parched plains. Beyond the hills once sacred to his people the plains stretched to a limitless horizon that petered out to the great desert marking the desolate and lonely heart of the ancient continent.

To Wallarie, the last full-blooded Nerambura clansman of the Darambal people, the sun was a spirit that marked each day of his tenuous freedom from the men who hunted him across the length and breadth of the colony of Queensland – a spirit fire that had marked the land for the twelve dry seasons he had known since the slaughter of his people by the Native Mounted Police under the command of the devil he had come to know as Morrison Mort. Since then the former police lieutenant had moved on to command a blackbirding ship belonging to the Macintosh family. But his evil went with him and its shadow still fell on the place where his small troop of heavily armed Aboriginal police had attacked and slaughtered the peaceful Nerambura clan by the waterholes one early December morning in 1862. No-one was to be spared and only a tiny group managed to flee the killers. Even they were gone now. Only Wallarie lived to remember the horror of that day: the screams of the women and children as the bullets scythed them down; the sickening crunch of bone shattering under the impact of a police boot and the sobbing of the survivors begging for mercy – to no avail. A dispersal was the name the white police called the brutal massacre.

The Nerambura warrior was also known to his hunters as the myall who had once ridden with the notorious Irish bushranger Tom Duffy. But Tom Duffy was long dead to the bullets of the Native Mounted Police.

Wallarie was alone to face the wrath of the British legal system. He had eluded his hunters until the younger Mounted Police recruits began to doubt that he actually existed; he was just a figment of the older troopers' imaginations, used to colour their stories of past exploits. Nobody could remember what he looked like and the wild bush blackfellas never spoke his name for fear that his spirit would come for them in the night.

But Wallarie was flesh and blood and felt the weariness of the hunted man. Nothing really mattered in his lonely life anymore except returning to the sacred site that nestled in the folds of the ancient volcanic hill. For there lay the timeless spiritual heart of his people.

And the beating heart could be felt in the place where the giant slab of rock concealed the cavern that held the fossilised bones of the mystical giant creatures that once roamed the land: the carnivorous kangaroo and the tiny, ferocious marsupial lions.

Wallarie had seen the bones and marvelled at the strange creatures that had existed in the time of the Dreaming.

In that sacred place his people had recorded life and death, things witnessed and events unexplainable as far back as the original Dreaming. Even the coming of the white squatter and his shepherds had been faithfully recorded by the last of the Nerambura elders. That was before they too fell to the guns of the invaders and destroyers of the land.

Wallarie faltered in his stride as he drew close to the hill. He could see the evil spirit which fed on death watching him with its reptilian eyes. Instinctively he raised a long hardwood spear to defend himself. But the crow cawed a lazy defiance at the frightened warrior's gesture, and hopped arrogantly away from the rotting carcass of a cow, to flap its wings and rise with a shimmer of purple-black light into the darkening sky.

The warrior lowered his spear and muttered a frightened curse on the crow as it flew on and up towards the craggy hills starkly outlined by the setting sun. This was not a place to be when the night came. The vengeful spirits of the dead roamed the bush in the dark hours. Although Tom Duffy had tried to convince him the night was their ally, Wallarie still avoided places of the dead.

Even the European stockmen of the Glen View run avoided the hills. A primeval superstitious dread, inherent in long forgotten memories, caused them to give the eerie place a wide berth. Had not six years earlier the owner of Glen View been found in the same area with a spear through him? The same magical spear that had killed Sir Donald Macintosh, had flown from the body of his son, to kill the tough Scot squatter. The magical spear of the spirit warrior Wallarie, who roamed in the night, seeking revenge on all those who should foolishly dare threaten the sacred site of the Nerambura people – or so the Aboriginal stockmen whispered amongst themselves. And via the station kitchen the whispered stories had been carried to the European and Chinese workers at the homestead.

Had Wallarie known of his elevation to the mystical world of legend he might have smiled sheepishly with embarrassment. Tom's laughter would have boomed around the ancient, eroded hills they once rode through in far off Burkesland. 'You black bastard. No-one will remember Tom Duffy. But old women will frighten kids to bed with threats that Wallarie will come and get them if they don't do as they are told. Long after we're gone from this world people will remember you, not me.'

And so it would be.

Tom was gone now. Also Mondo, Tom's Nerambura wife, who had borne him three children, Wallarie mused as he continued striding towards the ancient hills misted in the filter of red dust that hung in the air.

He knew about Tom and Mondo's children. It was his duty. They had the last remnants of Nerambura blood in their veins and were with the white woman called Kate O'Keefe who had been Tom Duffy's sister.

And there was a strange link with the white woman that Wallarie knew was one with the spirit of the white warrior of the cave. He did not know what the link was. Maybe the spirits of the cave would tell him this night as he sat cross-legged before the fire he would make in the cave. He would sing the sacred songs of the elders that only he and the possums living in the trees above the cave remembered.

In the early evening Wallarie climbed the old path and found again the entrance to the cave. He paused before entering the cavernous structure and gazed across the plains bathed in the soft silver glow of the rising full moon. He gazed across a land now occupied by the employees of the Macintosh companies: black stockmen who worked for tobacco, flour, sugar and tea. They had replaced the old-time shepherds who had once guarded the ill-suited flocks of sheep. Chinese gardeners tended the vegetable gardens around the sprawling timber and corrugated-iron residence. The homestead set on the land marked the permanent occupation of Darambal lands by the former tough old Scot squatter's new manager.

Wallarie hesitated. Was it that the surrounding bush had fallen into an expectant hush? Was it that he had been too long away from his country and that the sacred place might have forgotten him? He chanted a song asking permission from the spirit guardians to approach, took a deep breath, and forced himself to enter the darkness of the sacred place.

Fear pounded his heart and his head throbbed.

He trod cautiously as the smell of wood ash from long-dead fires, and the desiccated droppings of the animals which continued to visit the cool sanctuary of the overhang on hot days, drifted to him on the evening breeze. He felt the crunch of bones underfoot and recoiled in terror. His nerves were at a breaking point and he expected an evil spirit to rise up to meet him. But nothing happened. Wallarie froze until he could feel his heart pounding once again reassuring him that he was still in the lonely world of the living. He continued into the cave until at last his foot touched the dry ends of old logs.

Wallarie slid his hand inside his belt and his fingers wrapped around the only white man's invention he carried with him – a small tin of wax matches. In the inky, brooding darkness he pulled apart shreds of a log and stacked them into a tiny pile. The match flared and the wood caught alight.

He averted his eyes from the shadows that danced tentatively on the walls. For he needed the full and secure comfort of light before he dared view the sacred icons of his people.

Flames danced as brazen spirits greedily devoured the spirit of the timber. The spreading glow illuminated the interior of the cave as he sat cross-legged facing the wall at the back of the cave.

There! There they were!

The ancient images came alive as the light of the fire touched them and joined the fire spirit's dance in a corroboree. Ancient and mystical figures interspersed with the outlines of stick-like warriors hunting the giant kangaroos. And, always, the mysterious white warrior, alone with his spear poised seeking a target. An ochre panorama depicting all that was important to his people – earth, rocks, waterholes and the trees of the sprawling brigalow plains of central Queensland.

Wallarie felt cold awe grip him. The fire rose to the ceiling, revealing the scattered bones of Kondola, the old warrior, who had last sung the sacred songs to the spirits. The possums said that he flew to the cave as the spirit of the wedge-tailed eagle to escape the white shepherds who had hunted him long ago.

Wallarie did not look upon the scattered bones as he was afraid Kondola's spirit might be vengeful to any intrusion on his sleep. Instead, he began to chant the songs of his people. He clacked his two hard-wood nullahs together. The sound echoed eerily and soon the warrior heard the voices whisper to him from the corners of the cave.

He was no longer afraid of the awesome power of the sacred place and only felt an unfathomable sadness for the loss of all the children's laughter, the raised voices of the old people bickering in the spreading shade of the bumbil tree with its broad canopy of cooling leaves, and the soft murmur at night of a contented people with full bellies sitting around the campfires gossiping, laughing and recounting exploits of the day. Campfires, the ashes of which were long scattered by the hooves of stock searching for the life-giving water of the nearby creek.

In the distance the mournful, wailing cry of curlews drifted to the cave. But Wallarie did not hear them. He was absorbed in a world beyond the Dreaming where he saw things he did not fully understand. Strange things that he instinctively knew were linked to the future memories of his people. He chanted until he could chant no more then curled up on the cave floor and fell into a deep sleep.

The fire spirits died when they had devoured the spirits of the burning logs and Wallarie slept in a troubled sleep of visions until the first rays of the morning touched the face of the hill.

The warrior rose from his sleep and picked up his spears. The whispers in the dark had told him to leave the sacred place and trek north once again. They told him that his lonely journey was not over and that he must go to the country of the fierce warriors of the rainforest and the eucalypt plains of the Palmer River. He had a sacred mission passed on to him by the ancestor spirits: to find the last remaining blood relative of his people and warn him of the future. Wallarie knew his name. He was the one called Peter Duffy, son of Tom and Mondo.

The spirits had also told him that the spirit of the white warrior was restless. He had been awakened and had set out in his quest for vengeance against the blue-eyed devil known as Morrison Mort, the man who had carried out the terrible dispersal on Wallarie's clan.

TWO

The graceful clipper rose and fell. Under a mass of square-rigged sail her ornate bow slipped between the scrub-covered headlands marking the gateway to one of the world's most magnificent natural harbours. Once past Sydney's rugged sandstone cliffs, the captain tacked to port putting his ship on course for the busy southern shore.

The Yankee clipper *Boston* had made good time on the Samoa to Sydney passage and her captain was a happy man as his ship glided past the tiny sand-fringed coves. There would be a bonus for him at the end of the journey to reward him for his competent seamanship.

The clipper only carried a handful of passengers on this run. One of them, standing alone on the portside, was taking in the beauty of the harbour. He was a man who had taken leave rather suddenly from

Samoa and had the unremarkable name of Horace Brown, a name that seemed to reflect an unremarkable physical appearance. Of medium height, portly and balding, with spectacles perched on the end of a podgy nose, Horace Brown was not a man who stood out in a crowd. He was known to his fellow travellers as a remittance man, one of the lost sons of Britain who wandered the Pacific colonies endeavouring to live off the allowance sent to them by their wealthy – or at least moderately wealthy – families from the old country. Families who could not afford to have their sons at home for one scandalous reason or another.

Horace was no longer a young man. Nearing fifty he had long lost his youth and, in his middle years, lost the family which had banished him from their fold for his sexual indiscretions with similarly inclined young men.

But the nondescript man had an interesting history. That is, if he would ever talk about his life, which he was not prone to do.

Two decades earlier Captain Horace Brown had worked on Lord Raglan's staff in the Crimea. Although he did not ride in the great charges against the Russian infantry, nor stand shoulder to shoulder with the Thin Red Line repulsing the Cossack cavalry, the British Army could ill afford to lose a man with the uncanny skills that he possessed. An expert in languages and the subtle workings of the human mind, Captain Brown had controlled one of the most efficient intelligence networks on the Russian Peninsula. Although he had not claimed for himself the glory of the dashing cavalry officer, nor the stalwart infantry commander, he was probably responsible for many victories. An essential of waging war is to know the intentions of your enemy and Horace had made a lifetime career out of knowing what his country's enemies were thinking.

Since leaving the army and joining the Foreign Office in the service of Her Majesty he found his cover as a remittance man made him inconspicuous to those he spied on. He was well placed in the Pacific and Far East as he spoke Mandarin Chinese, Hindi, German, French and Russian fluently and with just the merest trace of an English accent.

Had he not commenced his working life as a soldier and developed a taste for adventure and intrigue he would most probably have taken a position as a professor in one of Britain's more prestigious universities teaching exotic languages. Now his considerable analytic and linguistic skills were used to assess the intentions of the French, German and American interests that might be considered a threat to British strategic interests in the Pacific and Far Eastern regions.

But for the moment, his interest was focused solely on an American gun dealer Michael O'Flynn, who also travelled on the Yankee clipper. A tall and broad shouldered man, Horace guessed O'Flynn was in his early thirties. He could plainly see why women would be attracted to the man with the eye patch. He had an open, handsome, clean-shaven face tanned by years in the sun and only slightly marred by a once-broken nose. But none of his imperfections seemed to detract from the man's obvious charisma.

The English agent wiped away the thin crust of salt spray from his spectacles and peered myopically along the ship's rail to where the big American stood gazing at the tree-lined shore. The day was exceptionally warm, but such days were not unusual for Sydney as Horace knew from his previous visits. He fervently hoped that the afternoon would see a summer storm, rather than the weather remaining uncomfortably muggy, as trailing a man as athletic as Mister O'Flynn could be hard work. Once ashore the American gun dealer would have to be followed until Horace was satisfied he had identified who he was meeting in Sydney.

He knew enough about Mister O'Flynn to arouse more than usual interest in the man. He knew that he was a New York Irishman who had fought on the Union side in the recent Civil War and that as a captain he had lost his left eye to Confederate shrapnel at the battle of Five Forks south west of Petersburgh in '65. But his gallantry under fire had earned him a Congressional Medal of Honour. A recognition of courage which was the American equivalent of Britain's Victoria Cross.

Although the American had a glass eye he preferred to wear a black leather eye patch to cover his disability. And he had not let the disability affect his skill with firearms. After the war O'Flynn had followed the great migration West and it was rumoured that he had also served as a mercenary in Mexico for the rebels under Senor Juarez.

O'Flynn had first come to the attention of the British intelligence networks when he had travelled to South America where he had got himself into a bit of a bother in one of the many small wars raging. He was a mercenary soldier whose skills were in great demand and he was now working for German interests in the Pacific. But what vital German interest had caused the Irish-American to sail across the Pacific from Samoa to Sydney? That was the question Horace knew he must find the answer to.

He had gleaned from his contacts in Samoa that the man was now working for the Prussian aristocrat Baron Manfred von Fellmann. Horace knew that the Prussian was one of the best intelligence agents the aggressively expansionist German chancellor, Otto von Bismarck, had in the Pacific. Until now the Iron Chancellor's ambitions had all been in Europe where he had waged war against his Danish, Austrian and French neighbours. So what was Bismarck up to by sending one of his best agents to the Pacific?

Horace turned his attention once again to the Irish-American with the black leather eye patch. O'Flynn was also a skilled card player, as Horace had learned to his dismay during the passage from Samoa. He had not let himself dwell on his loss at cards as he was able to learn much about Mister O'Flynn from the way he played the game of poker. Horace had a firm belief that a poker player's style was very much like the man himself and Mister Michael O'Flynn was exceptionally good at the game.

Horace had noted too that both married and

single women, charmed by his good looks and old fashioned courtesy, had vied for the American's attention. But Michael O'Flynn had discreetly side-stepped any shipboard romances.

This avoidance had intrigued Horace. He had wondered if the man might have similar sexual preferences to himself. But as he got to know the American better he strongly doubted that O'Flynn was inclined towards the sensual pleasures of the male body. It was as if the man could not afford to draw attention to himself in any way that might cause scandal.

Michael gripped the portside rail of the clipper and gazed at the harbour scenery, searching eagerly for the familiar landmarks of the city that had once been his home. Then he had been a younger man who had aspired to the gentle life of an artist.

But so much had happened in his life since those days. Instead of holding a paintbrush he now carried a gun. Rather than developing his creative talents sketching with a pencil, he had honed his skills to kill and maim.

Under the assumed name of Michael Maloney he had fled from his home eleven years earlier on a Yankee merchant ship destined for New Zealand. Since then he had adopted many names as a means of protecting his real identity. And even now he must remain living under an assumed name. He knew he could never resume being the dreamer the world had once known as Michael Duffy.

In the decade that had passed he had experienced the ugliness and horror of battlefields; from the dark and dangerous forests of New Zealand to the bloody carnage of the American Civil War, he had roamed and learned the arts of war.

When the cannons fell silent on the American battlefields he had drifted along the newly opened Western frontier to eventually travel south to Mexico as a soldier of fortune. His formidable reputation grew, but only to thrust him deeper into the world of international intrigue and, often enough, sudden and violent death.

Now he was home – albeit by accident rather than design – and he knew that his home town would not have forgotten that he was wanted for murder. At least if they believed him still to be alive.

The man who stood at the rail of the *Boston* was no longer the idealistic young man who had fallen in love with the dark-haired beauty Fiona Macintosh. Now Michael Duffy was Michael O'Flynn, battle-scarred veteran, mercenary and gun dealer called on a mission in the pay of the German Kaiser.

Horace cupped a cigar in his hands. The thick smoke was immediately blown away on the harbour breeze as he puffed contentedly and gazed at the busy shipping activity on the harbour.

Little had changed since he had last visited Sydney eighteen months earlier. The impressive man-o'-wars from Britain floated regally at anchor as symbols of the Empire. Plumes of black smoke billowed from the tall stacks of the busy little ferries as they dodged expertly between coastal schooners, brigs and barques steering for the open sea beyond the imposing headlands.

Horace watched crowded ships pass the clipper, their decks filled with hopeful miners seeking their fortunes on the newly discovered 'River of Gold' in the Colony of Queensland. The ships carried men, families and even single women, all with a dream of finding their fortunes on the Palmer. For an unlucky few it would be the last voyage they would ever make. Death would come for them at the end of a spear, starvation, fever or simply sheer exhaustion.

Some would only get as far as the goldfield's seaport of Cooktown where they would be prey for the armies of whores, unscrupulous publicans and shysters. In some cases, they would be recruited reluctantly to that army of human predators. But for now they were rich in their dreams as they watched the graceful American clipper glide into Sydney Harbour.

Australia's northern frontier was not even a consideration in Horace's thoughts as he idly watched the crowded ships leaving for Cooktown. He was still wondering how the American gun dealer was linked with the German government and, more importantly, just what the Germans were up to in this part of the world.

Michael Duffy's turbulent thoughts on the other hand were on coming home. He didn't know what was waiting for him. One thing he did know however: there were old scores to be settled with those who had taken away his dreams.

'You will be meeting the Baroness von Fellmann at a reception she is having for some Froggy official tomorrow, Mister O'Flynn,' George Hilary said as he poured Michael another rum. The Sydney gun dealer had a red and bulbous nose which Michael saw as a sign of a man addicted to strong liquor. 'The reception is being held at her home mid-afternoon.'

'My German isn't that good Mister Hilary,' Michael said as he accepted the generous tot of rum.

They were sitting at a table covered in gun grease and pieces of assorted rifles at the back of Hilary's gun shop. George Hilary was a Sydney gunsmith who had made his name supplying Snider rifles to the men going north to Queensland's dangerous goldfields. The Snider rifle was quickly establishing a reputation not unlike the Winchester rifle's reputation on the American frontier.

'You won't have to worry about your grasp of German. The Baroness is English,' Hilary said, eyeing Michael in a calculating way. He sensed that the Irish-American was a man he would not like to get on the wrong side of. His very demeanour was that of a man who had lived with violence for so long that it manifested itself in the way he related to everything around him. There was a wariness in him that threatened to explode at the slightest hint of trouble and he moved with the grace of a hunting leopard, ever vigilant and yet apparently relaxed at the same time.

Michael sipped sparingly at the strong rum. He would not allow himself to become inebriated as he had not been told the reason for his unexpected passage to Sydney. All he knew was that he had been promised an extremely lucrative job utilising his proven skills as a leader of men and his knowledge of jungle warfare, and that the model '73 Winchesters, destined for Baron Manfred von Fellmann in Samoa, had been re-routed to Sydney. He was being paid generously to escort the rifles to their new destination and did so without asking questions. Intrigue had long become a natural part of his life. He knew he would be told in good time why he was in Sydney and what he was to do.

Hilary was of little help in making clear just what was expected of him. The conversation was like walking through a hedge maze. So far Michael was not lost but he felt it could be easy to take the wrong turn if he were not careful. The Prussian aristocrat behind this mission had a reputation in Michael's world not unlike his own.

'I hear you brought some '73 model Winchesters with you Mister O'Flynn,' Hilary said. As a gun dealer he was interested in the rifle that might prove to be competition to the single shot Sniders he sold. 'I've been told the ammunition for them is a centre fire cartridge.'

'Yes. They're in storage until I hear what I'm supposed to do next. And I'm out of pocket for customs duties on them,' Michael growled irritably.

'The Baroness will no doubt reimburse you for your expenses when you tell her of the costs you have incurred,' Hilary said, refilling his battered mug. 'I hear she acts for her husband in Sydney on all business matters.'

'So you say. Will I be told everything when I go to this reception tomorrow afternoon?' Michael queried.

'You will be told as much as you need to know,' the gun dealer smiled sardonically as he leaned back in his chair. 'Because that's the way they work. But I'm sure they will look after you. They have been pretty fair in their dealings with me.'

Hilary had taken a liking to the man who sat opposite him. Maybe it was the effects of the rum that brought on the feeling of bonhomie. Despite the aura of violence the Irishman carried like a cloak he sensed a gentler and even compassionate man.

As far as Michael was concerned his questions were answered. He downed the remainder of his rum and excused himself from the company of the gun dealer and stepped out into the busy street.

Horse-drawn omnibuses, drays and pedestrians crowded him on the narrow city streets. The unseasonal warmth of Sydney's autumn day was oppressive and Michael felt sweat dripping down his chest under the starched shirt. He longed for the relative coolness of the hotel where he was staying. It was not far from Circular Quay and Michael considered spending the rest of the afternoon in the public bar. He had little to do until the following day when he would go to the Baroness von Fellmann's house for the afternoon reception.

He had considered a ferry journey to Manly

Village but decided against the visit. There were too many painful memories on that side of the harbour that he did not want to exhume from his past. Letting his family in Sydney know he was alive was definitely out of the question. He was still a wanted man.

More important was the uncertainty of his present life. To reveal that he was alive would only subject his family to a second grieving should the mission go wrong. No, it was better that he remain a distant memory so they could get on with their lives.

Michael was not aware that he was being followed along George Street by a short, slightly overweight man who was sweating profusely as he attempted to keep a discreet distance.

Horace had scribbled down the name of the gunsmith in his leather-bound notebook. There were many names and dates in his notebook. To any inquisitive observer the notes made little sense, they were all in code.

Nearer the Quay a breeze from the harbour swept up the narrow street and ruffled the Irishman's thick curls. When Michael reached the hotel he decided to go to his room instead of spending the afternoon in the public bar. The day had been long and Michael needed time alone to think about past, present and future.

Horace hailed down a horse-drawn hansom cab and directed the driver to take him to the military barracks at Paddington. There was someone he needed to consult on the matter of Mister O'Flynn's visit to the Sydney gun dealer.

THREE

Kate O'Keefe uttered a short prayer of thanks to God for creating the ox. Her long, plaited stockwhip snaked over the backs of the bullocks and cracked like a rifle, shattering the droning silence of the midday bush.

Spattered with dried mud her normally elegant and beautiful features were masked. Her grey, expressive eyes were as staring as those of the miners who had passed on the track, stumbling back to Cooktown, fleeing the hell that had been the Palmer River goldfields in the monsoonal wet season of '73/'74.

At first glance she appeared just another teamster, albeit one slighter in build than many who plied the track from the port of Cooktown to the goldfields along the Palmer. But on closer inspection any observer could see she had the curves that were distinctly female under the rough working man's clothing she wore.

Her eighteen bullocks strained to haul the massive four-wheeled wagon with its eight ton load of supplies. Behind her, a second wagon rumbled and creaked under the whip of Ben Rosenblum.

Ben was no longer the gangly boy who had set out six years earlier to learn the trade of the teamster. The arduous work had turned him into a tall, broad-shouldered young man of twenty-one and his dark good looks had attracted more than one admiring glance from the ladies in the dance halls, saloons and hotels of Cooktown.

Ben was the son of a widow who had recognised that her son would inevitably fall into a life of crime on Sydney's tough back streets and in an act of desperation had written to her sister Judith asking her for her help. Judith had responded by suggesting a job with Kate O'Keefe's Eureka company, and, as a favour to her dear friends Solomon and Judith Cohen who had stood by her in tough times, Kate had offered the boy an apprenticeship with her tough old taciturn teamster Joe Hanrahan. Ben's initial few months under Joe's supervision had proved successful, albeit a bit rough, as Ben came to learn that work was a discipline that could be installed by a fast right fist.

But Joe was two years dead now and buried somewhere west of Townsville. He had been killed when a wagon being hauled up a mountain track had rolled back and crushed him against a tree. The young Jewish teamster had buried him and said the prayers for the dead over his grave. He had doubted that God was particularly concerned that he had not used the correct procedure as he used Christian prayers from Joe's battered Protestant Bible. When the solitary service was over Ben had single-handedly continued with the task of getting the wagon and its load through to the outstations of the squatters.

Ben now walked with the long stride of a man. Gone forever was the pale city boy from Sydney's slums who Kate had hired. Once a surly city boy, he had joined the ranks of the tough frontier bushmen of Australia's northern colony. Between the two – Irish woman and Jewish man – they had laboured to haul the badly needed supplies over one hundred and sixty miles of ground left by God for the Devil to create.

By night they had taken turns standing guard against the possibility of an attack from prowling tribesmen. Kate would stand armed with a hard-hitting Martini Henry rifle and her little pepper box pistol, while Ben always carried the big Colt revolver in a holster strapped at his hip. It was the same pistol Kate had presented him with years earlier on his first trip west with the taciturn and burly Irish teamster Joe Hanrahan.

The long haul from Cooktown to the Palmer River goldfields had taken its toll on both Kate and Ben. Fording rivers still swollen by the monsoonal rains by day, and double-banking the wagons on the steep sections of the track, with the never-ending work of off-loading, then reloading stores, had sapped their reserves of strength. Often they would stumble beside the wagons like sleepwalkers while the big, stolid bullocks strained at the yokes hauling the wagons just that one mile more and then, just one more mile after that.

When those times came, and Kate's body screamed out for rest, she had talked to the big Irishman who walked beside her. He told her of other tracks in other places, of the devils that tempted with the promise of despair. He would urge her to keep going despite her despair.

Ben would see Kate talking to herself as she stumbled along. At first he thought she had been driven mad by the rigours of the trek, but he soon came to learn that she was talking to her long dead father who, sometimes gently and at other times harshly, encouraged his daughter not to give in.

Sometimes Ben suspected that the spirit of Patrick Duffy was speaking through his daughter when Kate refused to allow them to rest for even one day on the tortuous trail down to the goldfields. Day in and gruelling day out, they pushed forward with only the sounds of the wagons and the lonely bush as their companions.

'You hear that?' Ben cried as he stumbled forward. 'That sound coming from the south?'

Kate could hear the sound. It was a distant murmur of massed voices and clinking of metal against rock as picks chipped at stone. It was the welcome sound that told them they had finally reached the Palmer.

~

The bedraggled teamsters struggled into the town of white canvas tents and bark shanties. They hugged and Ben danced a little jig. They had brought with them supplies worth literally their weight in gold while stranded behind them were the supply wagons of their competitors, pulled by the big cart horses. Unlike the stalwart bullocks, the horses were unable to cross the flooded creeks. The bullocks had again proven their versatility.

Being first to arrive on the fields meant asking your own price. The two wagons were rushed as the word spread up and down the banks of the Palmer and its eroded gullies that the precious goods had arrived.

The miners came, gaunt and hollow-eyed, to jostle for flour, sugar, tea, tinned fish and meat. But mostly the miners came to purchase the most precious of all goods – tobacco. And when they came to the wagons they brought their gold with them.

Within a few hours sixteen tons of goods had been sold to eager customers prepared to pay the inflated prices Kate demanded.

Had Patrick Duffy lived to see his daughter trading with the miners, he would have smiled. His daughter handled the impatient, enthusiastic miners with firmness and fairness.

This was not the first trip Kate had made with Ben to the Palmer. Before the Big Wet they had come in late '73 when they had used two smaller bullock drays to haul supplies up the track from Townsville. A trek through hell as they had crossed the drought-parched plains and passed the long lines of hopeful miners walking with bed-rolls, pushing wheelbarrows loaded with their possessions, or riding on horseback.

For a fee Kate would carry the personal possessions of the miners on the drays. Together they would trudge past red-eyed men and women stumbling in the opposite direction, lost souls returning defeated to the relative haven Townsville offered. For here, on the drought-ravished plains, the biblical hell of fire and brimstone was preached. Here was a place on earth where a man or woman could be punished for their sins before they died, as they faced the relentless torment of heat, dust and endless plains of tortured trees.

On this visit Kate was astute enough to realise that she would not need all the bullocks for the return trip to Cooktown where she had established a depot. With half the bullocks she could get back to Cooktown with what would be lighter wagons.

When they had reached the newly established goldfields in '73 the excess bullocks were sold to a goldfield butcher for meat for the hungry miners, the bullocks themselves thus realising a massive profit. But although she had long hardened herself against sentimentality, Kate knew she would not be eating any fresh beef until she returned to the town on the banks of the Endeavour River.

With the cash and gold gained from the sale of both goods and bullocks, Kate had returned to Cooktown to purchase two four-wheeled wagons and new teams of bullocks. She had been acutely aware of the need to leave the Palmer before the monsoonal wet season came to cut the lifelines to the goldfields. But many of the miners were not familiar with the vagaries of the tropical monsoons. They ignored the warnings of experienced bushmen and foolishly remained to stockpile ore. But the ore was soon washed away under the constant hammering of torrential rains. In many cases so too were the lives of those who remained.

Kate was fully aware that as soon as the flooded rivers receded there would be a steady supply of food and goods to the goldfields and the glut of supplies would cause prices to fall. But she did not care as she and Ben had been the first to arrive and the starving miners had paid generously.

Kate carefully packed the delicate gold weighing scales into a small wooden case. The traded gold was now in small chamois bags and stacked neatly on the tray of her wagon. She did not need the gold scales for the last transaction as the wife of a miner paid her in crumpled currency. Twenty pounds for a bag of flour. The same bag would have sold for three pounds in Cooktown. A few of the miners also had paid in coins even though Kate preferred gold as she could make an extra five shillings on each ounce on the Sydney gold market.

The gold and money had come so fast this time that she hadn't had a minute to count her takings. But she knew it was a small fortune to add to her rapidly growing store in the bank vaults of Cooktown and Townsville. She was a very wealthy woman by any standards.

As Kate stood counting the pound notes by the

wagon she had the appearance of a hard and seasoned teamster more at home with rifle and bull whip than a lady in the genteel parlours of polite society, sipping tea from fine china. When she had finished, she folded the pound notes and turned to Ben. He was perched on the edge of the wagon with clay pipe in the corner of his mouth. His long legs dangled over the side while he cradled Kate's rifle across his knees. He was a formidable sight, armed with his Colt strapped at his hip and on the inside of his boot a long bowie knife. Like most of the frontiersmen he had a dark bushy beard as a sign of manhood, and while he sat guarding the gold even the most daring of would-be thieves steered clear of the wagon.

'Ben, sit on the takings until I get back,' Kate said as she placed the notes in a tin box kept for paper currency. 'I won't be gone long.'

Kate found some privacy a short distance from the miners' camp. When she had finished answering her call of nature she made her way back through the haphazardly arranged rows of tents and shanties. She noticed that there were few dogs in the camp to bark and yap at her heels. Most had been killed and eaten during the Wet by their owners.

As she pondered on the subtle changes in the camp she noticed a young girl dogging her steps. The girl gripped the hand of a hollow-eyed boy and attempted not to appear obtrusive. Kate had first noticed the two hovering around the wagon when she had sold the supplies to the miners and remembered how she had been struck by the pathetic sight.

Her heart had gone out to the young woman and the child. But she had quickly steeled herself against feelings of pity, they were just another two of many who had become the flotsam on the sea the devastating Wet had left in its wake.

The pair continued to follow. Kate pretended not to notice them until she was near the wagon, then she halted and turned to the girl who she could see was painfully thin. Her long, blonde tresses were greasy and matted. She wore a ragged, filthy dress but under other circumstances she would have looked pretty . . . And she had a strangely poignant expression with an intelligent look in her darkly shadowed eyes, and a very large strawberry birthmark that covered the left side of her gaunt face. Kate guessed that the young woman was about eighteen; at twenty-eight Kate felt old in comparison.

The boy, whose hand the girl held tightly, was a pitiful sight too. Kate guessed that he was about six years old. He was filthy and had a surly expression on his face as he glared at Kate through haunted eyes. Brother and sister Kate thought, as there was a distinct likeness between the two. 'Do you want to speak to me?' she asked.

'Yes . . . Missus O'Keefe. I . . . ' The girl was trembling and on the verge of tears, yet there the loneliness about her bridged the space between the two women. Kate could see herself mirrored in the girl who was somehow herself those many years before in Rockhampton when she had lived through fever and childbirth.

'Come with me to the wagons,' Kate said kindly.

'You both look as if you need something to eat.'

The young girl's eyes filled with tears of gratitude. Kate walked over to her and impulsively put her arms around the thin shoulders. The girl trembled under the touch and burst into deep and racking sobs. A woman's touch of compassion was not something she had ever known in her tormented life.

Kate guided her gently to the wagons as Ben watched curiously. 'Ben! Get a brew going and make up a stew. Enough for four,' Kate ordered. And he promptly obeyed.

Unlike many bushmen he did not think it unusual to take orders from a woman. Kate O'Keefe was not only his employer but also a woman who had long proved she was equal to any man he had met on the frontier. He was also just a little smitten with his employer who, when not on the track, was as beautiful as any woman he had ever seen, even more beautiful than the prettiest of Palmer Kate's painted ladies at the Cooktown brothels.

Palmer Kate ran a very different kind of business to Kate O'Keefe. She was a notorious madam and it was rumoured that she would meet the single women who sailed north seeking their fortunes at the jetty and offer them employment. The alternative to refusing her offer was to be thrown into the crocodile infested river.

Both Kates provided valuable service to the frontiersmen in their own ways.

Kate O'Keefe now sat the young woman on a stump of a tree now long gone for mining cradles, firewood and rough planks for the shanties. The boy squatted silently, watching Ben prepare the stew of tinned beef. He was like a dog waiting to eat scraps from the master's table. The stew of meat and onions tantalisingly wafted its aroma around the wagons arousing both hunger and suspicion in the boy who reminded Ben of some feral animal.

'You know who I am,' Kate said gently as the girl tried to wipe away tears from her face. 'But I don't know who you and the boy are.'

'Me name is Jennifer Harris. I came to the Palmer with me son,' she replied softly. 'I thought I could use the last of my money to find a fortune for Willie and me.'

Kate was confused. Who was Willie? Surely not the boy watching Ben. If he was, then the girl must have only been twelve or thirteen when she had given birth to him.

'Is that Willie?' Kate asked pointing to him. She saw a haunted look in the girl's eyes of things better not spoken about. Survival was a strong instinct and had the ability to overcome any rules of morality that men made. Kate knew without having to ask further how the young girl had traded for the meagre food that had kept her and her son alive. 'Where did you come from before the Palmer?' she asked softly.

'Willie and me come up from Brisbane. Before that we came up from Sydney with me dad. Me dad was a gardener. He got sick with the consumption. It killed him a few years back when we were in Brisbane. He left me and Willie some money, but it weren't enough and ran out. I used the last to come north. Willie and me come up together in December. That is when I first saw you. I thought you had a kind face. And when I saw you return . . .' She could not finish her story and began to sob again. Kate guessed she was remembering the horror of the past months. 'This place is worse than hell. The only way I could get food for Willie and meself was to . . . to . . .'

'You don't have to tell me,' Kate said, stroking her matted hair as if she were a child.

Her simple gesture was soothing and Jennifer cried until she could cry no more. Gone now were the grunting bodies of the men who had used her body for their relief. Gone were the men who in their lust had bitten her young flesh leaving the bruises as a stallion might leave on the neck of a mare. Now there was the empathy of a woman who seemed to understand her pain, a pain of having been brutally deprived of childhood by the perverted demands of the rich and powerful Mister Granville White.

The birth of Willie had come too early in her young life. In Kate's gentle touch she discovered a strange yet wonderful fleeting feeling of what it might have been to be a little girl safe from physical and spiritual pain.

'You want to travel with us back to Cooktown?' Kate asked gently. Jennifer nodded. 'It is not an easy trip. You would be expected to help pay your way with hard work,' she cautioned.

'I would take the place of your bullocks to get away from here Missus O'Keefe,' she replied with a bitter snort and glanced at her son. 'I would do almost anything.'

'And what do you plan to do when you get to Cooktown?' Kate asked. 'You do not appear to have any money.'

Jennifer sighed. Getting out of the Palmer would only put her and Willie in Cooktown. And from what she had heard of Cooktown's evil reputation it was on a par with the biblical towns of Sodom and Gomorrah. Hell had a seductive call. It had called firstly from the banks of the Palmer River and was now leading her deeper into its pits. The deepest section of the northern hell was Cooktown itself. The newcomers had laughed at how the brothels outnumbered the hotels – and there were over sixty hotels licensed in Cooktown!

'I don't know what I will do. I suppose anywhere has to be better than the Palmer.'

'Do you read and write?' Kate asked.

Jennifer looked at her with an expression of surprise. 'No, Missus O'Keefe. But I want Willie to learn one day,' she answered with a firmness that assured Kate the young woman would make it happen. 'All I'm good at is looking after young 'uns.'

'Then you have a job with me when we get back,' Kate said with a smile. 'If you wish to work for me, that is?' Jennifer opened her mouth to express her thanks but Kate cut her short. 'You might think the Palmer has more to offer when I tell you what I want to employ you for.' Jennifer reached out and gripped Kate's hands as Kate continued. 'I have a position for a nanny. But for a nanny who can look after three children. Two boys and one girl. It would also mean looking after four when we count Willie. Do you think that you could do that?'

'Yes, Missus O'Keefe. I would love to,' she replied without hesitation.

'You might not think the job is all that good when you meet them,' Kate smiled mysteriously. 'They are just a little bit wild. I've already had a couple of nannies give their notice. But I have a feeling that any woman who could survive on her own on the Palmer through the Wet might be just the person for the job.'

Ben soon had the stew ready while in the hot coals a blackened billy was full of steaming water ready for brewing tea. Although Jennifer was ravenous she had trouble keeping the food down. Her son had no such problem and volunteered to wipe the pot clean with a slice of damper bread.

While they were eating Ben stole glances at the girl. She was pretty, very pretty. And the birthmark did not detract from her beautiful oval-shaped face, pinched as it was with the privations she had suffered. He could also see that she was very self-conscious about the birthmark; she would try to let her long hair fall over her face to conceal it from the eyes of the curious.

As they relaxed by their campfire after the filling meal, they sipped on the hot tea sweetened with sugar, and listened to the sounds of the goldfields. From the depths of the night came the twanging sound of a jew's harp and somewhere a fiddle yowled out a tune. The voices of men and women joined in popular songs to celebrate full stomachs and another day alive. Laughter was becoming a more common sound on the goldfields as the terrible months of the Wet were rapidly forgotten by the miners. They looked optimistically to the promised golden days ahead. By the light of scattered fires, under the constellation of the Southern Cross, miners swapped stories, drank rum and smoked clay pipes. The clear night sky promised another day and with it the chance to resume the search for personal fortunes.

And it was by light of the campfire that Ben continued surreptitiously to glance with keen interest at the pretty girl Jennifer. But his interest was not lost on her. She would turn away quickly when their eyes met and talk to Kate as if she were not aware of him.

Kate smiled to herself when she saw the way Ben looked at the girl. He was like a guilty little boy. What would Solomon and Judith think of Ben's interest in a Gentile girl who had an illegitimate son, she wondered. But that was another problem and one of lesser concern for now. First they had the journey back up the track to Cooktown. They'd have to contend with fording rivers and creeks all over again. The only certainty was that the journey would not be easy.

Ben left their campfire for a short time to visit a miner he knew from his days hauling supplies to Tambo. When he returned he had a worried expression on his bearded face. He squatted by the fire and poked a stick into the red glowing coals to make a light for his pipe.

'Word's come back that the myalls jumped

Inspector Clohesy up the track at Hell's Gate,' he said, puffing on his pipe.

Kate heard his words and sipped at a mug of hot tea sweetened with sugar. Jennifer lay asleep with her head in Kate's lap while Willie slept with his head in his young mother's lap. The good food and comforting warm fire had caused them both to doze before falling into a deep and untroubled sleep. Kate did not have the heart to wake the girl and cradled her as she would a child. 'He had seven troopers with him when they attacked him on the Laura River,' Ben continued as he stared into the flickering flames of the fire.

Aboriginal tribesmen attacking a heavily armed party of police troopers meant they'd be more than prepared to attack two wagons and their escort of just two women, one boy and a man, Kate thought. She nodded gravely. They would not only have to traverse some of the most rugged land on the Australian continent, but they would also have to avoid the painted warriors of the north. It was ironic to think that the Aboriginal warriors would not be interested in the small fortune in gold they carried, that they would be more interested in their flesh!

Kate shuddered. The thought of what could be their fate if the tribesmen took them alive was horrifying. She had heard stories of how the tribesmen smashed the legs of their captives with rocks so that the victims could not escape and then roasted them to provide a feast.

Jennifer stirred when she felt the tiny shudder and opened her eyes. 'I'm sorry, Missus O'Keefe,' she slurred sleepily. 'I must have gone to sleep.'

Without thinking Kate gave Jennifer's shoulder a gentle and reassuring squeeze. Her mind was on the supply of rolled brass cartridges for her Martini Henry, a rifle capable of bringing to a stop the fiercest of tribesmen. Although it was a single shot weapon she was very skilful with the gun and it would be this skill that would matter most in the weeks ahead. Kate was a long way from the comfort and security of her uncle's hotel in Sydney. But then, she was a long way from the young girl she had once been before coming to Queensland to make her personal fortune.

She gazed down at Jennifer and the sleeping boy and was acutely aware that they had now become her responsibility. Glancing up at Ben squatting by the fire she felt somewhat reassured. Life had a way of bringing into her life capable men when she needed them most. 'Luke?' she whispered, and Ben glanced up from the coals of the fire.

'You say something Kate?' he asked in a puzzled voice.

'No, I was just thinking about something.'

He looked away and Kate realised that there were tears in her eyes. The American prospector Luke Tracy came so easily to her thoughts when she was lonely and frightened. He had always been like a tough yet gentle guardian angel, guiding her safely along the dangerous tracks of her life. She had long convinced herself that she had not loved him and that he was merely a dear friend whose company she sorely missed. He was six years gone, to where only God knew, and she had to accept that, like her dead brothers Tom and Michael, and her father Patrick Duffy, the American was just another sad memory in her life.

But sometimes his slow drawling voice would be in her head when she slept under the stars. Or she'd briefly see his face in the image of a miner walking the tortuous track to the Palmer. At those times her feelings for Luke were even more confused.

FOUR

So they called the place Cooktown, the lanky prospector mused as he stood at the edge of the dusty, bustling main street of the boom town. Might have been Tracytown, if I'd got to the Palmer first. With an ironic smile he hefted the swag onto his shoulders and strode down Charlotte Street.

Much of what he saw, heard and smelt brought back twenty-year-old memories of another great gold strike. It all had the same feeling as Ballarat back in '54: the hastily erected shops of bark and tin selling everything from laudanum to gunpowder, the numerous but less than salubrious places of solace for a man's carnal needs and the ever-present establishments to quench a thirst with fiery spirits. And always in the air an electric expectation generated by the newcomers preparing to go up the trail to the goldfields, convinced that a fortune awaited them at the end of their journey.

Six years he had been away from the land he had grown to know so well. A land where he had received his scar in the fierce battle on the Ballarat goldfields fighting the British army in an ill-fated rebellion against injustice. A land where he had searched for years for the elusive strike that would make him a rich man.

He appraised the eager faces around him and shook his head with a sadness for the bitter disillusionment he knew would be the fate for most. For this was not Ballarat within practical reach of the port of Melbourne and an easy road journey to the fields. This was the north where harsh jungles, mountains and monsoonal rains provided a natural barrier to even arriving on the fields. Luke knew. He had once attempted to reach the Palmer back in '68 – and failed. That prospecting journey had almost cost him his life.

Perhaps if he had not been betrayed by a treacherous lawyer by the name of Hugh Darlington he might have been the first and his name written into history. He would have returned to the valleys south of the Palmer River and finally on to the Palmer itself. If he had he would have found what the dying prospector had told him about: 'nuggets as big as hens' eggs just lying in the shallows of the river for the taking.' But the fever and the lack of supplies had driven him back when he knew he had been so close to his El Dorado. And a second opportunity to retrace his journey north had not presented itself.

Luke sighed for what might have been as he

remembered the events that caused him to flee the colony for the far-off sanctuary of the land of his birth. Before he fled he had entrusted a large sum of money to Kate O'Keefe's lawyer in Rockhampton – money made from the gold he had been given by the dying prospector. But Darlington had betrayed him to the police. Trading gold without official sanction brought heavy penalties.

Tall and rangy, Luke was now in the latter part of his thirties. His face was tanned from his exposure to the elements and the old scar that traced a line from his eye to his chin had become barely discernible with the passing of time. His blue eyes still had the look of a man accustomed to gazing at distant horizons. And although he did not have the classic handsome features of the refined gentleman, his face reflected a mixture of gentleness and savage strength. It was a face that was reassuring and easy to love.

'Mister Tracy?'

The question caused him to freeze. Had one of the constabulary recognised him? Had a poster been produced of his likeness? Were they still out to arrest him? He turned slowly and felt a sickening recognition.

The big man limped towards him. 'Sergeant James,' he answered with a note of despair. 'Long time since we last met.'

Henry James unexpectedly thrust out his hand. 'I thought it was you, even though you have shaved off your beard.' Luke accepted the handshake as Henry continued. 'It's not sergeant any more Mister Tracy. I was pensioned out of the police a couple of years back. Me and Emma work for Kate O'Keefe nowadays.' The mention of Kate's name caused Luke to feel giddy. 'You feeling unwell Mister Tracy?' Henry asked when he noticed the blood drain from the American's face.

'Yeah. Just getting my land legs,' Luke replied as he recovered his composure. 'How is Kate these days?'

'As well as can be, from the last time I saw her.'

'When was that?' Luke asked, attempting to sound indifferent.

'A few weeks back, before she went up the track to the Palmer with young Ben Rosenblum. They took a couple of wagons with supplies for the fields. Hoped to get through as soon as the Wet receded. According to all going well she should be on her way back by now.' Henry broke into a broad smile and dropped his handshake. 'I was down at the wharf checking on a cargo manifest when I saw you get off that ship out of San Francisco. Couldn't believe my eyes when I saw you. How long has it been?'

'Too long,' Luke sighed. 'Too long away from Queensland.'

'You have to come down to the depot and meet my family,' Henry said, slapping Luke on the back. 'I know Emma will be surprised to see you. She always figured you and Kate were a matched pair and wondered why you never got together.'

Luke let the big former policeman guide him along the wagon-rutted street through the jostling crowds that mirrored every nation and its citizens. As they walked Henry babbled on about events in the

Australian colonies that he felt Luke might want to know. 'You must have left the year that mad Irish Fenian shot Prince Alfred down in Sydney,' he said.

Luke nodded. He vaguely remembered something talked about around the Brisbane hotels while he was waiting for his ship to San Francisco. Something about the attempted assassination of Queen Victoria's second son who was on a goodwill tour of the Australian colonies. Some argued that the failed assassin was mad. Others stuck to the Irish Fenian plot to strike a blow against the English. No matter what, the man was eventually hanged.

A group of Europeans were struggling with a load of heavy supplies onto a dray.

'Could do with some of them Kanakas up in this bloody place as labourers,' Henry quipped. 'Those big blackfellas are used to working in the tropics but the bloody Queensland government has passed an Act protecting 'em. Think it had something to do with that massacre of sixty islanders aboard that blackbirder brig *Carl* back in '68. And we're not getting any more convicts to help out since you left. It seems England is deserting us,' he grumbled. 'Pulled out their army leaving us to fend for ourselves. And just when we need 'em to give the myalls a lesson in civilised behaviour around these parts. The government has been trying to round up the blackfellas but the myalls up here are a different lot to the ones I knew down south. Fight like those Spanish guerillas did against old Napoleon's armies in the Peninsula War. Hit and run tactics against the miners along the track to the goldfields.'

Luke listened with interest as Henry rambled on about the current status of the frontier. He had been away for just on six years and was learning quickly how things were different from what he remembered of the places beyond civilisation.

They came to one of the larger timber and iron shops at the end of the main street. Luke read the sign above the door: *The Eureka Company – General Merchants to the Palmer and Cooktown.* The name Eureka brought a smile to his face. The defiance was still in the Duffys. Henry ushered him inside the shop and Luke immediately found himself amidst a tidy cluster of goods. It was obvious from the well-stocked supplies that Kate ran a prosperous business. Men and women picked through the goods while a pretty young woman with startling blue eyes and long red hair tied back at her slender neck stood behind a heavy timber bench taking their money. She glanced up at Henry and then at Luke with a quizzical expression.

'This is the legendary Luke Tracy,' Henry said by way of flattering introduction. 'Mister Tracy, my wife Emma.'

Luke removed his broad floppy hat and mumbled a polite, 'Pleased to make your acquaintance ma'am.'

'Mister Tracy,' Emma said as she came out from behind the counter. 'I have heard many stories about you from the Cohens and Kate. Had matters worked in more fortunate ways I might have met you earlier when you were briefly in Rockhampton.'

'That was my misfortune,' Luke said, somewhat embarrassed by the special treatment being doled out by the Jameses. 'I knew your husband from those days.'

'You are an extraordinary man by all their accounts,' Emma said. 'I think Kate is very fond of you, more fond than most.'

Luke felt just a twinge of a blush under his tanned skin. If only they knew how much Kate meant to him. Not a day of his life had passed without her coming to his thoughts with her beautiful grey eyes and gentle smile. Not an hour when he did not ache to hold her and tell her how much he had loved her. His was a love that had begun the day they had stood together on a paddlewheeler steaming up the Fitzroy River over a decade earlier. And when riding the snow-blasted prairies of Montana in winter he had talked to her in his head. On the great paddlewheelers of the Mississippi the scent of lavender would sometimes drift to him from the pretty ladies and he would instinctively seek her out. In the forest-covered mountains of the Rockies she had been with him as he sat by his campfire. No, it had not been the news of the gold rush to northern Queensland that had really brought him back to the shores of Australia. It had been the inevitable search for the one true love of his life – Kate O'Keefe. But it was also a hopeless search because even if he found her there was nothing to say that someone else did not share her affections. Or that he – an almost penniless drifter forever seeking El Dorado – would amount to much in her affections. Even the mention of her fondness for him amounted to little more than feelings one would have for a friend. And what would he say to her when he sees her again? The thought somehow frightened him more than any of the numerous dangerous situations he had confronted in his past.

'Do you have lodgings?' Emma asked, cutting across his thoughts. 'If not then I know Kate would insist on you staying with us. We have a store room you can use until you decide on anywhere else you wish to stay.'

'Good idea,' Henry grunted. 'Kate would never forgive us if she knew we had not offered.'

'Thanks Sergeant James,' Luke replied gratefully. He had just stepped off the ship and knew from past experience on goldfields that accommodation was at a premium. 'I'll take you up on your offer.'

'It's Henry,' the former police sergeant said. 'Don't think formalities are in order with someone Kate holds in such high esteem.'

'Thanks Henry,' Luke said. 'Hope you'll call me Luke. Kind of nice to hear the name my mother gave me used by friends.'

Henry showed Luke to the spare room used to store bales of cloth. The American dropped his swag which was little more than a couple of blankets wrapped around the few personal items he carried. He glanced around and Henry could see that the American was pleased with what he saw. Although the heat in the tropics could be almost unbearable the plank walls had cracks wide enough to let in a gentle breeze yet keep unwanted visitors out. It was clean, protected from the elements and relatively comfortable when the bales of cloth were used to sleep on.

'We don't live here,' Henry said. 'We have a place up on the hill overlooking the river. You are expected for dinner tonight. Emma is a wonderful cook.'

'Thanks.' Fate had dealt him a good hand for once.

'I'll leave for now,' Henry said. 'Got to get back to the wharf. Expecting supplies on the next ship from Brisbane. Guess I will see you later after you get settled in.'

Luke nodded and when Henry left sat down on a bale. His head was reeling from the totally unexpected meeting with ghosts of his past. He had never in his wildest dreams expected to come so close to Kate simply by stepping off the ship in Cooktown. He had originally planned to try his luck on the fields and then head south to Rockhampton where he had last seen her years earlier. But luck had brought him to where he was now – within maybe days of finding Kate. All he had to do was head up the track to the Palmer and if his luck held out he would find her.

He unrolled the swag to reveal a leather wallet containing personal papers, a big Colt revolver and a sewing kit. He unwrapped a spare shirt that had been in the swag, found his shaving gear and thought about going in search of a bath. He felt content under the azure skies of tropical North Queensland. He felt that he had come home.

That evening at the James residence on the hill Luke met the progeny of Tom Duffy and his Darambal wife Mondo: Peter, Timothy and Sarah. He was impressed by the three children's manners. They were a credit to Kate, he thought, when informed how she had raised them with the help of governesses. He was also ruefully informed by Emma that they were a bit of a handful at times.

Luke also met Henry and Emma's son Gordon who he noted was very much like his father in his looks and mannerisms. When he asked the ages of the children he was told that Peter and Gordon were both almost twelve, Timothy ten and Sarah eight. It was obvious that the Duffy children and the James boy were as close as blood could be. Particularly Gordon and Peter.

Peter had the dark skin of his mother's people but the big build of his Irish father. His eyes were grey and he was a handsome lad. Timothy was fairer and very reserved. He did not seem to be as close as the others, Luke observed, and was less open in his way. But it was little Sarah who made the biggest impression on the American. Her skin had an almost golden sheen and she had the promise of growing into a beautiful young woman. But more than that, her nature was gentle and intelligent. She took an immediate liking to Luke.

Emma put the children in the care of a housekeeper who came in to assist at dinner times. The housekeeper, a good Christian woman who had lost her husband on the goldfields when a powder blast went wrong, had been hired by Kate to help Emma while she was away on the track. She was a big buxom middle-aged woman with grey hair and a no-nonsense approach to life and she quickly bustled the children off to bed.

Over a leg of roast mutton and vegetables Luke unfolded his plans to set out for the Palmer fields as soon as he had purchased sufficient supplies and had saved enough money to purchase a horse and new saddle.

Henry raised his eyebrows at the American's eagerness to get started but Emma smiled to herself. She had noticed with a woman's perceptiveness the change that came over the American every time Kate's name came up in conversation. It was no wonder he was eager to head out from Cooktown. He was a man desperately in love with the beautiful Irishwoman. But she frowned when she remembered the visit she had received two days earlier, a visit she knew would cause her friend a terrible pain in unleashing memories better forgotten.

Henry had been fencing a paddock for the bullocks at the back of Cooktown and she had been alone in the store. A big, handsome man had walked in and announced that he was Kevin O'Keefe, Kate's husband, and that he was looking for his wife. Shocked, Emma stated that Kate was somewhere on the track between Cooktown and the Palmer. He had stood for a moment appraising the store and left without any other conversation.

Reeling from the meeting Emma debated whether to tell her husband of the sudden reappearance of the man who had deserted Kate over a decade earlier. She was fully aware of the circumstances of the desertion as Judith Cohen had recounted the story to her when they lived in Rockhampton.

It was a pitiful story of a young and pregnant seventeen-year-old girl left alone at nights while her worthless husband went in search of good times at the local hotels and grog shanties. Judith and her husband Solomon had nursed Kate through a terrible fever at Luke Tracy's request. Finally Kevin O'Keefe ran off with the wife of a local publican, leaving his very ill wife to give premature birth to their child. The tiny baby lived only a few hours and was buried in a lonely grave outside Rockhampton. It had been the quiet strength of Luke and the loving care of the Cohens that had kept Kate going through the critical weeks following this tragic loss.

Emma had finally decided that she should not tell Henry of the meeting. Such was her husband's loyalty to their employer, she was just a little frightened that her big burly husband might become angry and seek out O'Keefe for a thrashing for all the grief he had visited upon Kate. And she sensed O'Keefe was a man capable of great violence. Her real fear was for Henry's safety should such a confrontation occur.

But now she had reason to feel an even greater disquiet. She remembered a story of a confrontation between Luke Tracy and O'Keefe. Years earlier a traveller to Rockhampton had told her of the incident. In some grog shanty outside of Brisbane Luke had pulled his gun on O'Keefe and threatened to kill him if they ever met again.

She turned her attention to the American puffing

contentedly on a cigar Henry had produced after the meal. He seemed at peace and she suspected that the possible proximity of Kate had a lot to do with his serenity. She knew that if she told him of the meeting with Kate's husband it might have a fatal outcome for the gentle American. Emma prayed that the two men would never meet.

FIVE

The reception at the von Fellmann residence was impressive. The house and garden had a panoramic view of the harbour. Shade was provided under brightly coloured marquee tents to keep the copious quantities of champagne chilled in buckets filled with ice imported from America. The champagne washed down succulent rock oysters freshly harvested from the harbour's foreshores.

The elegant guests picked at delicacies from silver salvers. It was obvious to Michael from the lavishly prepared reception that the German aristocrat was a man of considerable means.

Michael stood alone amongst the elegantly dressed guests. From his own flamboyant dress it was not hard to pick him as an American. But flamboyancy was not unique to him. Colourful military uniforms of colonial volunteer and militia officers, and their British brother officers on liaison duties to the newly established defence forces of New South Wales, also provided colour on the manicured lawns of the harbourside mansion.

Young ladies in dresses fitted over whalebone corsets flirted with the handsome and dashing young officers. More than one daughter of the landed or merchant gentry cast an undisguised look of admiration in the direction of the tall, splendidly built American with the exotic black leather eye patch. Coy whispers from behind ornate fans followed Michael as he walked alone to the edge of the lawn. From here he had a spectacular sweeping view of the harbour below. But he remained aloof from the guests. He had come on business. It did not pay to expose himself to inquiries about his past, however politely phrased.

He was not alone for long. A British army major joined him at the edge of the lawn. 'Mister O'Flynn I believe,' the officer said politely. 'We haven't met before but we nearly might have.' The English officer extended his hand. 'I'm Major Godfrey. Currently on liaison duty with the Duke of Edinburgh's Highland Volunteer Rifle Corps. I heard from a mutual friend that you once served with Phil Sheridan's command in the late war between the States. As it happens I had the honour of being one of Her Majesty's military observers in the same campaign where you regrettably lost your eye.'

Michael accepted his extended hand. 'You said a mutual friend Major Godfrey,' he replied guardedly, sizing up the English officer. 'I am not sure who that might be.'

'Ah, yes. You were only vaguely acquainted with Mister Horace Brown on the *Boston*,' the Major said as he gazed across the harbour. 'Mister Brown and I served together in the Crimea many years ago. I had the good fortune to run into Horace only yesterday at Victoria Barracks. He often drops in on the Officers' Mess when he is in town and tells me about his sojourns on the family's money.'

'Yes, I remember Mister Brown,' Michael said warily as he appraised the major. 'Poor poker player if I remember your friend rightly.'

Although the British major had the foppish manner of a gentleman born to command Michael noticed the colourful strip sewn on his jacket which belied the major's dilettante manner. He was obviously tougher than he looked as his ribands reflected the many colonial wars the major had fought in the interests of the British Empire: service in the Crimean War, the Indian Mutiny and the Second China War. He also wore the dark blue riband with a brownish stripe of the New Zealand campaign in which Michael had also fought under the command of the famous Prussian Count von Tempsky.

'I see you were also in the New Zealand campaign Major,' Michael said by way of conversation. The English officer gave him a sharp look of interest.

'I am flattered to think that an American would recognise the riband, Mister O'Flynn,' he said. 'How is it that you know the medal?'

Michael sipped at his champagne. A bad move to know such things. 'Knew a Limey once who had the same medal,' he answered quickly.

77

The Major did not pursue the subject except to say, 'I believe you were awarded the Congressional Medal of Honour by the late President Lincoln?'

Michael nodded and glanced away.

A short silence followed until the British major decided to restart the conversation. 'You and I should get together some time and share recollections on the Five Forks campaign,' he said. 'A fairly decisive encounter with the army of Northern Virginia by your army. I was rather impressed by the "Boy General" as your newspapers liked to call him. George Custer's attack on the Confederate right was a rum show. Now there is a young man with a big future. I have read lately that George Custer is doing a spot of duty chasing redskins in the Dakota territory. Damned fine chap for a colonial.'

Michael knew George Custer and did not like him. He considered the man a dangerous maniac bent on self-glory at the expense of the lives of his men. 'I believe *Lieutenant Colonel* Custer is doing so,' he replied with the emphasis on the lower rank as opposed to Custer's brevet general rank of his Civil War days.

'If ever there was a man to deal with your native problem then Custer will be the one to bring them to heel,' the British officer mooted with a note of admiration. 'We need a man like that here to deal with the damned savages up north. But the blasted darkies prefer to fight guerilla war against our courageous settlers. Won't stand and fight a battle.'

'Maybe George Custer will bite off more than he can chew some day Major,' Michael replied sardonically. 'I can tell you from personal experience that those redskins as you call them are, in the words of one of your own officers, amongst the finest light horsemen anywhere in the world. And man for man I would put my money on the injuns. So long as Custer has the numbers he will beat them. But pity help him if he ever has to face a united nation of the plains tribes.'

'Not likely to happen, Mister O'Flynn,' Godfrey scoffed. 'The Indians, fortunately for the white man, are little more than savages, without recourse to our superior tactics and technology. No, Custer will be the man to pacify the savages, mark my words.' Godfrey could see that George Custer was not a favourite of Mister O'Flynn and tactfully turned the subject. 'I am rather intrigued by your invitation to the reception Mister O'Flynn. How is it that you know our charming and, might I add, beautiful hostess and her husband the Baron?'

'I have not had the pleasure of meeting the Baron or his wife,' Michael replied. 'But I was invited to make the acquaintance of the Baron's wife by a mutual friend of the Baron and myself in Sydney.' What Michael said was partially true although he did not know if George Hilary had ever met the Baron or his wife either.

'Ah, I see,' the major replied, turning to watch the two women strolling towards them across the lawn from the marquees. 'Then I am pleased to say our hostess is approaching and I will have the honour of introducing you to the beautiful and generous lady.' Michael half turned and froze. His tanned face drained of blood.

Penelope White! And Fiona!

Penelope was smiling as she accepted the Major's patter of flattering compliments. She turned her frank gaze on Michael who saw a faint flicker of recognition in her eyes. Beside her Fiona had paled and appeared as if she might faint. The subtle exchange between Michael and the two women did not appear to have been noticed by the English major. 'Mister O'Flynn, may I introduce the Baroness von Fellmann and her charming cousin Missus Fiona White.'

Michael fought to regain his composure. 'You were right Major,' he replied calmly. 'But not generous enough in your praise of such a beautiful woman as the Baroness,' he said as he brushed Penelope's extended hand with a kiss in the Continental fashion. 'Nor did the Major speak of the beauty of the other ladies of the Colony of New South Wales,' he continued smoothly as he fixed Fiona with his single grey eye.

'What a charming man you are Mister O'Flynn,' Penelope said gaily as she withdrew her hand a little reluctantly from his. 'I have heard that you Americans can be more charming than my French guests. Isn't Mister O'Flynn charming Fiona?'

Fiona continued to stare wide-eyed at Michael and her cousin knew what had caused the painful reaction to the American. 'You seem to be somewhat familiar to us Mister O'Flynn,' Penelope continued.

Michael frowned and shook his head. 'I wish I was Baroness. But this is my first visit to Australia. It may be that I remind you of someone perhaps?'

he asked calmly, although he could feel his heart pounding with the fear of being exposed.

'Yes you do Mister O'Flynn,' Penelope said brightly, pursing her lips in a seductive manner while her eyes roamed over him. 'You bear an uncanny resemblance to a man Missus White and I knew many years ago. But I doubt you could be the same man. No, you are definitely not the man we mistook you for.'

Michael relaxed a little and appraised both women. Neither showed the passage of years except to mature and grow even more beautiful. They still made an interesting contrast: the dark-haired beauty of Fiona and the golden and more voluptuous beauty of the Baroness.

Fiona's emerald green eyes were wide still with what Michael interpreted as shock and her naturally pale and flawless skin whiter than chalk. He was uneasy, but was aware that he had changed dramatically in the intervening years since they last met. The ravages of war had changed his face and he now had the hard look of a man accustomed to living with death rather than the gentler expression of the young man who had once dreamed of being a landscape artist.

'I believe you are the gentleman my husband wrote to me about,' Penelope said in a more businesslike tone. She was composed and her expression displayed little more than a sensual appraisal of him. 'It will be my pleasure to discuss with you some matters of business. But you must excuse me today as I have to attend to my guests. Major Godfrey appears to be excelling at entertaining you for the moment. I would like to see you here tomorrow, six o'clock, if that is convenient to you Mister O'Flynn?'

'I think so Baroness,' Michael replied.

'Good! Please mingle and meet some of my other guests,' Penelope smiled enigmatically. 'I am sure they are intrigued by your appearance. I have heard more than one young lady mention how she would like to meet the mysterious American. You seem to have a magnetism for women Mister O'Flynn,' she said as she slipped her hand under Fiona's elbow.

'There is little that could be considered mysterious about me Baroness,' Michael replied modestly. 'But thank you for the compliment. I will take you up on the invitation.'

Penelope steered her cousin away. Not until they were out of hearing did Fiona finally utter, 'Penny, it was like seeing Michael come back from the dead.'

Penelope beamed a smile at a French naval officer who had consumed a good quantity of his national beverage and was feeling rather amorous. He said something to her in French and she replied fluently in kind before returning her attention to her cousin. 'I grant you that Mister O'Flynn has an uncanny similarity with Michael Duffy,' she said as they strolled in the garden back to the marquee.

Fiona still felt faint. Meeting the American had opened a floodgate of bittersweet memories.

Penelope again sensed her cousin's pain and leaned across to her as they strolled amongst the guests. 'Forget Mister O'Flynn, Fiona my love,' she whispered. 'While you are thinking of Mister O'Flynn you are only causing yourself to think of Michael. And Michael is gone forever. You only bring unnecessary pain for what is long past.'

Fiona knew Penelope was right. Michael Duffy was just a sweet, sad memory. Penelope was convinced that the likeness of O'Flynn to Michael Duffy was purely coincidental. And she was far too astute to make a mistake.

Michael kept up a pretence of a conversation with Major Godfrey but his mind was still reeling from his encounter with Penelope and Fiona. He was pleased when the Major saw a fellow officer and excused himself with a promise that both men should get together to talk of the war. Michael agreed, but neither man made any arrangements to meet.

As soon as the Major had excused himself Michael also made his exit. He was very aware that he was in territory as dangerous as any battlefield he had fought on. Recognition could mean being betrayed to the police and execution by hanging was still the penalty imposed for the capital crime of murder in the Colony of New South Wales.

But Major Godfrey had not dismissed the American so easily. He had watched Michael take his leave from the afternoon lawn party with great interest. Damn Horace Brown! Damn him for even mentioning his mission to shadow the American.

Major Godfrey had not given much thought to his conversations with his old friend from the Crimea until this afternoon when he had noticed

Michael O'Flynn amongst the invited guests of the Baroness. As an officer of Her Majesty's forces he knew it was his duty to keep an eye on the mysterious American.

Now he would have to take his reluctant leave of the party just as the champagne had made some of the younger and more eligible daughters of the colony less inhibited.

Michael did not notice the British officer take a cab to follow him. He was preoccupied with his unexpected meeting with Fiona and Penelope. What if Penelope had not been fooled? How much did she still dislike him? He hailed a hansom cab to return to his hotel. The last time they had met – a decade earlier – she had expressed her resentment of him in the most cruel way she could. Did she still dislike him enough to have him arrested? The uneasy thoughts nagged Michael as he sat brooding in the cab even though he was sure he had convinced the two women that he was Michael O'Flynn, American gun dealer.

That evening Michael drank alone in the bar of the hotel and no-one dared approach the one-eyed man. He did not have the appearance of someone looking for company.

When the bar closed Michael made his way up to his room and was annoyed to find that the door was not locked. He was sure he had locked it.

He carefully pushed the door open and stepped warily inside the darkened room. It took only seconds for his eyes to scan the room that was bathed in the soft shadows of a hallway light. The outline of the naked figure reclining on his bed caused him to catch his breath.

Penelope slid from the bed and padded across the dimly lit room to him. As she approached he could see the contours of her shapely hips and slim waist.

He did not resist when she pulled his face down to hers. The kiss was at first soft and moist, then savage as her teeth bit into his lip. He pulled away and could taste blood in his mouth.

'Hello Mister O'Flynn. Or should I say, Michael Duffy?'

'How did you know?'

'You might have only one eye Michael, but you still have the same soul,' she said, stroking his lips with the tips of her fingers. The touch stung where she had broken the skin with her teeth and she felt him wince. 'I knew you from the moment I looked into that eye and I saw the man you once were . . . and always will be. The same man that I had promised myself would be at my mercy one day. And now you are truly at my mercy!'

'Does Fiona know?' Michael asked as she tasted his blood on the tips of her fingers.

'I don't think so,' she purred deeply. 'My cousin is a romantic who would prefer to think that her lover died with his last thoughts being of her. Did you Michael?' she teased. 'Were your last thoughts of Fiona?'

'There have been many times in my life when I have had last thoughts Baroness,' Michael growled.

'But mostly of regret for not having had the opportunity to kill your brother. But for now I must confess that I am confused as to why you are in my bed. The last time I saw you you were expressing a deep and abiding hatred for me.'

'I want you Michael Duffy. I have always wanted you,' she said in a husky voice as she slid her hand inside his shirt to feel the hard muscle of his chest, 'from that day I saw you on the pier at Manly. But you were too besotted with my cousin to notice me then. And now I have you at my mercy as you fully know and can do with you whatever I wish. Even make you beg for me. Make you indulge me in my most depraved desires. And make you do whatever I want no matter how you should feel about any other woman in your life. Your life is mine because I know who you really are.' She drew his face down to hers and her kiss was hot and passionate.

For the moment he was totally at her mercy. Whether he had free choice was a moot point as the lingering scent of her body was the desirable and musky scent of a woman. He was losing himself to her desire. The years of living in a world of sudden death and extreme violence boiled over into a passion to create rather than destroy, to give pleasure instead of pain. It had been a long time since he had experienced the sweet and sensual pleasure of a woman's body. A long time since he had experienced the erotic pleasures she unleashed in him.

Penelope finally realised both a dream of revenge and a deep desire she had concealed even from herself. She drew him down onto the bed and her legs wrapped around his waist, locking him into her body. As he submitted to her will he was everything she imagined he would be: a magnificent lover who embodied all the maleness of a wild and untamed animal. She did not imagine love in the coupling of their bodies. No, her love was only for the dark-haired woman with the emerald green eyes who thought she had seen a ghost. She smiled triumphantly as she guided Michael's head down between her legs. Hers was the power of a woman to use her body to defeat her enemies – especially if they were men.

Michael did not think of Fiona. He had long learned to seize the moment in the turbulent and dangerous world that had changed him from being a romantic dreamer to a hard-bitten, cynical soldier of fortune. For him love was something he had lost with his dreams of marrying the dark-haired beauty Fiona Macintosh. At least with Penelope he understood the violence of lust. Lust, the satisfaction of which was paid for or occasionally granted freely in his troubled life as a soldier.

'The Baroness left immediately following the reception,' Major Godfrey said with an edge of envy for the American's luck in bedding the beautiful wife of the Prussian aristocrat. 'She is currently, shall we say, in the arms of Mister O'Flynn in his hotel room, lucky blighter.'

Baroness von Fellmann had a reputation for being very discreet in her amorous escapades as

Godfrey well knew. But visiting a man at his hotel was less than prudent. 'Do you think she knows Mister O'Flynn from some other time?' Horace asked him as both men conversed quietly in a corner of the Officers' Mess at Victoria Barracks.

Godfrey shook his head. 'I cannot see how that would be possible. As far as I know, the Baroness has never visited either Samoa or America. No, I would say the lady was smitten by our American friend. Nothing more.'

Horace frowned. He was not convinced that Mister O'Flynn and the Baroness had not met before. Although he could not say from personal experience anything about the sexual needs of a woman, he did know enough about the opposite sex to know a woman did not go to bed with a man she had only exchanged a few words with at a reception.

Horace was however in possession of information that she had first visited the gun dealer after she left her own reception party and then gone to the hotel where O'Flynn was staying. It was obvious that she had gone out of her way to locate the man and bed him. The whole situation was perplexing.

Mister O'Flynn seemed to have more of an interesting past than Horace had first suspected. He had a strange and intriguing accent under his Irish-American speech. One thing about being an expert in linguistics as Horace was, was the ability to read words and accents, as a hunter would interpret an animal's tracks. He strongly suspected that Michael O'Flynn had either spent a long time in Australia – or had visited before.

The visit by the Baroness to O'Flynn's hotel room seemed to confirm his theory that the American had been in Sydney previously although there was no record in existence to say so. So just *who* was Mister O'Flynn? The answer to that question just might prove more than valuable.

'O'Flynn tells me you are very good with the cards, Horace old chap,' Godfrey drawled, flashing a grin at his friend who was still brooding on the subject of Michael O'Flynn. 'Care for a hand or two? For a few guineas?'

'Dear chap,' Horace replied in a sad voice. 'One thing that I well and truly learned in the Crimea was never to play cards with an infantry officer. Sadly, you are not gentlemen like your brothers from the cavalry. No gentlemen at all.'

Godfrey gave his old friend a broad grin. 'It was worth a try old chap,' he sighed.

Horace finished his drink and excused himself from the Mess. Outside the barracks he hailed a cab. He was deep in thought during the trip back to his hotel. Manfred von Fellmann was up to something. What would the former Prussian officer do if he realised his Anglo-Australian wife was in bed with the American? Fortunately for O'Flynn the Baron was still in Samoa as far as he knew.

The English agent wondered at the intentions of the Germans and particularly of Manfred von Fellmann. He was Bismarck's most trusted intelligence agent for the Pacific region. Whatever the Germans were planning had to be of vital importance to their strategic interests in what most

European powers considered to be the backwater of international politics. Horace frowned as he passed by the tenement houses of Sydney. Why the hell had von Fellmann suddenly shifted his attention from Samoa to Sydney as British intelligence sources in Samoa had indicated? For whatever reason, he was sure that the mysterious Irish-American was the key to the whole enterprise. All he had to do was keep track of him and learn more about his past. He was sure that was the key to finding what was underlying the Germans' sudden interest in this part of the world. And Horace's keenly honed intelligence instincts told him too that O'Flynn was not all that he appeared to be.

Penelope lay in Michael's arms. She smiled when she remembered how only two nights earlier she had held Fiona against her naked body in a similar manner. She gazed down at Michael's battle-scarred body. How ironic that she and Michael had shared Fiona's body at different stages in their lives.

There was little chance she would betray Michael to the police. He was a key player in her husband's games of international intrigue. And besides, she mused as she watched him sleep, he was one of the best lovers she had ever bedded. She traced a long scar down his chest with the tip of her nail and smiled wickedly. 'Oh Michael,' she sighed softly so as not to wake him. 'If you only knew the games I have planned for when we next meet you would most probably rather face the gallows.'

SIX

Near closing time in the depot Luke heard the raised voice of a man and instinctively knew Emma was in trouble. He had just completed final preparations for his journey up the track to the Palmer River and sat on the edge of a bale in the room behind the store. He was packing his swag when the vaguely familiar voice of the angry man drifted to him.

Without hesitation Luke was on his feet. In seconds he stood in the depot, confronting a big, broad-shouldered man who was towering over Emma. 'You know when she will return,' he shouted down at her, turning with a frown to face Luke. 'You!' he uttered in his absolute surprise at seeing the American prospector. 'Thought you were long out of the colony.'

'O'Keefe you goddamned son of a bitch. I was kind of hoping you were dead by now.'

O'Keefe stepped away from an ashen-faced Emma whose trembling hands went to her face in shock. She sensed the meeting of the two men could only lead to bloodshed. 'A few have tried,' he snarled. 'But I'm still here, as you can see.'

'I also see you are still good at standing over helpless women,' Luke replied tensely. 'You ought to try and do the same to a man.'

'You call yourself a man,' O'Keefe snorted as he shook his head. 'You need a gun to back up your yellow streak.'

The blood drained from Luke's face at the insult to his courage. O'Keefe was around ten years younger than himself and much more powerfully built and Luke had no illusions about the possible outcome of a hand-to-hand fight between them.

But the challenge had cornered Luke who knew he was facing a deadly situation where his opponent would be the probable winner. He had only one hope, albeit a slight one. 'You still carry a knife?' he questioned as he slid his big bladed bowie from the inside of his knee-length boot.

O'Keefe grinned as he produced a double-edged blade from his waistcoat. Momentarily frozen by the speed and intensity of the confrontation Emma finally snapped to fling herself at O'Keefe's knife arm but he flicked her away as if she were nothing more than an annoying insect. Emma stumbled backwards and slammed into a pile of pots and pans sending them rattling in all directions. She knew she must fetch Henry to stop the fight before blood was spilled. But, as the two men circled, oblivious to her presence, O'Keefe blocked the doorway. Trapped, all she could do was watch helplessly. O'Keefe was grinning, taunting Luke who crouched slightly to balance himself on the balls of his feet.

'Vot is das?' a voice boomed from behind O'Keefe. 'Vot do you play games like kinder?' Luke let his attention shift for a split second to glimpse the figure in black framed in the doorway of the store. 'Mien vife and I come to buy goods. Not see two grown men fight,' the man in black with a great black bushy beard continued in a voice loud enough to shake the mightiest of gum trees loose of its leaves.

O'Keefe was poised uncertainly with the knife menacingly extended in his right hand. Luke could see that O'Keefe appeared unsettled as the voice behind him was an unknown quantity. Deftly, he slid the knife inside the sleeve of his coat, and turned to face the person who had spoken, a man around his own age, size and build. It was obvious from his accent that he was German and when their eyes locked it was also obvious that the stranger was not a man who displayed any fear. Without a word, O'Keefe pushed past the stranger and a pretty blonde woman who stood behind him and Luke slid the bowie back inside his boot.

'Thank you sir,' Emma said as the colour returned to her face. 'You have arrived at a very opportune time.'

She flashed Luke a look of concern and he returned a brief smile for her benefit although he felt far from happy. He had come close to killing Kate's husband – or being killed by him.

'Ach. It is nothing,' the man shrugged.

The pretty blonde woman smiled wanly at Emma as she took her place beside the big man in black.

'I am Missus Emma James,' Emma said. 'And may I introduce Mister Luke Tracy from America whose life you may have saved by your fortunate arrival.'

Luke rankled at Emma's presumption that he would be the one to be killed in a knife fight. It smacked at his male pride. But he said nothing and extended his hand to the man in black.

'I am Pastor Otto Werner and this is meine vife Caroline,' he said accepting Luke's hand. 'Vee are of the Lutheran missionaries sent out here.'

'Pleased to make your acquaintance,' Luke said shaking his hand. 'I hope you don't get the wrong idea about things around here. What happened was just a little misunderstanding between myself and the gentleman who just left. Nothing to do with the service in the store.'

Otto smiled knowingly at the American and released his powerful grip. 'I am sure vot you say is right Herr Tracy. I am sure this does not happen every day.' He turned to his wife and spoke in German. She smiled and nodded to Luke. 'Meine vife, her English is still learning,' Otto said. 'Vee haf come here to buy supplies. Vee are going to a country man's farm. His name is Schmidt and I believe his place is about fifty miles south of Maytown. Do you know him?' he asked.

Luke shook his head and looked at Emma.

'I am sorry Pastor,' she replied. 'But I don't think I can help you. I don't know the man. You could

94

possibly ask the Native Mounted Police at their barracks. They do a lot of patrolling in that country.'

The Lutheran pastor smiled and shook his head. 'I haf already asked. They say they do not know him. But vee vill find him,' he sighed. 'God vill guide meine vife and I to Herr Schmidt.'

Emma frowned. She was about to warn the pastor about the country south of Maytown. It was a dangerous land where a newcomer could easily get lost – or speared. But she refrained when she saw the set expression on the bearded face. He was a man of God and she sensed such warnings would be irrelevant to his mission. Instead she gave her attention to his list of supplies.

When they left the store Luke spoke.

'What did O'Keefe want with you?' he asked her. 'I heard him hollering. I was worried he might do you some harm.'

'He has been here before,' Emma sighed as she pushed back a lock of hair from her face. 'He accused me of not telling him the truth about Kate's whereabouts, said I knew where she was and wouldn't tell him. But I told him the truth. Kate is somewhere on the track to the Palmer.'

Luke frowned. 'If he returns tonight I want you to fetch me immediately,' he said. 'No need to get Henry tangled up in this.'

Gently Emma touched Luke on the arm. She could see that the American was protecting her husband from the likes of O'Keefe. 'Thank you,' she said softly. 'I will do that if Mister O'Keefe returns to the store this evening.'

Luke nodded. He felt guilty that he would be leaving at first light to search for Kate. It didn't seem right to leave Emma and Henry to face the man who was Kate's husband.

O'Keefe walked away from the store into the gathering night. He cursed the American's good luck being saved from what he perceived as the certainty of death on his blade. Whoever the stranger was who had intervened had an air about him of a man not to be intimidated. And the big man in black might have sided with the American had the James woman called on him for help. Not that it mattered. He would settle with Tracy at a later time. For now he had a business to run and more girls to recruit to his brothel. Given time – and the right bully boys – he would be able to open a second premises to accommodate the extra girls coming up from down south.

The night was dark and O'Keefe turned off the main street busy with the crowds of miners in search of a good time. The back alley took him into a narrow lane bordered by a Chinese joss house and the rear of his own establishment.

'O'Keefe!' a voice commanded, just a little nervously.

A smallish man stepped from the shadows of the joss house. O'Keefe stopped in his tracks and turned to confront him. He sneered when he saw who had called his name. 'You have some kind of problem I might be able to help you with,' he challenged insolently, letting the deadly knife slip into his hand from the sleeve.

The smaller man stood apprehensively in the shadows licking his lips as he watched the burly brothel keeper advance towards him. 'My missus is up there,' he croaked, and O'Keefe could see that the man was both drunk and frightened.

'I know you?' he frowned as he tested the grip on the bone handle of the knife.

'You took my missus to work for you when I was down on my luck,' the man said backing away from O'Keefe. 'She won't come home with me.'

'Then that's your bad luck mister,' O'Keefe said, baring his teeth. 'She's with a real man now.'

Suddenly the smaller man stopped backing away and stood very still in the shadows. From somewhere the two men could hear a woman's raucous laughter and the cursing of a drunken miner. Sweat beaded the forehead of the man in the shadows. 'No O'Keefe,' he said in a strangely disembodied voice. 'I think that's your bad luck.'

SEVEN

Captain Morrison Mort was not a man who reflected on the vagaries of life. If he had been, standing in the office of Granville White, he might have reflected that it had once been the office of David Macintosh.

That had been over a decade earlier and life as captain of the Macintosh barque had appealed to his health. At the beginning of his fourth decade of life he was tanned and fit with curling blond hair and pale blue eyes that had somehow captured the essence of sun and sea.

The office had changed little from the time that he had been given command of the *Osprey*. His employer Granville White sat in a big leather chair with his back to a window that overlooked the busy docks below. Granville now controlled the financial management of the vast Macintosh empire of shipping, property and stockmarket shares. In his mid-thirties he was a rather handsome man. A finely boned face and a receding hairline gave him an aristocratic appearance that women found appealing. And he carried with an arrogant ease an aura of genteel wealth and power. 'Welcome home Captain Mort,' Granville said with more formality than warmth. He rose and briefly extended his hand across the desk between them. 'Please be seated.'

Mort swept back his long navy blue jacket and sat down in one of the smaller leather chairs opposite his employer. 'Good to be back Mister White,' he mumbled without much conviction.

Sydney was not a place where he ever felt safe. Not since those years earlier when the Irish lawyer Daniel Duffy had attempted to indict him for murder. Only the power of the Macintosh name and their considerable resources had saved him from swinging on the gallows at Darlinghurst Gaol. As far as he knew Daniel Duffy was still active in attempting to bring him to justice. 'Your telegram I got in Brisbane said you had an urgent job back here.' Mort was not a man to mince with polite formalities. The meeting was about business and he got right to it.

A slight frown creased Granville's features. He lived with the genteel formalities of colonial society and Mort's abruptness was an affront to the social niceties of idle chatter as a preamble to business. 'You have a new assignment,' he said as he leaned back in his chair and puffed on a Cuban cigar. He had not bothered to offer one to the Captain who he knew did not indulge in alcohol or tobacco. The Captain was a man of spartan habits. 'The *Osprey* has been chartered by Baron von Fellmann as soon as he reaches our fair shores.'

'We are doing well with the kanakas,' Mort began in protest. 'The last shipment to Brisbane . . . '

'I accept that Captain,' Granville said, cutting the protest short with a wave of his cigar. 'But the Baron is prepared to compensate us generously for any loss of revenue. And besides, he is my brother-in law,' he added with a hint of sarcasm. 'One does not ignore my sister's requests.'

'Where does he want me to sail?' Mort grunted. He had resigned himself to obeying the obvious command.

'Cooktown,' Granville replied. 'After that only the Baron knows. But wherever he decides to sail you are to obey without question. He is, after all, paying for the charter.'

Mort raised his eyebrows. The assignment had an air of something wrong about it. Not that he particularly cared – so long as he was paid and commanded his ship. 'The Baron going after gold up on the Palmer?' he asked conversationally.

'Whatever the Baron's intentions are will not concern us,' Granville answered with a scowl. 'The less questions you ask the better you will get on with the Baron.'

Mort nodded his understanding. 'What I have to know Mister White,' he said, 'is what stores I will need and sailing times.'

Granville took a long puff from his cigar and blew a halo of grey smoke into the still air of the office. 'George Hobbs will have all the answers to your questions,' he replied. 'You can talk to him on the way out.'

Mort accepted that the brief meeting was at an end and started to rise from his chair. But Granville resumed speaking and Mort sat back down. 'Something of a somewhat disturbing nature has been brought to my attention in recent times,' Granville said. 'It appears your first mate Mister Horton has been saying things around The Rocks when he was on his last leave to Sydney. Things that are better left in the past.'

Mort felt a touch uneasy about the comment. He knew Jack Horton was a man who liked to partake of rum in the hotels around his old territory of The Rocks. When he was drunk he had a habit of becoming boastful of his adventures in the South Seas. 'What sort of things?' he asked.

'Things about that papist bastard Michael Duffy. And about my cousin David. Hints that they met with foul play.'

'Duffy was killed by the Maori in New Zealand,' Mort replied dismissively. 'And Mister Macintosh was killed by Chief Tiwi over five years ago. Got nothing to do with us.'

'Duffy I grant,' Granville agreed. 'But my cousin's demise might cause further questions to be asked, certainly in regard to the circumstances surrounding his death. My mother-in-law despises me enough to use her position to make things very uncomfortable for me. She might get it into her head to use her con-siderable resources to resurrect her own investigation.'

Mort knew that Lady Enid Macintosh believed that her beloved son had been murdered by himself on the orders of Granville White. Her hatred for them both was no secret in the company circles. Only the fact that Granville was her son-in-law – and so ably managed the vast financial empire – kept him temporarily safe from her wrath. But if something could be proved . . .

'Horton has a big mouth,' Mort agreed. 'It needs shutting.'

'Good!' Granville said. 'I am sure you can pension him off with an appropriate incentive to ensure his silence. You talk to him and settle the matter of his severance with the company. I am sure you can find a new first mate to your liking while you are in Sydney.'

George Hobbs sat behind his desk scribbling figures in his ledgers.

'Mister White says you have the information I need for the von Fellmann charter.'

Hobbs glanced up at the captain standing before his desk. He lifted a sealed envelope from the table and passed it to him. Mort ripped open the envelope and scanned the pages.

George Hobbs watched him from behind his spectacles. He did not like the *Osprey*'s captain despite his reputation for turning a handsome profit in the blackbirding trade for the company. Something about Mort made him feel decidedly uncomfortable in his presence. George shuddered involuntarily.

'Who's this Michael O'Flynn mentioned in the report?' Mort grunted without looking at him.

'I believe he is an American gun dealer who took a passage out of Samoa on the Baron's instructions. And, as far as I know, Mister O'Flynn is currently in town as a guest of the Baroness von Fellmann,' he replied. 'Other than that, I can tell you little more than what you have read, Captain Mort. The Baron is a rather private man, not inclined to divulge his business dealings.'

'And this cabbage eater, Karl Straub . . . ?' Mort queried further.

'I'm sorry Captain,' George shook his head. 'I know only as much as you and what is in the report.'

Mort stared hard at the little clerk behind his desk. He suspected that Hobbs knew more. But he also knew that his sympathies were with Lady Enid Macintosh. Why White had not dismissed David's private secretary made little sense to him. He could only conclude that dismissing Hobbs might confirm to Lady Macintosh that her son-in-law had something to hide. He looked into the bespectacled man's eyes and felt satisfied. Hobbs was a man who might have loyalties but he also understood fear. 'If Mister White requires my services in the next few days he can find me aboard my ship,' Mort said as he tucked the papers in his coat pocket and left the room.

After Mort's departure, Granville had remained sitting at his desk. He continued to puff at the big cigar, savouring its rich taste. Michael Duffy. He had not thought of the man for a long, long time. He was annoyed that the dead man's name should once again intrude in his life, albeit merely as a reminder of the unpleasant things he had to do to gain control of the Macintosh empire.

He stretched, stood and walked over to the window overlooking the wharves. From where he stood he could see the *Osprey* moored. And there was cousin David, he mused. Long dead to the world – but not to Lady Enid, his memory to her a potent obstacle to his own ambitions to rule the Macintosh fortunes.

His mother-in-law posed a real threat to his continuing ambitions to wrest complete and utter control for himself. But one day she would die, he consoled himself, and Fiona would inherit everything as the sole surviving Macintosh. And as Fiona's husband he would manoeuvre things so that he owned it all.

A dark cloud pervaded his thoughts when he reflected on his wife. He scowled and ashed the cigar on the floor. Fiona might be his wife but in name only. She was 'wife' to his sister Penelope. At every opportunity Fiona went to his sister's bed and continued to do so despite the fact that Penelope was now married to Baron Manfred von Fellmann.

Granville did not seem to care anymore that his wife had moved into another room. And he had long resigned himself to losing his wife's body to his sister's bed. What mattered was that Fiona had kept her word to be a publicly dutiful wife to him in his ruthless drive for power. He had after all, the solace of the bodies of the young girls he had procured in the Glebe tenements years earlier. A place where life was cheap and the patronage of the wealthy man a matter of survival for the families of the girls. The bestial pleasures he had taken with the prepubescent Jennifer Harris had long been forgotten for the pleasures of young Mary Beasley, eleven years old and already well practised in the ways of his perversions.

For a brief moment Granville thought about Glen View Station, a place he had never visited. Somehow the twists and turns of misfortune in his life could be traced back to a time twelve years earlier when Fiona's father, Sir Donald Macintosh, had ordered the dispersal of the Nerambura clan of Aboriginals on his property. A fateful day in November 1862 when the Native Mounted Police – commanded by none other than Morrison Mort – had slaughtered men, women and children without mercy. Very few had survived the massacre. And the pitiful handful that did were eventually hunted down like vermin and eliminated.

But from that terrible day rose the spectre of the Duffys. As witnesses and also unwitting victims they had become sworn enemies of the Macintosh family. Had all the misfortune visited upon him been the result of some obscure Aboriginal curse brought on by this slaughter?

The question was ludicrous but stubbornly persisted. As an educated and refined gentleman Granville knew such things were nonsense. But there had been a string of diabolical deaths over the years, albeit a couple he had actually conspired to. Both Sir Donald and his son Angus had died on the spears of a blackfella by the name of Wallarie. And even the hated Duffys had suffered their fair share of tragedy: Michael Duffy's brother Tom had been killed by the Native Mounted Police, his death graphically recorded in the southern papers weeks later.

If only the accursed Daniel Duffy could suffer some kind of death, he thought bitterly. Life would be much easier without his continuous crusade to bring the Macintosh name into disrepute.

The curse even seemed to reach into his life with his wife refusing her favours to him to procreate a son. Two daughters did not count. Females only counted as objects to serve his carnal desires.

The cigar had shrunk to the wrapper and Granville stubbed it on the window shelf. Outside the office life went on in Sydney. Maybe one day he would travel to Glen View and see for himself the supposed heart of the curse that was said to influence the lives of the Macintoshes and Duffys. He remembered long ago listening to Sir Donald rambling on about a strange cave on the cattle lease. What had amused him at the time was that Sir Donald actually had a look in his eyes as if he believed in the power of the site which was sacred to the Aboriginals.

But Sir Donald was a Scot, he scoffed as he turned away from the window that looked out onto the civilised world of Sydney. And the Scots were just as stupidly superstitious as the ignorant Irish.

~

Captain Mort walked the short distance to his ship. He noticed with some interest men and women clambering for berths on ships heading north to the newly opened goldfields on the Palmer River and the Queensland colony's far-flung territory on Cape York.

Mort knew about goldfields. He had once served as a policeman on the Ballarat diggings in '54. The damned miners had built a stockade and resisted by force of arms the British army and police, he remembered bitterly. But the Eureka Stockade – as they called their fortification – had fallen one hot summer morning to the might of British arms. He had been involved in the slaughter that followed.

Since that glorious day of killing Mort had led a colourful career, previously an officer of the Queensland Mounted Police, he was now Captain of a South Seas blackbirding barque. And in all his occupations he had been able to indulge his demonic madness for torture, rape and murder.

He soon walked to a wharf to admire the love of his life: his barque aptly named the *Osprey* – the sea eagle who had swooped on many an island to take either by persuasion or force of arms indentured black labour to toil in the sugarcane fields of tropical Queensland.

Jack Horton was nowhere to be seen when Mort boarded his ship. Not that he cared. His murderous first mate no longer had a job with the Macintosh companies. All he had to do now was replace him and it would not be hard to find a qualified man for the job as first mate in Sydney Town.

Mort leaned on the rail and gazed over the inlet

to the infamous slums of The Rocks. The jumble of old sandstone buildings had fallen into decay over time, moving enterprise away from the western side of the Quay. No doubt Horton was staying at his favourite boarding house. He knew where to find him – and how to terminate his employment.

Before he settled the matter of Jack Horton he knew it was time to visit The Rocks on a very special pilgrimage.

Morrison Mort knew The Rocks even if its residents did not recognise him. Not much had changed in the last twenty years or so, he thought as he casually strolled along the narrow streets. The sun was down and the night people had crawled out from under their sandstone rocks. Whores, sailors, pickpockets, a few well-dressed nervous young men seeking excitement and the surly gang members who ruled the streets.

The young toughs loitering in the dingy streets eyed the *Osprey* Captain walking amongst them. None attempted to accost him as he had the look of a man familiar with the place and its violence. Although he was a stranger to them he did not appear in any way nervous. Besides, he wore the dress of a sea captain, a man who was one of their own in a district with traditional connections to the sea. Mort had little reason to feel uncomfortable as he had come well-armed. He carried a small calibre pistol in his pocket and a razor-sharp knife inside his boot.

The stench of boiled cabbage, urine, vomit and

decay were familiar scents from his childhood. Here he had learned the lessons of the street before he was ten: to steal, lie and keep one step ahead of the police who came from time to time to snatch dangerous felons for the gallows at Darlinghurst Gaol.

He slowed in his purposeful stride in an alley between the close-packed tenements spewing the noises of despair: the constant wailing of hungry babies suffering flea bites in the dirty cramped rooms shared with the flotsam from the sea of poverty; the drunken raised voices of men and women squabbling over nothing and everything, and the occasional raucous, despairing laughter of gin-soaked whores sharing a bottle with customers.

Mort felt the fine hairs of his neck prickle. Although there was a chill in the night air, as he stood and stared into the doorway of the tiny tenement house with its dirt-grimed sandstone façade he was vaguely aware that he was sweating. Why had he let his feet guide him here, he wondered with a dread chill that shivered through his body. Was it that he had a need to face the most terrible ghost of his past and spit in her eye?

He recoiled in horror. *The ghost was real!* She came silently towards him from the darkness of the doorway and was smiling as she reached for him. 'Mother!' he screamed as he stumbled backwards in a desperate attempt to avoid the hands reaching for him. She was going to take him to the hell! A hell to which he himself had sent her so many years earlier.

'I'm not yer mother luv,' the ghost said. 'Me name's Rosie. An' I can give yer a good time if yer got the money? Wotcha want?' she asked, frowning, her arms crossed over small breasts concealed under a dirty cotton dress that was little more than a petticoat.

'You,' Mort hissed as the colour returned to his face. No, he thought with great relief, she was not the ghost he feared.

'Well, come in luv,' she said, turning her back on him, in order to walk back into the house. 'A good time will cost yer though.'

Mort followed. It was ironic, he thought, that in this very room he had murdered his mother. It was a tiny room, lit by two candles flickering shadows on a dirty well-used, straw-filled mattress in the corner. The loathing for the many times he had been subjected to the drunken sexual advances of filthy customers welled up in him. Times when his drunken mother had taken their money and laughed at his pain.

The fury was on him like a red haze when he looked down at the woman kneeling on all fours on the mattress, the hem of her dress pulled up over her hips revealing her buttocks.

'Yer want me this way?' she asked, looking up at him. For a second she felt a dread she had never experienced before. The pale blue eyes that looked back at her were like the windows to hell. She could find nothing to allay her sudden dread. It was as if she were in the presence of the devil incarnate.

'How you are will suit my needs,' the devil said as he let his hand slip to the razor-sharp knife in his boot.

No-one took much notice of the muffled screams that drifted out into the chilly night air.

Rats feeding on the body scuttled into the crevices of the room with protesting squeals at the entry of the two policemen. Sergeant Francis Farrell was a big Irishman and his bulk seemed to fill the tiny room.

He stood and stared at the pathetic body huddled in a corner in a vast pool of congealed blood. Her torn, blood-soaked dress lay in a crumpled pile beside her naked body. He felt little emotion as he stared. As a policeman of thirty years he had long come to accept that crimes of violence were as much a part of life as love and kindness were.

His presence had been summoned by young Constable Murphy who had found the body. The constable had been attending a dispute between barrow vendors at the Quay when a woman told him about a body in a room. The woman was a friend of Rosie's and Constable Murphy knew her as one of the prostitutes who worked the docks area around Sydney Harbour.

'Do you believe in ghosts?' the sergeant quietly asked the young uniformed constable who stood beside him.

Constable Murphy grimaced. 'Maybe it might be that I believe in the Little People, Sergeant, but not ghosts, unless you include the Banshee.'

'Well, a ghost did this,' Farrell said, aware that his comments concerning the world of the supernatural were confusing the young policeman. 'You see

Constable, I have been here before. I was about your age and The Rocks was my beat. Old Sergeant Kilford and I got a call to this very house one morning, and in this same room found a body mutilated in the very same way as this poor colleen. That must have been over thirty years ago.' Farrell frowned as the incident swirled back from almost forgotten memory to clear recollection. 'There was a boy at the time,' he continued slowly. 'A young lad no more than ten years of age. It was his mother who had been murdered.'

'Was not the murderer brought to justice?' Constable Murphy asked out of idle curiosity.

The sergeant shook his head. 'Thought it might have been one of her customers at the time,' he said. 'Some sailor, long gone on a ship by the time we found her. It's like that around here.' He stood in reflective silence as he tried to recall the boy. A blond-haired boy, he remembered. A boy who had stood in sullen silence in one corner of the room watching he and old Sergeant Kilford that morning. 'Always wonder what happened to the boy,' he muttered. The constable gave him a quizzical look and Sergeant Farrell returned his thoughts to the present. 'Start making notes on everything you see,' he said, without looking at the constable. 'Make a note of the poor colleen's wounds.'

Murphy wet the end of his pencil and commenced to try and describe in writing the hideous slashing of flesh, the frenzied mutilations to the mouth and private parts. So much blood that it splashed every wall of the room.

The Irish sergeant was reading the room with the many years of experience he had in such matters. What he read caused him to shudder, his first real emotion since entering the domain of death. 'He made her suffer,' he muttered as his eyes followed an invisible path around the room. 'Cut her and held her until she bled to death. It took a while and she tried to fight.'

Murphy glanced at the big sergeant. 'How do you know Sarge?' he asked, awed by the older man's perceptive observations.

'The blood marks tell me,' he replied. 'Over there on the mattress he inflicted the wounds, you can see from the way the blood is.' Murphy followed the sergeant's invisible chronology of events and began to see what his experienced colleague was unravelling from the blood trails. 'If you follow the blood you can see she tried to get away. But he held her and they ended up against the wall there,' he said, pointing to the body. 'She struggled in her pain and fear but he held her until she died from the loss of blood. He sat behind her and had his arms around her. Her blood soaked his lap.'

'A crime of passion,' Murphy commented.

Farrell shook his head. He was puzzled. He had seen many crimes of passion over the years and this was not one of them. Something very strange pervaded the room. The girl's killer had methodically inflicted the wounds to cause extreme pain and fear and then had remained to gloat on what he had caused. 'Not a crime of passion,' he finally said. 'The bastard who did this is a son of the devil himself.' He

113

sighed, wanting to be out in the alley where human sounds pervaded the air. 'Time we informed the detectives. It's their job to make the investigation.'

'Think they will catch the bastard?' Murphy asked as he put away his pencil and notebook.

Francis Farrell bit on his bottom lip. The question was reasonable enough and his reply far from flippant. 'Only if they believe in ghosts, Constable Murphy.'

Returning to the police station Sergeant Farrell kept remembering the young boy who had stood silently in the room the day they had discussed his mother's killer. He wished he could remember the boy's name. Not that it really had any bearing on the events of the current murder. Just something about the boy had haunted him for a long time after.

Ahh, but the old records would tell him who the boy was, he realised with a small amount of satisfaction. Maybe he would have a look at the file next time he was at the Darlinghurst lockup.

EIGHT

Two weeks out from the Palmer on the track to Cooktown and the journey was thankfully uneventful. Kate had decided to take a longer route as the Hell's Gate Trail was not a suitable track for wagons. The location of the attack on the armed gold escort was aptly named. A dangerously narrow defile on top of the Great Dividing Range over-looking the Palmer River, it was for many miners a tantalising glimpse of the River of Gold that was the closest they would ever get to their dream. For many, Hell's Gate would end in the nightmare of a spear or stone club.

During the journey a change came over Jenny. The gauntness in her face and haunted look in her eyes dissipated with the distance the lumbering wagons put between herself and the past horrors of the goldfields. The beauty that was her inheritance blossomed like a beautiful tropical lily on a northern billabong.

She also proved to be a capable companion on the slow journey east. She would cheerfully prepare the evening meals while Ben and Kate went about the end of day routine of unyoking the bullocks from the big wagons, and hobbling the beasts for the night. Jenny was an imaginative cook and the teamsters would return to stews seasoned with wild spices. Jenny explained how her father, who had been a gardener for a Mister Granville White, had taught her the use of herbs in cooking. She had found a discarded parcel containing dried herbs left by some weary miner on the side of the track. The lucky find proved better than the discovery of gold as far as Ben and Kate were concerned as they sat down each evening to a meal by the campfire.

During those times Kate noticed that Willie rarely left his mother's side. He hardly spoke unless it was necessary. She could see how jealously the boy guarded his mother, even against Ben whom he had befriended in a strange way. Kate guessed that the boy had witnessed many terrible things happen to his mother during the horrific months of the Wet on the Palmer. Although Willie had a distrust of men he would follow Ben like some faithful dog. Ben would give him meaningful tasks and the taciturn boy would do them with a begrudging gratitude.

The boy was a strange one! Kate reflected as she watched him help Ben hobble the big bullocks that were as good as any watchdogs. The scent of prowling tribesmen would cause the big beasts to become restless. Only once in the two weeks that they had been on the track had the animals alerted them that they were not alone.

It had been just on piccaninny dawn during the previous night when the bells around the beasts' necks had jangled more than usual. As the animals bellowed nervously both Kate and Ben became instantly alert. Weapons clutched in hands they had peered into the gathering dawn anticipating a deadly shower of spears. But a warning shot from Ben's revolver soon dispersed whoever lurked in the last shadows of the night and the spears did not fall.

When the sun rose that day Ben decided that Jenny should learn how to fire a gun. At a midday stop he decided to teach Jenny how to use Kate's rifle and chose a creek a hundred paces or so from the campsite. Kate allocated to Willie the task of finding firewood and issued him the obligatory warning not to stray far from the wagons in his search. The previous early morning incident had reinforced the vital need for alertness deep in hostile territory.

Standing close to Jenny by the creek Ben could smell the musky scent of her perspiration and fresh smell of her clean hair. It was now a familiar scent that he was acutely aware of whenever he was close to the slim young woman. A scent he had come to know ever since Kate had called a halt by a creek where both women had indulged themselves in the luxury of lathering with soap and washing in the creek. Ben had stood guard at the wagons a short distance away and had paused in his task of greasing the wagon axles to listen to the two women splashing and giggling with an uninhibited girlish delight. He could hear Jenny's laughter – like the sweet sounds of the butcher-bird in the first light of the day – and sighed for his unrequited desire to touch her. He imagined what it would be like to kiss those secret shadows beneath her breasts. Turning, he saw Willie scowling at him, as if the boy understood his lustful thoughts. Guilt flooded him and he had tried to think of something else.

After they had bathed Kate had presented the young woman with a clean dress. It was one which she had carefully packed for any occasion that might warrant its wearing. Not that any such occasion arose on the grinding, torturous trek along the track to the Palmer. But it was a small vanity that reminded Kate that she was still a woman, despite working in the gruelling man's world of the bullocky.

Jennifer had burst into tears at the simple gesture. No-one had ever given her a present in all of her eighteen years and the simple cotton dress without the rigid stays clung to the slim body in a provocative way that did not go unnoticed by Ben. Nor was it unnoticed by the miners who they occasionally passed on the track. Although Jenny preferred not to notice the miners' unabashed stares Ben had experienced twinges of jealousy for the attention Jenny was unwittingly provoking.

Despite his sometimes less than subtle interest in her he had remained aloof. He was afraid that if he showed any interest he might be rejected. And besides, Kate had spoken to him a couple of days out of the Palmer, and had explained that the girl might need time to adjust to the attentions of a good man. Indeed his boss had explained with such a knowing smile that it caused him to blush.

But now, standing next to Jenny and holding the heavy rifle into her shoulder, he was close enough to catch her scent and even touch her smooth flesh. The same disturbingly secret thoughts were back in his mind as he placed his hand self-consciously under the young woman's, gripping the wooden forestock of the rifle. Her long hair brushed his face and he had an overwhelming urge to hold her and kiss her on the lips. He was afraid of his feelings as he had never known a woman in the carnal sense. Kate had been like a surrogate mother keeping him away from the tempting fleshpots of Cooktown. Although he knew she was acting in his best interests the invitations from the painted ladies were hard to ignore.

Jenny was more acutely aware of Ben than he realised. He was not like the other men she had known in her life. He was kind and gentle in a shy way and had a wonderful laugh. But she did not consider herself beautiful when she remembered the strawberry birthmark. What man would ever want a woman with such a disfigurement?

Mister Granville White had not cared about the mark, she remembered bitterly. All he ever wanted was her prepubescent body. She still remembered the depraved things he did to her. Willie had been a product of those terrible times. But he was now a

119

part of her in a way that had brought only joy to her lonely life. Sometimes she shuddered when she looked at the boy and saw a part of Granville White looking back.

With the rifle butt in her shoulder she could feel Ben's big calloused hand under her own. As they stood at the edge of a shallow, stony bottomed creek she found herself wishing that the moment might go on for ever. She sighted the rifle at the fork of a drooping coolabah tree on the other side.

'You just let the gun rest in this hand and hold it steady with your other,' Ben said as he lowered his head to look down across her shoulder and along the sights. 'Remember,' he explained as his face pressed into her soft hair, 'when you squeeze the trigger do so with a gentle but even pressure.'

Jenny nodded as she closed one eye the way Ben had taught her. She was suddenly aware of a disturbing change in him. He was tense, something had distracted his attention from the shooting lesson. 'Jenny, I want you to walk back to the wagons with the rifle,' he said quietly but firmly.

She turned and gave him a puzzled look. 'Is something wrong?' she frowned.

'Maybe not,' he answered quietly. 'Just something I want to have a look at. Just go back to Kate and make sure Willie is at the wagon.'

She walked nervously away. On her right the rainforest marched up the craggy barrier that was the hilly spine between the Palmer goldfields and the ocean to the east.

The hairs on the back of Ben's neck stood erect.

He was acutely aware of a pounding in his ears and only when he could hear the distant sound of Jenny's voice engaged in a conversation with Kate did he walk cautiously with the Colt in his hand a short distance up the creek which flowed gently through a plateau of tall grasses and stunted trees. The swirling little eddies of mud in the clear waters had caught his eye whilst he had stood behind Jenny. And now he stared down the creek line at the other eddies of mud in the water.

There were hundreds of them! Footprints!

Prints so fresh that the creek had not had time to wash them away. Ten, maybe fifteen minutes old, Ben thought with rising fear. Either a very large war party or a peaceful tribe moving across the trail behind them. But it was not usual for the tribesmen to allow their women and children so near the track. No provocation was needed for the miners to indiscriminately shoot at any Aboriginal sighted in the bush. The idea that the only good black was a dead one prevailed amongst many of the white men of the frontier. Ben could only conclude that he was staring at the footprints of a very large war party stalking them.

He could see that the Aboriginal crossing had been made behind them when they had stopped for the midday break. The warriors had probably circled them and were now moving into an ambush position in the thicker scrub that edged further along the track towards Cooktown. His stomach churned. He was afraid and he had very good reason for that fear. Somewhere deeper in the scrub the painted warriors were moving silently into position with their spears, wooden swords, clubs and broad shields.

He could still hear Kate and Jennifer talking softly in the distance. Water burbled over the pebbles of the creek while in the thick scrub the little song birds shrilled. The serenity of the bush was deceptively mesmerising.

Ben edged away from the creek and began walking towards the wagons. He was acutely aware that with the next step he might hear the bloodchilling, black cockatoo war cry, as painted warriors rose up out of the ground wielding their weapons. The hundred paces to the wagons felt more like a hundred miles.

Kate saw the gun in Ben's hand as he approached and instinctively knew that something was terribly wrong. As he stood peering intently up the track to the stands of scrub she cast him a quizzical look.

'I think we are being watched,' he replied to her unspoken question. 'Saw signs of a big myall party that has crossed behind us when we stopped.'

Jennifer paled and with a stricken expression clasped Willie to her protectively.

'How many?' Kate asked calmly as she poured tea into an enamel mug and passed it to Ben.

'I don't know.' The mug shook in his hand. 'Maybe hundreds from the signs I saw back at the creek.'

Kate turned to scan the surrounding scrub. The heat of the midday sun high overhead caused the scrub to shimmer with an uncomfortable haze. 'I think they will be in the bush up ahead on the track,' she said calmly as she shaded her eyes against the glare.

'That's what I think,' he replied as he sipped the hot tea. 'I think they are just waiting for us to move on. Wait until we are well and truly within range of their spears. A short rush and they would be on us before we could get off many shots. The bloody grass helps hide them. We could just about step on one of 'em before we could ever see 'em.'

'Then we sit and wait here,' Kate suggested. 'Or we turn around and go back, or someone will come down the track and walk into their ambush. Then hopefully we will have extra guns to help us,' she added optimistically, wishing that she had purchased one of those American repeating rifles. She had been offered one by an American prospector who had been down on his luck and prepared to part with his Spencer for the price of his fare home.

Ben could see that Jenny, although pale and still frightened, was quickly regaining her calm. Willie stood protectively holding his mother's hand. He vowed silently that no man would ever again hurt her. Although he was not fully aware of what the tribesmen might do he did know that he would fight back somehow to protect her. Ben only wished that they had an extra rifle for Jenny. But all she carried was Kate's little pepper box pistol. It might get one warrior, but little else.

'Will the savages attack us here?' Jenny asked in a frightened voice.

'I don't think so,' Kate answered as she gazed up the track. 'At least not in broad daylight. They know that they would lose a few if they had to attack us across open ground. No, they will wait until either someone else falls into their trap. Or try to get us tonight.'

'What do you think we should do Kate?' Ben asked. He had a great respect for his boss's decisions. She had not accumulated a fortune without a sharp and perceptive mind.

Kate turned and walked across to one of the wagons where the boxes of cartridges were kept for the rifle. 'We fortify the wagons and wait,' she said as she opened the box of cartridges. 'If they come they will have to get at us under the wagons which should help stop their spears. And if we can keep up enough fire from under the wagons then it might be just enough to discourage them. From what I've been told it's not usual for them to keep up an attack against guns for very long.'

Ben was not so sure. Had not the tribesmen attacked a well-armed police party on its way back to Cooktown? Surely they were less prepared than the police who were trained and equipped to repel attacks from the myalls. But they had no other options. Although not very religious, Ben said a short and silent prayer for their deliverance.

'I think we should unhitch the bullocks,' Kate said hefting the rifle on her shoulder. 'And get them down to the creek.'

Ben agreed and Jenny stood guard while they hobbled the bullocks down to where they could graze on the grass and have access to the water.

~

The afternoon passed with an interminable slowness while the bells around the bullocks' necks jangled softly with a reassuring and soothing sound. The group kept an anxious vigil in both directions along the deserted track as surely there would be a traveller before sunset.

The tiny bush birds called to each other, oblivious of the drama unfolding around them, as the silence of the hot afternoon lulled the four into lethargy.

Towards sunset Jennifer, who was crouched under the wagon with Kate's rifle, heard the sound. It was a strange sing-song melody and coming from the Cooktown direction of the track. She nudged Ben who dozed beside her. He came awake with the revolver in his hand. 'I think I can hear someone coming,' she said excitedly as she rose to get a better view up the track.

'Chinamen!' Ben grunted, recognising the strange voices. 'Chinamen coming our way.'

'We've got to warn them,' Kate said as she took the rifle Jenny passed to her. 'Or they will be massacred if they get much closer.'

Ben pulled a face. He did not feel that it was worth risking their lives for people who the white miners detested as farmers would locusts on a field of grain.

'We need them, Ben,' she pleaded softly. 'If the myalls get to them first then that will only make it easier for the blackfellas to come after us later. You will have to warn them somehow.'

What she said made sense. Ben gazed at the

shadows creeping through the long grass. 'I'll use the creek as cover and skirt around the scrub,' he said as he unbuckled the holster from his waist. 'Make my way around to the track where the Chinee are and warn them. With that Irish luck of yours Kate, I might convince them that attack is our, and their, best hope of staying alive.' When the belt was unbuckled he passed it to her. 'You keep this. Jenny can use the rifle if . . . ' he trailed away.

Kate fully realised what the young man was doing. He was ensuring maximum firepower for the women. Without a gun he was virtually defenceless and was preparing to lay down his life for them. Courage and honour were the badges of the bushman and the protection of women and children an unspoken contract on the frontier. She reached out to the young man and touched him gently on the arm. 'No, Ben,' she said softly. 'You keep your gun.'

He shrugged off her offer in such a way that at first Jenny was confused by this exchange. Then it dawned on her why Ben had given Kate his gun. 'Benjamin!' she gasped as he slipped a wicked-looking bowie knife from the side of his boot.

'I've got this Jenny,' he said casually with a grim smile as he held up the knife. 'And I reckon I can outrun any myall from around here.'

She took a step forward and threw her arms around his neck. He could feel the pressure of her breasts against his chest and her lips were on his mouth as she drew him down to her. 'I have never met a man like you Benjamin,' she whispered hoarsely with tears in her eyes. 'Please be careful.'

126

He was stunned by her passion and stood with his hands at his sides. She clung to him with desperation. Events had moved too fast for the normal coy processes of courtship. All she knew was that it was important that *he knew* she cared more than she could admit to herself. He pushed her away gently. 'I hope you remember this moment when I return,' he growled softly.

Then he was gone.

Kate passed the rifle to Jenny. 'He will be back,' she said reassuringly as she slid the big Colt revolver from its leather holster. 'Ben is one of the best men out here.'

'I know,' Jenny answered in a small voice. 'I only wish I had told him before.'

Although Kate had expressed her confidence in the young teamster's ability to succeed in his task she could not feel as equally confident in the privacy of her thoughts. Was it that the strange curse on her family would take yet another she loved? She glanced down at the big Navy Colt in her hand checking that the percussion caps were in place over the revolver's chambers. 'God and Jenny's love go with you Ben,' she whispered softly. 'Come back for both of us.'

NINE

B en crouched and sprinted along a strip of dry sand in the creek bed. Where the sand ran out he was exposed up on the creek bank. Although his legs were strong from the countless miles of walking beside the big wagon, so too he knew were the legs of the hardy warriors. He prayed with desperate entreaty to God that the warriors in ambush would have all their attention on the column of approaching Chinese.

The knife in his hand felt lethal but he was also fully aware of how futile it was. It was unlikely any warriors would come close enough for him to use it in his defence. They would stand back and bury him under a shower of barbed spears. Worse still, they could rush him, and take him alive for one of their cannibal feasts! He shuddered with horror as he fought the terrible fear. The sprint in the late afternoon heat had taken its toll on his strength. But so far there had been no sign of the warriors and the long grass kept him hidden from their view.

He stumbled on a log and pitched face first into the ground, driving the wind from his lungs. As he lay gasping for breath he could hear the unintelligible sing-song voices chattering close by.

With some effort Ben rose from the ground. He could see the column of men above the sea of grass. Twenty, maybe thirty Chinese in their uniform blue trousers, shirts and broad conical hats. They jogged as they balanced bamboo poles with cane baskets slung across their shoulders while a few were carrying ancient flintlock muskets. They were being led by a giant of a man dressed in the bushmen's garb of moleskin trousers and red shirt. But the giant also wore one of those big American felt hats with the brim turned down, and he trailed a Snider rifle with a bandolier of ammunition around his waist.

'Hey!' Ben called and stood to wave his arms. The column came to a hesitant halt. Fear etched the smooth faces of the men who turned to stare at him and the armed Chinese levelled their muskets. 'You speakee English?' he called.

'Yair, I speakee good English Mister,' the giant at the head of the column bellowed in a voice deeply resonant with the accent of an Australian bushman. 'What the hell do you want?'

As Ben staggered towards the column, the bushman turned and spoke in Chinese to the men in the column. They were naturally nervous at the sight of the wild-eyed white man stumbling towards them.

The lurid stories that circulated around the Chinese quarter of Cooktown of white men who ambushed and killed Chinese for the gold they might be carrying were fresh in their minds. It was rumoured that sometimes the white men would leave Chinese bodies with Aboriginal spears in the bullet holes in an attempt to make it look as if the natives had killed them. They watched suspiciously as the white man approached.

Ben was surprised to see that the man dressed in European clothing was part Chinese although at first glance this had not been noticeable. He was around Ben's own age and clean shaven. The man's eyes were a coal black and his appraisal of Ben like a deadly taipan snake's of a mouse. The Snider rifle the giant Eurasian carried looked like a toy in his broad hands. 'The name's Ben Rosenblum,' Ben panted when he reached the column. 'And you are just about to be bushwhacked 'bout two to three hundred yards up the track.'

The Snider was casually levelled at his chest as the Eurasian eyed him suspiciously. 'Myalls?' he asked without taking the barrel of the rifle off him.

'Yair. Myalls,' Ben replied, ignoring the threat of the rifle. 'Maybe a couple of hundred of 'em.'

Ben could see that the man was obviously the leader of the party. When he spoke the others reacted quickly. The men with arms closed on him while the others in the column squatted obediently in line waiting for further orders. The fear in the Chinese coolies' eyes now turned to terror as they remembered the stories told in Cooktown of how the northern Aboriginal tribes preferred Chinese flesh to that of the Europeans. Around the opium houses, restaurants and brothels of the Chinese quarter fellow Chinese regaled tales to wide-eyed and frightened men going up the track to the Palmer, stories of others captured by the painted warriors and strung up by their pigtails from trees to await slaughter.

'My name is John Wong,' the Eurasian said without offering his hand. He let the rifle drop to his side. He had seen no guile in the other man's eyes and decided to trust him. 'Tell me what the hell is going on.'

Ben briefly recounted his discovery of the tracks in the creek while John listened and surveyed a stand of stunted trees on the grassy plain between them and the distant wagons. Cynically he realised that the teamster's warning had only been given because he needed the Chinese as an ally to ensure his own survival; he was acutely aware of the European's dislike of the Chinese.

When Ben had finished outlining the situation John turned and addressed those of his men armed with muskets. The Chinese looked fearful, although they listened without questioning their leader. When he had finished addressing his men, John turned to Ben. 'I've told them that we are going to advance in a line against the myalls. I figure that if we go in shooting, the myalls will decide there are easier pickings up along the track and will run.' He flashed Ben an evil grin. 'But if I'm wrong and they stand and fight then the myalls are going to have an interesting supper tonight. White and yellow meat,' he added with a chuckle as he cocked the hammer of his rifle. He turned to his men and barked brief orders. The Chinese responded – if somewhat reluctantly – and fanned out into an extended line.

They advanced cautiously across the grassy plain towards the scrub which now lay under a soft golden glow from the setting sun. The men with the muskets advanced ahead of the line and Ben kept close to John.

For the first hundred yards there was nothing except the sound of the bush birds warbling, and the swish of the long grass under foot. The Chinese were as tense as hunting dogs searching for game. The long barrels of their muskets thrust forward as if hoping they might ward off the hidden warriors. Ben's nerves were at breaking point.

The ear-splitting screech of the black cockatoo rent the late afternoon air and simultaneously lines of yellow and white painted naked warriors rose from the long grass immediately ahead of them. The heart-stopping spectacle of the hundreds of warriors armed with their array of deadly weapons caused the advancing skirmish line to freeze in its tracks.

The Chinese teetered on the verge of panicked flight and, without firing a shot, turned to flee the superior numbers of black warriors confronting them. John's voice roared above the Aboriginal war cry. He tried to rally his men as he fired his Snider into the massed ranks of painted warriors. A warrior crumpled with a yelp of pain as a bullet took him in the chest. But then a shower of deadly barbed reed spears hissed through the sky falling amongst the ranks of Chinese.

Ben felt a spear pluck at the elbow of his shirt and saw one of the Chinese musketeers nearby fall as a spear found its target. The stricken man dropped his flintlock as he desperately plucked at the spear buried deep in his lung. But the deadly barbs held firm against his futile efforts to tear the shaft out. The initiative was with the tribesmen and Ben knew the situation was extremely grim.

The volley of spears was followed by a full charge of warriors screaming their black cockatoo war cries as they surged forward brandishing clubs and wooden swords.

Ben scooped up the dying man's musket and levelled the long barrel at a painted warrior who was charging towards him wielding a wooden sword and shield. The ancient flintlock fired true and the warrior spun as the lead ball took him.

Ben's shot was followed by a rattle of fire by the Chinese musketeers as John bullied them back into a semblance of a line to face the phalanx charging towards them. A lethal shower of lead ripped through the warriors' ranks and three warriors cried out their despair.

When they fell they were snatched up by their comrades who dragged them to the rear of the line which was by now faltering in its determination to close with the men who had rallied to fight back. Behind their own ranks the tribesmen stuffed the bullet holes with grass in a futile attempt to stem the bleeding.

John was firing his single shot Snider as if it had been one of the new repeating rifles from the Winchester company of America. With practised hands he fired, then flipped open the breech to slam in a cartridge. He did not have to take careful aim as the warriors were massed on the grassy plain in front of them.

Ben gripped the musket by its long barrel and stood his ground. He would wield the weapon as a club when the tribesmen reached them. Around him the Chinese musketeers scrabbled for powder and shot to reload their cumbersome weapons. They held their ground as they poured a spasmodic fusillade into the ranks of the charging warriors.

Then a distant crash of gunfire erupted behind the tribesmen. Kate and Jenny had joined the battle from the cover of the wagons. The combined weight of cross-fire unbalanced the momentum of the attack. The leader of the painted warriors could see that the Chinese had now rallied and appeared determined to sell their lives dearly. Bullets plucked at the grass and the men around him and he realised that the situation would only lead to unacceptable losses on his side.

It was not a lack of courage that caused the warrior chief to break off the attack but rather a thorough knowledge of the European way of fighting. He knew well the limitations of their own weapons. He knew that it was only through the use of stealth and ambush that they held any hope of success in their warfare against the invaders of their lands. On his command the warriors broke off the attack and turned to retreat with their wounded for the safety of the surrounding thick bush on the hill-sides overlooking the track.

The gunfire from John's Snider tapered off as the tribesmen melted into the bush. A wispy cloud of gunsmoke drifted on the still air. The victorious Chinese broke into an excited babble at the sight of the retreating Aboriginal warriors. Through the babble Ben could hear the distant voices of Kate and Jenny calling to him from the wagons. As he stood with the ancient flintlock in his hands, he realised that he was shaking uncontrollably. It had been so close. If John had not rallied his men and Kate had not joined the fight they would have been swamped by the screaming ranks of warriors.

He was vaguely aware of Jennifer's cotton skirt swirling around her knees as she ran towards him across the grassy plain that had moments before been a battlefield. He tried to smile bravely as she flung herself into his arms and smothered him with kisses. He held her and knew he would never let her go.

'I don't know how I can thank you enough for help-ing us Mister Wong,' Kate said, as she passed him a slab of jam-covered damper. He was not only a big man but he also had a big appetite. The jam dripped through his fingers onto his lap as he sat on a log beside the campfire under the canopy of brilliant stars.

'Tucker like this is thanks enough, Missus O'Keefe,' John answered gratefully, as he licked at his sticky fingers. 'I've been on rice and dried fish for the last week. The tucker of my Chinese cousins isn't what I'm used to. Man gets a craving for the food he was brought up on.'

Kate was surprised to hear him talk about his Chinese 'cousins' because he did not look very Chinese. Yet, he did have a Chinese surname, and there was the faintest trace of the Orient in his strong and handsome features. 'You say your countrymen Mister Wong, but you don't sound or look like them,' she commented politely. 'Although I must presume you have Chinese parentage.'

'I'm half Irish half Chinese. My mother met my father on the Ballarat goldfields back in '54. I was born there. Guess you could say I'm between two worlds,' he reflected, as he stared into the flickering flames of the campfire. Kate glanced at him with surprise. It was hard for her to imagine someone of Irish blood also having Oriental blood. John noticed her bemused look. 'I get to celebrate twice as many holidays,' he chuckled when he came out of his introspection. 'I even got drunk last Saint Pat's day in Sydney with some of my mother's relatives.'

Kate felt a little foolish talking about John's mixed blood when she remembered that she herself was raising her brother Tom's three children. They also lived between two worlds.

John finished the damper and washed it down with sweet black tea. The fire crackled in the silence and he stared contentedly into the flames. A full stomach of European food and the company of the legendary Kate O'Keefe sufficed for the moment.

Even those in the Chinese quarter had heard of Kate O'Keefe. Her compassion crossed racial lines and the young Chinese girls working for the tongs had been recipients of her charity from time to time.

Ben and Jennifer had gone for a short walk into the dark to sit and gaze up at the brilliance of the southern sky. But they had not wandered too far from the protection the wagons afforded, just far enough to talk privately away from the hearing of the others.

Young Willie remained by the fire staring at John. He had attached himself to the charismatic man. The Eurasian bushman had taken the boy to his camp a short distance from the wagons and the Chinese had made a fuss of him, offering him some of their precious supply of candied ginger.

Willie had been wide-eyed at the strangeness of the men who had pigtails like girls and spoke in a language he did not understand. The Chinese were a relative novelty on the northern goldfields in the early months of 1874.

Now Willie sat at John's feet savouring the tangy sweetness of a lump of candied ginger he had brought back from the Chinese camp. For once he was not clinging protectively to his mother, as Kate astutely noticed. But the excitement of the day and a full stomach caught up with Willie. He quietly slipped away to make his bed under Kate's wagon while she sipped her tea and watched the shadows dance in the fire.

'You know, I miss the company of my European brothers from time to time,' John said reflectively.

'But lately I've been starting to think in Chinese. Haven't done that since I left my father in Melbourne years ago when my mother died.'

'What are you doing travelling to the Palmer with . . . ' Kate hesitated as she did not know the appropriate word to describe John's fellow travellers.

He glanced up and smiled. 'You mean with the Chinks,' he said, to relieve her embarrassed discomfiture in casting him as Chinese. 'Well, as a man between two worlds, I have value to Soo Yin, my boss. Mister Soo uses me to act as his go-between in his dealings with the Europeans who ship the coolies out here. Very soon there will be thousands coming here and I will be the man to help organise their migration from Hong Kong. I don't suppose that will make me very popular with the white miners.'

Kate had heard of Soo Yin, a wealthy and very powerful Chinese merchant operating in Cooktown. She had also heard that the Chinese merchant ran brothels and gambling houses for the Chinese, although Soo Yin did not discriminate against the white men who wished to avail themselves of the services he provided in the Chinese quarter. There were also whispered stories about Chinese secret societies in Cooktown, of which Soo Yin was reputed to be a leader. *Tongs* she had heard them called. 'So you are a kind of interpreter Mister Wong,' she offered conversationally.

'Interpreter, adviser, supervisor and a few other things. Soo needs the European side of my mind to help him deal with the Europeans,' he continued. 'I suppose you can say I translate one idea on one side

138

of my head into another idea on the other side. And vice versa. Right now I'm on my way down to the Palmer to establish a base for Mister Soo's operations. My men who carry the arms are to be . . . gang bosses I suppose you could call them.'

'What will you do?' Kate asked. 'When you have reached the Palmer?'

'Return to Cooktown. Maybe sail for Hong Kong to see . . . ' He hesitated. He had almost mentioned the existence of the tong he was working for, although he was not a member as his European blood made him suspect in the eyes of the Chinese purists. '. . . Well, to see about another batch for the Palmer.' Then he fell silent.

Soo commanded the Lotus tong in North Queensland. John's father had recommended his son for the employment on account of his dual knowledge of both Chinese and European ways. But John had always felt more comfortable in European ways, having grown up with the scent of the gum tree rather than the sandalwood incense stick. He spoke relatively fluent Chinese with a European accent. And his size commanded respect from those who were told to obey him. Soo had made a wise decision in employing the young man as had been proved in the encounter earlier that afternoon. He had the brains of his Chinese father's people – and the brawn of his Irish mother's side.

'Missus O'Keefe,' he asked now, 'I don't want to sound like I am poking around into your business, but did you have a husband back in Cooktown?'

Kate cast him a startled look. 'I had . . . I have a

husband. But I have not seen him in over ten years. Why do you ask such a curious question Mister Wong?'

John stared down into the fire to avoid her eyes. There was something on his mind and he wondered whether he should say anything at all. His question certainly had aroused Kate's curiosity. 'Why do you ask? Do you know something about my husband?'

He continued to stare into the fire, struggling with a matter that he knew he should stay out of. However he decided to tell her and took a breath. 'There was a fella looking for you in Cooktown a while back. Said he was your husband.'

'Kevin!' Kate gasped. For so long he had gone from her life. Now he was back!

'Don't know his first name,' John continued. 'Just that he was a big fella. Good with the cards.'

'Is he still in Cooktown?' Kate asked, her feelings a confused jumble of emotions. She had grown to detest Kevin O'Keefe for leaving her on her own just when she needed him most. At the same time, she still remembered how she had felt as a sixteen-year-old girl madly in love with the handsome son of Irish convicts.

John gazed at the glowing coals of the fire. 'I'm afraid the fella I met will be permanently in Cooktown, Missus O'Keefe,' he said bluntly. 'Got himself killed over some married woman. Seems her husband shot him and then took off.' Sudden and violent death was a part of John's existence on the frontier and he knew no other way of telling her the facts.

Kate swooned. John tensed as if to spring to her side, but she waved him off to reassure him that she was adequately composed. 'I'm sorry it was me to break the news to you Missus O'Keefe,' he said apologetically.

'It is all right Mister Wong,' she replied in a weary voice. 'The inevitable has happened. I think I have always known that my husband's life would end in that manner.'

A shooting star blazed across the night sky causing Kate to glance up at the long trail of sparks. *A spirit trying to return to the earth* an old Aboriginal had once told her in Townsville. She shuddered, hoping it was not her husband's spirit returning to haunt her and said a silent prayer that his soul should rest in peace. Strangely, she felt resentment that his death had denied her the opportunity to confront him at least once more. Besides, his death had left her with unresolved issues about her own feelings.

John could see the grief etched in her beautiful face and wisely excused himself from her company. 'Good night Missus O'Keefe,' he mumbled, before returning to his men camped a short distance from the wagons.

As he walked to his camp he wondered whether he had actually seen grief in the woman's face. Or had it been relief mixed with a little bit of anger? Who knew with European women? He shrugged his broad shoulders. But who knew with women of any nationality, when it came to that?

Kate sat staring at the fire, thinking about her life. Kevin was dead. She was free to start a life with any man she chose. Not that being married to Kevin had stopped her from going to Hugh Darlington's bed years earlier. Living like a nun had not appealed to her passionate nature.

But into her life had come Tom's children who kept her occupied as they would any mother. She had grown to love the three as if they were her own. They in turn eventually responded to her with their love.

Little Sarah was growing up with only the faintest of memories for her natural mother. Although Kate had tried to tell her who she was, young Sarah had the resilience of her birth mother and coping with the reality of her present life meant the little girl repressed terrible memories.

But the two boys did remember their mother and father. They had not forgotten the night when they saw both their parents die from the guns of the Native Mounted Police.

Kate had grown to accept the responsibilities of a parent but she still yearned for the love that she could share with just one special man. And she yearned again to feel a life growing in her body and a baby at her breast.

The fire had burned down to a softly glowing log when Kate heard the curlews crying to each other in the night. She shivered against the cold and pulled an old woollen shawl around her shoulders. She remained by the fire until even the night sounds were muted before rising stiffly to retire for the night. The morning would come soon enough.

TEN

Tiny as the kitchen of the Erin Hotel was, it had witnessed many memorable family gatherings of the Duffy family, and Sergeant Francis Farrell felt at home as he sat at the old worn table.

For years he had been a guest of the publican Frank Duffy. On cold nights when the big sergeant had been a constable walking his beat around Redfern's splendid streets and narrow alleyways, the back door to the hotel had always been left open for him. It was a sanctuary from the bitter cold where he had sipped a warming rum with the publican and talked of bygone days in dear old Ireland.

Although Frank was dead, the tradition of hospitality of the publican's son, Daniel Duffy, continued and the back door remained open to the police sergeant.

It was of mutual benefit for the two to meet from

time to time. The Erin was the ideal place to swap information concerning Sydney's criminal under-world – information to convict or acquit, depending on the trade-off between police officer and legal representative. For Daniel Duffy was a young man with an enviable reputation around Sydney Town as a highly successful criminal lawyer.

In his early thirties, Daniel was tall, clean shaven and slightly stooped by his years of academic study. But he had the Duffy trademark for toughness in his professional dealings and was grudgingly respected by even a waspish colonial society that normally looked down on the Irish.

His face reminded many of his cousin Michael Duffy; the same grey eyes and handsome features – albeit less marked than Michael's face – battered by his short career as a bare knuckle boxer. Many would also describe Daniel as a serious fellow who rarely smiled. But it was known to the Irish patrons of the Erin that there was a heathen curse on the family and it was no wonder the lawyer rarely smiled.

After years of exposure to the Duffys, Francis Farrell had become an unofficial member of the clan. Had it not been for his non-intervention in Michael's escape from Sydney back in '63, then the young man might have dangled at the end of a rope for a killing that was not his fault. The vagaries of jury decisions could well have found Michael Duffy guilty of murder when he had, in actual fact, killed Jack Horton's brother in self-defence.

Daniel sat at the table toying with a tumbler of rum. He was smartly dressed in a three-piece suit that marked him as a senior member of the legal firm of Sullivan & Levi – Solicitors. One day he would be a partner. That is, if he did not choose to enter politics as many would like him to do, given that he had another trademark of the Duffys – a quiet charisma.

Sergeant Farrell was dressed in his heavy serge uniform and his hat lay on the table between the two men. 'I swear if a ghost had jumped out at me from the page I would not have blinked,' he said and took a long swig of his tot of rum. 'The name was there all these years under our noses.'

'Morrison Mort,' Daniel hissed. 'He was the boy in that murder case you used to scare us kids with all those years ago. It was his mother that was murdered.'

'Don't know why I even bothered looking up the report,' Farrell sighed. 'Must have been the ghost of young Rosie who was guiding me to the archives.' He glanced self-consciously at Daniel. Admitting ghosts might exist was blasphemy to the policeman's creed of only believing in those things of the temporal world. All else was speculation for priests and women. 'But then,' he added quickly, 'it made sense to look up old Sergeant Kilford's notes. Same trademark in the same place. Too much to be a coincidence on its own.'

Daniel frowned. It was absurd to think that a boy barely ten years of age could have the mind or motivation to carry out such a hideous crime. It was a case that had frightened and thrilled him and his cousin Michael. Both boys would beg the big policeman to tell them about the gory goings on in the world of crime. And Francis Farrell was a born storyteller. His description of the mutilations – although veiled in the telling – had caused the two boys to have goose bumps and nightmares. Now the same story had resurrected those goose bumps of his youth. 'Could it be . . . ' Daniel trailed away as he tried to comprehend the almost incomprehensible evil in a child. It was even recognised as a legal impossibility in his own profession. A child under ten was deemed as incapable of *mens rea*, the Latin term for the concept of intent. He glanced at the police sergeant for an answer.

'He was present then,' Farrell shrugged. 'And I know his ship is back in Sydney now.'

'But could he . . . ' Daniel paused as he attempted to understand the full horror of what might have happened years earlier. '. . . God almighty! A boy could not have the mind to inflict so terrible a death on his own mother. It has to be impossible. Even for Mort!'

'A couple of my informants tell me a sea captain was seen in The Rocks around Rosie's place the night she was killed.'

'Did they say it was Mort?' Daniel asked, his professional interest aroused.

Farrell shook his head. 'Didn't – or don't want to – recognise him. They said it was too dark to make out his features.'

Both men well knew the reluctance of The Rocks' residents to be involved in any police investigation. It was a place closed to official scrutiny by the law, and information from residents could only be obtained by bribe or threat, neither of which was a reliable means of gathering evidence for a court of law. 'If you are thinkin' we might bring him in for questioning,' Farrell continued, 'I doubt that we would get him to confess. He's got the luck of the devil himself.'

Daniel impatiently waved off the suggestion. 'I know the problems Sergeant Farrell,' he said. 'All Mort has to do is deny his involvement and without witnesses you would be hard pressed to present a case.'

Farrell glanced down at his empty tumbler. 'I know what he has done to the family but we still have the law for the likes of him,' he growled. 'However we can pay him a bit of attention while he's in Sydney Town. He might even go after another girl.'

Daniel shuddered at the last statement made by the police sergeant. How many poor souls would the demonic killer wrench from living bodies before he was brought to the gallows? 'Pray that it is not someone we love,' Daniel said softly.

Mort sat in his cabin staring at the straight-bladed infantry weapon lying unsheathed on the chart table amongst the maps. It had been with him since '54 when he had won it in a game of cards from an unlucky young officer destined to storm the Eureka Stockade. The blade was oiled and ready to be returned to its scabbard to be hung once again on the wall of the small cabin.

Mort reached out and ran his fingers along its length. If only he had the sword at his side when he had killed the whore. Oh, she would have screamed like the others had in the past. Like the nigger girls from the police barracks when he had been an officer in the Native Mounted Police. And the brown-skinned beauties he had taken from the Pacific islands as a blackbirder. They had all screamed for their lives, begged him for the mercy that was not his to give to the species of creature that had caused him so much pain as a child living with his prostitute mother in The Rocks. But she was dead, her filthy mouth that had laughed obscenely at his pain, mutilated by a knife. And that unspeakable part of her that gave pleasure to her customers torn apart by the same knife so that it could never give pleasure again.

Carefully, Mort sheathed the silver blade in its scabbard, and held it in his arms as he crooned a tuneless song. They would never lead him to the gallows. The old Aboriginal who came to him in his dreams had told him so. No, he would meet the white warrior of the cave and only then would his fate be decided.

Mort grinned, his handsome features contorted into a grimace. He shrugged off the old Aboriginal's assuredness that the white warrior would be the cause of his demise. No living man had that power. Neither heathen white warrior nor civilised lawyer would ever be the cause of his demise. Not when his sword was unsheathed.

He rose and placed the sword on the rack over his bunk. He would not be needing it tonight. The matter of his first mate's severance from the company was even now hopefully being settled.

Hilda Jones was as hard as the men who sought board at her establishment. She was also a big woman, big enough to intimidate most of the boarders who stayed under the roof of her run-down boarding house at the edge of the infamous Rocks.

Hilda had little time for the traps. But it had been her message to Detective Kingsley that had brought the policeman somewhat reluctantly to the front door of her establishment.

There was a man bleeding his life away in one of her rooms. And she wanted him out. She had tried to get the badly wounded man to leave but the knife that he flashed – and the evil in his eyes – made her think twice. He had demanded that she fetch a police detective to talk to him. Not one of the beat police, but a detective. Well, at least now the traps would deal with him and rid her of his worthless carcass.

The detective followed the broad back of the woman as she waddled down a narrow fly-specked hallway to a room at the back of her boarding house. He tried not to gag at the putrid and overpowering smells of boiled cabbage, urine and vomit. The stench seemed to fill the air like some ghost of a long-dead boarder.

''e come in las' night wid 'is guts 'angin' out,' she said as she pushed open the door to the tiny room. From a single iron bed with a blood-soaked mattress on sagging springs, a man turned his pain-filled face towards the door. The movement caused him to grimace. 'At least 'e's paid up to today,' Hilda Jones said with some relief. 'From the look of 'im he ain't goin' to see tomorrow.'

Detective Kingsley peered into the semi-gloom of the room which had only a broken window high in the wall for ventilation and light. The dirty wooden floor under the cot was thick with blood that had pooled into a dark stain. Skulking rats scurried away to places that only they knew; they would return when the intruders had departed.

'You a trap?' the dying man asked in a hoarse whisper. He was thirsty from a combination of blood loss and a hangover.

Kingsley said he was and the man asked for water to quench his raging thirst. Hilda was reluctant to leave the room, half of which her massive bulk occupied. She was curious as to why the man had demanded to see a police officer. But Kingsley spoke harshly to the landlady and she left to fetch the man a drink. The detective moved closer to the bed so that he could hear the barely whispered words of the dying man. 'Me name's Jack Horton an' I know I'm dyin'. Must be, to be talkin' to a trap on me own accord,' the man rasped hoarsely, trying to cough. But no sound came from his dry throat and his shoulders heaved, causing the blood to flow even more heavily.

'What happened Mister Horton?' the detective asked with a note of respect, although he suspected that Horton was a man with some kind of long criminal record. It was obvious that the man might have a lot to say before he departed this world and all good police were natural agents of intelligence gathering.

'Don' matter what 'appened anymore. Jus' say I was a bit slow an' the other bastard a bit fast. Maybe some day 'e will end up like me.' The words came painfully. His adversary's knife had slit the dying man from hip to chest. 'What I want you 'ere for is to tell you 'bout a treacherous bastard who set me up to die like some stuck pig. An' me bein' 'is first mate an' all. I knows he was behind me killin' as sure as I knows me name is Jack Horton.'

Kingsley was losing interest. So the man just wanted to squeal on a mate who had probably deserted him during one of the many knife fights in The Rocks. It was unlikely the police would ever find his killer.

Horton could see the detective's lack of real interest in him. But he knew how to get his attention. 'You ever 'ear of Lady Enid Macintosh?' he asked in a whisper.

Kingsley showed immediate interest. Yes, he had read of the Macintosh family from time to time in the newspapers. They were powerful, influential people in the Colony. 'Yair, I've heard of her,' he replied. The dying man's expression showed pleasure at the fact the name had caught the detective's attention. 'Big nob in Sydney,' the detective added.

'Yair, well, I'm gonna tell you some things, that will make yer 'air stan' on edge. 'bout the Macintoshes, an' the bastard Morrison Mort that works for 'em. Matter of fact, I'm goin' to tell you a lot of things before I go. So youse better start takin' notes . . . '

Before he died Jack Horton revealed all he knew to the detective who listened like a man stunned by a blow to the back of the head. Horton's motive for telling what he knew was simple: to revenge himself on Mort whom he suspected was behind the sudden ambush in an alley behind the hotel where he had been drinking. For some time he had been uneasy. Something about his captain's aloofness had warned him treachery was afoot. No, Jack Horton was not making a death-bed confession to ease his conscience. He was taking a final act of revenge on the people he had always hated for their manipulative power.

Kingsley was glad that he had closed the door against the nosy landlady. What the dying man had told him in confidence was information that had to be carefully evaluated for its monetary worth. It was information that could be of great assistance in establishing friends in the right places. The call to Horton's death bed was one of the luckiest things that had occurred in all his years of policing Sydney's seamy streets. There was certainly a silver lining in every cloud! Even in run-down boarding houses in The Rocks!

ELEVEN

As he rode out of the rising sun, Kate paused to glance at the approaching horseman. All she could see however was a tall man framed by the fiery glow. The glare hurt her eyes so she returned to packing the cooking pots into a box under the wagon and dismissed the horseman as just another traveller heading for the Palmer River.

Ben, Jenny and Willie had gone down to the creek to fetch water for the trip while the Chinese under the command of John Wong were moving out onto the track and already heading south. The horseman would probably overtake them very soon, Kate thought idly.

The departing Chinese laughed and waved to Willie who watched them from the banks of the creek. He was disappointed that they were taking their precious supply of candied ginger with them and was tempted to run after them and ask for more of the sweet. But he sensed that he could not leave Ben alone with his mother. She had been acting very strangely since the previous evening.

'Hello Kate. Don't you own a dress?'

Startled, Kate swung around, dropping the pots on the ground. With the rising sun still at his back the horseman seemed to tower over her. She had not heard him approach and shaded her eyes to focus his face. For the first time in her life she saw the full extent of the scar that ran from the corner of his eye down his cheek.

'Luke!' she gasped. 'You no longer have your beard!'

'Yeah,' the tall American replied, with a slow smile on what Kate thought was the most wonderful face of any man she had ever known outside the men of her family.

'Beards aren't all the fashion back home.'

She began to cry, although without knowing why. Nevertheless it felt so good to cry!

Luke flung himself from the saddle to go to her side but she waved him away angrily. 'Why didn't you write?' she sobbed bitterly. 'You just ride out of our lives. Six years and not a word. Why?'

Luke hung his head and stood self-consciously wringing the brim of the broad felt hat in his hands. He had not expected this reaction from the woman he had dreamed of seeing again for so long. He'd thought that maybe she might be mildly annoyed. But not tears and anger. 'I didn't think you cared,' he mumbled. 'I just didn't seem to get around to writing, that's all.' Kate did not reply but turned to stoop and pick up the pots and pans. He bent to help her. 'I'm truly sorry Kate,' he said, placing his hand over hers.

Kate sniffed defiantly and used the long sleeve of her shirt to wipe away the tears. 'It doesn't matter,' she said, as she stood with a handful of pots. 'It was just that the Cohens were concerned for you, more than anyone else.' Luke placed his hat on his head and turned away lest she see the pain in his face. 'Why did you come back?' she asked, as he strode towards his horse.

He paused in his stride and turned to face her. 'Heard about the Palmer while I was in the Montana territory,' he replied bitterly, disguising his pain. 'Realised some other bastard had discovered my river of gold. Had to come back to see if any was left. That's the only goddamn reason I came back!' He lied to protect himself. To have travelled so far only to have Kate reject his love was more than he could face.

'I see,' Kate whispered. 'You are welcome to travel with us,' she said in a louder voice. 'That is, if you wish to return to Cooktown for any reason.'

'I might,' he growled. 'As a matter of fact I do have some unfinished business back there. The Palmer can wait for a while.'

'Then tether your horse to the wagon and walk with me,' Kate said with less anger in her voice. 'You can tell me where you have been for the last six years. And how you came to be on the track.'

Luke nodded and led his horse to the wagon.

'Told you Kate. I was going to have a look at *my* river of gold, that's all.' He thought he could see a flicker of disappointment in her eyes at his answer. But it was not likely, he told himself. 'You know, I almost got to the Palmer six, maybe seven years back,' he said tethering his horse. 'Just bad luck and a bad case of the fever drove me south. But I met a poor bastard who got there. Can't remember his name. Buried him with a myall spear in his leg, out beyond the hills south of here,' he said with a wave of his arm. 'Things might have been different if I had pushed on,' he added wistfully. 'I might have got rich. But that's all past.' And you might have seen me as more than a down-and-out prospector, he reflected sadly to himself.

Goddamn you Luke Tracy, Kate thought angrily as she took in the outline of his face. Goddamn you for just coming and going in my life. It was all too confusing, her feelings an untidy mess which could only be sorted out when time allowed. For now she had the task of getting her two wagons back to Cooktown. People other than Luke required her attention for the moment. It was not the time or place for her to explore what she felt for the man she had always tried to deny she loved.

Although Luke walked with Kate beside the bullock wagon little was said. For Luke, talking was one of those things people did when they had nothing better to do with their lives. Besides, he had a personal score to settle with the man who had caused his flight to America. Before his departure from Cooktown, Luke had learned that a Rockhampton solicitor by the name of Hugh Darlington was scheduled to visit and consequently the American's brooding thoughts did not make him very talkative. Especially since he was focused on the deadly confrontation he planned with the man he had since come to learn was once Kate's lover.

That evening they camped by the track. Luke assisted Ben in unyoking the bullocks and hobbling them for the night while Kate and Jenny prepared the evening's meal.

The awkward silence between Kate and Luke created a tension not lost on Ben. He had never known his boss to be so unsettled and aloof. He had heard from his aunt Judith how the American had been such an important part of the young Irishwoman's life. His aunt had even ventured that Kate loved Luke Tracy. 'But that she refuses to admit as much to herself,' his aunt had sighed.

Ben had taken a liking to Luke. He had an easy way about him that inspired confidence and it was not hard to see why his uncle Solomon spoke so highly of the Yankee. A couple of years back his uncle had told him how Luke was forced to flee the country because of some kind of treachery by a Rockhampton solicitor. But he would not elaborate and the subject was forgotten. And Jenny had shyly told him of how she had first met the American prospector on a Brisbane River wharf six years earlier. His generosity to her and her father was something that had touched her. The fact that he had reappeared in her life again made her feel as if everything would turn out well for Willie and herself in the future. It was like an omen.

So if the American had been so important to Kate why was she now treating him as if he were a leper, Ben puzzled. He could only conclude – as had countless men past and present – that it was the mysterious and unfathomable nature of a woman to do so.

Kate patted the dough into a flat cake. As she prepared the damper bread to be placed in the hot ashes to bake, she found herself gazing at Luke going about the task of hobbling the bullocks. Tall and lean with a face that reminded her of a noble eagle, Luke's dark blue eyes always seemed to be seeing things beyond the distant horizons. His face was tanned and his long hair, shot with grey streaks, hung down to his shoulders. It was not a handsome face but one that spoke of gentleness backed by a toughness of a man others respected for his physical courage. The long scar inflicted by an English soldier's bayonet had faded considerably with time but was still a reminder to the world of his stand at Eureka twenty years earlier.

It was a face she had grown to love, Kate now grudgingly admitted to herself. Those same eyes that watched the distant horizons could suddenly brim with laughter, and his slow drawling voice filled her with a yearning to be held by him. Strong, gentle, funny, intelligent and caring, she thought, when she put words to what she loved about him.

But he was also impulsive, foolhardy and a born

drifter. Dangerous and lonely enterprises guided him in his perpetual search for gold and he seemed to have little in the way of ambition to settle down. He was everything a woman should avoid.

As Luke strode towards her, his saddle over his shoulder and trailing his rifle, Kate looked away. She did not want him to see the love in her eyes.

'Can I do something Kate?' he asked gently as he settled his saddle and rifle beside the fire.

'I have gone this long without a man's help,' she replied. Luke flinched. Without a word he picked up his rifle and saddle and walked away.

Kate bit her lip. She didn't mean it that way! Why was it that she could not tell him of her love? The word 'defence' echoed as a bitter self-recrimination. She had a need to defend her feelings against the pain of him leaving her life – as others had – forever.

Kate's wagons rumbled into Cooktown, the big wheels creaking and groaning along Charlotte Street. They passed the numerous bawdy houses and hotels that had sprung up on the banks of the Endeavour River to cater to the appetite and thirsts of those who had come in search of a dream. But despite the sordid reputation of the boom town, Kate felt that she had arrived home.

Dust rose in a permanent cloud, finely coating all who ventured onto the main street. A babble of accents merged into an excited din of sound; the guttural accents of the Nordic visitors mingled with the sing-song voices of the Asian miners, the brogue of Scots and the twang of Americans.

Ships of every nation were anchored in the river just off the main street, having disgorged their cargoes upon arrival in Australia's far north. The ships were as crowded as the crush of humanity on the shore; coastal steamers, Chinese junks and small sailing ships competed for anchorage in the muddy brown waters that ran into the opal-like Coral Sea.

Luke, leading his horse, strode beside Kate down the busy street. Ben, Jennifer and young Willie followed, trudging beside the second of Kate's wagons. Through this melting pot of humanity the big wagons rolled until they neared the depot where Kate handed over control of her wagon to Luke. She had led her little band of travellers to the depot that stored the precious goods of the frontier: shovels, picks, gold cradles, candles, tinned meat, nails, kerosene, cloth, canvas tents, medicines, tobacco, tea, coffee, rice, sugar and flour. 'I have something to do before I arrive at my store,' she said mysteriously.

'Kate, there is something I should tell you,' Luke said, with a stricken expression clearly stamped on his face. Kate returned his expression with one of puzzlement. She had never seen him express such pain before. He had always been a man who kept his feelings very much to himself. 'I really came back because I wanted to see you again.' She could see that he was groping for words and sensed in his simple statements a great depth of feeling. 'I love you Kate. I always have. For what it's worth.'

She gently touched his face with her fingers, and turned to walk away without a word. This was not the time to deal with their feelings for each other.

Now she must go in search of a place she knew she must visit before she could find peace in her life.

Finding her husband's final resting place had been difficult. There were so many freshly dug graves around Cooktown with little to mark who lay beneath the earthen mounds. But luck was on her side when she caught sight of a young woman placing a posy of wildflowers on one of the graves.

The young woman had a face aged by her profession and a pallid complexion indicating that she rarely saw the daylight hours. She was pretty, in a hard way, and Kate felt that the woman would have been attractive to a man like her husband. The young woman stared down at the unmarked grave. There were no tears, only an expression of regret when she glanced up at Kate.

'I'm looking for the grave of someone I once knew,' Kate said gently. 'A man called Kevin O'Keefe.'

The woman glared. There was hostility and resentment in her darkly shadowed eyes. 'You know him too?' she sniffed angrily. 'Not altogether surprised. The big bastard had an eye for pretty women.' She glanced down at the grave and a tear splashed from her eye. 'That's him there,' she said, indicating the grave at her feet. 'Stupid bastard got himself killed.' The woman choked and could not continue her grief-stricken tirade.

Kate guessed that she was the woman John Wong had said her husband had got himself killed over and felt an empathy for the woman who had made the fatal mistake of falling for Kevin O'Keefe's charm just as she had all those years earlier. She felt no animosity towards her, only a deep sadness that Kevin's life had come to nothing more than this unmarked grave on the Queensland frontier.

She walked away, leaving the young woman to grieve for the handsome and charming rogue, knowing she would never return to visit the site again. It belonged to the other woman who wept openly for him as she could not. It was time to go to the depot that was her home and be with the living.

The interior of the depot felt cool after the weeks toiling with the bullock teams. Kate sat on a bale of hay in her store reflecting on the visit to her husband's grave. She found her thoughts drifting to Luke, the Cohens and the Jameses who had all become so much a part of her existence and wondered what she would do without them. The loss of any one of the people who had come to share her life since that fateful day she had stepped ashore at Rockhampton – eleven long years past – would have been a loss greater than that of the man she had married. Had time hardened her against her past? Or was it that she had nothing in common with the girl she had once been?

She gazed at Emma James who had greeted her with an outpouring of unabashed joy for her safe return. She felt a touch of envy for Emma's wonderful life with Henry. They may have had little in the way of money but Emma had her husband's gentle love.

When Henry was discharged on medical grounds from the Native Mounted Police, he and Emma had accepted an offer to work for Kate managing the Cooktown depot. The depot was used for the storage of goods to be hauled down to the Palmer River and out to the homesteads of the squatters, as well as to the little towns springing up in the hills and on the plains of North Queensland.

The rush to the Palmer had stripped Kate of teamsters to work with her small fleet of wagons but she had been able to recruit Ben back to her business, even though she knew he had intended to try his luck on the fields. Ben gave up his ambitions to make his fortune prospecting, his unstinting loyalty ensuring that she continued to build on her fortune. But it was a fortune tied up in capital investment: land, wagons, cattle, mining shares and a string of supply depots. Her business enterprises now overlapped with those of the Cohens who had expanded into hotels and even shares in enterprises in Sydney and Brisbane. The informal partnership proved extremely profitable for Kate and the Cohens and was firmly established on nothing more than a handshake of trust.

Emma reached over and touched Kate's hand. It was a familiar gesture between them and she returned the gentle gesture with a weary smile. 'I will be all right Em,' Kate said. 'The trip back was a little rough.'

Emma worried for her friend who drove her self so hard. There was not a bad bone in the woman, she thought with a sigh. Her only fault was that she worked like a man and denied the woman in her. Kate's once flawless pale skin was now tanned to a golden hue and her hands were callused from the tough, physically demanding work of handling the bullock teams. But the gruelling work could not dim the beauty of her grey eyes which burned with an intensity touching all around her with their light. Emma could see that she was depressed about all that had happened in the last few days. 'Your husband came here a couple of weeks ago,' Emma said. 'He said he would catch up with you when you returned.'

'Instead I caught up with him,' Kate replied wearily, as she stretched her long legs and reflected on her visit to Kevin's grave.

'The children missed you,' Emma said, by way of letting her know that there were people who needed her. 'Sarah in particular,' she added.

At eight years Sarah seemed already a young woman with her own mind. Although she played rough and rowdy games with her older brothers Tim and Peter, she was a serious young lady, with big brown eyes and a pert nose. And she idolised her aunt Kate and followed her whenever she could.

Life had not been easy for the children. To many of the white children they were 'darkies', and Kate's three adopted charges found themselves cruelly isolated in the town.

Young Gordon James proved the exception. The son of Henry and Emma, he was a constant companion of the three Duffy children. So when Kate had moved temporarily to Cooktown to oversee the hauling of stores to the Palmer, she had brought the three children with her, rather than leave them in the care of a stranger. All three had inherited much of their father's rebelliousness, which had brought about the resignation of more than one nanny.

Of the three children Peter proved to be the most difficult. He preferred to roam the bush and often camped with the wandering Aboriginals on the outskirts of the town. He was growing fast and already showed the promise of his father's muscled build.

Gordon was only nine but big for his age. Often he would disappear with his best friend Peter to go bush where the two lived the life of the Aboriginals who accepted the boys into their nomadic life. The Aboriginal men taught both boys the skills of the bush. Gordon was a quick learner and better at tracking than Peter. Little Sarah secretly adored him. Indeed, she knew, even at her tender age, that she would always love the son of Henry and Emma James.

The news that her aunt Kate was home had reached Sarah. She ran all the way to the store, wearing a dress covered in dirt from the rough games the boys played. She burst in. 'Aunt Kate, Peter and Gordon have run away again,' she said breathlessly, as she gave her aunt a crushing hug.

'Stop telling tales on your brother, Sarah,' Kate said with a gentle squeeze. Kate was not concerned about the disappearance of the two boys. They always came back after a couple of days. Or, if not, Henry would track them down and bring them back by the scruff of their necks. Besides, they rarely went any further than the Aboriginal camps just outside of town. 'Where is Henry?' Kate asked Emma. She had not seen him at the store.

'He's gone off to see someone about a prospecting job or something like that,' she replied with a worried expression. 'At least that is what he told me.'

'He is finding it hard to work in the store?' Kate asked sympathetically.

'He misses the bush so much Kate. He misses all the excitement of his days with the police. But he does not miss the work he did for that horrid and evil Lieutenant Mort. Henry is like a man haunted,' Emma added with a frown. 'He lives with a terrible guilt for what he has done to the Aborigines on the dispersals. He is not a bad man. Just a man who feels that he did bad things in the name of the law. I do not understand it but he loves the bush out there and wants to return to his days roaming the tracks. But I know you need him here to help out and I feel guilty that my husband would even think about deserting you for a job in the bush.'

Kate gave her friend a reassuring smile. Both women knew it was really Emma who did most of the work around the depot when Kate was out with the bullock team, even though Henry was useful when he was needed. 'I think I know how he feels Em,' Kate said as she remembered her experiences on the track. 'There is something beautiful out there which you have to experience to understand.' How could she put into words the majesty of freedom on the track. Sure there was danger. But there was danger in the almost lawless frontier town on the Endeavour River. 'Did he say what he was going to do?' she asked out of a sense of curiosity.

'No. He just looks for jobs that his past experience might suit,' Emma replied.

Kate shrugged. She wondered how he would cope with his almost crippled leg if he did get a job back in the bush. The old war injury had grown worse with the passing of the years and gave him a lot of pain. But he rarely let on about his suffering from the shrapnel wound. She could see that Emma was worried and hoped that Henry would not get the job back in the bush for Emma's sake. Knowing Henry as Kate did, she surmised that there would have to be an element of danger to get his interest.

'I think I will attend to the correspondence before I wash and change,' Kate said, as she stroked Sarah's long dark hair with her fingers. 'Then I can go and sleep on a real bed.'

She heaved herself wearily off the bale of cloth and stretched. The trauma of the last few days had taken a greater toll on her reserves of strength than she had admitted to herself. But she had reason to smile when she remembered that Luke had come back into her life. It was still like some wonderful dream.

The smile turned to a frown however as she allowed a doubt to creep into her thoughts. There was a nagging question that neither had resolved as they had walked side by side with the big wagons. Luke had said so little, but she had sensed a tension in him that she could not reach. And yet when the sun was gone from the tropical skies they had sat together discussing little other than the events that had transpired in their lives. Why did it have to be so difficult? Why was it that neither seemed to be able to reach out without the fear of failure? For now she would attend to the mundane business of running a company and put aside thoughts of him.

She found a pile of correspondence Emma had placed in an old chocolate box kept under the counter and wearily shuffled the piles of invoices and receipts looking for personal letters. She found two. One was from Sydney and she recognised her cousin Daniel's handwriting. The other was from Hugh Darlington. She was surprised to find a letter from Hugh and opened his letter first. She read it and groaned. It was not possible, but it had happened. Another blow! This time it was financial.

Despite his past betrayal of her trust she had re-employed Hugh's law firm to handle her legal matters after the death of Sir Donald Macintosh. Better the devil she knew, she had rationalised at the time. He was after all the best in his business on the northern frontier. But now, as she stared at the contents of the letter she wondered if she had not made a huge mistake in her decision to hire him once again. What else could go wrong? According to his letter her former lover would be in Cooktown within a fortnight. When she glanced at the date on the letter she realised he was already in town. She hoped Luke was not aware of her past relationship with the suave Rockhampton lawyer.

TWELVE

Detective Kingsley's meeting with Lady Enid Macintosh proved to be interesting. He was served cucumber sandwiches as he sat in the parlour of the great mansion overlooking the harbour.

Lady Enid was all that the detective imagined a titled lady would be – and he had to admit that she was a beautiful woman for one he guessed must be in her fifties. Her flawless skin was unwrinkled and her jet dark hair only beginning to show the grey streaks of time. But it was her striking large emerald green eyes that he noticed above all her features.

She was aloof but polite to the likes of himself. He was pleased to see the faintest crack in the obvious contempt she had for mere working class police detectives when he related how Horton had told him that her son-in-law Granville White was behind the death of her son David Macintosh years earlier.

Before he died Horton had managed to tell him of how Mort had left David on the beach to be butchered by the natives and that the *Osprey* captain had once had a conversation with Granville White about what might happen to David Macintosh on such a trip. Lady Enid's son-in-law had hinted heavily too that any 'accident' would not be held against the captain of the *Osprey*.

Horton also mentioned that Granville White had hired him and his half-brother to kill an Irishman by the name of Michael Duffy. But Duffy had instead killed Horton's brother in self-defence.

Enid interrupted the detective. Michael Duffy was dead, killed in the war against the New Zealand Maoris. So the information that Horton had confessed to Duffy's innocence was of no value. Unfortunately Kingsley had not corroborated the confession with a witness and it would come down to only his word in any court of law. Kingsley himself did not know of the Duffy case but guessed that the records would probably be held by the Darlinghurst police.

Enid listened impassively. At least that is how she appeared. So Granville was instrumental in the death of her David. For that he would pay dearly! The policeman was only confirming what she had always suspected and the wheels had already been set in motion for her son-in-law's demise as a power in the colony. Revenge would come slowly but surely. Granville would pay dearly for the murder of David, she vowed. And so too her daughter for siding with him.

'I realise that what this Jack Horton told me could prove to be an embarrassment to the good name of yourself and your family, Lady Macintosh,' Kingsley said, balancing a teacup and saucer on his knee as he munched at a cucumber sandwich. 'So I thought it best to tell you first. Only fair.'

Enid stared coldly at the man across the room from her. His manners were atrocious and his feigned servile demeanour insulting. She well knew why the detective had come to her with the information instead of going to his superiors. 'I know I am speaking for my late husband when I say how grateful we are for your consideration in this matter, Mister Kingsley,' she said politely. 'I am sure a gift of money might express our gratitude for your discretion.'

Kingsley could detect the contempt in her voice. In his job he had long learned to read the difference between a person's words and the way they said them. A cunning look came over his face. 'Any amount Lady Enid,' he replied solicitously. 'I trust you know how much my discretion is worth. But no cheques. I prefer that you pay me in the legal tender of the colony.'

She nodded her understanding. The policeman was shrewd and this might be a sign of some intelligence – hopefully enough for him to realise that reneging on the deal to remain silent could prove detrimental to himself as much as to the Macintosh name. 'I happen to have enough to pay you presently. If you wait here I will fetch it,' she said, rising to go to the library.

When she returned she passed the notes to the

detective. He stuffed the money into the pocket of his trousers and scooped up the last of the sandwiches from the silver salver.

'There is one other thing,' Enid said as the detective prepared to leave. 'I will be needing your services as a policeman in the future.' Kingsley looked surprised. 'Although we both understand the rather sensitive nature of what has been confided to you by Mister Horton, I may have recourse to call on you to give evidence in a court of law as regarding Captain Mort's involvement in the murder of the native girls.'

'Of course, Lady Macintosh,' Kingsley replied. 'It is my duty to give evidence in criminal matters.'

'Then I would like you to speak to Mister Daniel Duffy of the law firm Sullivan & Levi. They are located in the city.'

'I know Mister Duffy,' the detective growled. 'He and I have had occasion to clash over cases in the Petty Sessions.'

'Then you will appreciate Mister Duffy enjoys somewhat of a formidable reputation as a practitioner of the law,' Enid said with just a touch of satisfaction. 'I would like you to tell him in confidence all that you have told me here today, with the exception of matters relating to the conspiracy to kill Michael Duffy.' Kingsley frowned and Enid added, 'Michael Duffy was Mister Daniel Duffy's cousin. I have my reasons for your silence on that matter.' Kingsley nodded his understanding and after the maid had shown him out Enid stood and walked across to the big bay window to look down on the policeman walking down the crushed gravel driveway. The information concerning Michael Duffy's innocence had come too late for the unfortunate man, she thought idly as she watched the policeman disappear through the wrought iron gate. But even if he had been alive she doubted that she would have revealed what she knew of his apparent innocence. No, Michael Duffy might have proved to be a formidable man to deal with had he lived, she realised, recalling his magnetic attraction to her daughter Fiona, an attraction that had been powerful enough to produce a son.

She dismissed any thought of declaring Michael's innocence to Daniel Duffy as she could see no value in the proposition. It was not in her nature to have the man who had stolen her daughter's heart perceived as a martyr. She turned away from the window and let a rare smile purse her lips. The ironies of life, she thought. That the son of a man who she had once hated with the venom of her class for Papists was the key to destroying her most hated of enemies – her own daughter and her daughter's husband. Very soon it would be time to activate a contract formulated so long ago in the Botanic Gardens between herself and the Irish lawyer Daniel Duffy.

The house that Fiona White shared with her estranged husband had been a wedding gift to her from her father. A two-storey stone house with a sweeping coachway, it was in many ways a replica of the elegant family mansion of her estranged mother

Lady Enid Macintosh. And, as with her family estate, Fiona thought of it as a house rather than a home.

In the early hours of the evening an elegant carriage brought her to the entrance of the house and Fiona was helped down by her driver who bid her a good evening as she walked up the broad steps. At the front door she was met by a maid who followed her through to the drawing room where her two daughters, Dorothy and Helen, sat with their nanny, happily playing with porcelain dolls. Dorothy, the elder at nine years of age, was very much like her aunt Penelope in appearance and had also inherited her extroverted nature. Helen, the younger at eight years, took very much after her mother with her dark looks and emerald green eyes.

With grave faces her daughters bid their mother a good evening. Spontaneous expressions of delight were not encouraged by the nannies. Young ladies must learn to control their emotions.

Fiona asked polite questions about her daughters and was assured by the stern woman that the two girls had been veritable angels. Fiona gazed at their serious little faces staring back at her and gave them an impulsive hug. She watched as her daughters were bustled up the stairs by the nanny who chided them for their unladylike outburst of delight when their mother had embraced them.

The two girls were growing so fast and Fiona reflected guiltily on how little time she had spent with them. She had promised herself that her daughters would receive the attention that her own mother had denied her. But there always seemed to be functions to attend, dinners to organise and the constant social visits to support Granville's growing position of prestige in colonial society. Indeed the nanny saw more of the girls than she did, just as her own gentle Molly O'Rourke had spent more time with her than her own mother had. And now she was growing daily in the same mould as her severe and unyielding mother. If only Molly could be there to advise her.

But the gentle and loving Irish nanny was long gone. Fiona missed her more than she missed any person in her life. It was not a yearning she could admit as Molly had been little more than a paid servant carrying out what was expected of her. Often she would find herself searching for Molly in the areas of Sydney where the Irish tended to congregate. But she was never among the faces she saw pass by her carriage. Molly had simply disappeared and her mother remained tight-lipped as to her whereabouts.

Fiona hated her mother even more for the silence that denied her a chance to confront Molly. She wanted to ask the woman she had trusted above all others in the world just one question. Why had she betrayed her, the person who she professed to love above all others? Why had she conspired with her mother Lady Macintosh to have her newborn disposed of at one of the infamous baby farms?

When the two little girls had been tucked into bed by their nanny, Fiona dismissed the servants for the night, and went up to her room. She had not shared her bed with Granville since the night six years earlier when she had slept with her beautiful cousin Penelope.

Fiona shed her cumbersome clothes and stood naked before the mirror. She admired her body as she knew her cousin admired her in the privacy of their world – Penelope's bed. The birth of her two daughters had done little to alter her soft shape except to fill out her small breasts. She cupped them in her hands and was displeased to feel that they sagged a little more each year. Even so, Penelope found her desirable, and that was what mattered most.

Fiona sat on her bed and sighed. She ached to feel Penelope's body against hers, to feel her moist lips on her breasts and the sweet taste of her mouth on her own. But Penelope had made excuses for not being able to be with her this night. Had her desire been prompted by the unexpected memories of Michael Duffy that the meeting with the mysterious, handsome American provoked? His uncanny resemblance to Michael aroused bittersweet memories of the younger man whom she had briefly loved. And she found herself thinking about the son who had been taken from her at birth.

How different things might have been if only Michael Duffy had lived to be part of her life. But she knew that Michael would not have forgiven her for allowing Enid to dispose of their child. The child had probably been sent to one of the infamous baby farms where unwanted babies were slowly starved to death. Had her baby lived he would have grown to be a young boy by now, eleven years old! What would he have looked like? Like Michael, or would he have had the Macintosh looks?

The thoughts of her lost child brought bitter tears to her eyes. She had often hoped that her son was actually with a good family, growing into a young man who would search for her one day. She forced away the tears and refused to allow her thoughts to dwell on her loss. Still, she wondered what life might have been with him if Penelope had not touched that hidden part of her. Was it that her desire for another woman had always been just below the surface? She knew the sensual love between two women was wrong. But Penelope's bed was a different universe, not part of the world she knew in her day-to-day life. How could the feelings her beautiful cousin aroused be wrong in the eyes of her unforgiving Christian God? Had not women in past times and cultures shared with each other that special kind of love that only one woman could give another?

Fiona sighed, slipped between the sheets and drifted into a troubled sleep.

George Hilary's young apprentice fetched his boss to the front counter. A potential customer was perusing the stocks of rifles on display and had asked some particularly difficult technical questions beyond the knowledge of the apprentice gunsmith.

Hilary entered from the back of his shop, beaming his customary smile for anyone prepared to buy his lethal merchandise. He was greeted with the promising sight of a well-dressed, portly gentleman carrying a silver-topped cane, all of which appeared to indicate some moderate financial means. A potential customer for one of the more expensive sporting guns, Hilary calculated, rather than the stock of ruggedly functional Snider rifles for use on the frontier. 'Yes sir, and what can I do for you?' Hilary asked by way of greeting.

The portly man turned from a display case of expensive English Tranter pistols. 'You are Mister George Hilary I presume sir,' he said, 'the proprietor of this shop.'

Hilary nodded. 'I am sir.'

'Good! I prefer to do business with the proprietor rather than the servant,' Horace said, extending his hand to the gun dealer.

Hilary quickly wiped his greasy hand on his trousers before accepting the extended hand. 'I am Mister Horace Brown. Gentleman wanderer of these parts.'

Remittance man, Hilary thought as he shook hands. Still, they usually had some money and a lot of idle time to spend shooting. 'I see that you were looking at the Tranters. Good choice for personal protection,' Hilary said, removing one of the weapons from its case. He held it at arm's length and pointed at the busy street through the glass pane splashed with his name and occupation. 'Five shot double action, gun of choice for any man who wishes for the best insurance on his life.'

'The gun of choice for the bushranger,' Horace said with a smile.

Hilary dropped his arm and gave a short cough to clear his throat. 'Men who know their guns Mister Brown,' he retorted defensively. 'The only insurance they have.'

'I was looking more in the line of a rifle,' Horace said, turning his attention to a rack of Sniders. 'Preferably one of those new Winchester repeating rifles that load a metal cartridge.'

Hilary replaced the revolver in its case where it lay surrounded by smaller compartments containing tins of percussion caps, lubricated bullets and a flask of black powder. 'I'm afraid I do not stock Winchester rifles Mister Brown,' he replied. 'But I can sell you a Spencer in good condition. A carbine favoured by the Northern forces in the late war between the American states.'

'It was just that I had the good fortune to voyage from Samoa,' Horace said, 'with a gentleman from America who dealt in Winchesters. I thought he might have been selling them to Sydney gun dealers. I regret now that I did not take the opportunity to purchase one from him when we were aboard the *Boston*.'

'I'm afraid Mister O'Flynn's merchandise was not for sale,' Hilary frowned. 'They have already been sold.'

'Ahh. You know the man I speak of,' Horace said with a disarming smile. 'A true gentleman.'

The gun dealer glanced sharply at the portly little man with some suspicion. 'We have met,' he replied shortly, 'on a professional basis.'

'A pity to learn that Mister O'Flynn has already

sold his rifles to someone else,' Horace said casually. 'I don't suppose you might extend me the courtesy of telling me to which Sydney gun dealer he has sold his consignment so that I might inquire as to the purchase of one of those splendid guns.'

'The Snider is more effective in stopping a myall if that is why you wish to purchase such a gun,' the gun dealer replied grumpily, as he sensed that he was about to lose a customer. 'The Winchester is little more than a glorified revolver. Fires a light round. Won't stop a savage blackfella.'

'That might be,' Horace mused. 'But the Winchester fires a lot of bullets.'

'Well, I am afraid I cannot help you,' Hilary growled. 'I don't know who Mister O'Flynn sold his consignment to.'

'Isn't that rather unusual?' Horace retorted. 'I would have assumed such a large consignment of Winchester's latest rifles would have been the cause of great interest amongst gun dealers such as yourself, sir.'

'If that is all I can help you with, sir,' Hilary replied in a manner which indicated that the conversation was at an end, 'I regret that I must get back to my business and no doubt you to yours. Good day sir.'

'I will also bid you a good day Mister Hilary,' Horace said with an audible sigh to show his disappointment. 'I am sorry that we could not do business together.'

On the footpath outside the gun dealer's shop Horace paused to consider what he had learned from the brief encounter with O'Flynn's first Sydney contact. Not much at all. But somewhere in the colony there were enough repeating rifles to equip a small force of men with considerable firepower. For whatever purpose they had in mind.

Inside the gun shop George Hilary scowled as he watched the portly little man standing in deep thought outside his shop. He had felt uneasy about the seemingly innocent remarks by the remittance man. Should he get a message to the American about the encounter with Mister Brown?

He rubbed the back of his neck and shook his head. Surely a man as insignificant as Mister Brown could not be a threat to the likes of the tough American.

That evening Michael Duffy sat opposite Penelope von Fellmann at the dining table in her home. The flickering candlelight gave him the devilish appearance of a man well acquainted with life's vices and his eye patch gave him the rakish look of the old-time English pirates, Penelope mused as she appraised him across the table. During her visit to his hotel room she had seen the scars that covered his muscled body and her long fingers had traced the ugly welt that ran along his ribs. Michael had flinched at the touch of her sharp curved nails.

'Reb bayonet,' he had growled.

'And this one?'

'Maori axe.'

'And how did you lose your eye?'

181

'Shrapnel. Not sure if it was ours or the Rebs',' he answered, as her fingers had lovingly stroked the scars and welts of his naked body.

With her tongue she had traced the scar from a Commanche knife along his ribs. His body read like the saga of some mystical warrior. A wicked, fleeting thought of the women of ancient Rome who were reputed to have drunk the blood of the gladiators fresh from combat in the arena had crossed her mind, causing her to shiver with a delicious ecstasy for the pleasures she and her Roman sisters had experienced. Lust associated with violence – and Michael her modern-day gladiator.

'Well, Baroness, I guess you will tell me why I am here,' Michael said, fixing her dreamy gaze through the soft glow of the candles.

The polished teak table reflected his image as clearly as a mirror. Penelope snapped back to the present, now musing that he was much like the reflection on the table. Two men: one a very dangerous warrior; the other a gentle and creative lover.

'I like it when you call me Baroness,' she replied with a slow smile of satisfaction for the power she wielded. 'It makes me feel as if I am your mistress to command you as I will. To call on you for any service I should desire.'

'Right now, I am hardly in any position to upset you,' he growled quietly, 'knowing what you know about my past.'

'You are right in that assumption Michael,' she said haughtily. 'I dare say the police in Sydney would be more than surprised – and pleased – to know that you are alive and able to stand trial for murder.' She hesitated when she noticed the dangerous change in his expression as Michael toyed with a crystal goblet of burgundy wine in front of him. 'But I can promise you that I am not about to reveal your identity,' she added quickly.

They were alone after the meal. The servants had been dismissed from their duties after the table had been cleared. Penelope was wearing one of her more revealing dresses that showed her large but firm breasts to their best advantage. She was proud too of her narrow waist and wide hips. But she could see from the way the Irishman toyed with the crystal glass that his mind was elsewhere and that he was not entirely smitten with her as she hoped he would be. 'What are you thinking Michael?' she probed. 'Are you thinking about Fiona?'

He glanced up at her, surprised, as if she had read his thoughts. 'Yes. I guess I was,' he answered.

'Fiona did not recognise you,' Penelope frowned. 'She saw only a ghost, and ghosts frighten her. But apart from anything else, any future with my cousin was doomed from the very beginning. You must have known that you would never be socially acceptable to the Macintosh family.'

'But I'm "socially acceptable" for you to go to bed with Baroness,' he mused, staring into her eyes with a grim smile on his face.

'You do not know my reasons for wanting to have you Michael,' Penelope said, dropping her eyes. 'Now, I am not so sure myself. At first I thought I was . . . ' She tried to find the reasons: a desire to prove to him that he was no more than another of her play things to discard; an unconscious desire to hurt Fiona for being a Macintosh? 'I wanted you, that is all,' she concluded, as if dismissing the muddle of reasons in her own confused thoughts. 'I suppose it would come as no surprise, if I asked what became of you,' she said.

'That is a long story and I am not about to bore you with its account,' he replied mischievously. 'Let us say that it pays to make the right kind of friends.'

'But why the report that you had been killed?' she queried.

He ceased smiling and stared into the crystal goblet. Burgundy and blood had the same rich colour. 'Because when you are dead people soon forget about you. Even the traps,' he replied softly.

'Then what happened in your life when you left New Zealand, as you obviously did?' she persisted. She found the mysterious man more fascinating than she dared admit to herself and wondered how much of himself he would reveal.

Her question evoked pain in his face as he took a deep breath and let it out with a visible heave of his broad shoulders. 'Then I found myself in America. Right in the middle of another war. Too much has happened since then to talk about,' he answered, dismissing any further discussion on the matter. 'Maybe some day I might tell you. But I don't think so.'

Even as she listened to Michael answer her questions she could feel her physical desire rising for him. The damned man had that effect on her. Who was in fact master of the situation between them, she wondered irritably.

But it was time to get down to the business and other more pleasant diversions would have to wait for the moment. 'I think we should discuss why you are here Michael,' she said formally.

'So you aren't interested in a narrative of any further scars tonight?' he asked with a wicked hint of mockery in his voice.

She preferred not to answer. The feeling of being filled by him was still with her.

'My husband has a task that requires a man of your experience,' she replied, ignoring both his gentle taunt and her own desire.

'My experience?' he asked with interest. 'What do you mean by my *experience*.'

'Manfred had been informed of your, should we say, colourful exploits in South America, as well as your illustrious war record in America,' she explained. 'He felt that you would be the right man to help him in a matter of great importance.'

'You know about my "exploits", as you call them, in South America?' he echoed, in awe of the Prussian's knowledge of his supposedly secretive career as a soldier of fortune.

'My husband has many contacts in America. And there is little he does not know about what you have done there. He felt that you had the right kind of experience to help him in his mission. But I think he would even be more impressed if he knew all that there is to know about Michael Duffy.'

Michael pulled a candle towards him to light one of the cigars that had been left on the table. As he puffed at the cigar, a halo of blue smoke curled around his head. 'I think it would be better for us all if your husband just knew about Michael O'Flynn, Baroness. Michael Duffy died a long time ago, as we both know.'

'If that is your wish. Then I will respect it,' she replied as she watched the smoke around his head and tried not to smile at the strangely symbolic shape. Michael was certainly no angel!

'This mission your husband has?' he asked bluntly. 'What is my role?'

'That I am not at liberty to tell you at this stage,' Penelope answered guardedly. 'I am only in a position to offer you the job – and the money. Would two thousand dollars American interest you for, say, two months' work?'

The Irish mercenary raised his brow as an expression of interest. Two thousand dollars for two months' work was a lot of money! He had long learned not to question closely the nature of such highly paid work. But he knew this job must be either very dangerous or unlawful. 'I suppose it would be a waste of time inquiring any further into what I am to do for the money,' he said, as he took another puff of the cigar.

Penelope could smell the rich smoke and guessed his kiss would taste of cigar and burgundy. 'I wish I could tell you more but my husband does not share *all* his secrets with me and I have learned not to ask him about certain matters. But I do know Manfred has a mission that might change the nature of things. A mission of great importance to Germany. I do not know exactly what things will change,' she confessed, and Michael could see that she was telling the truth by the puzzled expression on her beautiful face as she explained her husband's wishes. 'Will it bother you to take German money?' she asked. He shook his head. 'Good,' she added, with an expression of relief. 'I do know that Manfred has the greatest respect for your reputation and that is why he wants you to work for him.'

Michael fell into a silence as he contemplated all that she had told him – which was not a great deal. Two thousand dollars, however, was. 'What happens next?' he asked as he emerged from his silence.

'Next week you will take passage on the *Mary Anne* sailing for Brisbane. There, you will change ships and sail for Cooktown. When you get to Cooktown you will meet a gentleman by the name of Herr Straub and recruit six men. Six men you deem to be not unlike yourself in experience. You will be authorised to pay them well and will have access to money from the Bank of New South Wales in Cooktown,' she explained as she leaned forward in such a way that he was able to admire and remember the firmness of her breasts. 'The men will be outfitted when Manfred arrives. But you will supply the rifles I believe you have brought from America with you. They have been paid for, as you will see when you check with Mister Hilary in George Street. As for the rest, Manfred will inform you when he arrives in Cooktown.'

'Cooktown. Your husband planning on a bit of claim jumping up there?' Michael asked wryly.

'If I know Manfred,' Penelope answered, ignoring

his attempt at witticism, 'he will be playing for far greater stakes than a mere gold mine.' She did have a suspicion of what her husband was planning but preferred not to confirm it as this would only put her in conflict with loyalties to herself and her empire. She was pleased that Michael asked few questions. 'There is one other very important matter I think I should mention,' she said drawing a breath. 'I sense that you have a great need to take your revenge on my brother for what he has done to you.'

Michael looked up sharply. She could see the grey eye staring at her with a cold hate. 'Would you expect any less of me?' he snarled.

'You will not harm him Michael,' she replied calmly. 'For all that he has done to you he is still my brother and the father of Fiona's daughters. And, if it is any consolation, I suspect that the ghost of your memory haunts him anyway. You will promise me that no harm will come to my brother at your hand.' She could see the raging turmoil reflected in his face. His personal and abiding hatred would have to be tempered by the cold logic of the tactician.

'I promise I will not harm him whilst I am in the employ of your husband,' he reluctantly conceded. 'After that time, all bets are off,' he added savagely.

Penelope felt the tension flow from her body. The promise would hold him for the moment and it was the moment that counted in her experience. Now that she had passed on her husband's instructions and settled the matter of her brother there were other more pleasurable matters to pursue.

She rose from the table and with a mysterious

smile took Michael's hand in hers. With the cigar and the goblet of burgundy in hand he followed her upstairs to her bedroom. Penelope closed the door. 'Take off your shirt and lie on the bed,' she commanded in a throaty voice.

Michael placed his goblet on a bedside table and crushed the burning end of the cigar between his fingers. Something in her eyes worried him as he lay back on her big bed with its silk sheets. She had the expression of someone detached from their own body.

Penelope began to slowly shed her clothes, all the time fixing Michael with an enigmatic smile. The candlelit room cast strange shadows that made him uneasy. He could sense something dangerous around him but could not describe it in logical terms. 'Did you play games when you were a little boy?' Penelope asked as she stood naked before him except for a pair of long silk pantaloons split at the crotch. Her hands were behind her back and she stood with her legs apart.

'Of course I did,' Michael replied with a slight frown. The feeling of danger was increasing in the room. He had always had a sense for dangerous situations and in the past the instinct had given him an edge to survive. Now all his instincts told him to walk away. His fears were confirmed when Penelope's hands came from behind her back and he saw the light flicker along the edge of a thin-bladed dagger. He felt his body tense as it prepared to fight or flee of its own accord. Penelope was smiling as she advanced slowly towards him.

'This is a beautiful knife,' she said softly. 'I was given it by an Italian Count when I was in Italy some years ago. He told me that it is called a stiletto, a favoured weapon of the assassin.'

'I have seen them before,' Michael said, attempting to sound calmer than he actually felt. 'A woman's weapon,' he added scornfully.

Penelope now stood at the end of the bed with a dreamy expression of complete detachment on her face. 'We are going to play a game Michael,' she said, as if from afar. She climbed onto the bed. 'A game where you will experience the ultimate pleasures of life. Exquisite pleasures that you will take to the grave with screams of rapturous joy.'

She is going to kill me, Michael thought in alarm. She has planned this for a long time as her way of revenge. But revenge for what? She had him at a disadvantage and he knew he must remain calm. He must play down the situation until he could strike and disarm her. 'What game are we about to play?' he asked with a confident smile. His seemingly fearless expression seemed to satisfy Penelope.

'A game of absolute trust,' she replied, as she knelt facing him with her legs apart. He could see that she was highly aroused and despite the continuing fear felt his own arousal. 'But involving some physical pain. I am sure you will be able to bear it. I know you are a man well acquainted with pain.'

Their eyes locked across the short distance between them as he attempted to explore her soul. He searched for malice but, oddly, he saw none. Just a smouldering lust for pleasure.

'I may be the world's greatest fool or a man who gives you his complete trust,' Michael said softly. 'We both know that you hold in your hand an instrument of death.'

'I will not kill you Michael,' Penelope said. 'That I promise you. But I will promise you pain.'

'Then what is your game?'

'I will show you.'

She turned and edged her way up to his head where she straddled his face. He could smell the strong perfume of her arousal and taste the wetness of her desire. Suddenly he felt a stinging pain as the needle-sharp point of the stiletto raked his chest. His body arched and he muffled a cry of pain. 'Taste my sweetness,' Penelope ordered as she leaned forward. Her long blonde hair brushed his chest as her tongue sought out the tiny river of blood spilling down to his stomach. 'As I will taste you.'

With maddening and deliberately frustrating slowness his tongue probed her body above him. The damned man was deliberately showing his power over her rising desire, she thought, as the blood from the wound covered her face, matting the ends of her hair. He was tormenting her in a way that made her want to have him fill her. His exquisite torture was an eternity of pleasure. She was hardly aware that he had turned her on her back and was entering her from above.

The ecstasy continued through the night, into the early hours of the morning. When sleep at last came to them Michael once again walked the terrible corridors of his recent life. There was a young man screaming as he held his bowels in his hands. He was staring at Michael with the despair of a man who knows he is dying. Fourteen, fifteen. Did age matter on the battlefield where every man was locked in the absolute terror from the unseen? Which battle had it been when he had lost all hope for his soul? In the forests of New Zealand? Or was it in the blood-soaked cornfields of the American South? Red was the paint of his life, not the brilliant blues of the paintings he had once dreamed of exhibiting to the world. And sleep was not always a welcome guest.

This night was such a night and Penelope wondered at the world Michael had entered as he twitched and moaned beside her. But it was not something that was new to her. Her own husband occasionally slept as fitfully as Michael did now. She had come to accept that it was just something that soldiers who had seen combat suffered from.

Before sunrise she awoke. Michael was still sleeping and Penelope gazed down at his sleeping face. Terrible, uninvited thoughts came to her and a frown clouded her face. This wonderful and intelligent lover – sensitive to a woman's deepest desires – could be dead within a couple of months, she thought sadly. Such were the missions her husband was prone to embark upon. She might miss Michael for a short time, she grudgingly admitted to herself, but his death would be in the best interests of those he once knew. For Penelope realised that the man who lay beside her was as dangerous to women as he was to men. Should he ever meet again with Fiona . . . Penelope felt a chill in her soul and shuddered. The consequences were too terrible to even consider.

Gently she stroked his chest until he awoke. At least for now she could use his body for her own pleasure in love while her husband used his body in war.

'Where did you learn to play your games Baroness?' Michael asked sleepily as he stirred beside her.

'From a man not unlike yourself,' she answered, as she remembered that memorable night when Morrison Mort had stroked her with his sword. 'A man just as dangerous as you Michael.'

THIRTEEN

Peter Duffy followed his best friend Gordon James up the hill along the winding narrow track overhung with rainforest giants. The two boys were stripped to their trousers and their chests streaked with scratches from the sharp vegetation that plucked at them as they climbed with great effort after the black warrior leading them upwards into the hidden places of the jungle.

'Hey Gordon, slow down,' Peter called irritably, as he puffed with exertion. 'You're going too fast.'

Gordon turned his head to flash him a triumphant smile. Where the climb turned in on itself in places hardly recognisable as a path he continued making his way up the track hand over foot. Although they were friends and as close as true brothers the competition between the two boys had always been the same. Around town they were an inseparable pair – and a duo the other town boys had come to respect for their ability to fight when forced to. Like his father who would not tolerate the sneering references to young Peter being a half-caste, Gordon would not tolerate jibes at his friend's mixed race parentage.

The Aboriginal ahead of them paused and turned to ascertain the two young boys were still following. He stood watching the white boy clamber ahead of the Darambal blood boy with a sense of uneasiness. He knew who the white boy was, as his identity had been revealed in a dream. This was not a good sign, he thought, as Gordon reached him sweating but obviously still with the reserves of strength to go on, while Peter lagged badly as he struggled to keep up.

'Peter Duffy, son of Tom and Mondo, you must beat the white boy,' Wallarie said.

Peter did not understand the strange language and yet the sound was familiar to his ears as if he had been born to hear the words spoken in the Nerambura dialect. 'If you do not beat him now he will kill you one day.'

Peter glanced up at Wallarie standing up the hill from him. Yes! He knew the words and now remembered the man who spoke them. 'Wallarie!' he called wide-eyed up the hill.

The big warrior grinned down at him. 'Baal you forget Wallarie,' he replied in English, grinning with pleasure at the boy's distant memory of another time and place. 'Wallarie not forget you.'

Gordon watched the exchange with boyish

curiosity. He had originally wondered why Peter had insisted on following the Aboriginal who had stepped out from the ranks of the Kyowarra tribesmen they had befriended on the outskirts of Cooktown and gestured for them to follow him away from where the tribe was camped a safe distance from the townspeople and miners. Now there was a hint of an answer in the apparent connection it seemed that the Aboriginal had with his friend Peter.

The boys had stumbled on the Kyowarra campsite in one of their many far-ranging explorations of the surrounding thick bushland. As they were merely boys, the normally wary tribesmen recognised that they were not a threat to their safety and accepted their presence without fuss. It was obvious to the tribe that one of the boys had Aboriginal blood from some other tribe. And the Darambal man amongst their number confirmed that the Kyowarra were right when he identified the one he called Peter as having Darambal blood.

Peter reached Wallarie who turned his back and continued to climb the hill. This time Peter called on all the strength he had to get ahead of Gordon. A tacit agreement was reached between the two boys that they were in a race to the top.

Grunting, sweating and ignoring the sharp sticks that lashed their bodies the two boys vied with each other and called on their respective spirits to win the race. Neither had understood Wallarie's actual words of warning. But still they had understood his meaning.

~

Gordon was first to the top of the hill. He had conveniently tripped, causing Peter to stumble and roll back just far enough for Gordon to take the lead.

Wallarie squatted in a small sun-dappled clearing shadowed by the rainforest giants. He stared at the two boys gasping for breath as they kneeled in the rich compost-like earth, regaining their breath once they had reached the summit. So the white boy had beaten the son of his white brother Tom Duffy, Wallarie thought sadly. And so it would always be. Peter's eyes, glazed from the exertion of the climb, came to settle on Wallarie's dark eyes watching him speculatively.

'I have come for you Peter Duffy,' Wallarie intoned in the Nerambura dialect. 'I have come to teach you the spirit ways of your ancestors who once sat under the bumbil tree and told the stories. But now I must also teach the ways to the son of the man who killed our people in the shadow of the sacred hill of the Nerambura people,' he said. And his eyes shifted to Gordon who he knew did not understand what he was saying. Gordon frowned in his puzzlement and glanced at Peter who listened with an expression of rapt attention to the words he was once again beginning to recognise. Wallarie continued to intone the message from the ancestor spirits.

'What's the myall saying?' Gordon whispered.

'He's saying things you wouldn't understand,' Peter replied in an awed voice.

'You understand his lingo?' Gordon asked switching his attention back to Wallarie whose body glistened with sweat and was marked by many scars as he continued to drone his message in a lilting voice that was the sound of the bush creatures.

'I think I do. It's like things in my head are starting to make sense,' Peter said slowly. 'Things I remember when I was a little kid when the troopers killed my ma and da. Wallarie is telling me things I have to do. He says you and I have to go with him when the Kyowarra go north on walkabout.'

'My dad will give us a hidin' if we go with him,' Gordon whined. 'And Kate will give you a hidin' too.'

'We have to go with Wallarie,' Peter scowled. 'Because he is going to teach us things I have to know.'

'You can bloody well go,' Gordon swore. 'But I don't want my dad givin' me a hidin' down at the wood pile. And he will give you one too because your aunt Kate will tell him to.'

'I don't care,' Peter retorted. But his resolve was beginning to crumble at the thought of Henry James's heavy leather belt around his backside and legs. 'I am going without you. You can run back to your dad like a girl if you like but I'm going with the Kyowarra and Wallarie.'

Gordon took a couple of paces in the direction of the track. 'See you back at the store then,' he quipped over his shoulder. He hesitated when he noticed that Peter had not budged from the clearing, turned and walked slowly back to his friend. 'Well, I'm bloody well going with you,' he said with a resigned shrug of his shoulders. 'I beat you up the hill and you bloody myalls aren't as smart as me anyway.'

'I always beat you at counting and spelling,' Peter bridled. 'I'm smarter than you at school.'

Gordon scowled. It was true that he was smarter than him by a long shot when it came to school work and that didn't seem right when Peter was a half-caste.

'Yeah, but I'm better in the bush than you,' Gordon retorted angrily. 'You might get lost.'

Wallarie smiled. He had observed the interaction between the white boy and the half-Nerambura boy with interest. In the end it had been Peter's will that had won out. The white boy would follow and the signs were good for the time ahead.

He rose from the earth and turned to Peter. 'You and the white boy will follow me now,' he said. 'We will leave for the hunting and fishing lands of the Kyowarra in the morning. You will be safe and in time return to the white man's town. But for now you will learn many things and one day use what you have learned. And you Peter Duffy,' he said, fixing the young boy with his smouldering dark eyes, 'will have to learn more because one day the son of Henry James will kill you if you don't.'

Peter shuddered with a terrible fear and glanced at Gordon standing beside him. It was obvious that his friend had no comprehension of the words that Wallarie had uttered.

With mixed thoughts the boys followed Wallarie wearily back down the narrow, winding bush track to the camp of the Kyowarra. They were aware that in accepting the invitation to go north with the last of the Nerambura clan they would be defying people who loved them. But they were both excited by the mysterious quest that lay ahead.

Four days passed and the boys still had not returned home.

Neither Kate nor the Jameses had felt any real concern for the boys' welfare when they had not returned in three days. They had long accepted that the two boys were just as much at home camping in the bush as they were sleeping in their own beds. Once before they had disappeared into the bush and had returned after three days only a little worse for their experience. Hungry and covered in insect bites, they had received hugs and kisses from the women – and a visit to the wood heap with Henry. Needless to say, they had promised not to stray at any time in the future for more than three days. But four days had now passed and both Kate and Emma were growing more anxious with each passing hour.

Only Henry remained unperturbed by their absence. They were after all both boys with a keen sense of adventure and a proven ability to look after themselves in the bush. But his complacency changed when, in a chance conversation with an old German prospector at the store, he had been reliably informed that both boys were last seen camping with the remnants of the Kyowarra tribe a mile or so from the town. Henry knew the old prospector had a good understanding of the differences between the tribesmen. He was a veteran of the north who had often camped with the tribes – and he had added that the Kyowarra had upped camp and gone walk-about two days earlier.

The Kyowarra — like the Daldewarra — were fiercely independent warriors who rarely came close to the white man's civilisation. Their traditional hunting and fishing grounds were along the stretches of the Normanby River north west of Cooktown. The old German prospector's news chilled Henry but he did not tell either Kate or Emma of his apprehension. Nor did he tell them about the boys being with the Kyowarra.

Kate, however, was suspicious of his feigned calm. She noticed that he had packed many days' supply of rations — and extra ammunition — in his saddle bags before riding out of town with the transparent excuse that he was just going on a week's hunting trip.

Emma also knew something was terribly wrong but both women had faith in the former police sergeant's chances of finding the boys. Still, Emma prayed as she had never prayed before that God would make a special point of protecting her husband in his search for Gordon and Peter. The lives of the two boys were in God's — and Henry's — hands and there was nothing anyone else could do.

As Henry rode north west of Cooktown into the rugged rainforested hills he felt his unease increase by the minute. Not only for the fact that he was riding in hostile country, but for an unease that was very much spiritual. It was as if a voice was calling to him from the forests, speaking of a distant memory, of a horror he would rather forget.

Sweat ran in rivulets to sting his eyes and his leg throbbed from the unnatural angles it was forced to endure keeping his balance on the treacherous hills as he walked leading his horse. His shoulders ached from hauling down on the bridle to keep the big horse reluctantly moving forward, and many times he had been forced to stop and hack at the tangle of rainforest scrub with a machete.

It was slow and laborious work with only tiny tunnels to show for hours of back-breaking effort. But they were tunnels that allowed him to cut across the ridges and down onto the Normanby's flatter floodplains, shortcuts to make up distance and time between himself and the Kyowarra. He knew they were somewhere ahead of him from the numerous signs he stumbled on of recently abandoned camps.

His gruelling trek through the jungle-covered hills finally proved successful. The previous evening he had watched the Kyowarras' campfires from the ridge. He had seen the flickering figures celebrating a corroboree in the shadows of the night. The Kyowarra had been so close that he had smelt the delicious aroma of fat river fish cooking in the coals of the fires and heard the laughter of people with full stomachs.

The sound of the corroboree had been haunting. Only when the clack-clack of the hardwood song-sticks had ceased in the early hours of the morning did Henry snatch a few hours of sleep.

At the rising of the sun he was able to see the distant smoke of cooking fires. The vegetation had changed dramatically and he now looked over the sparser scrub lands of the Cape. He stood with his horse, gazing out at a broad valley where he could clearly see members of the nomadic tribe rising to meet the day. It was an impressive sight as hundreds of men, women and children chattered and laughed as they prepared to join once again with the diurnal spirits of the land in their never-ending quest for survival.

Gazing down on the Kyowarra Henry felt his stomach knot with fear. He knew that he was alone against the impressive numbers of heavily armed warriors. And he was a long way from the safety of civilisation, in territory that the tribesmen had not conceded to the white invaders of their traditional lands.

Leading his horse, Henry descended the steep slope to the river clearing below. When he reached the grassy plain he mounted his horse to ride towards the main camp to confront the tribe.

Startled by the appearance of the lone horseman, hundreds of brightly painted tribesmen rose from the grassy plain with spear, war club and wooden shield. They stared at the approaching white man with a mixture of curiosity and animosity.

Remembering the terrible times when the white men's guns brought death to their warriors daring to stand against the miners' guns, women and children stood wide-eyed and fearful, staring at Henry. Now one of those same white men was boldly approaching their camp astride his horse with a rifle resting across the saddle.

As Henry rode slowly across the plain he scanned the wall of armed warriors spreading menacingly in a defensive screen across the front of their camp. He could clearly see that he was not welcome. He was an intruder on the land they still tentatively controlled.

He was acutely aware of the predicament he had deliberately exposed himself to. Should they launch an attack he knew he had little hope of escape. He might take one or two with him into death before being overwhelmed by the sheer weight of numbers. But he also knew that he had no other option than confronting the hostile tribesmen if he was to ascertain if the two boys were with the tribe.

He calculated that he was a couple of hundred yards out from the line of warriors. He also knew that another fifty yards would put him within range of their long, deadly spears. As if by tacit mutual agreement neither he, nor the warriors standing silently in their ranks watching him, seemed eager to close the gap.

Henry stood in the stirrups and scanned the ranks of tribesmen fingering their spears nervously and muttering amongst themselves. The sound was like the growl from the belly of a dangerous animal. 'Gordon! Peter!' he called. His call carried to the warriors who fell ominously silent.

'Dad! Uncle Henry!' the twin response came to him across the open space of the plain. Henry felt a wave of exhilaration that momentarily overcame his fear. They were alive! The days of sweating and ankle-twisting tracking in unfamiliar territory had been rewarded. For a brief moment he hated himself for harbouring the doubt that he may never see his son or Peter again, a doubt that had been a strange and superstitious fear creeping to him in the dark nights on the lonely tracts of primeval rainforest. A fear that the land and its people would claim his son from him as a cruel punishment for his role in dispersing the dark people of central Queensland.

Henry's nightmares had caused him to wake and scream protests at the spirits of the night. He would wake in a lather of sweat and stare into the blackness. He would see the flitting shadows and hear whispers discussing the death he had brought on a helpless people. He had begged them not to claim his son for the sins of the father. But as the day crept above the jungle and the mists lay on the river like smoke from the night spirits' fires, he would reassure himself that all in the night was but a dream of his own guilt.

Gordon stepped forward from the line of warriors. His young body was lean and hard. He was covered in animal fat and dirt. His hair was matted and except for a tattered pair of shorts he was to all intents a white Kyowarra. Behind him stood Peter in a similar condition.

Both boys appeared healthy and unharmed. For this Henry felt gratitude to the fierce tribesmen who stared malevolently at him. At the same time he also fully knew that the same courtesy was not being extended towards him. The warriors were notching spears to woomeras and the eerie silence in their ranks was broken by a murmur of low growling voices.

'God! Not now!' Henry whispered. He could see

his son's terror-filled face as he realised what was about to happen. He was about to see his father cut down by the Kyowarra warriors!

Henry raised his rifle above his head as the spears rattled on the woomeras. He held it high so that the warriors had a clear view of the weapon. Then he tossed the rifle to the ground as a gesture that he meant them no harm. But his gesture seemed futile as the warriors' murmur turned to a loud growl.

Hopeless despair swept over Henry as he faced the ranks of warriors surging towards him. His mount shifted nervously under him as it sensed its rider's fear. In seconds the Kyowarra would bridge the gap and Henry would never see his son or his beloved wife Emma again. He also knew that any attempt to retrieve the rifle in the grass was futile, and that the big Colt he carried barely matched the range of the spears, that would in seconds fill the early morning sky with their whispering death.

A single voice rose above the din of the warriors. It seemed to berate the Kyowarra tribesmen. And it was a voice vaguely familiar to Henry. 'Wallarie!' it hissed. Although six years had passed the voice had burned its fear into his mind forever. There was a distant memory of a black face behind a rifle pointed at him as he lay in a world of pain and imminent death brought on by the snake's bite.

As suddenly as the attack had been launched it miraculously ceased. The line opened to allow a single warrior to stride forward with the two boys beside him. Wallarie stopped at the forward edge of the ranks of Kyowarra and turned to Peter. 'The man who is my enemy has come for you,' he said. 'It is not his time to die yet. You will return with him to the white woman who is sister to my brother Tom Duffy, your father.' He then turned his attention to Gordon who stood trembling beside Peter. 'He has the spirit of the wild dog. One day he will be as his father was – a killer of black people.' His voice seemed to come from a place beyond him. 'You and he will travel together. But the day will come when a choice must be made as to which of you lives. I do not know which of you that will be. But I do know I will come to you again in my lifetime. I will come to you on the wings of an eagle, as old Kondola did when the white men hunted him in our lands. He flew to the sacred place of the Nerambura Dreaming and sang the songs for the others who could not. Go now and remember all that you have been taught.'

Mesmerised by the transformation that had come on Wallarie, Peter stood rooted to the earth, staring into the dark eyes of the warrior. He saw flashes of the Dreaming and for the first time in many years the confusion returned as to who he was. Standing on the grassy plain – so far from the world of Europeans – he saw his other spirit. It was wild and free. As old as the Dreaming itself.

The transformation in Wallarie's face seemed to dissolve. He was once again the man Peter vaguely recalled in childhood memories, the man who had stood beside his white father on the plains of Burkesland. But now nothing more could be said and Peter walked hesitantly with Gordon towards Henry astride his horse.

Henry could not take his eyes from the tall Nerambura warrior who stood in the front rank of Kyowarra tribesmen. It was as if they were in communication without words being said. Just a mere presence was sufficient to understand each other.

Wallarie had given him back the two boys as a gift. Without his timely intervention Henry knew that he himself would have surely died. And yet the message that came to him from the Nerambura warrior was not of the forgiveness that he so desperately sought for his past wrongdoings. It was a message that only his death would suffice as penance for what he had done. That only his spilt blood could satisfy the spirits of the sacred places of a land where the crow and goanna lived amongst the bleaching bones of a long-dispersed people.

Was it guilt at confronting the last of the Nerambura clan of the Darambal people that caused him to experience the feeling of dread? Henry knew the answer could never come in ways a white man could understand. 'I will pay the price for my life Wallarie, but spare my son,' he muttered defiantly. 'He was born of this land like you.'

The boys reached Henry's mount and stared up at him somewhat sheepishly. They were no longer young Kyowarra warriors but two schoolboys caught in the act of truancy. Henry sighed as he gazed down at the grubby face of his son who was not only a reflection of himself but also a stranger. A child of the new land and belonging to this new world of harsh places.

For the first time he realised that Gordon would

never be a part of a land he still occasionally yearned for as 'home'. Not for Gordon the neatly terraced green fields of England. It was even possible that his son would never see a field under snow or walk amongst the forests of oak. Strange thoughts for a strange time, Henry told himself. He turned his attention to Peter whose grey eyes were those of his father Tom Duffy. His dark skin that of his mother's people. Here stood the true native of the new land, he realised with a dawning insight.

In Peter's blood flowed the conqueror – and the conquered. Half-castes, they called the new breed of children. But there was an exotic beauty in this union of people that both cultures had spawned – and then spurned. Henry glanced up to seek out Wallarie. But the Nerambura warrior was gone.

He did not turn to face the boys as he did not want his son to see the tears that splashed down his bearded face. Instead, he growled from the saddle that they should follow him back to the ridges and wheeled his horse. As the boys followed him across the plain, the tall grasses gently bent to the will of the wind spirits.

As he rode away, Henry felt the sorrow for the certainty that he would not grow old to see his son become a man. For Wallarie had told him violent death would be his fate. It was as inevitable as the sun setting across the plains of brigalow scrub that were the lands of the Darambal people.

FOURTEEN

It has not changed much over the years, Michael reflected as he stood with his hands in his pockets, staring at the Erin Hotel. He wondered what his family would be doing right at that moment. Aunt Bridget was probably poking at the fire in the kitchen preparing for the Saturday afternoon lunch. Uncle Frank would be down in the cellar grumbling to Max about anything and everything while Max ignored him. And Daniel? Daniel may have left home. By now he would be qualified as a solicitor if he had persevered with his articles.

The front door opened and Michael saw two young boys spill out onto the street. A petite, red-haired woman followed them out and by her maternal manner he could see that the two boys were obviously her children.

But the red-haired woman was a mystery.

Michael had not seen her before. One look at the smaller of the boys, however, was enough to convince him that he was looking at a replica of his cousin Daniel. He smiled with warm pleasure. So Daniel was a father and the pretty red-haired woman was most probably his wife. He had done well for himself!

The woman went inside the hotel, closing the door behind her, and the two boys jostled with each other on their way up the narrow street. It was Saturday morning and they had all day to roam. Michael knew exactly where they were going and followed at a discreet distance. If the paddock was still at the end of the street then the boys were bound to start there. Had not he and Daniel done likewise when they were the same age?

As Michael followed the two boys, however, he was unaware that he was in turn being trailed.

Horace Brown yawned as he set off behind the damned American who kept odd hours. Mister O'Flynn had not always been predictable in his movements around Sydney over the last fortnight whilst awaiting a sea passage north. Horace knew about the voyage. Acting on a hunch he had checked shipping manifests to see if the American had plans of leaving the colony. His hunch paid off when a shipping agent came up with his name booked for a passage to Cooktown. An extra coin slipped to the agent produced the fact that the passage had been booked by the Baroness von Fellmann. So, Michael O'Flynn was scheduled to visit the northern frontier, Horace had pondered, as he left the shipping office.

But O'Flynn's visit to the Irish section of town to stand on a street corner was very strange indeed! What link did he have with the Erin Hotel? He would attempt to find that out when he made discreet inquiries with some of the patrons. For now he would follow O'Flynn and see where he was going.

Michael smiled. He was right! The boys had led him to Fraser's paddock where the old gum trees were still standing as they had from the first days of settlement with their solid trunks scratched smooth from the myriad of little feet that had climbed them. The big branches drooped permanently from the years of weight of the many boys who had used the limbs to sit on and to talk about things near and dear to a boy's heart: of annoying sisters and little girls whose very existence demanded teasing, of plans to raid the Chinese kids in the next suburb and pull their pigtails. Many an adventure had been planned amongst those branches, Michael remembered fondly.

The bigger of the two boys scrambled up the oldest of the gums. He perched himself on a low branch and called to the smaller boy to join him. But the smaller boy seemed reluctant to risk climbing the gnarled tree and declined the invitation. He remained under the tree staring curiously at the man with the eye patch who was walking across the paddock towards them.

'Morning boys. Having a good time?' Michael asked in a friendly tone.

The boy sitting in the branches answered bluntly. 'You talk funny mister.'

Michael flashed a wry smile up at the boy who obviously referred to the American accent he had acquired. 'Yeah, guess I do talk funny,' he said.

'Why do you talk funny?' the boy asked.

'I suppose because I come from America,' Michael answered. 'Most of us talk funny over there.'

'You're a Yankee!' the smaller boy standing below the tree exclaimed. 'Have you killed any Injuns?' he asked in an awed voice. Martin Duffy knew a lot about cowboys and Indians. He had overheard men talk about them at the hotel when they were discussing the Yankees.

'A few,' Michael answered, less than modestly. He knew this was one way of getting the boys' attention and was proved right as both boys suddenly appeared impressed.

'Did the Injuns knock out your eye?' Patrick asked from the tree branch.

Michael shook his head. 'No, but that is another story. My name is Michael O'Flynn. Who sir, may I be addressing?'

'I'm Patrick,' the boy on the tree branch answered boldly. 'And this is my brother Martin. We live at the Erin Hotel.'

'Ahh. I used to know some people who lived at the Erin Hotel,' Michael drawled casually. 'There was Francis Duffy and his wife, Bridget. And there was a man called Max and another man called Daniel.'

'That's our da!' Martin exclaimed with boyish excitement.

Michael smiled. So the boys were definitely Daniel's boys. 'Do you have any other brothers and sisters?' he asked politely to keep the information flowing about his family.

'We've got a sister. But she's a pest,' Martin chortled. 'Always wants to play with us. But we run away and hide from her. Mum gets angry when we do.'

'She doesn't know where we are today. Her name is Charmaine,' Patrick added.

The two boys were a mine of information, Michael realised. 'Is your father a lawyer?'

'Yes. He works in town in a big office,' Patrick answered still eyeing Michael and his mysterious eye patch. 'When did you know our da?'

'A long time ago. I was visiting from America and met your da then,' he lied. 'What is your mother's name?'

'Ma . . . I mean, Colleen,' Martin answered, correcting himself. 'She's at home.'

'And your grandfather?' Both boys went silent.

'Grandpa died last year,' Patrick answered with a frown. 'Got sick and died.'

Michael felt a stab of pain. He had always felt a great affection for his uncle Frank who had practically reared him as his own son. The boys did not see the mixture of tension and emotional pain in his face. A precious part of his world had gone and they were not to know. 'What about your grandma?' he asked, recovering as calmly as he could from the shock of learning his beloved uncle was dead.

'Grandma is helping ma in the kitchen,' Martin replied.

Michael felt a surge of relief to hear that she was still alive. She had been the only mother he had really known. His own mother had died on the sea voyage from Ireland when he was very young and his aunt Bridget had filled the gap, lavishing tender love on a little boy as only a woman can.

'Does Max the German still work at the Erin?' Michael asked.

'Uncle Max teaches me to box,' Patrick said proudly, warming to the stranger who knew all the people that he knew. 'Max says I will be as good as Michael Duffy some day.'

So I'm not entirely forgotten, he thought sadly. At least remembered for my fighting prowess if nothing else. 'Do you know who Michael Duffy was?' He was curious to see how much the boys knew about him.

'Not much,' Patrick answered uncertainly, adding that he wished he had known more about his uncle Michael so he could tell the American all about him. 'Except that Uncle Max says I am just like him.' Michael looked closely at Patrick. Yes, he mused. It was as if he was looking into a mirror that reflected the past – except that the boy had very green eyes! Obviously a characteristic of his mother's side of the family. But those eyes brought back a painful surge of memories. They were so like Fiona's! 'What happened to Michael Duffy?' he asked.

'He went away to a war and was killed,' Patrick answered simply.

'Does anyone ever talk about him at home?'

'Grandma prays for his soul almost every night,'

Patrick answered. 'And Da said that Michael Duffy was a good man. That's all.'

Michael felt depressed. He regretted querying the boys about himself. Never before had he felt so much like a ghost. 'Do you have an uncle Kevin and an aunt Kate?' he asked as he shook off his melancholy.

'Aunt Kate lives in Queensland and she is very rich,' Martin answered with great pride for the aunt he had heard a lot about but had never met. 'But Uncle Kevin went away a long time ago before I was born. I heard Grandma say so.'

Michael was not surprised to hear O'Keefe had deserted Kate. Married life was not Kevin O'Keefe's style.

'Well lads. Thank you for telling me all about your ma and da. And about your uncle Frank and aunt Bridget. And you, Patrick Duffy, do as Max tells you when you are boxing because he knows all there is to being a fighter. Some day I think you might be better than Michael Duffy himself. Remember that.'

Young Patrick gave the man a quizzical look. The Yankee looked like he was very sad and was going to cry like a girl, he thought, with a touch of embarrassment. 'I have something for you boys,' Michael added. 'But before I give them to you, you both have to promise not to tell anyone I was talking to you.' He gave each boy a silver dollar. They had a vague understanding of the value of the American coins and mumbled their thanks with promises to remain forever silent. 'Some day you can buy something for your ma and da,' Michael suggested. 'As well as Aunt Bridget and Max. Maybe at Christmas time.'

The boys glanced at each other as Michael walked away.

'Grandma isn't our aunt,' Martin said. 'The Yankee must be crazy.'

From a street adjoining Fraser's paddock Horace had watched the American talk to the boys. He wished that he could have heard what was being said. O'Flynn was seemingly deep in thought as he strolled along the narrow streets past the tenement houses of Redfern.

The past was buried forever. Now there was only the present Michael thought. He wished that the ship sailing to Cooktown was leaving before sunset instead of two days hence. The pain of being so close to those he loved without being able to reveal himself to them ached at his soul more painfully than any war wounds he had ever received.

Horace watched Michael walk out of sight. He was tempted to cut across the street to ask the boys what the American had said to them. But he decided against such an action. It would not pay to reveal himself to those O'Flynn had contact with lest he happened to talk to the boys again. Young boys had a habit of remembering and relating unusual incidents. He would try the Erin Hotel instead. Alcohol and gossip were bedmates.

In the hotel Horace found a handful of working men sitting in a corner with their heads down over their glasses of rum. Behind the bar stood a powerful-looking man with a face that had obviously seen a lot

217

of physical hurt in its time. He stood polishing glasses with a cloth and glanced at Horace with just the smallest sign of curiosity.

Horace had a great belief in saloon keepers and barmen as sources of valuable information. They saw a lot – and knew a lot – about the people who frequented their establishments. But gaining the confidence of barmen was no mean feat. They were people who tended to keep what they knew to themselves. Although generally reluctant to talk, they were nonetheless only human, and every man had his weakness, even taciturn barmen.

Horace plonked himself at the bar and the barman approached. Despite his bulk he moved with the feline grace of a dangerous leopard. Instinct told Horace that the barman was a very dangerous man to be on the wrong side of.

'Vot you vont?' he asked.

Horace's practised ear picked up the slightest nuances in the accent. Probably once a resident of Hamburg.

'A schnapps if you have it,' he answered in fluent German, which caused the barman to cast him a curious look.

'You speak good German. For an Englishman,' the barman replied in his native tongue, and Horace was just a little miffed that his fluent grasp of German was not good enough to fool him. 'But we do not have any schnapps, my friend. You can have rum or whisky.'

'Is it Irish whisky?' Horace asked and the German nodded.

'The best thing to come out of Ireland,' Max said as he poured his customer a shot and pushed the glass across the highly polished and much-used bar top. 'Better than those damned brawling Irishmen whose heads I have to knock together every night.'

Horace grinned at the German's observation. He was obviously in a predominantly Irish expatriate drinking house. 'How is it that an Englishman speaks German so good?' Max added. 'You live in Germany?'

'My father was born in Bavaria,' Horace lied. 'I grew up in England. But my love is to the fatherland, my friend.' Having established his false identity Horace slipped easily into the new man he had created for the situation. 'The name is Franz Neumann.'

'I am Max Braun,' Max said, offering a big beefy hand. 'Hamburg was my last port in Germany.'

'Have you been in the colonies for long?' Horace asked, drawing the German into a conversation.

'Since '54,' he answered.

'Skipped ship to join the rush for the Ballarat fields?'

'Ya. Got my head busted by you damned English at Eureka.'

'Ahh. But a sad mistake in history my friend,' Horace sighed. 'Maybe I could buy you a drink as by way of a belated apology for my English blood.'

Max broke into a broad smile, revealing where he had lost most of his teeth over the years from a bad diet at sea and too many fights on land. 'I will accept your apology Herr Neumann and will join you in a toast to the brave Germans who fought you English at the stockade.'

'My loyalty is to my German blood,' Horace gently reminded his new-found friend. 'Not my English blood. So here's to the brave men who fought at the stockade.'

He raised his glass as did Max. But Horace secretly toasted the red-coated soldiers who had fought and died that terrible day. Not the rebels. They swilled back the whisky and Max promptly refilled the glasses for which Horace paid handsomely.

'Tell me Mister Braun?' Horace said, toying with his generously filled tumbler. 'How is it that you came to be working in a hotel in the colonies instead of returning to Hamburg?'

Max eyed the little man on the other side of the bar and wiped his lips with the sleeve of his shirt. 'Mister Duffy's brother saved my life at the stockade,' he answered. 'He was a good man like my old boss Frank Duffy who owned the Erin until young Daniel took over. And Missus Duffy, Frank's wife, is the best cook outside Hamburg. Why should I go back to Germany when I have a job where I get well fed, drink grog and get to break a few Irishmen's heads now and then? No, my family is here.'

'You have a wife and family?' Horace asked, as he sipped lightly on the good Irish whisky.

'No my friend. My family is the Duffy children, all of them.' The big German smiled sadly. 'They are like my own. Young Michael who I taught to become the best fighter in Sydney. That was until he went away and was killed in New Zealand back in '63 by the Maoris. And there was his brother Tom who the bloody mounted police killed in '68. But I still have my little Katie who is a very important woman in Queensland,' he added, with obvious pride for Kate O'Keefe's considerable financial achievements. 'And I have all of Frank's grandchildren who live here at the Erin. I am teaching young Patrick to be a fighter like Michael Duffy was.'

Horace listened as the barman rolled off the names of his adopted family's children with the fierce pride of a beloved uncle. But something Max had mentioned caught his attention, albeit only slightly. 'I can see that the Duffy family has a history of tragedy from what you have told me about the two Duffy brothers,' he said sympathetically. Max sighed before swilling his whisky and refilling the glass. Recollection of a great sadness had brought on the need for another drink.

'They have a heathen Aboriginal curse on them,' Max said. 'I don't know how this could be, but it's true.'

Horace blinked at the German's obvious sincerity in relating the cause of the tragedies that seemed to haunt the Duffy family. But he was not about to openly scoff at a man whose brawny arms were as thick as Horace's own legs. 'Surely an Aboriginal curse would not reach out to New Zealand?' Horace queried. 'Surely such a thing would be restricted to this land alone.'

'A curse can follow you anywhere in the world, Herr Neumann,' Max smiled sadly shaking his head. 'Evil spirits do not know international boundaries like us in the living world. Michael Duffy was killed as surely by the curse in New Zealand as he would have been had he stayed here.'

'This Michael Duffy, was he a soldier with the British army in New Zealand?'

'No,' Max cast him a look of contempt. 'Michael would never have joined the British. He would have died first. His father fought the damned English in Ireland. No, he fought with the Prussian Count von Tempsky's Waikato Rangers.'

Von Tempsky. A Prussian just like Manfred von Fellmann, Horace thought. An interesting but most probably unimportant coincidence. His line of questioning about the Duffy family was going nowhere and, as intriguing as the tragedy was in the family, it had little to do with the Irish-American Michael O'Flynn. He would steer the conversation with the barman on to the subject of any Americans who might have frequented the hotel in the past.

He was about to pursue this line of questioning when the big German was called by one of the patrons to refill his glass, leaving Horace to sip his whisky and gaze around the interior of the bar. It was like most he had known in Sydney. The same strong smell of tobacco and stale beer, of ingrained vomit and unwashed working men's bodies.

On the walls were a few sepia photos of wooden-faced bare knuckle fighters posing with patient stillness. One photo held pride of place above the bar. It was of a handsome and sturdily built young man posing in the classical style of the bare knuckle boxer: naked from the waist up and wearing the tight trousers and sash of the men who others envied for their brutal courage in the bloody contests where the last man standing was deemed the winner.

The English agent could not help but admire the handsome young man's superb physique: broad shoulders, a muscled chest and arms that rippled with strength. The proud face was intelligent and strong. There was just the hint of a smile at the corners of the eyes despite the fact the subject had been forced to stand very still for the exposure. Horace almost choked on the whisky.

The face!

It was the face of Michael O'Flynn! Albeit with two good eyes and just a little younger!

'You look as if you have seen a ghost, Herr Neumann,' Max said when he returned to pick up his tumbler of whisky.

Horace quickly regained his composure. 'Who is the young man in the daguerreotype above the bar Mister Braun?'

Max turned to gaze up at the photograph of his beloved Michael 'That is young Michael Duffy when I was teaching him to fight. He could have been the world champion if he had not been killed.'

'Why did he go to New Zealand if he had such a splendid future as a fighter?'

'He was falsely accused of a killing,' Max scowled. 'But he was innocent as everyone knew, except the police. He had no choice but to get out of New South Wales before he was arrested and hanged.'

'Have you seen him recently?' Horace ventured.

Max stared at the Englishman as if he was some

kind of *dummkopf.* 'How could I Herr Neumann? I have already told you, Michael Duffy is dead.'

Horace quickly finished his drink and thanked the big German barman. He left the Erin with his head swimming from a combination of good Irish whisky and the knowledge that he had stumbled onto by sheer coincidence. No wonder Michael O'Flynn had been so aloof on the *Boston.* Horace had assumed rightly that he was a man who harboured a secret he did not want exposed in New South Wales. He was a fugitive from the hangman!

Horace smiled to himself. Next time he played poker with Michael Duffy he held the winning hand.

Daniel Duffy, first cousin to the supposedly dead Irishman, lay against the pillows of the double bed admiring the long auburn tresses of his wife. As she sat at the edge of the bed carefully combing her hair with an inlaid mother-of-pearl brush, her hair shimmered with the fiery light of the lantern.

Daniel waited patiently until his wife had counted the obligatory one hundred strokes before she slipped between the cool sheets of the bed to join him. Their room had already lost some of the heat of the hot summer's day and the sheets were refreshing to the touch. 'What was the boys' explanation for the American dollars?' he asked, as she pulled the sheet up to cover her breasts.

'They said that an American man with one eye gave the money to them at Fraser's paddock this morning,' she answered, snuggling into her husband. 'It's a strange story, but I think they are telling the truth.'

Colleen had been told of the money by her young daughter Charmaine who had been miffed that she did not have one of the pretty coins like her brothers. And with the subtlety of Ghengis Khan on a rampage across the Russian steppes Colleen had interrogated the boys until Martin broke, telling the story of their meeting with the American stranger. He had received a threatening glower from Patrick for his betrayal of their oath. But oaths had no validity under the persistence of a mother's interrogation. At least they would be able to keep the dollars. Colleen did not have the heart to deprive the boys of their small fortune. They had piously promised to spend the money on the family the following Christmas.

'The American told the boys not to tell anyone of the meeting,' she explained. 'Your mother was with me when Martin described the man to me . . .' She paused if uncertain whether she should continue with what had eventuated. 'The strangest thing happened . . . your mother almost fainted. She insisted that Martin repeat word for word everything the American had said to them.' Colleen struggled with what she was about to say because none of it made any sense. 'Your mother said it was Michael Duffy the boys had met. She said that Michael's ghost had come back from far away where it had been lost and roaming.'

'Ghosts don't have American accents,' Daniel said

scoffing at this interpretation of the boys' encounter with the stranger. 'Or hand out silver dollars. He was in all probability a sailor who had once visited the Erin.' But for the life of him Daniel could not think of any such meeting in the past.

'Daniel?'

'Yes.'

'I think you should talk to your mother,' Colleen said in a concerned voice. 'And get this foolishness out of her mind. I don't think it is good that she continues to believe the boys met the ghost of Patrick's father.'

'I will,' he sighed. 'First thing in the morning.'

That night Daniel's sleep was troubled with dreams. When he awoke in the early hours of the morning the sheets were soaked with his sweat. That damned talk of ghosts! He sat in the dark room, attempting to erase the haunting memory of the dream. He would definitely have to convince his mother that the man was not Michael's ghost or otherwise he would probably keep having the same damned dream.

But the trouble with the women in the Duffy family was that they had a primitive attitude to matters of the supernatural. His mother and Kate firmly believed in powers beyond those of the natural world. Daniel on the other hand was an educated man. He knew that the persistence of such beliefs was a legacy of the Celtic tradition they clung to, a means of interpreting what could not be immediately explained by science.

When he confronted his mother the following morning and tried to reason with her that the American was just a stranger who had befriended the boys and not Michael's ghost, she merely smiled and patted her son condescendingly on the cheek. Daniel knew he was wasting his time trying to rationalise with her and shook his head in despair. Next it would be bloody leprechauns living in the back of the Erin!

He stomped away leaving his mother to believe Michael Duffy had come back from the grave. At least he had spoken to her as his wife had asked him to.

Bridget felt sorry for her son. It was sad that such an intelligent boy could not see that there were worlds other than those that existed on earth. But that he could only believe Michael had returned to them. His poor soul must be in torment, searching for those he had loved and left.

She made ready to attend church and bustle the boys out of bed. Young Martin was always eager to kneel and be absorbed by the Latin mysteries of the mass. However Patrick's feeble attempts to feign illness went unheeded by a less than sympathetic Bridget. She scolded him for his lack of faith as he lay groaning in his bed. What would the good fathers think to know that one of their students was not prepared to drag himself from his bed to receive the Eucharist!

When all were assembled they were trundled off to the church where the pagan superstitions of Bridget's Celtic past were reluctantly acknowledged as almost impossible to stamp out. A thousand years of staunchly imposed Catholic dogma had not killed off the Banshee. The Irish Angel of Death co-existed in the Irish psyche as surely as Saint Patrick had driven the serpents out of the Emerald Isle itself.

FIFTEEN

The Kate O'Keefe who sat in the tiny office of the Bank of New South Wales at Cooktown had little in common with the bullocky she had been weeks earlier. Prim and proper, she was dressed in an eggshell-blue coloured dress that rustled when she moved. Her long dark hair was piled on her head in a manner that accentuated her slender neck. Only the golden tan of her face denoted a life beyond the constraints of the drawing room.

The man who sat behind his desk poring over the great ledgers of account with their neat copper-plate columns of figures was the epitome of a bank manager. Dressed in a three-piece suit more ideal for cooler southern climes, he occasionally adjusted the spectacles at the tip of his nose and unconsciously pulled at his ear. Mister Dixon was barely in his forties, yet the great mutton chop whiskers down the side of his face had grey streaks, indicative of the responsibility he carried on his shoulders in Australia's far northern frontier. Vast sums of gold accumulated in his safes and credits dominated his ledger entries.

Kate was as anxious as a schoolgirl awaiting her yearly conduct report as the manager continued to frown. Finally he looked up at her with what might be interpreted as a smile. 'It's good news, Missus O'Keefe,' he said as he leaned back in his chair. 'The gold has been converted and I have the pleasure to inform you the mortgage on Balaclava Station is almost acquitted.' Kate sighed, the relief making her feel just a little light-headed. 'But,' he added ominously, 'you are not, as they say, out of the woods yet. Some of your other investments have not fared well and you may be required to shift assets to cover them. That may yet mean selling Balaclava.'

Kate felt her euphoria turn to a sour pessimism. She had been warned by the Cohens that she was over-extending but she had played their fears off against her will to make money out of the gold diggers. She could never imagine ever selling Balaclava as it adjoined Glen View Station, which was still under the control of the Macintoshes. Kate had sworn an oath years earlier to one day own the land where her beloved father lay buried in an unmarked grave. 'To put it bluntly Mister Dixon,' she said, 'what is my overall financial position?'

The bank manager broke into a beaming smile. 'Extremely good Missus O'Keefe. So long as you do not have to call on a cash flow. You are currently in a position to absorb some losses from your other investments so long as you do not follow bad money with good. And be a little less generous with the charities you support up here.'

He hated adding the matter of the charities. Only he and Kate knew how the considerable cost of providing monies for the families of destitute miners strained her cash flow. Food and medicine cost dearly in the far north and so far she had paid without counting the pounds.

Like many others in the colony, Dixon had heard the stories of the young pregnant seventeen-year-old girl who had come north in '63 to establish a pub. Instead, she had lost a baby, a husband and ended up working as a barmaid in a Rockhampton hotel for a couple of years until a windfall from an old bullocky had provided her with the capital to establish a financial empire in her own right. Most young ladies would have taken the rather large bequest and gone south to Sydney or Melbourne as the estate would have provided a moderately comfortable income. But not the legendary Kate O'Keefe. She had teamed up with the Jewish merchants, the Cohens, and with the sweat of her brow and against all odds forged an empire. A beautiful saint, she was also Queen of the North, he thought when he tried to label her. It was impossible not to admire such a woman.

'Despite what you say Mister Dixon,' Kate replied quietly, 'the account for the miners' families continues as normal.'

'I expected you to say that Missus O'Keefe,' he sighed. 'In anticipation I have prepared papers for you to transfer a small amount of your cash to that account. I don't think it will put any great strain on your finances at this stage.'

'Good,' Kate said. 'And I want you to transfer an amount to an Ironstone Mountain account I wish to open.'

'Ironstone Mountain?' Dixon was puzzled. 'I don't think I have heard of Ironstone Mountain.'

'It is an area discovered by the Archers of Rockhampton a while back at the headwaters of the Dee River. I heard about it when I was working in Rockhampton.'

'What made you interested in such a place if I may inquire?'

'It's a mountain,' Kate replied, 'and I have a fascination for mountains, Mister Dixon. Somehow I feel that Ironstone Mountain is worth looking at in the future.' She did not know exactly why she had singled out the hill situated a relatively short distance west of Rockhampton. Maybe Luke's disease of seeking the metal he so highly prized had infected her, and that listening to him so often talk about potential gold ore areas, had rubbed off. Or was it that she had found a way to give him a gift as precious as the love she felt for him? 'I have a man who has the experience to explore Ironstone,' she added. 'He might just find something of worth.'

Dixon raised his bushy eyebrows as a silent expression of disapproval. Kate noticed his gesture and felt just a little concern for her impulsive act. But she had made risky decisions in the past and this was just one more of them. 'It will be done,' Dixon grudgingly conceded. 'I only hope that it does not put any greater strain on your cash flow.'

'Thank you Mister Dixon,' Kate said, as she rose with a rustle of skirts. 'I know my money is in good hands with you.' He smiled self-consciously at her compliment.

Kate left the office and walked to the busy street where Luke leaned against a verandah post with his arms crossed idly watching the townsfolk parading before him. One of his evil cheroots was stuck in the corner of his mouth. When he turned to see Kate walking towards him he flung the cigar into the dust of the street.

'Is everything okay?' he asked with a frown.

'Everything is fine,' she replied with a warm smile. 'I am not destined for the poorhouse.'

'Good.'

As they walked down Charlotte Street Kate agonised over whether to tell Luke what had transpired in the bank manager's office. All was not well. Any call on her by a major creditor could cause her to lose Balaclava.

She glanced at Luke. Since they had arrived back in Cooktown he had not mentioned any plans to go down the track to the Palmer goldfields. Instead, he had worked at odd jobs around the town, and camped on the fringes with the transient miners of the small tent city. Her proposal as raised in the bank manager's office to prospect Ironstone Mountain had a mercenary edge. But it was also rooted in deeper feelings for the man who was walking with her back to her depot.

She knew he would not see the proposal in direct terms as her gift to him. She fully knew that if he did, his fierce pride would be badly wounded by the gesture. When they were on the track to Cooktown he had talked about raising cattle suitable for the tropics. But he had also admitted that he had not been very good as a cowboy back in Montana. But, he'd added brightly, owning your own spread was a different matter. Kate had smiled at his optimism. He had some ambition after all.

But she had to be honest with herself. Men like Luke Tracy were born to see the far horizons, and to love them was to love their nomadic souls. And she was not sure if she was prepared to love him body and soul. To do so could bring the pain of loss back into her life. It seemed all she had allowed herself to love was constantly being taken from her.

'I have a proposal for you,' she finally said as they neared the depot. 'I have spoken to Mister Dixon and asked him to allocate funds for you to go south and prospect Ironstone Mountain.'

Luke stopped in his tracks and turned to her. 'I know the hill,' he said in his surprise. 'Just out of Rockhampton. I've been around it.'

'But have you ever been on it?' she asked.

He frowned and slowly his frown turned to a smile. 'Can't say that I have.' He grasped Kate by the elbows. 'You'd really grubstake a down-and-out prospector Kate?'

'Why not,' she replied with a broad smile. 'After all, you only just missed out on claiming the Palmer.'

They commenced walking towards the depot

and Kate could feel his excitement and felt a surge of happiness. Yes, she had done right by him.

'You know,' he said, 'I once thought about having a look at that old hill. Should have.' He stopped and looked down into Kate's eyes. 'I have a good feeling about that hill Kate. Your investment will pay off.' Then suddenly the excitement drained from him as he realised a reality. 'But I would be away from you Kate. I don't think I could do that ever again.'

She touched his face and fought back her tears. 'Knowing you as I do I also know that you were born to search for what the earth hides from us. When we are separated, at night I will be able to look up at the stars and know we will be seeing the same heavens. I know that when you have found your El Dorado, you will finally be content.'

'I know why you are doing this Kate,' he said in awe, 'and I don't think I have loved you more.'

'I'm doing this to make a profit,' she sniffled with a laugh. 'I just think I have employed the best goddamn prospector in the colonies to make that profit for the Eureka companies.'

'You have,' he replied, albeit less than modestly. 'I won't let you down Kate O'Keefe.'

She slipped her arm into his and together they walked in silence to the depot.

Jennifer was aware of Ben's feelings for her. Since their arrival in Cooktown the young man had used every excuse to be around her and his presence made her uneasy. Not that she did not have strong feelings for him. She knew, that under other circumstances, she might have even called her feelings love. But love was something between a good woman and a good man and in the equation Ben was the good man, she the bad woman.

Her inexplicable coolness towards him after the emotionally charged moment when they had faced the warrior tribesmen on the Palmer track together persisted. It was as if nothing had happened between them. Although confused and hurt Ben refused to concede defeat. All he knew was that he loved Jennifer Harris more than he had loved any woman. Not that he had ever loved a woman before – at least not in the Biblical sense.

He stood in the small, hot kitchen of Kate's temporary home in Cooktown, watching Jenny bending over a big round tub going about the business of washing dishes. She was so absorbed in her duty that she was not aware of the young man standing behind her. Working for Kate was not considered a chore for Jenny compared to the past months of her traumatic life. No more the terror of rape and no more the fear for the life of her son. Under Kate's roof she had discovered the gentle warmth of caring and sharing. Even her son Willie had left his world of nightmares to play in the sun with Kate's adopted children.

He and young Tim had forged a strong friendship. They were both outsiders to the tight clique of Sarah, Peter and Gordon and found themselves happy in each other's company, which pleased Jenny as much as it did Kate who had long been worried about Tim's exclusion from the triangle.

'Jenny,' Ben said quietly. Startled, she swung around from her washing. 'Could I talk to you?'

She wiped her hands on an apron. 'Of course Ben,' she replied with a pleasant but distant smile.

'Kind of hoped we might go for a walk to the river and look at the boats,' he said hopefully. 'It's pretty down there.' Jenny untied the apron, which Ben interpreted as an acceptance of his invitation. She patted down her old but clean dress and followed him out of the kitchen.

They walked in an awkward silence down to the river. Between them was a tension as if they both knew why Ben had appeared in the kitchen this day. Neither seemed to be aware of the people they passed on their walk. It was as if a fuse was burning towards a powder keg located on the banks of the Endeavour River. When finally they came to the river, Ben sat down in a small clearing fronted by stands of mangrove trees with their gnarled roots reaching down into the sand and mud of the tropical waters. Through the trees they could see the big ships of every kind at anchor and the bustle of smaller boats moving between them.

Spreading her long dress Jenny sat down beside Ben and stared at the colourful flotillas. The fuse had burned to the edge of the powder keg, as they both knew.

'I love you Jenny,' Ben said setting off the explosion. 'Always have from the moment I saw you on the Palmer.'

'You cannot love me,' she replied in a voice laced with pain. 'I am not a woman fit for the love of a good man.'

Ben turned towards her and she saw in his expression a terrible pain not unlike her own. 'Why can't I love you Jenny? To me you are the most beautiful woman in the world. I have never seen any woman as beautiful as you.'

'How could you love this?' she said savagely, pulling away the long tresses of her hair to reveal the strawberry birthmark covering the side of her face. 'How could any man love a woman with this?' Ben's eyes brimmed with a desperate need to be believed for what he was about to say. She could not bear to see his pain and glanced away. Her long golden hair fell back across her face as she sat with her head down.

Ben reached across and gently brushed her hair from her face. She did not resist his gesture. 'I don't care about the mark,' he said softly. 'All I know is that I always want to be with you, for as long as I live. I want to marry you.'

Tears welled in Jenny's eyes and she covered her face with her hands. 'I can never marry you,' she sobbed. 'I could never marry any man. I'm used goods.'

'I don't care,' Ben said gently. 'I don't care anything about you except for what I see and know now.'

Jenny ceased crying and swung on him bitterly. 'You don't know what I'm talking about. If you knew you'd run a mile.'

He did not know what she alluded to, although Kate had hinted when they were on the track to Cooktown that things had happened to young Jenny that were best not spoken about. Now he wondered indeed if her past mattered. He took a deep breath. 'I don't care,' he said. 'I don't care about anything except you.'

'And what about Willie? Would you say that if you knew how he was born?'

'It don't matter,' Ben persisted stubbornly. 'Nothing matters except how I feel about you, and Willie. And all the things you said to me back on the track when we fought the myalls. Didn't any of that matter?'

Jenny wiped away her tears with the back of her hands. She was trembling and Ben placed his arm around her shoulders. A delicate little sunbird flashed black and gold as it hovered near a flowering tree on the river bank. She stared at the bird – only fractionally larger than a hummingbird – with its long beak inserted in the heart of the flower.

'I meant what I said then,' she replied quietly. 'But that was then and this is now. You and I could never be together in towns where people would talk about how you married a woman like me.'

'I don't intend to stay in towns,' Ben said close to her ear. 'I'm saving to take up a lease down south on the Flinders River. Run cattle to supply meat for the goldfields. Kate is going to help finance me next year. She said it was worth the risk for me coming back to work for her instead of panning for gold on the Palmer.'

Jenny felt his gentle and confident words against her cheek. For the first time since they had walked away from Kate's house she flashed him a wan smile. 'You really do love me!' she said. 'You would take me as your lawful wife to work with you.'

'I've even got a name for our new place, when we get it,' he said, with a broad smile across his sun-tanned face. 'I'm going to call it Jerusalem.'

'Why a name from the Bible?' she asked. 'Isn't that where the Jews live?'

Ben bowed his head and stared bleakly at the river before answering. 'I'm a Jew. At least my mother says I am. But she never told me much about being a Jew except to say people called Gentiles don't like us. They reckon we killed their Saviour.'

'I don't care if you are a Jew,' Jenny said, taking his hand in hers. 'I don't think you would have killed Our Lord if you had been around then, not that I know much about being a Christian anyway.' They looked at each other and burst into laughter. The fragments had settled around them and they both remained unhurt by the explosion. Jenny leaned across to Ben and kissed him on the lips. 'I always loved you too, Ben,' she said. 'From the first time I saw you by the fire looking at me the way you did. You had a kind look, not like the other men in my life who hurt me. I felt safe when you looked at me.'

'You don't have to tell me about what happened before we met,' Ben said. 'That was the past and all I know is that this is now. I think we should get married and take up a lease on the Flinders.'

Jenny flung her arms around the young man and

crushed him to her. 'We will,' she said and, for the first time since she could remember, felt true love. That unknown feeling she had always suspected existed – but was afraid to find, lest it hurt her.

That evening Jenny sought out Kate and told her of the love she and Ben felt for each other. Her news was met with a long hug from Kate and the conferring of her blessing on the future for them both.

When Kate was alone she reflected on the happy news. It was a good union. She had always sensed in the young girl a wonderful, if partially hidden, strength very few possessed. Jenny would make a fine wife for Ben and stand by him through good and bad times. She wondered miserably why it could not be so between herself and Luke. A tiny voice told her that she had to trust her heart more than her head. But for now her head ruled and her heart took a secondary role in her busy life.

SIXTEEN

Miss Gertrude Pitcher did not like Mister Granville White. A stern woman with a permanently pinched face and silver-grey hair, she had strong ideas on the raising of young ladies. For some time now she had sensed something in the girls' father that was not quite right, an intangible evilness about the man when he was around his daughters. But she dared not express her misgivings to Missus White for fear of reprisal, although she would do everything in her power to protect the girls from harm.

The nanny felt disturbed as she stood in the drawing room of her employer's house, suspiciously eyeing Mister White and the young girl who stood brazenly beside him in her cheap dress staring defiantly back at her.

'Mary is a little friend I have brought to meet

Dorothy,' he said, almost too casually for her liking. The girl did not have the look of a young lady but more of one of those trollops from the working class suburbs of Sydney. She had long dark hair that flowed loosely around her shoulders and her cherubic expression seemed to mask a worldly wisdom. 'She and my daughter Dorothy,' he continued, 'will spend some time together this afternoon in the library with me. I would like you to fetch Dorothy to join us there Miss Pitcher.'

Miss Pitcher did not know why she should feel uneasy except that Missus White was away for the next two days with her younger daughter Helen visiting friends at Camden. Dorothy had been left in her care because she had been running a slight fever and was not up to the coach trip to the country with her mother. But why the concern, she wondered with a frown, her female intuition telling her something did not bid well. 'Do you not think that Miss Mary is possibly a little old to be a friend to Miss Dorothy?' she asked coldly 'Miss Mary appears to be . . .'

'Miss Mary is eleven years old and my daughter is nine, Miss Pitcher,' Granville cut across icily, asserting his dominance as her employer. 'And I think it is my position as Dorothy's father to decide who my daughter should befriend. Don't you think so Miss Pitcher?'

'Very well Mister White,' Gertrude conceded reluctantly. 'I shall fetch Miss Dorothy.' She turned her back and swished from the room with the imperious air of her position as nanny to a budding young lady of good breeding.

Granville scowled at the back of the departing nanny. He would have to think of some way of having her dismissed if she maintained her insolence. The woman did not know her place.

Dorothy stood uncertainly in the library. It was not a place where she was normally permitted and the invitation to the sacrosanct room made her feel uneasy. Granville smiled at his daughter as Miss Pitcher closed the door behind her. He rose from behind his desk to cross the room and thought how much his daughter was like Penelope at the same age. He took his daughter's hand and led her to the big leather couch. Dorothy had the same golden ringlets of his sister and the same exquisite beauty.

'Have I done something wrong Papa?' the little girl asked in a tremulous voice, as her father sat her down on the couch.

'No Dorothy,' her father answered in a tight voice, giving his daughter a gentle hug of reassurance. 'You are here because you are a good girl my little darling.'

Dorothy felt like crying with relief. She loved the man who had always been so distant in her life and yet always there to protect her world. The soothing words and gentle embrace flooded her with a sense of well-being. 'I am a good girl Papa,' she answered, with a slight tremor of relief that the call to the darkly mysterious and forbidden room was not to chastise her for unknown transgressions. 'I love you Papa.'

'I know my little darling. And I know you will never tell anyone about the games we will play together in this room. No matter what happens. Because if you do I will have to punish you and send you away forever. You will never see your mother or sister ever again. Do you understand what I am saying?'

Confused, Dorothy listened to the soft words of threat with a terrifying realisation that in fact she had done something terribly wrong to cause her father so much anguish, although what she did not know. She did know however that her father knew everything, and if he said he would send her away, then he would.

She stared at him standing over her and her tremor became a trembling. She wanted to burst into tears but she knew she must not. She had been taught that a young lady should not display her emotions. Ashen-faced, she watched in stunned disbelief as the strange girl in the room took off her clothes. She stood naked displaying herself with a leering smile. Dorothy wanted to run from the room and run forever. Horrified she sat and stared imploringly, hoping her father would make what was happening go away. But when she stared into her father's eyes she saw only the strange, glazed expression of someone she did not know. It was as if a devil had come to take her father away. The creature leering at her, with the sweat glistening on his forehead, was as totally alien as the strange girl who came to her. Mary knelt and ran her hands up Dorothy's legs inside her dress.

'You will like what Mary is going to do to you

my little darling,' her father crooned, as his lust rose at the sight of Mary kneeling before his daughter. Mary's naked buttocks spread enticingly before him. 'Mary will do things to you that will feel nice. And Papa will do things to you that you will like.'

With mounting, helpless terror, Dorothy felt the older girl's hands force her legs apart and her fingers touch that place forbidden to all. She wanted to scream out. How could it be that the man she most trusted in the world could be taken away and the devil come to his body?

Granville groaned as he watched Mary smiling her pleasure for him. It was so easy, he thought, as Mary caressed his daughter with lewd words of encouragement. It was as easy as the first time with his sister all those years before in England. And now he had another Penelope to pleasure him. It was so easy. With casual and brutal indifference to his daughter's terror he began to unbutton the fly of his trousers.

Miss Gertrude Pitcher had always prided herself on her absolute self-control. But now she felt her steel-like resolve dissolve. What she had seen in Dorothy's bedroom a short time after she had returned from the library was beyond all control.

Granville sat smugly, watching her across the library with the eyes of a predatory animal as Gertrude's rage boiled into words. 'Miss Dorothy has been . . . been . . . ' she faltered in her attempt to dredge up words to fit what she had witnessed in the

246

little girl's bedroom: a face turned to her with eyes that had seen a horror only the devil himself could conjure from hell. She'd had an experience so unspeakable that Miss Pitcher wondered if the little girl lying huddled on her bed would ever speak again.

'My daughter has not been harmed Miss Pitcher,' Granville replied self-assuredly. 'She has had a little fright when I had to chastise her. That is all. And I would hope for your prospects of continuing employment in my house that you remember that well.'

Gertrude stared disbelievingly at the monster before her. How could he lie so blatantly when the signs were obvious that the man had interfered with his own daughter? This man that she had once admired, not only as her employer, but also as a leading gentleman of colonial society feted for a future knighthood – how could he destroy the innocence of a child as gentle and trusting as little Dorothy?

Granville calmly opened a drawer of his desk and produced a box of fine Cuban cigars. Casually, as if indifferent to the presence of the enraged nanny in the library, he lit one. 'You have nothing else to say, Miss Pitcher,' he said, softly blowing smoke into the air and turning his attention back to Gertrude who stood stiff-backed and lost for words. 'If not, I would take this opportunity to give you some advice that I would hope you would consider wisely. And my advice is that you keep to yourself any unfounded suspicions you may have in your filthy mind.' He leaned forward with his arms on the desk and his tone changed. His words came as a snarl. 'You see, Dorothy will tell you nothing, as there is nothing to tell. And you will definitely not make any reference of this day to my wife. If Dorothy should behave in unusual ways in the future, I would expect that you will be able to provide my wife with a satisfactory explanation.'

Gertrude Pitcher gaped at the almost unbelievable arrogance of the man. His presumption that she would condone the unspeakable acts which had caused the little girl to lapse into a catatonic state. 'I will be telling Missus White of my suspicions as soon as she returns,' she said firmly. 'I am sure she will know what to do.'

'I can assure you that no such thing will happen Miss Pitcher,' Granville said, as he watched a halo of blue smoke rise slowly in the still air of the room. 'For if you speak of unfounded allegations I will use my considerable power to ruin you. Or worse still, you may have an unfortunate accident, as it seems many people around me do from time to time.'

'You dare threaten me Mister White?'

'I do not threaten Miss Pitcher,' he snarled. 'I do.'

Gertrude felt the heat of his malevolence scorch her soul with real fear. It was true that people around Mister White suffered unsavoury fates. She shuddered. Her personal fear for her life was now greater than her rage.

Granville smiled as he watched the expression of sanctimonious indignation dissolve on the stern nanny's face. The extraordinary wealth at his disposal, thanks to his growing influence in the Macintosh companies, gave him unlimited power over the likes of the nanny and others of her penniless ilk. But he also knew he must guarantee her silence – and by means other than fear alone.

He reached into the drawer of his desk and removed a wad of bank notes. It amounted to a year's wages for the nanny. Fear and greed were worthy allies to a man like Granville, who lived by both. He placed the wad on the desk and tapped it with the stub of his cigar. 'All this is yours Miss Pitcher,' he said. 'It is yours to keep and use in any way you may wish. But I must point out that there are conditions attached.'

Gertrude opened her mouth to speak. Granville raised his hand to silence her. 'I will finish speaking Miss Pitcher. The first condition is that you remain in my employ for as long as I desire. And by remaining in my employ you will – how do I put it? – protect my interests in the matter of my love for Dorothy, no matter how much you may find the way I express that love distasteful. I can assure you, that she will learn in time to appreciate what we do together and view it as a genuine expression of my affection. Needless to say, I hope that I can come to rely on your support immediately. That is all I have to say. I will leave you alone now to think about all that I have proposed.'

He rose and pushed past Gertrude who stood stunned by all that had transpired. Granville went to his daughter's bedroom. Dorothy needed reassurance that what had transpired between her, Mary Beasley and himself was their little secret.

When Granville returned to the library ten minutes later, Miss Pitcher was gone from the room, and so too was the wad of bank notes.

The cedar-panelled boardroom of the Macintosh offices had an ingrained scent of rich old cigar smoke. Moments earlier the boardroom had been filled with men wearing expensive suits and grim faces. After the meeting was adjourned they left behind a haze of blue smoke and two people sitting opposite each other at the solid teak table.

Lady Enid Macintosh sat straight backed and stared hard at the man opposite her. He felt decidedly nervous under her unrelenting gaze and wished that the board of directors had chosen anyone but himself to speak to her. He had known Lady Macintosh for many years and wondered how she did not seem to age as he had in the same period. She still had the flawless complexion and dark hair of a woman much younger than one in her late fifties whereas time had given him a paunch and thinned his hair.

'You have been in discussions with my son-in-law Mister McHugh,' she finally said, breaking the silence. 'And I presume he has convinced you all that I am a mere woman, incapable of managing my late husband's estates.'

McHugh pulled a pained expression as if attempting to ward off her unrelenting stony stare. 'It is not my personal opinion that you should step aside Lady Macintosh,' he replied. 'But the general feeling of the shareholders is that a man, such as your son-in-law, should be granted exclusive power to decide future enterprises. Mister White has a proven record for increasing profits, which you no doubt must acknowledge. It's just that a strong man is needed at the helm to steer the Macintosh companies. You are not growing any younger Lady Macintosh, and the strain of managing your late husband's companies must weary you.'

Enid's unrelenting stiffness in the presence of the spokesman for the shareholders softened noticeably. Was it that the woman was finally seeing his point of view?

'I concede that I may not be growing any younger Mister McHugh,' she said with a faint smile. 'But I do not concede my son-in-law is the man to take control of my late husband's companies.'

'But there are no other men in your family to take the reins when you have . . . ah . . . passed on,' he implored. 'Surely you can see that. Mister White is the only close male blood relative you have and, after all, he is married to your daughter.'

'What if I said that you were wrong about Mister White being the only close male blood relative I have,' Enid said with a mysterious smile. 'What if another existed who I could prove was of my blood. Would that alter your opinion about Mister White being the only one capable of taking absolute control in the future? What if even now I had chosen one with Macintosh blood to be groomed for the company's management?'

'What you propose seems somewhat hard to

251

understand,' McHugh replied, hoping that his feeling of disbelief was not apparent in his face. 'From what I know of the tragic circumstances of your family's history none of your sons left children. Unless . . .' The possibility of illegitimate offspring was not something one expressed and he let the question hang between them.

'I do not intend to go any further with this conversation Mister McHugh,' Enid said quietly. 'And under the circumstances I can only request that you do not mention outside these walls what has transpired between us. All I ask you is to go back to the shareholders and reassure them that I will *not* be stepping aside for my son-in-law. And reassure them that there will be another of Macintosh blood to take over from me in the years ahead. One whose breeding has produced qualities far superior to Mr White.'

McHugh frowned and pursed his lips. It was all very mysterious. But Lady Macintosh was not a woman who made a statement without being able to back up what she said. 'As the major shareholder of Sir Donald's estates I must accept that what you request be respected,' he smiled. 'I do not know how this suggestion you make could eventuate. But I do know your reputation well enough to be able to return to the shareholders and ask for an extension of time before the matter of you stepping aside be put before any formal meeting.'

'Good, Mister McHugh,' Enid said. 'I can assure you that my son-in-law will never have total control of my husband's companies while I am alive. Or even when I am dead, for that matter. He is an evil man who I have many reasons not to trust. Nor should you,' she added.

McHugh shifted uncomfortably. He was a hard Scot who had strong views on issues of morality. As it was he did not like Granville White. The rumours that White had a controlling interest in a Sydney brothel did not bide well with him. In his business dealings with White he had come away less than impressed with the man's pompous manner. To be able to return to the shareholders and ask them to defer any formal request for Lady Enid Macintosh to step aside suited him well enough. 'I shall bid you a good day then Lady Macintosh,' he said, as he rose from the table and tucked a leather satchel under his arm. 'If it is any consolation please be assured that my personal opinion is that the best person to manage the companies has been – and always will be – you, or whoever you shall deem to take your place in the future.'

Enid glanced up at McHugh. 'Be assured that you will not be disappointed,' she said with a warm smile. 'I trust that you and I will be able to work together in the future.'

McHugh nodded and made his departure from the boardroom leaving Enid alone to ponder on the meeting. Somehow Granville had planted the seed for her to step aside, she thought angrily. He had guided the mood of the shareholders in a subtle campaign to undermine her authority. But now she had played her ace card against her evil son-in-law. It was not a card he knew about however, and the time was nigh to produce the ace. Enid rose from the table with a grim expression on her delicate face. It was time to contact the law firm of Sullivan & Levi.

For the last five years Daniel Duffy had made the visit to the Botanic Gardens to meet with Lady Enid Macintosh. The meetings had been a secret that only they shared and over that time the tough courtroom lawyer had almost grown fond of the dignified matriarch of the family sworn enemy to his own.

At each meeting they had strolled amongst the flowers whilst pretending to be accidental acquaintances. And as they strolled, Daniel had talked about her grandson Patrick Duffy, while she had listened quietly, stopping occasionally to admire the flowers.

But this meeting was different. There was a degree of tension as they strolled together: the tall and slightly stooped young lawyer walking beside the straight-backed matron. This meeting would be the last of such meetings, as they had agreed those years earlier. At their first clandestine meeting Enid had proposed taking over the rearing of young Patrick. The illegitimate son of Fiona Macintosh and Michael Duffy would enter into her privileged Anglo-Gaelic's Protestant world, to be groomed for riches and power beyond the dreams of the Irish-Catholic Duffys. Sealed in formal legal documents, their pact guaranteed to Daniel that his nephew would receive the very best education the British Empire could offer – and eventually an opportunity to take over the management of the vast Macintosh financial holdings. The young lawyer had an unmovable faith in Patrick's innate strength to remain true to his faith – and his Irish family – in the years ahead. In his opinion Lady Macintosh had grossly underestimated the strength of Patrick's Celtic roots to withstand any persuasions of the Anglo-Gaelic's heritage. In so many ways young Patrick was the image of his true father.

'How is Patrick with his studies?' Enid asked, as they strolled past a gardener busy with the task of planting seedlings. 'I hope he has improved since last year.'

Daniel smiled when he reflected on what had prompted her remark. 'He has Lady Macintosh,' he said. 'The good fathers decided not to expel him.'

Enid glanced at the lawyer with just the hint of a smile in her eyes. 'From what you told me last year it seems young Patrick had a spot of bother with some of the older boys at his school.'

'He gave three of them a thrashing,' Daniel grinned. 'It appears he was only acting in defence of young Martin. The trouble was that the boys were the sons of some well known and influential businessmen. Patrick made a promise to the good fathers that he would atone for his sins by getting the highest marks for Latin in his year. And he did so. He is an extremely bright boy, but allows his fists to rule his head from time to time.'

'One could say from the tone of your voice Mister Duffy,' Enid said mildly, 'that you seem to approve of Patrick's pugilistic ways.'

Daniel stopped walking and turned to her. 'He is a Duffy, Lady Macintosh. Like his father. And like his father – and his father before him – he is a fighter.

It is part of the Duffy heritage to fight for causes.'

'Then young Patrick will have another cause to fight for,' Enid said. 'When he is older. A cause that will require the best of both his Scots and his Irish blood.'

Daniel raised his eyebrows at her statement. He did not think that he would ever hear the staunchly Protestant matriarch of the Macintoshes admit that Irish blood had any redeeming qualities. 'By that I presume you mean opposing your son-in-law?' he asked.

'And his own mother,' Enid replied with a touch of bitterness. 'As well as those such as Captain Mort who ally themselves with my son-in-law. We do have common enemies Mister Duffy.'

'Ah, Captain Mort,' Daniel said quietly, and stared away into the distance. 'A man as evil as can be, with the devil's luck.'

'I was sorry to hear that your firm was unable to bring the man to justice those years past,' Enid said sympathetically. 'Both you and I know he was responsible for my son's cruel death at the hands of the natives. I prayed you would be successful in bringing him to the gallows.'

'We lost our prime witness, the Reverend Macalister, at the same time that you lost your son,' Daniel sighed. 'And a short time later found our moves to bring the matter to the courts blocked by *your* legal representatives Lady Macintosh.'

'May I reassure you,' Enid said quickly, 'that I had no part in that Mister Duffy. The matters were initiated by my son-in-law at the time without my knowledge. Had I known I would have instructed our solicitors to stand aside in the matter. You must realise that it was just as much in my interest to see Mort hang as it was yours. As it is you will soon receive a visit from a Detective Kingsley. He is in possession of certain important information that I think may finally bring Captain Mort to justice. I would like your firm to pursue the matter with some discretion.'

'Could it be said that you are happy to see Sullivan & Levi do so,' Daniel said with a touch of bitterness in his voice, 'rather than cause a scandal to your family name?' He could see that he had touched a raw nerve and Enid glanced away guiltily. 'Not that it matters anymore,' he continued pessimistically. 'Captain Mort will probably remain free from the law. And free from the punishment he so richly deserves for the murders of so many people in the past.'

'God will find a way to punish Captain Mort if you don't,' Enid said softly. 'Otherwise I might doubt that there is a God.'

'I pray you are right,' Daniel agreed. 'But I fear Mort will grow old and have to await his punishment in the next life. For now we are both in the shadow of the *Osprey*, Lady Macintosh, and its shadow is death.' He paused and turned to Enid. 'But there is one glimmer of hope,' he added. 'There was a rather gruesome murder in The Rocks some days ago and a reliable informant has told me that he feels Mort was the man who committed the murder.'

Enid's face expressed a sudden interest. 'How sure is your informant of the captain's complicity?'

'Very sure. He feels from his considerable

experience that The Rocks is a place where people know things but do not talk. It's their code.'

'All people understand greed Mister Duffy,' Enid said serenely. 'Tell your informant that I am putting up fifty guineas to any witness who should come forward and volunteer information that might incriminate Captain Mort. Of course I expect the matter to be handled discreetly.'

Daniel smiled and shook his head. 'You realise that your offer is rather generous but not exactly ethical Lady Macintosh.'

'Neither is the murderer of my son remaining unpunished, Mister Duffy,' she replied bitterly. 'I will personally guarantee the money.'

'I will pass on your offer,' he said. 'Other than that we have very little else.'

Enid stepped off once again and Daniel followed her. 'We have Patrick,' she said, as they walked slowly between the flower beds. 'And in time he may right what is wrong.'

Daniel nodded. 'Then it is time you met your grandson,' he said quietly. 'According to our agreement.'

Enid glanced at the lawyer. Was it that she sensed a common need to work through this young boy towards a future resolution of vengeance, she wondered with a flash of insight. How strange life was when she found herself allied to a family that indirectly had brought so much suffering to her own over the years. 'Yes Mister Duffy,' she replied. 'I would like that to happen as soon as possible.'

~

Granville heard the muffled exchange of voices which he recognised as being those of his wife and the nanny. He sat at his desk in the library and felt the tension of the moment pass him by as slowly as the steady tick-tock of the clock on the wall. Would Miss Pitcher renege on the deal they had struck as to her silence and future complicity? He found himself straining as if to detect any nuances in the exchange below that might indicate his betrayal.

Long moments passed. The tension was unbearable and he noticed that his hands were trembling. Damned if he was going to sit around and wonder, he scowled. The only way was to go downstairs and, in a sense, confront Fiona.

He rose from behind the desk and made his way to the drawing room where he found his wife sitting with his daughters. Behind Dorothy and Helen stood Miss Pitcher.

'Hello Granville.' Fiona greeted his entrance with the cold voice she usually reserved for him. 'You do not appear well. Is it that you have the same illness as it seems Dorothy has?'

Granville paled. Was she being facetious?

Miss Pitcher came to his rescue. 'Mister White has not been well ma'am,' she said quickly. 'I observed that he and Dorothy both developed the symptoms about the same time as each other.'

Fiona glanced down at Dorothy who stood staring forlornly at her father. 'Are you feeling ill now Dorothy?' she asked with a frown.

The little golden haired girl shook her head. 'No Mama.'

Fiona missed the subtle exchange of looks between her husband and the nanny. On Granville's face was an expression of triumph and smug satisfaction; on Miss Pitcher's an expression of hate and guilt for the evil pact she had entered into.

Granville felt the tension leave him and the colour returned to his face. He even allowed himself to smile and hold out his arms to his younger daughter Helen. She was in many ways a replica of his wife with her dark hair and green eyes. 'Have you missed papa?' he said with a beaming smile. The little girl ran to him. It was not often that her father expressed his paternal feelings so warmly.

'Yes Papa,' she squealed as she threw her arms around his legs.

Dorothy watched her younger sister hug her father and began to tremble. Miss Pitcher noticed the change in her and she quickly made excuses to bustle the two girls from the room. The warmth of the two little girls' presence went with them. Left behind in their wake was the usual frostiness that existed between the pair who were husband and wife only in name.

'I trust your visit went well?' Granville said to break the cold silence.

'It did,' Fiona replied. 'Did my mother agree to step aside for you while I was gone?'

Granville frowned and thrust his hands in his pockets. The news relayed by McHugh after his meeting with Lady Macintosh was not promising. Something ridiculous about her nominating a proxy. 'I'm afraid not,' he answered. 'Your mother thinks she will live forever. She told that simpleton McHugh that she would nominate someone to replace me in the future. Damned ridiculous, I know, as the terms of your father's will do not allow her to do so. If anyone is to replace me it could only be a son of ours, which we do not have,' he added bitterly, as he reflected on the circumstances that had brought about the unbridgeable rift between them.

Fiona ignored his bitterness. He was no longer of any consequence in her life, except as the relatively competent manager of her family's substantial fortune and the father of her two daughters. 'I am sure it will all be yours one day,' she said patronisingly. 'As for my mother's threat, I'm sure she is bluffing. The only male heir of her bloodline was the son that I gave birth to. And she made sure that he was disposed of,' she added bitterly, looking away. 'I suppose the only consolation I have is that my mother destroyed all chance of *her* bloodline being carried forward in the way of a grandson.' Fiona paused when she noticed her husband pale. 'What is wrong?' she asked, although not out of concern for his health so much as curiosity as to why her normally undemonstrative husband could suddenly appear so stricken.

'Are you sure your mother had the Duffy brat sent to a baby farm?' he asked, almost in a whisper.

Fiona frowned in confusion. 'I wish it had been otherwise,' she replied quietly. 'But when Molly disappeared, I knew why. Molly would never have left me if she had not conspired to have my baby killed. That is why I am so sure.'

But Granville was not so sure anymore. It was

something that his mother-in-law had once said to him years earlier. Something about *her* blood returning to destroy him. He shook his head. No, it was impossible to envisage. Enid Macintosh could never consider using the Duffy brat – if it were still alive – to be part of her sanctimonious world. 'You are right,' he muttered. 'It's not possible.' But why was it that he could see the face of a young man swimming before his eyes – the face of Michael Duffy, laughing at him.

BEYOND THE
FRONTIER

SEVENTEEN

Wallarie knew that this would be the most dangerous section of his trek south. He was in the territory dominated by the swarms of gold prospectors, and the land of the ferocious tribesmen, who fought a guerilla war against all who should trespass upon their sacred lands.

Hunting had proved fruitless. He had been hampered by the need to move stealthily in enemy territory and game was in short supply. He was weak with hunger and what he had been able to scrounge from the earth in the way of insects, tubers and small marsupials had been barely sufficient to keep him alive.

He sat with his back against a rock that provided little shade, and gazed at the heat shimmering off the undulating rocky hills, covered with stunted, dead-looking scrub. Tom Duffy had once taught him to count, so Wallarie now knew he was at least twenty-five days south of where he had left the Kyowarra tribesmen. His mission – to seek out and warn Peter Duffy – was completed. Now he yearned to return to the brigalow plains of his ancestors where he would camp by the billabongs and live off the bounty of his people: the fat fish and ducks of the water; the small wallabies and prickly echidnas whose delicious flesh was much prized; and, if he were fortunate, the dark honey of the small bush bees.

But he knew it would not be easy as now the white man dominated his ancestral lands – a price paid in the blood of Wallarie's people, slaughtered a dozen years earlier by the Native Mounted Police, and the armed shepherds of Donald Macintosh.

He sat and dreamed of food. The heat and silence, like a comforting blanket, lulled him into a doze.

Suddenly he tensed. The voices were unmistakably European. With no discernible movement Wallarie gripped a spear. He calculated that the voices belonged to two men located at about twice the range of his spear. Slowly he turned to see the two prospectors clumsily approaching along a low ridge. One of the men carried a rifle. If he remained still they would probably not see him in the tangle of scrub and rocks. They would pass, oblivious to his presence and continue blithely on their way.

Against all the caution that he should have exhibited for his survival in hostile territory however, Wallarie thought about the food they most probably carried in the swags slung over their shoulders. The white man's tea and sugar was too tempting to resist.

When they had passed he stood up without his weapons. 'Hey whitefellas, you got baccy?' he called. The two men spun to face him with expressions of utter surprise and fear in their bearded faces. Wallarie grinned reassuringly. 'Me good blackfella boss,' he said showing his empty hands. 'No baal blackfella.'

The two men heard the words spoken in broken English from the tall and muscled Aboriginal standing unarmed a hundred paces away.

'A bloody myall,' the man with the rifle muttered to his companion who glanced furtively around the scrub.

Maybe it was an ambush, he thought fearfully. 'Watch him Frank,' he hissed. 'I heared they drag their spears between their toes. When they get up close they use 'em.'

'This darkie's not gonna get the chance,' Frank said, raising his rifle to his shoulder, 'he's gonna be dead.'

Wallarie knew instantly that he was in serious trouble and cursed himself for allowing his hunger to overcome his caution. He turned to run but the shot took him through the flesh just below his armpit. The impact knocked him off his feet and he was flung into the hot earth.

'You got 'im!' he vaguely heard, as he slammed into the sandy ground. 'Bloody good shot!'

Wallarie was well acquainted with European firearms. His dead brother Tom Duffy had claimed

267

he was a better shot than he when they had ranged the Gulf country years earlier as men outside the law. He knew that the rifle the prospector used was a single shot and would need time to reload. Despite the terrible pain that was threatening to overwhelm him, he forced himself to his feet, and ran.

'Jesus!' Frank blasphemed. 'He's getting away.' The bearded prospector fumbled with a cartridge which fell from his hand. His error gave Wallarie valuable yards to lengthen the distance between them.

Frank's companion tugged at his sleeve. 'I think we should get out of here,' he said fearfully. 'He might be goin' for help, bring back a lot more of his darkie mates.'

Frank scooped up the cartridge and slammed it home in the breech. 'Think you might be right,' he replied. With frightened glances over their shoulders both men hurried away.

When he was satisfied he was not being followed – and that he was safely out of range – Wallarie collapsed amongst the rocks. He felt the waves of pain swamp him, as they had so many years earlier, when the devil Morrison Mort had shot him in the side. Any movement of his left arm caused him to cry out in his pain. The bullet had passed through the flesh between his ribs and shoulder. It had lodged firmly in the muscle. 'Bloody bastards,' he groaned, as he gritted his teeth and swore. It was an English expression Tom Duffy had used when he was most angry. 'Bloody bastards shoot a blackfella.'

Weak from hunger and loss of blood Wallarie was hardly aware that he was slipping from consciousness. The flies and ants came seeking nourishment from his wound. But Wallarie did not feel their bites. He was slipping into a world of visions.

A little over two weeks out of Sydney Michael stood alone on the Cooktown jetty gripping a battered carpet bag. He wondered how his contact would recognise him in the mass of eager, newly arrived miners disembarking with him who forced their way through disillusioned miners fighting to get a berth on the ship that had brought them north. Some had even foolishly leapt into the river inhabited by the giant saltwater crocodiles to swim towards the boat before it had docked. The disembarking miners looked upon the departing ones with bewilderment. What was ahead that could cause them to be so desperate to leave?

Cooktown had the same raw feeling of the frontier towns that Michael had once known in his years travelling in the American West. It was a town of freshly cut timber buildings, tents and roads rutted by the wagons at the end of the Wet season. On the mangrove banks of the Endeavour River, the town had exploded from the earth with the hardiness of a pestilent weed, and taken root at the foot of the forested hills surrounding the settlement.

'Mister O'Flynn?' The voice called to him from the crowded river bank. Michael found himself being pushed backwards as the miners stampeded the gangplank to board the ship. The man who had called to Michael had to fight his way through the frenzied crowd. But he was a big and formidable man and, between the two, they were able to get ashore with Michael's luggage.

'Mister O'Flynn. May I introduce myself,' the man said when they were clear of the wharf. 'I am Herr Karl Straub. I work for Baron von Fellmann.' Straub was about Michael's age and had short clipped blond hair. He was clean shaven and had a distinctive and impressive Teutonic appearance about him that made him stand out from the sun-tanned and bushy-bearded miners. He thrust out his hand. His grip was strong and brief.

'Ich nehme an, sie sind Herr Straub,' Michael replied and the German appeared surprised to hear his native tongue used by the Irishman.

'Sie sprechen Deutsch,' he commented. 'Mit einem Hamburger Akzent.'

'I picked up some as a kid,' Michael said switching back to English. 'From an old friend who happened to be from Hamburg.'

'You speak German very well,' Straub complimented, as he guided Michael away from the jostling crowds around the river bank. From the way Straub held himself – his straight back and measured pace – Michael guessed that he was a military man. Most probably an officer.

As they walked along the busy street Michael took in the sights, sounds and smells of this new environment. Cooktown was beginning to take on an air of permanency, if not respectability, he mused as he compared it to similar boom towns he had known in his travels on the American frontier.

Bordering the street he could see that man's basic needs were well catered for. There were hotels, saloons and grog shanties for the thirst the tropics brought on and the less than subtle signs of houses where a man's carnal needs were taken care of. In between these less salubrious places of business were merchant stores, pharmacies, butchers, bakers and other more respectable businesses.

Large signs hastily nailed up advertised wares eagerly sought by the men and women heading down the track for the Palmer River goldfields. There was even a touch of the Orient about the town with the faint scent of incense and Eastern spices on the tropical breezes.

'The Baron has written to tell me that I am to look after you,' Straub said as the two men made their way along Charlotte Street. 'It appears that you impressed the Baroness while you were in Sydney.' Michael flinched. Sleeping with another man's wife was not something he normally found honourable. The wound that Penelope had slashed across his chest now formed a scar, a reminder of her ownership of him.

'I must thank the Baron sometime for his courtesy,' he replied as they passed a melee of drunken men brawling in the middle of the street. 'And compliment him on his choice of such a charming wife. She was most generous with her courtesy towards me whilst I stayed over in Sydney.'

But Straub did not seem unduly interested in

Michael's response. He appeared distracted and unimpressed by the behaviour of the brawling miners. 'It is like this day and night,' he scowled. 'The law is unable to control the miners. They are ignorant men who gamble away their gold. Or end up dead in some backyard with their throats slit. I should warn you that Cooktown is not a place to tread heavily Mister O'Flynn. There are many here who would slit your throat for nothing more than the clothes you wear.'

After a short time of dodging drunken miners spilling out of cheap hotels and brothels and declining the invitations from hard-faced women on the street to go with them to secluded and private places, the two men arrived at one of the better hotels. It was a two-storey wooden plank building with an upper wrought iron railed verandah that faced across the street to the mangroves of the river.

Straub ushered Michael inside the hotel where men lined the bar conversing in raised voices. As it was only mid-morning Michael wondered what the hotel would be like at night. A veritable riot, he mused.

'We go upstairs,' Straub said bluntly. 'You have a room here. Rooms are not easy to get.'

Michael was pleased that he was not paying the bill for the room when Straub ushered him inside. It would have cost a small fortune in a place where men paid for their drinks with gold nuggets.

The room was simple and clean. It opened onto the wide verandah overlooking the street. A gap between the buildings opposite allowed Michael to catch a glimpse of the river and feel the strong breeze that blew through the town, without which he guessed Cooktown could prove to be as hot as an oven under the tropical sun.

He dumped his bag on the sagging bed and followed Straub outside onto the verandah. They slumped into comfortable weather-beaten cane chairs and it was good to be off the cramped deck of the ship that had brought him north.

While he had been forced to wait a couple of days in Brisbane on his journey north, Michael had learned much about his brother Tom's life and tragic death, as well as his sister Kate O'Keefe's rise to fame. Both were now legends in their own right. Very few old timers whom he had talked to in the hotel bars and on the waterfront had not heard of them both. To those of Irish blood Tom Duffy was a hero. To any others he was nothing more than a murdering thief who had thrown in his lot with an equally vicious blackfella. But all had to agree that Kate O'Keefe was beyond reproach.

'How did you know who I was when I got off the ship?' he now asked Herr Straub, snapping back to the present once they were both comfortably seated on the verandah.

'I did not expect to see many men with an eye patch disembark from the ship, Mister O'Flynn,' Straub answered with a chuckle. Michael smiled. He sometimes forgot that his eye patch made him stand out in a crowd.

'So here I am Herr Straub. And here I get told why I am here,' Michael said wryly, as he gazed across the rooftops of the buildings adjacent to the river choked with ships of every shape and description.

'Not completely Mister O'Flynn,' the German cautioned. 'I am to tell you what you are to do next. But not why. You are being paid good money I believe, to obey orders.'

'Orders are things issued to soldiers Herr Straub,' Michael said quietly. 'And if I gather correctly *you* know a lot about giving orders.'

Straub stiffened. Michael's remark had hit a nerve. 'It is not important who I am,' he replied. 'Better you ask only questions, how you say, relevant to what you are to do for the Baron.'

Let them play their games, Michael thought peevishly. They were, after all, paying the bills. 'Seems reasonable Herr Straub,' he said, shrugging off Straub's formal sense of secrecy. 'So what do I do?'

Straub rose from his chair. 'First I will get us a drink. What is your drink? Rum, gin?' he asked politely.

'Rum will be fine,' Michael replied gratefully. He was thirsty and the thought of a drink sounded like a good idea.

When Straub left to get the drinks Michael removed his coat. In the side pocket of his jacket he carried a small Colt revolver. He was never very far from some kind of firearm. Guns were his living – and might possibly be his death.

Straub returned shortly with a bottle and two glasses. Michael could see that it was good rum. The Baron was certainly looking after him – or was it Penelope's doing, albeit through her husband?

Straub poured them both a generous tot. 'Cheers,' he said, and Michael responded by raising his glass. When they had both emptied their glasses Straub refilled them. 'You can get anything in this cursed town. So long as you have the money,' he said as he took a sip of his rum.

'Reminds me of other places I've been,' Michael reflected. 'All life gets measured in how close to the top of the dung hill you are. But if you are not careful you can get buried under it.'

Straub glanced quizzically at him. 'I do not understand this philosophy,' he frowned.

'Doesn't matter Herr Straub. Just a thought on life,' Michael said, as he finished the tot and refilled his glass.

The German followed suit and leaned forward in his chair. 'Tomorrow Mister O'Flynn, you are to start recruiting six men,' he said, as if he were reciting a military order. 'They are to be bushmen who have preferably had military or police experience, men of sober habits and who are prepared to obey orders without question. You will be given an account with one of the banks here to pay them. The account is in your name. The men must be prepared to undertake a prospecting expedition but they do not have to be proven miners. Their ability to live under harsh conditions is preferred above all other qualities,' he concluded.

'I would have thought their mining experience would be preferred, if we are looking for gold,' Michael said facetiously. His sarcasm was not missed by the German.

'As I said Mister O'Flynn, no questions, unless they are on matters directly concerning your briefing,' he replied in an even tone, ignoring the Irish mercenary's gibe.

'I understand,' Michael answered. 'Is there any more that I should know?'

'That is all I have to tell you. Except that should at any stage you be asked, you are to say you are organising a prospecting party,' Straub answered. 'The Queensland government pays rewards for discoveries of gold here. That should be good enough to stop any further questions. I need not tell you, that you do not know me or the Baron. I think that goes without saying.'

Michael nodded. After all he had taken the job for the money. Legal or not – it paid well.

Before they had finished the bottle Straub briefed him on details of the bank account and how much he was to offer each man. It was a generous amount. And as they talked together the Irishman had the feeling that he was the appointed commander of a small private army under the overall generalship of the Baron. It had all the odour of a military expedition and nothing to do with prospecting. But if it was an army, who were they going to fight?

Michael had killed many men over the years. From the forests of New Zealand to the jungles of South America, he had learned and practised his deadly profession. He no longer moralised on political issues; he was after all a soldier of fortune.

Straub finished briefing him and answered as

many of Michael's few questions – covering technical matters relevant to the recruiting and equipping of his select group of fellow adventurers – as he could. When they were satisfied that they had exhausted the briefing, Straub invited Michael to take lunch with him in the hotel's excellent dining room. The meal was excellent: fried steak with boiled potatoes and cabbage, and the two men switched to imported English beer with their meal.

Over lunch Karl Straub proved to be a different man from the one that Michael had known on the hotel verandah and was extremely interested in the fact that Michael spoke German. Michael used their time at lunch to practise his rusty German and Straub proved to have a rich sense of humour, along with interesting observations of the Australian colonies. But although they talked on many subjects of local interest, Straub gave nothing away about himself. Michael was able, however, to ask questions about his employer the Baron, Straub having decided that information on the Baron's personal life was not as confidential as his public life.

From Straub Michael learned how Penelope had met Manfred von Fellmann while she was staying with relatives in Prussia. The Baron had married her on the eve of the Franco-Prussian War where he served with distinction against the French. After the war Penelope had returned to Australia with her husband whose family had commercial interests in the Pacific. From his base in Sydney the Baron roamed the Pacific, managing the considerable family financial interests in the region.

The rum and beer had loosened the normally reserved nature of the stiff-necked German and Straub spoke of the Baron in an almost familiar way. It was the intimate knowledge that Straub seemed to have of the Baron that surprised Michael most; he spoke of the Baron as one would of family. Even so, Michael was sure that, in some way, a formal military relationship existed between him and Herr Straub.

After lunch the two men retired from the dining room and returned to the verandah to enjoy the river breezes. They continued to empty another rum bottle between them and the sun was setting before Straub left for his hotel.

Michael was left sitting alone on the verandah to enjoy the gentle breeze that accompanied the lengthening shadows. Up and down the busy street voices grew louder and more raucous. The residents of Cooktown were rising from the day like nocturnal beasts in search of prey and pleasure. The rum and beer, coupled with the tranquillity of the tropical sunset viewed from the comfort of his cane chair, soon took their effect on Michael and he fell into a deep and peaceful sleep.

The vision came to Wallarie as he lay on the cooling earth under the constellation of the Southern Cross. It was the warrior spirit of the sacred cave calling to him to say that he was to return to the northern forests. The time of vengeance was near and the spirit warrior would need his help. The vision faded and Wallarie slowly opened his eyes. All was a sparkling blackness above him and a coolness that was refreshing around him. A dingo howled and a night bird called a lonely song to the moonless sky.

He lay on the earth and groaned. Not only for his all-consuming thirst and throbbing wound but also because the spirit warrior was asking the impossible of him. He was too weak in his present condition. He needed life-giving water and knew there was a patch of damp ground in a dry watercourse not far away. With all the strength he could muster he dragged himself along, allowing his acute sense of smell to guide him to the water.

The brackish water restored his body but the constant hunger reminded him he must also eat to stay alive. The two whitefellas had food, he knew. But they had preferred to shoot him down rather than share it.

Hatred and hunger combined caused a new strength to surge through the emaciated body of the Darambal warrior. 'Bloody bastards,' he swore as he struggled to his feet. The bleeding had ceased but his arm was still too numb to move effectively. With stumbling steps he made his way in the dark to where he had left his weapons.

Armed once again, he turned his attention to the north. That is where the prospectors had been travelling when they had fired on him. And that is where he must go to meet the warrior spirit of the cave. When the sun once again rose over the hills he would find their tracks and hunt them down. They had forfeited their right to live.

EIGHTEEN

Night was descending over the harbour and the Macintosh barque rose and fell gently on the tide. Channel bells clanged softly and muffled voices drifted on the evening breeze from ships moored nearby. The clip-clop of horses pulling drays, wagons and carriages from the nearby streets adjoining the Quay were becoming too frequent for Captain Mort, who sat alone in his cabin poring over charts and tide tables. He always felt uneasy in Sydney — and with good cause. It was a place where the law was mustered against him. But soon he would be sailing. As soon as the German Baron von Fellmann arrived from Samoa.

Henry Sims stood uncertainly outside his captain's cabin. He was the replacement first mate for the *Osprey* and had much in common with his predecessor Jack Horton. Like Horton he had been born and brought up in the infamous Rocks area of Sydney. He was a tough, brutal man in his prime who had lived on the wrong side of civilised norms. Unlike Horton, however, he was not fully aware of his captain's murderous madness.

His experience with the intricacies of sailing ships was limited. But that is not why he had been given the job that promised lucrative rewards. His abilities with a knife – and unquestioning loyalty – had brought him employment with Mort. All he had to do was dispose of his predecessor. A dark back alley, a drunken victim and the flash of a blade, was all that was required to register him aboard.

The first mate's uncertainty was fuelled by his knowledge that Mort did not like being disturbed whilst he was in his cabin. As for visitors coming aboard and demanding to see the captain – well, that was another thing. But this visitor was different, and even the relatively dull-witted former Rocks thug was overawed by the woman's aura of power. 'Cap'n Mort?' he tentatively called through the door. 'A lady to see you on deck.'

'Who wants to see me?' Mort replied irritably.

'She don't give her name. She jus' said you would come up an' see 'er.'

There was a short silence and the cabin door opened. Mort appeared dressed in his full uniform with his jacket undone and thrust his face at Sims. 'What the devil does this woman want?' he asked belligerently.

'Says she wants to see you. That's all.'

Mort buttoned his jacket and followed the first

mate. Some bloody whore come peddling her wares, he thought as he clambered on deck. He would send her packing.

But his belligerence dissolved very quickly when he saw who was standing beside the gangway gazing back at the shore. A cold fear gripped his kidneys. With a scowl he dismissed the first mate so that he might be alone with the woman. 'Lady Macintosh,' he said deferentially. 'What, if I may inquire, brings you to my ship?'

Enid turned to face him. 'If I may correct you Captain Mort,' she said coldly, 'the *Osprey* belongs to me. It is not your ship by any means.'

Flustered by her reminder Mort mumbled, 'I am sorry for my unintended presumption. It's just that the *Osprey* has been under my command for so long now, that I have grown to feel responsible for her, in every way.'

'An admirable quality Captain Mort,' Enid replied, without any hint of compliment. 'But that is why my son-in-law pays you so generously. It is what we expect.'

'If I may ask again Lady Macintosh, what brings you to the *Osprey* this evening?'

'I must admit that I have never stepped foot on the *Osprey*'s decks,' she replied, quickly glancing around the barque. 'But I decided this was an opportune time to do so.'

'Opportune time?' Mort asked suspiciously. He noticed that she was alone on his ship. But down on the wharf he could see her carriage and a burly driver looking up at them. 'Opportune time for what?'

Enid fixed him with her emerald-green eyes. To Mort they were the colour of a dangerous sea. 'Just to inform you,' she replied coldly, 'that should you be brought before the law on charges of murder I will need to seek another captain to replace you.'

Stunned by the woman's calmly delivered statement he gaped at her.

Enid had prayed for this moment for a long time. It was not that she would not have paid anything to see him dangle at the end of a rope, but being able to cause him fear was her personal means of exacting revenge for the death of her son. 'As this is most probably an imminent situation,' she added, 'I will require that you ensure all papers pertaining to the *Osprey* are secured safely with the company secretary George Hobbs tomorrow morning. Failure to do so will give me recourse to immediately dismiss you from your post. I hope for your sake that this does not happen.' The last statement was a lie. Enid well knew anything to hurt the murderer of her son would give her joy.

'Mister White might have something to say about your threat,' Mort snarled like a cornered animal. 'You do not have the power to threaten me.'

'I suggest that you ask my son-in-law who still controls the Macintosh companies Captain Mort,' she replied in an icy tone. 'He does not own the *Osprey*. I do. He merely manages its affairs. Nothing more.'

They stood staring at each other, the air thick with mutual hatred. Hers for the man who had probably acted on orders from Granville White to kill

David. And his for the woman who he sensed had the power to deprive him of the only thing he had come to love in his life – his ship.

'Should I be brought before any magistrates in Sydney, Lady Macintosh, what then becomes of the Baron's expedition that the *Osprey* has been chartered for?' Mort asked. 'Will you replace me?'

A cold smile preceded her words. 'In the unlikely event that you are not arrested for murder,' she replied, 'then you will still captain the charter. The Baron has paid handsomely for our services and, if nothing else, I know you are capable of seeing that his mission is successful.'

'Thank you Lady Macintosh,' Mort replied sarcastically. 'I am sure you will not be disappointed.'

'I am sure I will not be disappointed,' she replied, still holding her cold smile. 'The Lord has given me the means to see to that. And now I will leave your presence Captain Mort with the knowledge that I *know* you killed my son. You may not answer to the law for that, but you will answer to my God when your time comes.'

Mort did not attempt to deny the charge she had brought against him. Any denial would be a waste of time with a woman like Enid Macintosh as she was made of unbending steel dressed in velvet. He watched her walk away with a confident spring in her step as if his hanging were an inevitability.

When Enid reached her carriage the driver stepped down from his seat to assist her into the finely crafted conveyance. She thanked him and settled back against the leather seat for the ride home. Now she would savour the discomfort she had caused the murderous captain and later sleep in the knowledge that he would not sleep. His nights would be haunted by the uncertainty of his fate. It was only a matter of time – and the legal brilliance of Daniel Duffy – to compile the evidence Detective Kingsley would present. As far as Enid was concerned the matter was settled.

Now she was free to go after her own son-in-law for his conspiracy in the murder of her son. And it would be another Duffy who would be her ally in Granville White's demise as a power in the family. The irony of life was not lost on Enid. Once the name Duffy had been an unspeakable abomination in her family. But time had changed all that. Time and the strange curse that bound the two families in a series of violent deaths.

Mort watched the carriage rattle away from the wharf. He turned and went to his cabin where he slumped onto a stool. Uncertain as he was about what exact evidence Lady Macintosh had against him, he was certain that she would not have come to gloat, unless she was right.

Mort stared at the sword on the wall above his bunk. He brooded on her words and presence aboard the *Osprey*. For an inexplicable reason he had a rec-ollection of a hot and dusty morning in central Queensland. November '62, he remembered. A big and bearded Irish bullocky by the name of Patrick Duffy manacled to a tree with his nigger boy. The sword sliding into the Irishman's belly as Duffy fixed him with his dying hate and spat a curse on him. Something about him dying an equally painful death.

Mort shook his head and laughed. The maniacal sound echoed throughout the bowels of the *Osprey*.

He was tall and broad shouldered for a boy almost eleven years old, and there was a certain defiance, not servility, in his emerald eyes. He had the promise of dashing, handsome looks that could bring him the choice of any young lady in English society – or colonial society – for that matter.

Enid could see in the boy what had attracted her daughter to his father. 'What has your . . . what has Mister Duffy told you to call me?' she asked young Patrick as he stood before her in the library.

'Lady Enid,' he replied.

She nodded. Good! One day he would know all. But for now he seemed to accept the confusing events in his life. He had the stuff of the Macintoshes to adapt to difficult situations. After all, her blood ran in his veins, and he was the next generation to pass on that same blood to a long line of Macintosh heirs. 'I will call you Patrick,' she said with just a touch of grandmotherly tenderness. 'Has Mister Duffy told you what is going to happen to you next month?' she asked gently, as she sat in her chair behind her desk.

In many ways the first meeting between the two

of them was more like a business meeting. She had considered whether she might have done better to see the boy in the drawing room, rather than the sombre library, with its cases of leatherbound books covering the walls.

But in many ways this *was* a business meeting. For a moment she could see that the boy appeared apprehensive – not frightened like a child – but apprehensive as an adult calculating his future in a business deal. She did not want him to feel that way.

Patrick could not be less than awed by the surroundings of the Macintosh mansion. He had never dreamed that a house could be so big and beautiful. Even the library was like some treasure cove with all its books and strange ornaments made of metal and wood. There were Aboriginal spears and clubs, shields and throwing sticks. It was like a museum and Patrick loved museums. The thought of going away from his family made him sad. At the same time he was excited by what he was discovering in this new world his father had brought him to 'I have been told that I will be going to England with you so that I might get an education there,' Patrick replied. 'Father said I would be gone for a long time.' She could hear just the slightest quiver in the boy's reply.

'But you will be coming back,' she said to allay his fears. 'And you will be able to write to your family from England whenever you wish.' She felt that she should try to help him look forward to what was in the future, and shifted the conversation back to the present. 'Mister Duffy has told me that you like reading books.'

'And I like boxing,' Patrick replied brightly. 'Uncle Max teaches me. He says some day I will be as good as Michael Duffy who he once taught to box.'

'I do not think that boxing is really something for gentlemen,' Enid said, with the faintest of smiles. 'I think that you might learn other things. You might learn to ride with the hounds some day. Now, that is much more suited to a gentleman.' No, she thought wryly. It would not do to have the heir to the Macintosh empire known as some back street pugilist!

Enid spent an hour with Patrick chatting in the library, and by the time they had exhausted subjects dear to a boy's heart, she was quite enchanted by his natural charm. She even felt a strange urge to call him David.

When Daniel came to the library he noticed that she was a very different woman from the stern Lady Macintosh he had left Patrick with. He saw a soft glow in her expression and suspected that it was a reflection of her grandmotherly pride.

Patrick was taken by a maid to the kitchen to feast on cream buns and drink buttermilk while Daniel and Enid made arrangements for his sea voyage to England. She repeated to him that Patrick would be looked after as her very own grandson, and that he would be able to relay his impressions to his own family, at the Erin Hotel. Daniel was reassured that the decision to allow Patrick to be educated in England was in the boy's best interests.

As Daniel left the Macintosh house with Patrick

he could not help but smile at a distant memory of another young man. While Patrick lived – so would Michael! And the boy could charm the pants off the devil's wife herself – just like his father.

Enid watched the carriage trundle down the driveway through the big front gates. She could see Patrick gazing back in open-mouthed awe at the house. Yes, some day he would realise just who he was, she thought with some contentment for the first time in many years. And the Macintosh name would continue through his blood line – her blood line!

NINETEEN

Michael was not sure what brought him out of his deep sleep. But years of living on the edge had honed his survival instincts; a cracking twig or the sudden silence of the insects in the night could alert him to danger. He was asleep among the less than subtle night sounds of a brawling frontier town: women's voices raised in ribald laughter; men swearing and shouting; the sounds of dance halls with their tinny pianos and whoops of drunken men dancing parodies of the Irish jigs and Scottish reels; somewhere a child crying incessantly as a wagon rumbled past the hotel on the street below.

No, it was not a sound that brought him out of his deep sleep, but the skin-crawling feeling that he was not alone, a feeling of immediate and close danger!

'If you are thinking about your gun Mister

Duffy,' the voice said in the night, 'you need not because I have it.'

Michael opened his eyes, blinking away the sleep, and focused on a vaguely familiar face. 'We meet again Mister Brown,' he said when he was able to get a clearer picture of the Englishman sitting in the chair vacated by Straub late that afternoon. 'Hope you have a bottle with you. Or at least a good reason for taking my gun,' he drawled casually, desperately trying to gather his wits fogged by an excess of alcohol. He was puzzled at something that the Englishman had said to him. Something important. Then it came to him with a shock. Adrenalin surged through his body, forcing his senses fully awake. Brown had called him Duffy!

'Sorry Mister Duffy, or may I call you Michael,' Horace said casually, although he felt far from being at ease. The more he had learned about Michael Duffy the more he respected the man's ability to kill. 'That way, only you and I know who you really are.' Horace had guessed that the Irishman would be armed and he was proven right.

Michael's small revolver was nestled in his lap and he considered the option of attempting to recover his gun. But he also sensed that the Mister Brown that he knew from the clipper ship, was not the Mister Brown sitting in the semi-dark of the hotel verandah.

Unexpectedly Horace passed the gun back to him. 'I don't think you will be needing this with me,' he said cheerfully. 'I haven't come here to do you any harm.'

Michael accepted the pistol. 'If you think I am this Duffy person then you are taking a great risk Mister Brown,' he said, as he held the pistol in his hand.

Horace smiled and shook his head. 'I don't think so. I think you also know that it is a waste of time for you to deny that you are Michael Duffy, formerly of Sydney and one of Von Tempsky's Rangers. Also former member of the Army of the United States of America and now a roving agent for German interests. You need not try to deny who you are as that would be futile with me.'

Horace spoke so calmly, and with such intimate knowledge of his past, that Michael did indeed know it was futile to deny who he was. 'I won't insult your intelligence by denying I am who you say,' he replied calmly. 'But that brings me to who you really are. Remittance men don't normally follow me from one end of the Pacific to the other. So I doubt that you are a remittance man Mister Brown. If that is your name.'

'My name really is Horace Brown,' he sighed. 'And I *am* a remittance man, of sorts. At least I am to my family.'

'But who are you to the rest of the world?' Michael asked suspiciously.

'Let us say I have a great interest in this part of the world,' he replied, with careful consideration for how much he could reveal. 'An interest probably stronger than a lot of friends I have back in England. You know, you and I have a lot more in common than you would think Michael. Except that I am not wanted for murder . . . Or should I say, *was* wanted for murder. But warrants don't apply to dead men do they?'

'You know that,' Michael answered with a growl. Brown was a man of mystery but already he was beginning to form his suspicions of who, or what, Horace Brown was.

Horace removed his spectacles and wiped them on the sleeve of his shirt before replacing them on the tip of his podgy nose. 'Some day you will have to tell me how you got the Von to feign your demise,' he said. 'I heard he was killed by the Maoris back in '68. Regretfully I never had the opportunity to meet the somewhat colourful commander of the Waikato Rangers. But I heard a lot about him from his colleague Captain Jackson. Yes, I would have given much to have shared a drink with Gustavus von Tempsky. A very unusual man,' he mused as he kept Michael under his scrutiny. 'Not unlike yourself Michael. A soldier of fortune one could say. A former officer in the Prussian army turned guerilla fighter against the Spanish regulars in Nicaragua. And finally a commander of the Forest Rangers in New Zealand. And, like you, he was an artist of some note. Ah, but you never did get the chance to become an artist, did you? Oh, and he was very much a ladies' man. Yes, I can see that you would easily become friends with such a man.'

Michael was stunned by the little Englishman's intimate knowledge. His detailed information on his military experience with von Tempsky's Forest Rangers could only come from access to military records. The more Brown revealed information about him the more he actually revealed intelligence on himself. 'Who do you work for Mister Brown,' Michael asked bluntly, 'the British Foreign Office?'

Horace did not shift under his relentless gaze. 'Let us just say that I work for the best interests of Queen Victoria, God bless her, and all who raise the flag on her birthday. Which brings me to you and I. And the Baron.' Horace now shifted his seemingly casual rambling to that of hard-edged business. 'In *your* best interests Mister Duffy,' he said, leaning forward, 'I think you should cooperate with me. I think you and I will have a long and happy future if you do, like a good marriage, one could say. But if you decide there is no chance of consummation then I am afraid to say divorce could be very messy for you.'

Michael understood the Englishman's analogy all too clearly. Either he cooperated with him – or he would suddenly find himself ending up in some uncomfortable police lockup awaiting extradition back to the Colony of New South Wales. That he might even be shot attempting to escape custody was also a possibility. There was something very dangerous about the man that belied his clerical appearance. Michael fully understood dangerous men and knew that he was dealing with one. 'I think I would like to hear what you have to say, Mister Brown,' he replied. 'Somehow I don't think I have much choice.'

Horace smiled and visibly relaxed as he sank back into the cane chair. 'I think you should start our "marriage" by dropping the formality of "mister".

My name is Horace and I would deem it an honour from a man of your considerable reputation if you called me Horace. But not Horry. My nanny used to call me that.'

'Horace, I must tell you that today I have been feted by the Germans, threatened by a representative of Her Majesty's government. And now here I am an Irish-Australian, with an American accent, it's all very confusing,' Michael concluded with a short and bitter laugh.

Horace smiled. The man has a sense of humour, he thought and could not help but like the man for his easy-going manner and past proven courage in war. He felt comfortable in the company of men like himself: men who lived on the edge in a world far too civilised to accommodate daring and courage. 'I must confess that I have lied to you Michael,' he replied. 'I said that I didn't have a drink for us when you asked.' He produced a silver hip flask. 'I presume you will join me in a toast to our mutual future. And I can assure you that working with me will bring financial rewards commensurate with your rather peculiar skills. When we have made the toast, I will ask you some questions the answers to which, I assure you, are of critical interest to both the colony of Queensland and England.'

Michael found an empty glass beside his chair and Horace poured the brandy. He raised the hip flask. 'Her Majesty, God bless her,' he toasted, raising his hip flask to the night.

'Saint Pat. And damn the English to hell,' Michael responded as he raised his glass. With toasts aside,

Horace got down to business, and the next meeting between them was arranged.

The evening was cool and pleasant when Horace left Michael to return to his hotel room. He had urgent work to do as a result of his meeting with the soldier of fortune. A fat, translucent pink gecko on the wall of the hotel room shrilled its startlingly loud staccato chatter.

Horace flinched at the shrill cry. He knew that his nerves were on edge and sighed as he sat staring at the fresh paint on the wall of his hotel room. He pondered on how much he had gleaned indirectly from Michael Duffy – and the chain of contacts the Irishman had made from Samoa to Cooktown. He knew that the Germans were planning something of great importance. Something that had the potential to seriously interfere with British interests in the Pacific. But what?

Bismarck's unified Germany was a rising power in Europe and Horace knew that historically such powers required empires. But Bismarck had not taken any real steps towards colonisation in the Pacific. His Hamburg merchants had spread across the Pacific. So too had France, Holland and even the United States of America, even though it always denied its interests in colonisation. As such Samoa had become a microcosm of conflicting interests between the Americans, Germans and British.

One day, Horace believed, England would find herself confronting Germany on the Continent.

And when that day came, where the Germans had financial interests, they would also have military bases. But his radical views had been laughed at by his colleagues in the Foreign Office. France was the traditional enemy of England – not Germany, they had scoffed. He had reminded them of the crushing German victory in the Franco-Prussian War. But nevertheless, the fools could not see that Bismarck was looking at those places on the world map not yet shaded with British red!

Horace Brown did not keep a journal but he did produce pages of reports for dispatch to London. He commenced his report, 'Intentions of German Interests in the Pacific: Future Problems.' He paused and placed the nibbed pen to the side of the blotting paper, stretching as he watched with interest as the gecko darted for a moth that had foolishly landed on the ceiling nearby.

He considered all that he knew to date. Michael Duffy was acting for von Fellmann to recruit other men who had martial skills. Duffy had said that, if questioned, he had been instructed to say that they were organising a prospecting expedition. To where? For what? Not even Duffy had that answer. Herr Straub had the distinct markings of a military man – an officer in most probability. The *Osprey* – under the command of one Captain Morrison Mort – had been chartered to sail to Cooktown with the Baron aboard. Horace had been briefed by Major Godfrey about Mort and knew that he was definitely a shady character capable of taking money for any purpose.

When he put all that he knew together the

revelation came to the Foreign Office man like a divine inspiration. The party of heavily armed men with bush experience or martial/police skills . . . the *Osprey* . . . Michael Duffy's knowledge of the jungles from his experience in South America and a ruthless ship's captain experienced in working in hostile waters amongst the natives. There was one place where a man would need to be heavily armed or have an armed party always at hand. Only one place of strategic interest to an expanding German influence in the Pacific.

New Guinea!

The huge island directly north of eastern Australia was mysterious – and unexplored. Reputed to be a land of head-hunters and cannibals, it was an island of jungles with a massive mountain range along its spine, rising into the clouds. Should the Germans annex the island they could garrison it with troops only a stone's throw away from a vital British holding. Such an annexation would pose a decisively strategic threat to the security of the British Empire in the Pacific.

But it was all supposition. He knew his theory needed corroboration and Michael Duffy was the only man he had been able to recruit inside the Prussian's organisation, although Duffy was not exactly a volunteer to British causes. He was, after all, little more than a soldier of fortune, and mercenaries were notoriously unreliable in their loyalties to patriotic causes. Money and survival primarily guided their loyalties.

Horace knew that he needed more to ensure

Michael Duffy stayed on his side. He needed to find a cause that would ensure he remained loyal to his ultimate aim of stopping the Germans if indeed they were planning to annex the island of New Guinea to their Pacific empire.

The British agent picked up the pen and scribbled down a series of options. The answer had been with him all the time when he reviewed his list. The *Osprey* captain was the key! He was the key to obtaining Duffy's total compliance in terms of stopping the Prussian agent. When in Sydney the English agent had dug further into the mercenary's past and Mort's name had cropped up like a deadly weed in the Duffy garden.

With a satisfied smile Horace Brown recommenced his report to London. Whether the fools at the other end accepted his opinions was irrelevant. By the time the report reached London the Germans might have completed their mission and it would all be too late for British interests. But at least he had an idea of how to stop the Baron from succeeding in his mission. *How* would not be included in his report as his ideas were not always condoned by the niceties of international law.

TWENTY

Kingsley was surreptitiously taking in the rich decor of Daniel's office. Like Enid Macintosh, Daniel did not warm to the presence of the police detective. There was something very mercenary about the man. Kingsley had been evasive when he had quietly interrupted and raised the question as to whether the dying criminal had mentioned Michael's name at any time, Daniel thought, as he completed the notes he had taken concerning the policeman's conversation with Jack Horton.

'What do you think Mister Duffy?' the detective asked.

Daniel frowned and stood to stretch his legs. He walked to the door and glanced out at the clerks hunched over their ledgers in the adjoining room. 'I'm afraid Mister Kingsley,' he replied, turning back to walk across the room to his desk, 'that all you have told me is old and unprovable news.'

Kingsley scowled. He did not like lawyers and the off-hand manner in which this one treated his visit only confirmed his bitter dislike for them. 'What about Horton's confession that he and Captain Mort murdered all those darkie girls? What about that?'

'Proof is a direct witness account of what someone has actually seen or heard,' Daniel replied in a tired voice. 'Not hearsay in the third person. But as a policeman you should know that. So I'm afraid all we have is confirmation of suspicion, nothing more. No real evidence.' He slumped in his chair and added, 'I truly wish I could tell you otherwise.'

Kingsley scowled as he rose to his feet. Somehow he knew he would not be getting any more money for his assistance – especially from the likes of Mister Duffy. 'I will bid you a good afternoon Mister Duffy,' he said abruptly.

Daniel nodded. He did not bother to escort the policeman to the door but sat dejected staring at the wall. When Kingsley was gone he shuffled the papers in front of him. If only Sergeant Farrell could have produced evidence to link Mort with the murder of the prostitute, he thought pessimistically. Something more recent with all the elements that might sway a judge to pass sentence of death on Mort, should the jury find him guilty. But that opportunity seemed as remote as man's chances of flying to the moon. Daniel felt a need for a stiff drink. Evil seemed to have a way of surviving – like the rats that plagued The Rocks.

~

Lathered in sweat Granville White awoke in the early morning hours. The persistent dream haunted him and, alone in his bed, he cursed Michael Duffy's memory. It was as if the damned Irishman was laughing at him from beyond his grave. It might be that Michael Duffy was dead, he thought with a shudder. But was there a possibility that his bastard son had survived – despite what his mother-in-law had said about the brat's fate at a baby farm.

Granville eased himself from his bed, slipped a smoking jacket over his pyjamas, and made his way to the library. The rest of the household was asleep, and Fiona was away for the night, leaving their daughters in the care of the nanny. She's probably with Penelope, he thought bitterly as he lit a lantern. The lantern light flooded the library. This was his special place of privacy where he could be alone to ponder on the fate of his enemies and take his perverse pleasures. But for now it was a place for thinking.

The recurring nightmare of the dead Irishman had haunted him since his mother-in-law's threat to challenge his position and had been heightened by the mysterious hint of a successor selected by her. If the Duffy bastard were still alive where would the old Irish nanny Molly O'Rourke have taken him for sanctuary? He sat on the couch staring at his desk and smiled grimly. It would have to be Michael Duffy's family! The Irish were like that – clannish and devoted to family – and he knew where to find the Duffys!

Granville had long ago learned that real power was the ability to buy life and death and that a man's power was the aphrodisiac that attracted women, who didn't really care how dangerous that power was. He stroked the big leather couch considering what he must do. As he felt the smooth animal skin under his hand the bestial cravings in his dark soul stirred. With Fiona away the house was his for the night. He needed to relieve his tension and it would be a pity to waste the opportunity. He rose from the couch and padded to his daughter's bedroom.

Captain Morrison Mort preferred to remain in the cabin aboard his ship. The quietly assured threat from Lady Macintosh had the outcome she had hoped and planned for. He was a man haunted by paranoia. Every rattle of a carriage on the wharf was a police van; every footstep on the deck above his head the traps come to arrest him.

Sims had delivered the ship's papers to George Hobbs as ordered by Lady Macintosh as nothing short of the ship sinking would bring Mort out of his cabin. Only a summons from his boss Granville White to meet him at an infamous brothel superseded his crippling fear.

Mort had taken a hansom cab to a dirty hovel of a tenement house in Glebe where he alighted to be met by a tough-looking doorman who he followed inside. They passed tiny doorways in a long hallway, where Mort could see unkempt women lying about in the rooms on palliasses waiting for their customers. Mort sneered at the manner of the establishment. It had no class. He had seen better whore houses in conservative Melbourne.

'Come through to the office,' the tough said.

Mort obeyed, stepping into a room where Granville White was sitting on a bed, a room that Mort casually noted was in a much better state than those he had passed along the hallway.

Granville did not rise. 'I am pleased to see that you answered my summons so promptly Captain Mort,' he said, dismissing the escorting tough with a wave. 'I would offer you a chair but as you see there are none in this room. So I am afraid you must stand.'

'That'll be all right with me Mister White,' Mort answered diffidently.

'I need your special services once again,' Granville said. 'It has been a long time since I called on you for a favour.'

Mort shifted uneasily. Had the matter been of a routine business nature, he knew that his employer would have called on him at his ship. But since he had demanded to meet elsewhere, it had to be of an extremely confidential nature. Literally a matter of life or death. But whose death?

'I heard about the unfortunate demise of your first mate Jack Horton recently,' Granville said. 'Did you kill him? Or did you have someone else do it?'

Mort stared hard at his boss. He was not afraid of Granville White but knew he owed him much – including saving his neck from being stretched on the gallows. 'I'm not saying I had anything to do with his demise,' Mort lied. 'But it was a good thing when all is considered.'

Granville smiled knowingly and dropped the

subject. His question had been answered and his appreciation would be demonstrated later with a bonus in the captain's pay. It was good to have employees who could use their initiative. 'To ask about Horton's demise was not the reason why I organised this meeting,' he said. 'The reason you are here is because I would like you to attend to a very important matter, before you sail with Baron von Fellmann for Cooktown. A matter involving a name I know you are familiar with.'

'Who would that be?' Mort asked guardedly.

'Duffy.'

Mort blanched. The name haunted him for reasons he would be unable to explain to a sane person. There had been too many nights at sea when an old Aboriginal wearing feathers and daubed in ochre had appeared and stood in the dark corners of his cabin just watching him. The figure had always come in that time between sleeping and waking. And always the name Duffy seemed to jump into his head 'You know I do,' he answered. 'You want something to happen to that bastard Duffy lawyer?'

Granville shook his head. 'No, he is no threat,' he replied. 'I want you to organise people I know you are acquainted with to find a young boy who would be around eleven years of age by now. The boy is most likely the son of another Duffy I had the misfortune of being acquainted with some years ago, Michael Duffy. Not that you would have personally known him as you were with the Native Mounted Police at the time. I now strongly suspect that the boy is alive and being raised by his family at the Erin

Hotel in Redfern, where his uncle Daniel Duffy lives. I want you to ascertain if the boy exists.'

'What if I find him? What then Mister White?'

'You take appropriate action to remove him permanently from this world.'

Mort frowned. It was not that he had any qualms about killing a boy, but that the risks were great when it brought him close to the lawyer who had almost succeeded in having him hanged years earlier. 'I can make arrangements,' he said. 'But I cannot risk being personally involved. Lady Macintosh came to the *Osprey* recently to warn me that I may be arrested for the death of her son. I don't know how she knows, but I do know she was not bluffing. I hope you understand why I have to keep my head down.'

'I fully understand Captain,' Granville said sympathetically. 'I am only calling on your assistance to arrange for the right people to do the job. I can also assure you that my mother-in-law has nothing in the way of evidence to link you to my dear cousin David's death. She is just a bitter and helpless old woman clutching at straws. I can promise that given time, Captain Mort, she will be stripped of all power in the companies, and I will have sole control of the Macintosh enterprises. So you need not worry about her threats. There is one other thing I should add that I think will please you,' he added smugly. 'Carry out this task of disposing of the Duffy brat, if he exists, and I will have papers drawn up signing the *Osprey* over to you on the demise of my dear mother-in-law.'

Mort tensed and looked sharply at Granville. Had he heard right? The *Osprey* would be his! Never in his wildest dreams had he imagined such a prize. He would own the only thing he truly loved in this world! His sharp look turned to suspicion. 'Lady Macintosh would never approve of such a contract,' he said in a surly tone.

'Lady Macintosh does not have to know,' Granville replied with a cold smile. 'The papers will be drawn up in secret. They will be legitimate, with a little legal intrigue, and you will have a duly signed copy with my signature. I am sure that the contract will stand up in any court of law.' Mort relaxed. Despite his distrust in everything and everyone he did have a respect for formal papers. 'Oh,' Granville added, 'I do not have to impress upon you the need for the utmost confidentiality in this matter.'

'That goes without saying Mister White,' Mort scowled. 'I will attend to the matter we have discussed straightaway.' He glanced around the room and added, 'Kind of surprised you would meet me in such a place as this Mister White. Thought you might find somewhere better.'

Granville smiled ruefully. 'One does not make a profit by spending on luxuries,' he replied. 'One supplies the product and the customer is satisfied whether they be in a harem or in this place of ill repute. So if you have no further questions I will organise the money for your venture.'

Mort had no further questions. Finding a boy – and killing him – required little in the way of knowledge. All it required was an acquired brutality.

~

The man Captain Mort hired was good at his job. His name was Charlie Heath and although he was reputed to have killed on two other occasions he had never been brought to justice. He was a big, vicious-looking man who frequented the pubs around The Rocks where he lived off the vice and violence of the area. Besides being physically very strong, he had an inborn cunning that, in another world, would have made him a slick politician.

Heath's appearance in the bar of the Erin Hotel caused Max Braun some curiosity. The man was not a regular patron and his overheard questions concerning the Duffy family caused more than a twinge of suspicion with the burly barman.

'Vot you vont to know about Duffy family?' Max asked aggressively when Charlie stepped up to the bar for a drink. 'I hear you ask too many questions mein friend.'

Charlie eyed the barman with an insolence born of the self-confidence to inflict pain. 'None of yer business cabbage eater,' he answered with a sneer. 'Just a few friendly questions is all I ask.'

Max fixed the other man's eyes with his and Charlie was surprised to see no hint of fear in the German's face. 'You be vise to ask your questions elsewhere,' Max said. 'None of the Duffy business is yours. Now I ask you to leaf or I throw you out.'

Charlie bridled at the obvious challenge. But his cunning overrode his instinct to pull a knife and slash the broad face pushed into his. 'I'm going cabbage eater,' he sneered. 'I don't like yer face. And if I ever see yer out on the street you and I will settle up.' He turned his back and walked away.

Max watched him depart and filed his face in his memory. He was a man he might like to kill before he grew much older. The former Hamburg seaman was no stranger to violence himself. He had seen it all on some of the toughest and most dangerous waterfronts of the '50s before he jumped ship in Melbourne and fought the English army at the Eureka Stockade.

He picked up an empty glass and polished it with a clean rag. His mind was not on the task at hand but the face he had just seen. Something about the man worried him. What information about the Duffys could be important enough to warrant the man's strange questions about Patrick and Martin? They were, after all, only boys. Had the questions been about Daniel then he might have understood. Lawyers had a natural way of making enemies with dissatisfied clients.

With a fixed smile on his face Charlie Heath walked away from the Erin Hotel. He had learned enough to know that the boy Patrick was in all probability the one that Captain Mort wanted dead. Now it was just a matter of identifying what Patrick Duffy looked like. Then all he had to do was plan the time and place to kill him. An eleven-year-old boy was not a problem. It would be the easiest fifty quid he had ever earned!

Charlie Heath passed on his information to

Captain Mort who in turn informed Granville White. Once the existence of the son of Michael Duffy was confirmed, Granville's nights grew even longer. This time there would be no mistakes, he fumed, as there had been with Michael Duffy years earlier. Duffy might be a ghost haunting his life – his bastard son was soon to join his father in death.

TWENTY-ONE

'There's nothin' out here except rocks and flies Harry,' Frank said to his companion squatting beside him, chipping at a lump of quartz rock with a miner's pick. 'Rocks, flies and darkies,' he added.

Harry grunted as he stood to take the stiffness out of his back. Their expedition away from the established goldfields of the Palmer had proved to be fruitless. That is, with the exception of the blackfella they had bagged the previous day. He stood and gazed around them at the seemingly endless panorama of stunted trees, rocks and shimmering heat haze. 'That darkie you shot yesterday spoke English,' he said, expressing something that had nagged him through the night. 'Bit unusual don't you think, for a myall?'

Frank tried to spit but his mouth was too dry. 'Don't mean he could be trusted,' he replied. 'All blackfellas should be shot on sight.' He stood and hurled the piece of quartz at a lizard basking on a rocky shelf. 'How's your water supply?' he asked, as he wiped the sweat from his brow.

'Not good,' Harry replied, swishing the canteen in his hand. 'Enough for a day and that's it.'

'About the same with me. Think it's time we headed back to that creek we passed a day back. Fill up and head back to the Palmer.'

Harry nodded. Neither had expressed their concern previously. So intent had they been to seek out another gold lode that they had pushed themselves beyond the limits of safety. Food was not a problem. They carried a good supply of flour, tea, sugar and tinned meat. Water was the vital concern in the semi-arid country they had traversed.

Both men heaved their swags onto their backs and turned to retrace their steps. But they had not gone more than a dozen paces when Harry stopped, shaded his eyes, and peered at the horizon. 'Frank,' he said softly. 'I think I can see a blackfella up there, on that ridge ahead of us.'

Frank stopped and stared in the direction that had been indicated. 'By Crikey yer right,' he said. 'I think it's the one I shot. Thought the bastard would be crow bait by now.' He raised his rifle and took careful aim at the tiny figure watching them from the rise.

Wallarie saw the puff of smoke and a second later heard the bang. He smiled grimly at the two tiny dots below him. Stupid bastards should know that he was out of range of the Snider, he thought with bitter satisfaction. Maybe he should teach them how to shoot.

'He didn't even move,' Harry said in an awed voice. 'It's like he's not scared of us.'

'We need to get closer,' Frank said, as he reloaded the rifle. 'Then we'll see him do a dance.'

But Harry was not so sure. There was something very disconcerting about the wild myall on the ridge. It was as if he knew things that they did not. A cold fear gripped his body. 'Maybe we just leave him alone and maybe he will leave us alone,' he said with a shudder. 'I don't like the look of this, Frank. He might have some mates somewhere, just waitin' for us to go after him.'

'You've got that Le Mat,' Frank said. 'It's more than enough to keep any darkie at bay.' The Le Mat was a powder and ball revolver with the addition of a small shotgun device attached underneath the barrel – a weapon favoured by the Confederate officers of the American Civil War. But its shortcoming was its limited range.

'I have Frank but I don't like the idea.'

Frank glanced at him with an expression of contempt. 'I'm going after the black bastard and finishing him off,' he said, as he strode away towards the ridge. 'If yer any kind of mate, you'd come with me.'

Wallarie watched the two men on the flat below him. They appeared to be arguing. His appearance had provoked them as he had planned. He felt further satisfaction when the two men began trudging in his direction as he had hoped they would.

Although his left arm was still too stiff and sore to use effectively he was not worried. He would not need to use it for now as he trailed his long spears in his right hand. All that was important was that the two men pursue him. In doing so he would wear them down and then strike at a time of his choosing. He smiled as the two men struggled up the rocky slope under a blazing sun. 'Bloody bastards,' he swore with a chuckle in his curse. 'Wallarie wait for you.'

All day the spectre of the wild myall taunted them. His image danced in the shimmering haze just out of rifle range as the men stumbled in the body-sapping terrain.

'He's leading us away from the creek,' Harry gasped through cracked lips as he slumped to his knees for a rest. 'The bastard's playin' us like a fish on a hook.'

Frank went down on one knee, using his rifle as a prop. He too had come to realise the situation. The black bastard was cunning, he had to admit to himself. He had altered course in subtle ways and eventually turned the hunt in a direction away from the creek bed. 'Think it's time we let the darkie go,' he reluctantly conceded as he lifted himself to his feet.

~

Bitterly disappointed, Wallarie watched the two men change direction and walk away from him. He had hoped to keep up the chase until nightfall. But he knew where they were going. Like the birds of the arid west at sunset they were in flight for water.

As disappointed as he was Wallarie still felt some satisfaction. He had seen the way the two men had moved across the terrain. He knew that they were weak and thirsty from the arduous pursuit. And a thirsty man was preoccupied with slaking the unbearable torment a raging thirst caused.

In a loping stride, Wallarie set out for the creek so that he would be between them and it just before sunset. For his plan to work he knew he must take a terrible risk, even though his original plan had been to decoy the two men away from the source of life-giving water until the night came. Driven almost mad with thirst they would have been easy to dispatch. But now the odds had unwittingly changed in favour of the prospectors.

Wallarie no longer smiled with grim satisfaction. All commonsense told him that he should withdraw from his plan. But commonsense was not strong enough to overcome his need to wage his own personal war on the Europeans who had once slaughtered his people.

Outnumbered, out-gunned and with his left arm dangling by his side, he did not break his stride. He loped with a distant memory of a night when he and Tom Duffy had set out to hunt down and kill the men who had butchered the last survivors of the dispersal. Against all the odds they had succeeded.

Wallarie hoped Tom's Irish luck was still with him. He knew that the warrior spirit of the cave was; it had told him so the previous night in his visions.

The sun was low on the horizon when Wallarie scrambled up the last ridge. Before him was the apparently dry sandy creek bed and he grinned his satisfaction. He knew that he was ahead of the two prospectors who he had watched wander aimlessly in the scrubby land throughout the day. The shimmering heat and the need for water had meant their condition deteriorated as they had struggled with the rugged terrain. And coupled with nature's pitiless disregard for them was the unspoken fear that dogged their every step: somewhere out there a man was hunting them as they had hunted him. Critical hours passed before the two prospectors finally found their bearings.

The dull ache of Wallarie's wound caused him to groan from time to time, an involuntary reaction caused by the relentless strain that he placed on himself to reach the creek before the two white men. But now as he crouched below the rise the pain was forgotten. All that preoccupied him was his plan to place himself precisely where the land worked in his favour. If he were wrong he knew that death was an inevitability.

He slipped his spear on the woomera. The balance felt right and all that was left now was to wait in ambush.

~

The Le Mat in Harry's hand felt heavy as he trudged a few paces behind Frank. The horizon ahead was a soft blur of mauve shadows creeping through the gullies and the sun a soft orange ball touching the ridge directly to their front. As Harry squinted against the glare Frank took on a strangely elongated shape at the centre of an orange ball. Unable to continue watching him, Harry dropped his eyes to concentrate on his partner's boot prints which marked the trail they followed. Like a man sleep-walking, he followed the tracks in the dry earth and thought about water. Cool, wet water. The strange myall was forgotten.

Frank's strangled scream snapped Harry's obsessive thoughts. Suddenly he felt a fear like none other he had ever experienced.

'I'm slain Harry,' Frank choked, as he stumbled blindly into the orange ball.

Harry could vaguely discern that his partner was gripping something that inexplicably was growing out of his front. It was long and slender and Frank gripped it with both hands as he slumped to his knees. Harry froze and blinked against the glare of the setting sun. For a second he saw a ghost-like shape beyond Frank. But it was gone before he could react.

'Oh Jesus!' he heard himself gasp. 'The bastard's speared you!'

Frank knelt forward against the shaft. His agonised groans grew rapidly weak until they petered out into a low moan. He toppled sideways and Harry instinctively knew that his partner was dead.

Frantically he searched about himself with the pistol raised. But all he saw was a silent land of stunted trees, rocks and red earth. He did not have the strength in his legs to run. Fear had rooted him to the ground as surely as if he were one of the prickly trees around him. Only the unconscious action of firing his pistol – until it eventually clicked on an empty chamber – brought him out of his petrified state. Only then did he drop his gun and run wildly back the way they had trekked.

Wallarie watched the panic-stricken man. 'Stupid bastard,' he muttered, shaking his head. He had used another one of Tom Duffy's favourite expressions. The prospector curled on the ground did not move. He was most probably dead. At ten paces – with the sun at his back – he could hardly miss when the prospector had ascended the low ridge. Wallarie remembered the brief second when the man had squinted uncomprehendingly at the shadow materialising out of the sun. It had been like that, those many years earlier, when he had speared the white squatter Donald Macintosh at a waterhole. The prospector had been in the process of raising his rifle when the spear took him through the chest, his rifle clattering amongst the rocks unfired.

With a grunt of pain, the Darambal warrior rose from amongst the rocks and walked cautiously towards the body. In death Frank still gripped the spear shaft, his opaque eyes staring at Wallarie's feet.

Satisfied that the man no longer posed a threat, Wallarie squatted beside the body, and tugged away the bed-roll wrapped around the dead man's shoulders. He unlashed the rope that held it together and grinned at the treasure that spilled out: tea, sugar, flour and tinned meat. And even better still, a twist of dark brown tobacco to savour, after he had eaten the man's supplies.

With a contented sigh Wallarie used the dead man's knife to open a tin of meat and wolfed down the warm fatty contents. When his hunger had been sated he gathered the remaining food supplies into the blanket. He ignored the rifle; he knew its possession would mark him as a dangerous blackfella to the army of Europeans around the Palmer. To all intents and purposes he would be an inconspicuous, solitary myall trekking through the land they now claimed as their own. That way, to most he would not be perceived as a threat.

As he walked into the night Wallarie chuckled. Maybe some whitefellas might find the body. They would probably not recognise the distinctive spear barbs as belonging to Wallarie the Nerambura warrior from down south. That was a pity as the local blackfellas would get the blame and his personal war against the Europeans go unrecognised.

Some time during the night Harry collapsed as he wandered aimlessly under the canvas of the southern constellations. He lay on the cooling earth, whimpering his fear and despair. All the horror that was the northern frontier surrounded him in the night.

He and Frank had been good mates who had left the southern city of Melbourne to seek their fortune on the northern goldfields. Out of luck as latecomers to the Palmer, they had set out to claim from the land what they felt it owed them. But they were not men born of the bush. The vast and lonely spaces were as alien to them as the city would have been to Wallarie. The frontier was a place of horrors. And the greatest horror of all was the loneliness of the vast land. For Harry true hell was dying alone and never being found.

TWENTY-TWO

French Charley's stood out in Cooktown as an elegant and sophisticated place of entertainment. An oasis in a desert of uncouth and bawdy outlets of diversion for the frontiersmen.

It was rumoured that the proprietor, Monsieur Charles Bouel, was in Cooktown to avoid 'Madame Guillotine', for one reason or another. Those who could afford to patronise his establishment cared little for the Frenchman's past transgressions. They came for the excellent food and wines, the lavish entertainment and the prettiest girls in the north. French Charley's was by far the best restaurant in Queensland's north. Well-travelled gourmets and raconteurs said it was by far the best in all of the Australian colonies.

Monsieur Bouel was said to have tutored his girls in the French accent and to dance the notorious cancan. The imported furnishings that decorated the palace of pleasure gave the visitor the illusion of being in the best of continental parlours. And it was to French Charley's that Hugh Darlington had invited Kate to dine whilst he was visiting from Rockhampton.

Kate dressed appropriately for the supper engagement at the elegant restaurant. Gone was the grubby teamster who had worn moleskin trousers. Now the beautiful young woman appeared wearing the latest in bustle designs from England.

When she swept into the restaurant as regally as visiting royalty, her extraordinary beauty turned the heads of the bearded miners. She was escorted by no less than Monsieur Bouel himself who met her at the front entrance. He was renowned for attending personally to those up on their luck and who therefore could afford to wine and dine at his salubrious establishment.

The French proprietor was impressed by the young woman, not only on account of her famed beauty but also her reputation as an astute business-woman. Although Kate could easily afford to dine at the restaurant every night, it was not normally a place a single woman would go, unless she was look-ing for a job entertaining the wealthier miners, a job of helping them dispose of the weight of their gold in their pockets when their trousers came down.

Kate swept across the room with all the grace and dignity of one born to command the attention of all those around her. She knew that her entrance had turned heads. She also knew her beauty had brought on the glowering looks from the painted ladies who sat with the bearded miners. But Monsieur Bouel's ladies consoled themselves with the knowledge that the famous Kate O'Keefe was not in competition with them for the attention of their temporary beaus.

Hugh Darlington felt a painful pang of regret for the fact that he had let the beautiful woman slip from his life. A handsome man in his mid-thirties, his delicate hands and patrician appearance bespoke of a cultured man, so different from the rough and ready miners around him. Cooktown was not a place he would have normally visited. He was only in town to represent a powerful mining company which was preparing to buy out mining leases for future deep mining operations on the Palmer.

He rose to his feet as Kate was escorted to the table. They had parted as lovers five years earlier and their parting had been fiery. But business dealings put them in contact again when they had met in his Rockhampton office to discuss the purchase of the Balaclava Station adjoining Glen View. Bostock's next of kin in England wanted the property sold and so Kate had made a generous offer to buy the property. But their meeting had been purely professional and cool. Kate would never forgive him for his betrayal of her trust. He had inadvertently exposed his true allegiance to the wealthy Macintosh clan, not for any sentimental reason, but one based on the lawyer's nose for money and power. He had seriously underestimated the determination of the young woman to successfully forge her own financial empire. Her continuing distrust of him had been very apparent, by the fact that he had been in Cooktown many weeks without her attempting to contact him – until now.

'Kate, you are even more beautiful than when I first met you,' Hugh said gallantly as he brushed her hand with a kiss. She smiled and thanked him for his courtesy. Monsieur Bouel pulled out her chair for her. 'I took the liberty of ordering for us just before you arrived,' Hugh said. 'I only hope your tastes in food have not changed as, alas, your feelings may have towards me.'

'Times change and so do we Hugh,' Kate replied looking him straight in the eye.

'Sadly for us both the changes are irreversible.' The lawyer smiled pensively. At least her attitude to the irreversibility of their past torrid relationship in Rockhampton made it easier for what he must do this evening. 'Whatever it must be Kate,' he said with a shrug. 'I only wish things had been different. But you chose to follow your path.'

Kate could see that he was still as handsome and charming as ever. The tiny fear that she may allow herself to remember the old yearnings she once had for him, niggled at her. But that had been six years earlier, she reminded herself, and much had happened since then to sweep away any fond memories.

An immaculately dressed waiter hovered diffidently nearby holding a napkin-wrapped bottle of champagne. Hugh signalled to the waiter, who poured the wine with a stylish flourish. 'I have ordered a local fish with oyster sauce and vegetables in season,' Hugh said, as Kate sipped from her glass. 'To be followed by fresh fruit and mocha.'

She was impressed by his choice of food and wine. 'It all sounds very nice,' she commented pleasantly. 'At least we have something we can enjoy together before you raise the reason of why I am here.'

The lawyer shifted uncomfortably. 'Ah, yes. I am afraid what I have to tell you may spoil your appetite,' he said. 'So we should leave business until the coffee arrives. What do you think?'

Kate considered his proposal. But after weeks on the rugged and perilous track to the Palmer, anything he had to say could not be half as threatening. 'No. I think you should tell me now what your business with me is. I doubt that whatever you have to say could spoil my appetite.'

He coughed lightly and took a deep breath. 'Kate, I must tell you that you should consider selling Balaclava Station. The Macintosh companies are not happy that you own property adjoining theirs.'

'Is that all?' she replied serenely, as it was of little concern what the Macintoshes thought of her. She was at war with them and the fact that her ownership of Balaclava was unsettling pleased her.

'No. I'm afraid I must also insist that you repay me the money I loaned to help you get started. With appropriate interest accrued since '68,' he added self-consciously. He was uncomfortable asking her for the money which was not in fact his. But Hugh had aspirations beyond those of a country solicitor. He needed every penny he could put his hands on to further his campaign for a seat in the colony's parliament. But the so-called loan to Kate was Luke Tracy's money, entrusted to the Rockhampton lawyer who was acting at the time in Kate's legal affairs. Luke had insisted that Kate not be told the source of the money. His strong male pride prevented him from revealing himself as the source; he felt Kate might interpret his generous gesture as an attempt to buy her love. But the unscrupulous lawyer had capitalised on the secrecy. Darlington feigned to be the source of the money, casting himself in the light of one who truly cared for her. At the time the lie had worked to help cement her feelings for him.

Kate felt her anger rising. 'You told me the loan was given interest-free,' she said in a carefully controlled voice. 'Now you make me feel as if the money was only an inducement to get me to go to your bed. Do you know how that makes me feel?' Her voice rose angrily. 'You have made me no different from the women sitting around us now,' she said savagely, as she cast her gaze at a table where a pretty young red-haired girl was making a point of allowing the miner dining with her to see her milk-white breasts exposed above the low-cut dress.

'It is not like that Kate,' he pleaded. He was embarrassed by the attention being turned on them by the diners. 'At the time things were different. You must have known that.'

She turned her attention back to Hugh who nervously toyed with his crystal champagne flute. 'What if I refuse to pay interest?' she demanded. 'Oh, I always knew the principal would be due. But this matter of interest was never mentioned. Your letter only said that you wanted to discuss the return of an amount of money. I thought you meant some outstanding fees.'

'You do not have much choice,' Hugh replied menacingly. 'If you refuse I will take action. And you cannot win against me Kate. I am a lawyer and I know the law.'

'You bastard!' she hissed, her aspersion on Darlington's parentage not missed by a grinning miner at the next table. He knew Kate O'Keefe from his time on the Palmer. He had a healthy respect for the woman who could manage a bullock wagon along the dangerous track to the goldfields. He almost felt sorry for the man she cursed.

Hugh glanced around, feeling decidedly uncomfortable. He now bitterly regretted choosing French Charley's. It was all turning sour on him! 'Kate, I don't think this calls for a situation,' he pleaded. 'We are talking business and I know you understand business. I doubt that the interest will send your company broke. You forget, I know your financial situation.'

Kate glared at the man she had once thought so desirable. She wondered how she could have ever found the slimy lawyer attractive. 'Then you know that my money is tied up in the Eureka company,' she replied quietly. 'Cash is something I cannot readily obtain at the moment.'

'That is your concern,' Hugh said bluntly. 'I can give you two weeks to come up with the money and the interest. If you don't I will be forced to put you before a court.'

Before Kate could reply the waiter returned to ask politely if they were ready to dine. Hugh said that they were. He hoped that she might be more reasonable on a full stomach. As the waiter retreated a stony silence fell between the two.

The waiter returned shortly bearing a large red emperor fish which swam in a sea of dark, salty oyster sauce on a silver platter. The baked fish was surrounded with tiny boiled potatoes and fresh vegetables steamed with a delicious touch of ginger. But the delicious aroma of the steam rising from the rich platter did not stimulate Kate's appetite.

'You will get your money,' Kate said, not attempting to conceal her anger. 'Is that all you have to tell me?' she added.

'Ah, no . . . ' Hugh said, as he sliced a section of succulent white flesh from the fish. 'I have some advice for you. Advice that I pray you will take with the good intentions that I give it.'

'Tell me, and I will decide,' she replied, watching him pile the fish on his plate and wondering at his appetite.

'If you wish to be accepted by your peers in Queensland, I suggest that you make a break with your business partners, the Cohens. It does not bide well with certain powerful people in the colony that you have a strong association with the Jews. I say this to you as a friend.'

Kate was aghast at the man's condemnation of the two people with whom she partly shared her financial empire. Solomon and Judith Cohen's business association went beyond a mutual convenience.

It went beyond even simple friendship. They were as close to her as her own family in Sydney.

'I will tell you something Mister Darlington,' she said, her angry voice carrying beyond the nearest tables as she rose with the half-filled champagne flute in her hand. 'I owe my very life to the love and care those Jews as you call them granted to me when I first came to Queensland. If it had not been for the Cohens I might be long dead by now. And in many ways, I owe my considerable financial success to their considerate counsel, in the management of the Eureka company.' Kate paused for a split second and a colourful curse she had once heard Luke mutter came easily to her lips. 'You are nothing more than a goddamned flea on the back of a hog, you slimy bastard.'

The lawyer was too slow to react to the champagne flute shattering on the table. Champagne spattered him in an exploding shower of crystal. A cheer rose from the tough miners who had followed the beautiful young woman's rising anger with interest. 'Good on yer girlie,' came the chorus from them. They had little time for the likes of Hugh Darlington, who they viewed as one of the uppity townsmen living soft and protected lives, far from their own physical and dangerous lives.

Hugh hung his head in acute embarrassment. Kate had humiliated him in public and he would not forget. No, he would not forget.

Kate swished from the restaurant, pushing past the French proprietor who gallantly promised that Monsieur Darlington would be barred from his establishment. No-one could be forgiven for upsetting the legendary Kate O'Keefe. She appreciated the Frenchman's chivalrous gesture. At least in the north of the colony she had more standing than the lawyer. North Queensland was her country!

The evening air was cooling to Kate's angry, flushed face as she strode along the busy street. Big wagons headed for the Palmer track rumbled past her while men, drunk with liquor and new-found wealth called to the beautiful young woman, with invitations to share their money and their bed. At least their motivations were forthright, she thought bitterly as she walked deep in thought along Charlotte Street to her store.

Kate reflected on how much more she was a part of the frontier than she would ever be in polite and genteel society. Her troubled reflections drifted to the only two men who had shared her bed. Both had proved to be worthless. First, there had been Kevin, her husband, who had sworn a life of fidelity. A promise which he broke in just under six months of marriage. And then came Hugh Darlington. She had been seduced by his handsome looks and polished manners. This same man, only moments earlier, had promised to put her before a court of law.

She scowled at the memory of the two men. Men were useless creatures! But she wavered in her attack on all men when she remembered the men of her family – and Luke Tracy. She slowed her pace as she reflected on the American's meaning to her life.

He had never taken from her. Luke had only ever given of himself without asking anything in return – and he had been with her when she needed him most. But he was a restless and roaming spirit, shifting like the tropical breezes. Could such a man ever be content to settle in one place?

Luke had a fierce, infuriatingly stubborn male pride that had inevitably surfaced. He had returned to her a day after her offer to bankroll a prospecting expedition to Ironstone Mountain and expressed his reluctance to allow her to fund him. She had protested but he quietly told her he had made a serious mistake in accepting her more than generous offer. He had told her he had money and it was just a matter of getting it back. But the whereabouts of that money remained a mystery to Kate as he had changed the subject.

The strong and independent woman stopped and sighed. She realised that she might turn the old dog of the track into a lap dog. Old dog! She smiled to herself. Yes, he was like an old dog – faithful, scarred, protective and loving. But like an old dog he had a bad habit of wandering. Was his talk of settling down a feeble attempt to convince her he was finally prepared to stay in one place? Or would he become like Henry James, and yearn for the days in the saddle, riding the long and lonely tracks of the frontier?

Henry was carrying out a routine check on the store when he found Kate sitting alone in the dark. As he held up the lantern she wiped away a tear. 'Are you feeling unwell?' he asked in his concern.

'Thank you Henry,' she replied with a sniff. 'I was just about to leave.'

'Bad night?' Henry asked, sitting down beside her on a keg of nails.

'Bad life more like it,' she answered with a short and bitter laugh.

'I wouldn't say that,' he said, trying to cheer her up. 'Look at what you have achieved in the space of a mere six years. You have one of the most prosperous businesses in Queensland. Enough money that you never need work again. And a lot of friends in this part of the world.'

'I know. But there are things money cannot buy,' Kate said sadly, touching him on the arm. 'I've learned that now. You know Henry, I have always envied you and Emma for all that you have together.'

'Not a real lot,' he shrugged. 'The bloody police pension doesn't go far. Emma and I appreciate what you have done for us with this job.'

'It's not charity,' Kate quickly remonstrated. 'You both work very hard. And I don't know what I would have done without your help. You and Emma have been wonderful.' She appreciated his concern for her and remembered the conversation she had with Emma about Henry being restless in his present employment at the store. Even now she sensed that he was just a little uncomfortable in her company. 'I heard from Emma that you have applied for a job working for that American that I have heard so much of around town. I just want you to know that I understand and don't mind.'

'I don't know for sure whether I've got the job

yet,' Henry mumbled, feeling just a little guilty for applying for the job. 'O'Flynn told me he had to get final approval before I was in.'

'I have to admit that I hope you don't get it,' Kate said gently. 'From what I've heard of this Mister O'Flynn, he is not a very reputable kind of character. The word around Cooktown is that he is recruiting for a very dangerous expedition to God knows where! If anything were to happen to you . . . you know Emma and Gordon would be devastated. No, Henry. You left all that kind of thing behind when you left the Native Mounted Police.'

'You know Kate,' Henry said with a grin. 'O'Flynn struck me as a very capable man. In some ways he reminds me of you. I think that if you had been born a man you might have been very much like Mister O'Flynn.'

'I don't think we sound very much alike at all,' she answered, shaking her head vigorously. 'Mister O'Flynn sounds like a real rogue.' They both laughed.

Kate could be a rogue when she put her mind to it, Henry thought. 'I think you should come home with me and talk to Emma for a while,' he said, as he rose stiffly from the keg of nails and stretched his war-damaged leg.

During the walk to his house Kate told him what had happened with Hugh Darlington and about his insistence on her repaying the loan with interest. He laughed when she related how she had caused the lawyer to become the butt of the miners' jeers.

~

Luke was visiting the James residence when Henry and Kate arrived. Kate greeted him rather coldly and immediately sought Emma's company. The men shrugged and tacitly decided that it was time to go outside and sit on the wood heap.

'Kate's had a bad night from what I can gather.' Henry said.

Luke nodded. 'Bloody women,' he grumbled. 'I don't know what I've done wrong. One minute she looks as if she is glad to see me then . . . '

Henry made sympathetic noises and produced a bottle of rum, pouring Luke a generous tot in a battered tin cup. They swigged the dark liquid and Henry unravelled what he knew about Kate's meeting with the Rockhampton lawyer.

'So that goddamned snake-oil salesman wants his money back,' Luke growled savagely. 'Money not even his own.' He fished in his trouser pocket and passed Henry a very worn scrap of paper. 'It's a receipt signed by Darlington for a lot of money,' Luke explained. 'And from what you tell me he only gave Kate half of what I told him to give her. The bastard probably spent the rest.'

Henry handed back the receipt. 'That the reason you took off for America back in '68?'

'I was so close to being there before Hahn and Mulligan,' Luke answered ruefully. 'If it hadn't been for that goddamned son of a bitch I would have been on the Palmer back in '68. I would have been known as the man who *discovered* the Palmer. But that low-down bastard Darlington put me into the traps at Rockhampton for dealing in gold without a licence.

Solomon Cohen tipped me off that they were after me. I had to get out of Queensland. Had to leave Kate . . . ' he tapered off. How could he tell another man his deep feelings for the woman he loved? 'And here I am now, broke and needing a stake to prospect down south.'

'Kate was going to finance you,' Henry said. 'What happened?'

Luke bowed his head and stared at the ground. 'Couldn't take money from a woman,' he mumbled self-consciously. 'Especially Kate.'

'If you need a stake I know a man who might have a job for you,' Henry said quietly. 'I think you have what he wants and the money is good for the job.'

Luke glanced up at him with interest. 'Is it legal?' he asked quietly, and Henry grinned at the question.

'Was selling gold the way you did legal?' he countered.

'Not rightly.'

'The man is looking for bushmen to go on a prospecting expedition, somewhere north it seems. But he only wants men with military or police experience.'

'I don't have military experience,' Luke answered bluntly.

'You got that scar fighting at Eureka, didn't you?' Henry reminded him. 'Weren't you with the California Revolver Brigade? They were a military force. Even if they were rebels.'

Luke stared away into the night. 'Yeah,' he answered wistfully. 'Maybe this fella recruiting might be sympathetic to veterans of the Eureka, no matter which side they served on.'

'I think he might,' Henry added, finishing the last of the bottle in one gulp. 'He's a Yankee like you. Kind of reminds me a bit of Kate in some strange way. His name's Michael O'Flynn. I'll take you to meet him at his hotel tomorrow.'

'If I get the job,' Luke said staring into the star-lit night sky, 'there is something I have to do first. I'm going to need your help. It concerns that son of a bitch Darlington.'

Henry listened to his friend outline the plan he had for the fate of the Rockhampton lawyer. When Luke finished he only had one comment. 'If things go wrong you'll either die in the dust from a bullet or end up hanging anyway. Not many other choices left for you.'

'You'll help me?' Luke growled.

Henry shrugged and stood up. 'I guess you love Kate a lot more than any other man alive to do what you have planned. Or you are completely insane. Either way I will stick with you Luke.' Nothing more needed to be said between the two men. It was the way of mateship.

TWENTY-THREE

Opponents of the Chinese miners and merchants complained that Cooktown was rapidly becoming the Canton of the South. Out of Hong Kong on Robert Town's ships they came in their thousands for *Sin Chin San* – the New Mountain of Gold as the Chinese called Queensland. And they came with little else to lose other than their lives.

Hard-working people who kept to themselves, the Chinese went where the Europeans left ground considered to be worthless. And from this supposedly worthless ground they extracted gold – reason enough to cause the animosity of the miners who felt cheated by their success.

The presence of the Chinese manifested itself most noticeably in Cooktown's China Town, a rambling quarter made up of Chinese eating houses from which wafted the aromas of exotic oriental spices and strange foods. From the opium dens and brothels came the pungent scent of opium mixed with the incense of joss houses. Doll-like girls with tiny, painfully bound feet waved delicate fans against the tropical heat as they rested from the places that employed their bodies to provide services to both Chinese and European miners. The Chinese quarter was an Asian world unto itself ruled by the secretive tongs.

Michael Duffy's guide was a surprising young man. At first Michael had taken him for just another miner – a big man with broad shoulders, golden skin and coal-black eyes. But it was obvious that his guide was a Eurasian when he said something in Chinese to one of the tiny young women outside a brothel. She laughed shyly from behind her fan and John grinned.

Michael followed John Wong through the quarter to a ramshackle building of corrugated iron. Inside, Michael was aware of the close-packed smell of sweating bodies, opium and dried fish. It was a heady mix. Alien, but not unpleasant.

A huddle of Chinese men squatted around a square sheet of tin with oriental calligraphy along the sides. They wore loincloths and little else in the stifling heat.

'Fan tan,' Michael commented. He had seen the game played by Chinese on the ship steaming north from Brisbane.

'You play fan tan Mister O'Flynn?' John asked.

'No,' he replied, as the players chatted and sweated around the board. 'Never learned how to play but it looks interesting.'

'It's a fairly simple game,' John explained. 'The figures on the sides of the board are numbers one to four. The player selects the side he wants to put his money on and the banker, as you would call him, has a few dozen brass coins which he uses as counters. You see now, the banker tosses the coins in a pile on the floor.'

Michael watched with a gambler's professional interest. The banker placed a cup over some of the Chinese coins he had scattered and brushed the rest away with a deft movement. He then lifted the cup and quickly sorted the coins into sets of four. When he had completed the counting, one of the Chinese players at the metal board grinned triumphantly, and was patted on the back by the men behind him.

'What happened?' Michael asked. He was mystified by the outcome.

'It's pretty straightforward,' John grinned. 'When the last pile is counted, the number of coins left over corresponds to one side of the board. The winner gets three times what he put on. I suppose you could say each player has a one in four chance of winning. Not bad odds.'

'You play much fan tan?' Michael asked.

''I prefer poker myself,' John chuckled. 'You see, I have an inscrutable Oriental face that gives me the edge when playing against you Europeans. I hear you play a pretty good game of poker yourself Mister O'Flynn. At least that is what Mister Horace Brown tells me. Some day you and I should sit down to a few friendly hands.'

'Did Brown teach you to play poker?' Michael

asked. John shook his head. 'Then that's too bad,' Michael sighed. 'Against you, I have a feeling I might come off second best.'

John smiled at the compliment. There was a trustful feeling about the big Irishman, he thought. John was good at sizing up men, an ability which came from twenty years of living in a world where his mixed birth made him an outsider. He had always been cautious in his dealings with both Orientals and Occidentals. He instinctively recognised those who accepted him and those who did not. This man he sensed, accepted him.

He led Michael through a low doorway and both men were forced to duck their heads. The room they entered could have been anywhere in the East; the scents of sandalwood incense and opium mixed to fill the air. Michael could see the incense sticks smouldering in front of a shrine to Buddha. A Chinese man, who Michael guessed could be anywhere between thirty and sixty years of age, reclined on pillows. He had the eyes of a viper and Michael instinctively sensed that he could be dangerous. Reclining beside him, Horace spoke softly in Chinese as the man closely watched Michael approach. Soo Yin was both a wealthy merchant and the Cooktown representative of a powerful tong based in Hong Kong.

'Ah, Michael,' Horace said in a slightly slurred voice. 'I see Mister Wong got you here without any problems.' Michael guessed that Brown had been smoking opium. His eyes had the faraway look of a man who had seen many beautiful dreams while still awake.

'I'm here,' Michael replied, as he cautiously scanned the dim interior of the room. 'Your choice of meeting place surprises me Horace. But then, I can see you are right at home.'

'Mister Soo and I have mutual interests and share a mutual pastime as you can see,' Horace said, pushing himself with some effort into a sitting position. 'Although I think it is rather ironic that we should force opium on the Chinese and then condemn them for using it. I myself find it preferable to rum or gin. But my preferences have little to do with our meeting so sit down and make yourself comfortable. We have a lot to talk about.'

Michael felt awkward sitting on the floor with his knees under his chin. John sat beside him, his long legs crossed in the style Michael had seen depicted in the figurines of the Buddha. Brown was able to sit cross-legged easily, and he wondered how the short, squat Englishman could manage the position, without any obvious signs of discomfort.

'Mister Soo does not speak English,' Horace explained. 'But he has kindly allowed us to use his place to meet from time to time. Here, there is little chance of people knowing of our meetings. Anyone seeing you come to this part of town will think you are visiting one of the, ah, establishments of Oriental carnal delights. It's not uncommon for the miners to do so.'

Michael had to agree that Brown's choice of meeting location was well chosen. Much better than one of the European places where they might be seen by anyone with more than a normal curiosity.

'Thank you John,' Horace said, dismissing the young man. 'Mister O'Flynn and I will speak alone with your boss.'

John nodded and rose to his feet. Soo continued to puff on the opium pipe and slip into the dreams the drug would bring him as he watched the two Europeans converse. He knew that Brown would tell him anything relevant that he should know. Besides, he also knew that John Wong would only be a short distance away and in a position to eavesdrop on the conversation. Trust was not something the tong leader believed in. But he valued Brown's friendship. He was an interesting man who had been able to open bureaucratic doors for him in Hong Kong with the British administrators. The opening of such doors came at a price, but Brown's price was surprisingly little – just information. He guessed that Mister Brown was a spy. This did not matter, as he valued the financial opportunities their relationship gave to his enterprises, both in Hong Kong and Queensland.

'Your Chinese friend Mister Soo has the look of a rattlesnake,' Michael said quietly.

'You can believe that Michael,' Horace replied grimly. 'He is not a man to cross. In India there are men who can control the cobra with music. Seen them do it m'self in the marketplaces. And I suppose I could compare Mister Soo to a cobra under my control. That is to say, he is quite capable of biting me if the music stops.' Michael understood the analogy. Horace lived in a world of delicate balances based on reward rather than patriotism. 'I suspect,' he continued, 'Mister Soo has John listening to what we are discussing right now. But that does not matter as we will be discussing matters Soo has little interest in.'

In the days since Michael had arrived in Cooktown he had recruited six men of the calibre required by Straub. He had little trouble finding them among the unsuccessful miners awaiting a berth out of Cooktown. In the tent city on the outskirts of the town, and in the many bars, the word had gone around about a big, one-eyed Yankee looking for men to join a prospecting expedition. The money was more than generous for the right sort of man and the mercenary recruits flocked to his hotel room to apply.

Michael passed Horace a sheet of folded paper with the names of the six men he had recruited. Beside each name he had jotted a short outline of their experience. Horace unfolded the paper and scanned the names. He knew only one of the men – at least knew of him. 'How well do you know the man second on your list?' he asked, as he showed Michael the sheet and pointed to the name.

'He says he fought in the Crimea and that he was once a trap in the Native Mounted Police,' Michael replied warily. 'Heard I was recruiting and turned up to see me. Big fella with a limp but says it is not a problem to him. Used to be a police sergeant, he tells me.'

'Well, you have a problem with Henry James,' Horace said quietly. 'I think there are some things you don't know so I am going to tell you because, if what I know is right, Mister James would be a dead man if he ever stepped aboard the *Osprey* when she gets here.'

'What in the hell is the *Osprey*?' Michael asked, annoyed for being kept in the dark by both Brown and Straub.

'A blackbirding ship under the command of one Morrison Mort. Does the name Mort mean anything to you?' Horace asked, knowing full well that it did.

Michael paled. 'Was this Mort ever with the Native Mounted Police?' His good eye had taken on a strange, terrifying depth that made Horace feel somewhat afraid at what he was unleashing.

'Same man Michael,' he answered grimly. But inwardly Horace rejoiced that the mention of Mort's name had brought about a reaction. Yes, he thought. He knew now that the Irishman would give his full cooperation.

'That murdering bastard!' Michael hissed savagely. From his discreet inquiries around Brisbane on his stop-over, Michael had pretty well confirmed that the man had murdered his father. Although Tom had died, as the result of a bullet from an Aboriginal trooper's carbine, it may as well have been Mort who pulled the trigger.

'I suspected you would like to even scores with Captain Mort,' Horace said. 'For the woes he has brought to your family. I doubt that you would ever win justice in a court of law.'

'You know that,' Michael snarled. 'Any settling will be done by me.'

'Good!' Horace replied serenely. 'Then you will be interested in what I have planned, should the *Osprey* be sailing to New Guinea with the Baron as I strongly suspect it will be.'

'You said that this man Henry James would be a dead man if he went aboard the *Osprey*. Why is that?' Michael asked.

'Ah yes, our Mister James. Well, it is a long story. In the short version, Henry James virtually had Mort cashiered from the Native Mounted Police about ten years ago. From what I can gather Captain Mort has a bit of a cloud over his head when it comes to leaving dead bodies, mostly black, around him. Appears he killed a trooper who James was a bit close to. I can understand how he felt. I was close to a darkie fellow once. Got himself killed and I took it personally. Happened in Samoa.' Horace's voice trailed away as he remembered the young man who had been his lover. He had died when his village was shelled by a German warship that had anchored off the coast and blasted the helpless villagers with high explosive gunfire. 'There is something else I gather you do not know about Mister James,' Horace added. 'Or you would not have employed him in the first place. Henry James works for your sister in Cooktown.'

'Kate!' Michael gasped. 'But Kate is in Townsville. That is what I was told while I was in Brisbane.'

Horace shook his head. 'At the moment your sister is working out of a depot she has set up only a street from where we sit now. It seems your sister is a remarkable woman. I have been told that she has built a small fortune all from a dray and team of bullocks. Apparently she has taken on the family tradition of being a teamster. The young man who brought you here has met her when he was on his way down to the Palmer. Helped get her out of a spot of bother with the natives, I believe.'

'Does he know who I am?' Michael asked, still recovering from the shock.

'By now he does,' Horace replied with a wry grin. 'That is, if he is still listening to all that we say. But before we discuss as much as I know about your family,' Horace continued, 'I think you and I should agree on a few things first. One, that you recruit someone else to replace Henry James. I would hate to have to go to the funeral of a fellow Crimean campaigner. And two, that I have your total loyalty. No more taking von Fellmann's money with some foolish idea that you owe him anything. I suspect that it is in your nature to be loyal to an employer. For your sworn loyalty to me I will give you my word that I will provide the means to settle with Captain Mort. Permanently.'

Michael stared at the little Englishman sitting like a small Buddha on the pillows. He had toyed with the idea of getting out of Cooktown and out of the reaches of British law. It would have been easy to doublecross Brown when he was away from him. But now the Englishman was playing him like a hooked fish. 'How do you plan to help me settle with Mort?' he finally asked. 'You know I will personally kill him.'

'That is your affair,' Horace replied casually. 'But I think you could arrange to have Captain Mort go down with his ship, when you blow it up.'

'Blow it up!' Michael exploded, as Horace had not even blinked when he uttered his statement so casually. 'You mean with a bomb?'

'Yes. I believe that is how you blow up a ship,' Horace replied calmly. 'And now I will tell you all you have to know to accomplish the mission.'

Michael listened attentively as Horace outlined his plan. It was fraught with extreme danger to all concerned and Michael guessed that the plan did not have the sanction of those in the British Foreign Office. He guessed that Horace was not about to inform his masters of how he planned to sabotage German operations in the Pacific. Like Michael he was a man used to living on the edge. What his civil service masters did not know could not hurt them.

But Horace was also acutely aware that only the pawns in the global chess game of strategy got burned – not the kings and bishops. And he knew that he and the Irish mercenary recruited to his cause were mere pawns where the moves left blood on the board.

Michael stood across the street from a modest building of pit-sawn timber and corrugated iron. A recently painted sign over the entrance displayed the words 'The Eureka Company General Merchants to the Palmer and Cooktown'.

He gazed with mixed emotions at the building. There was a feeling of absolute joy for being so close to the sister that he loved dearly but, at the same time, a deep sadness for his inability to cross the street and back into her life. He was but a ghost of a memory to his sister – and one whose resurrection might be temporary. He well knew that the mission he was to undertake was extremely dangerous. Better he remain nothing more than a memory to her rather than reveal his existence and needlessly bring grief to her a second time.

He fished in his waistcoat for a small silver box of cigarillos. He lit the dark tobacco stick and remained standing under the shade of an awning, staring vacantly at his sister's depot. With a deep sigh he prepared to walk away. He would keep his gentle memories.

He froze. Kate! He had no doubt that the beautiful young woman who walked out of the store onto the street was his sister. Even though over a decade had passed since he had last seen her, he recognised her distinctive long raven hair. She even had the same faint splash of freckles over her pert nose that summer in Sydney would bring to her pretty face. Stunned, he stared at her from across the street. A pretty little girl of mixed Aboriginal and European blood came out from the store. Smiling, Kate took her hand.

Michael was perplexed by the obviously close relationship. 'The little girl with your sister, I reckon, is your niece,' a voice at his elbow said quietly. Startled, Michael spun to confront John Wong. 'Daughter of your brother Tom and his myall woman,' he added. 'Figured you would come here after you got through with Horace. Also thought you might need a guide.'

'What's the little girl's name?' Michael asked.

'Sarah,' John replied, recalling his conversations with Kate on the track. 'I think you have a couple of nephews too, but I can't think of their names. I remember a story getting around the hotels recently of how Henry James had to go after one of them – and his own son – up in the Kyowarra territory. Got them back okay.'

Michael returned his attention to the store where Kate stood in animated conversation with his niece Sarah. Yes, he thought. He could see the family resemblance in the little girl. One day she would also be a beautiful young woman – a bit like his own sister.

'I guess you aren't going to make your presence known,' John said bluntly. 'Not with what you and Horace are planning.'

'Would you?' Michael countered. 'Considering what's at stake.'

'I don't suppose so,' John replied slowly, as if considering something profound. 'My Chinese relatives believe in ancestor worship so I figure if you were Chinese like me then your relatives would be providing you with lots of free rice meals on your grave. It's not a bad way of living,' he grinned. 'Beats working. Better to remain dead to them.'

Michael smiled at John's self-effacing jokes about his heritage. 'Been tough for you,' he said. 'Like it's going to be tough for my little niece over there.'

'Yeah, it will be tough for her,' John sighed. 'But I think she has the right kind of blood to deal with what people will say about her in the years ahead. I've seen your sister handle things most men couldn't. And I grew up on the stories about Tom Duffy the bushranger. Now I've met you Mister O'Flynn.

With that kind of blood in her veins I can feel sorry for the rest of the world.'

Michael noticed that his niece was pointing at him from across the street. 'You said you played a bit of poker Mister Wong?' he said. 'I think it's about time I found out how good you are.' As John grinned Michael saw a flash of warmth behind the dark eyes.

He walked away with no sense of grief. Although Kate was only thirty paces from where he stood, she was, in fact, a lifetime away. He could see nevertheless that his sister was a woman all the Duffys could be proud of.

'That man is staring at us Aunt Kate,' Sarah said, pointing to Michael across the busy street. 'He looks funny. He has one eye.'

'It is rude to point,' Kate gently chided. 'Especially if the poor man is partly blind.'

'But he is staring at us,' Sarah protested. 'And you told me staring was a rude thing.' Kate's curiosity overcame her need to exemplify manners. She followed the direction of her niece's finger to see a tall, broad-shouldered young man in the company of John Wong. For just a fraction of a second, Kate saw the face of the stranger standing beside John before they both turned away from her. There was something hauntingly familiar about it.

Surely Mister Wong would have greeted her, she frowned. She raised her hand to wave to him but a big wagon came between them. By the time it had passed, both he and the stranger were gone from the street.

'Do you know him, Aunt Kate?' Sarah asked, aware of the subtle shift in Kate's attention.

'No,' she replied uncertainly, 'it's just that he reminded me of someone I once loved very much.'

'Mister O'Flynn,' Henry said. 'This is a mate of mine by the name of Luke Tracy. He's a Yankee like you and he stood with the rebels at the stockade back in '54. He's looking for work.' The appearance of the former police sergeant on the verandah felt poignant, given that he had come from Kate's store.

'I knew an Irishman who fought with the California Brigade back in '54,' Michael said, as he appraised Luke. 'Fella by the name of Patrick Duffy. Did you know of him?'

'Yeah, knew him personally,' Luke replied. 'Big Irishman. A bit like you as a matter of fact. When did you meet Patrick Duffy?'

'A long time ago,' Michael answered. He walked over to the railing of the hotel verandah to gaze down on the busy life of the frontier town; a never-ending stream of men and women heading down the dangerous track to the Palmer as they came off the ships docking daily at the Cooktown wharves. He turned away from the railing. 'I have a team of men Mister Tracy and we sail very soon. Under other circumstances you might not have got a berth but you are in luck today. A vacancy has just come up and I don't have time to go out and find someone else.' Michael turned to Henry. 'You are out of the expedition Mister James,' he said bluntly. 'Mister Tracy will take your place.'

Henry stood stunned. 'I'm what?' he exploded. Michael felt a twinge of guilt for sacking the former soldier and police sergeant. But he could not afford to risk the life of someone close to his beloved sister.

'I regret that I had to make the decision Mister James,' Michael said, as gently as he could. 'But I've made my mind up and am not about to tell you why. You just have to accept it.'

For a brief moment he expected the Englishman to swing at him. There was a cold anger in the man's eyes. But Henry shook his head in resignation and stormed away. Michael turned his attention back to Luke. 'I will see you here tomorrow afternoon at four o'clock. You will be briefed and given your kit.'

Luke nodded. No words need be said – at least not to Michael O'Flynn. The words needed to be said to Henry, as it was Henry who had suggested that he approach the American recruiter. Neither had expected this outcome, and he felt a sense of misguided betrayal. He mumbled a thanks for the job and hurried away.

Michael watched them leave the hotel and walk across the street. The meeting had disturbed him. That the American Luke Tracy had stood with his father at the Eureka Stockade brought back memories. However, he was pleased that he was able to put Henry James off his team. He sensed that the situation would become very dangerous in the near future, and although he intended to put the lives of his team foremost, there were no guarantees, only that a man's life did not go on forever.

The *Osprey* was due to sail into Cooktown in the next few days, according to Karl Straub, and Michael knew he would finally come face to face with the man who he knew in his heart was responsible for his father's murder. He wondered how he would react to such a meeting. He would have to wait to find out.

There was little to do in the waiting. Everything was in place for the mysterious expedition. The purchase of the components for a bomb caused few questions in a town that sold mining equipment. Horace had even fused his device, a lethal package of blasting powder normally used to break rock in search of gold ore. In this case the bomb was designed to blow the bottom out of a ship.

Michael walked away from the railing and slumped in a cane chair. He had a strange feeling that some mysterious force had drawn him to this time and place for a reason. So many strange coincidences: the meeting with Fiona and Penelope in Sydney; his beloved sister Kate in Cooktown; the fact that he was soon to confront the man who had brought so much misery to his family; the chain of terrible events that led back to the dispersal of an Aboriginal tribe in Queensland, unleashing misery on both families.

He thought about the stories he had heard of a myall curse, stories told by the bushmen around the hotel bars in Brisbane that had become part of frontier lore. Maybe there really was a myall curse. If so, whose side would the fickle avenging myall spirits be on, when he met the man who he was always destined to kill – or be killed by?

TWENTY-FOUR

Sergeant Francis Farrell felt like dancing an Irish jig. But before he did, he would relate to Daniel Duffy the grand news that for so many years they had hoped for. He hurried to the offices of Sullivan & Levi where he was immediately ushered into Daniel's office. All at the law firm were familiar with the big Irish police sergeant's mysterious visits. The clerks had often speculated amongst themselves on the relationship between the Sydney policeman and the leading criminal lawyer. Most presumed he was on a retainer to provide inside information. Not that they voiced their suspicions. To do so would be killing the goose that laid the golden eggs crucial in winning cases for the defence.

Farrell's waxed moustache fairly bristled with excitement and his eyes glowed with triumph as he took a chair in the office. 'We've got him!'

he exclaimed, leaning forward to Daniel. 'Lady Macintosh's reward worked!'

'Mort?' Daniel asked. 'You have evidence that will stand up in court?'

'Two eyewitnesses,' Farrell said with the broadest of grins. 'Two men who volunteered Mort as the man they saw coming out of Rosie's place immediately after they heard her screams cease. Said they were on their way to visit her when they heard her screaming. Said it put the fear of God in them and that they were too frightened to find out why she was screaming. So they hung back, and minutes later saw Mort come out with blood all over him. Better still, they said they saw a knife in his hand.'

'Did you suggest to them that it was Mort they saw?' Daniel asked impatiently. The answer was critical to a prosecution case.

Farrell's broad smile turned to a knowing grin. 'Didn't have to,' he replied. 'They named Mort themselves. Said they saw him with a mate of theirs by the name of Sims who is now first mate on the *Osprey*. They don't know how he got the job as he had no real sea experience except for a short time on a brig out of Sydney a few years back. Sims that is.'

Daniel frowned. 'How do they explain their sudden recollection?' he asked, leaning back in his chair. 'Other than the fact that we know the reward money has cleared their memory.'

Farrell scowled. 'That is a bit of a problem,' he said. 'Seems they both want fifty guineas apiece for giving evidence against Mort. They aren't prepared to share the reward.'

'I'm sure Lady Macintosh can accommodate their request,' Daniel assured. He knew Enid would stop at nothing to see Mort hang and money was her weapon to ensure this happened. 'Corroboration is the noose for Mort's neck so you can tell them it's fifty apiece if we ever get the opportunity to see that happen.'

The smile returned to Farrell's face. 'Good! I have their statements and it's now only a matter of arresting Mort. Danny boy, we finally have him.' But the smile began to fade when he noticed the glum expression on the lawyer's face at the mention of Mort's imminent arrest. 'What is it? he asked. The news should have caused only ecstatic joy.

'You don't know?' Daniel said. 'Do you?'

'Know what?'

'The *Osprey* sailed a couple of weeks ago,' he said bitterly. 'Mort is on his way north and sailing out of our jurisdiction.'

'Holy mother of God!' the sergeant exploded. 'The devil protects him again!'

'It seems so. If only we had had this evidence weeks earlier everything might have turned out differently. But now we have to go through a tedious process of tracking him down, probably in Queensland, and undertaking an extradition. Somehow, I think Mort does have the devil protecting him, as you say, and he will simply slip away to another country. No, Sergeant Farrell, he has beaten us again.'

Farrell leaned back in his chair, completely deflated of his triumph. There would be no Irish jig this day to celebrate. Instead, he would probably join Daniel Duffy at the Erin Hotel, where they would get rolling drunk to drown their bitter disappointment.

Penelope took afternoon tea at Fiona's house. They sat in the pleasant surrounds of the garden, enjoying the mild Sydney day. Normally they would have met at one of the city's fashionable restaurants to chat about the inconsequential things in their lives – social engagements and fashion. Manfred had sailed into Sydney from Samoa and was now on board the *Osprey* bound for Cooktown. The little time Penelope had shared with her husband had been filled with organising his expedition north. And when they had made love it had been a brief but exciting interlude spiced with just a little something extra for her husband's benefit. The interlude had included Fiona.

With Manfred now sailing north on the *Osprey* Penelope preferred to share a quiet, private moment with her beloved Fiona away from the crush and mill of Sydney society. In the background she could hear the babble of Fiona's daughters playing hide and seek in the garden under the stern eye of Miss Gertrude Pitcher. As Fiona served tea from a fine porcelain china pot, Penelope gazed at the two little girls squealing with delight in their play. A frown clouded Penelope's face. 'Is there something wrong with Dorothy? She does not seem to be the same little girl I once knew.'

Fiona paused pouring the tea and glanced at her

cousin. 'I do not know what you mean,' she said. 'You don't think she's unwell do you?'

'No,' Penelope said slowly, as if attempting to analyse the subtle change in Dorothy's demeanour. 'I suppose it is just that she is growing up so fast, that the changes are noticeable. Nothing more than that.' But she was not so sure. Something about her niece touched distant and disturbing memories of her own life at that age. There was something about the haunted look in the little girl's eyes that only one who had experienced similar could recognise. Penelope shook her head. The vague and troubling thoughts could not be entertained. Surely not her brother again! Not his own daughter!

'I suppose you are missing Manfred,' Fiona said, too casually trying to hide her jealousy. 'He never seems to be able to spend much time at home with you.'

Penelope leaned forward to her cousin. 'You have no need to be jealous my love,' she reassured softly. 'Manfred is my husband. And I suppose I love him in my own way. He is strong and powerful, a man amongst men, but it is you I love with my heart. I provide Manfred my body to sate his desires and it is that which binds us when all else is considered. Not the love that the romanticists write about in those silly novels you so much like to read.'

Fiona placed the teapot carefully on the table. 'Was it that apparent?' she asked quietly, with a plea in her emerald eyes for forgiveness.

'I understand you better than any other person alive,' Penelope smiled gently. 'I suspect even better than your own mother.'

'It's just that night . . . ' Fiona tapered away and turned to gaze at her daughters.

'That night was a special kind of sharing my love,' Penelope soothed. 'Manfred is a man of peculiar tastes. To watch two women making love is something that satisfies him in a way we may not understand. But I suspect, that in your own way, having my husband watching us heightened your own desire for me.'

Fiona blushed as Penelope reached over and took her hand. 'I do not understand how you make me feel so much,' she said hoarsely. 'All I know, is that I want to be with you forever. But I know this cannot be, because I have duties to my family.'

'We are together forever,' Penelope said gently. 'Even when we are apart. It is you who I think of when I am alone. No-one else. And now that Manfred will be away for so long I think we should meet more often.'

That she already spent so much time with Penelope caused Fiona a twinge of guilt. But she recognised how much Penelope meant to her very existence. Was it that she was obsessed by her rather than in love with her? Would the situation ever arise where she might be forced to choose between Penelope and someone – or something – she loved? Fiona glanced guiltily at her daughters. Had her long absences from them already forced that choice?

Granville White preferred to meet people in his office. In his own domain he felt he had the edge.

Across the desk from him sat the priggish McHugh, his hostile glare barely concealed. Not that it mattered to Granville as the tone of the meeting would not be overly friendly.

'I have been informed by one of the shareholders,' Granville started icily, 'that you were unable to convince my mother-in-law to step aside and allow me free rein to manage the companies.'

McHugh shifted uncomfortably under the unrelenting gaze of the man he both detested and was afraid of. The dark rumours that circulated in the smoking room of the Australia Club had given him reason to entertain loathing and fear. White had somewhat dubious contacts with the rougher elements of Sydney's vicious gangs feared even by the police. He cleared his throat. 'Lady Macintosh has recently informed me that she has someone under consideration to take over from her,' he replied nervously, 'should she ever step down. I felt that it was not my place to question her ladyship any further on the matter.'

Granville leaned back in his big leather chair. 'Her ladyship, my mother-in-law, has no-one she can replace me with in the future,' he scowled. 'She has simply lied to you to deliberately sabotage my efforts for future expansions in the Macintosh enterprises. And if she remains we will all suffer the consequences of a feeble woman's inept efforts to manage something well and truly beyond the natural capabilities God gave woman.'

'I must disagree with you Mister White,' McHugh bristled. 'In the past, even when Sir Donald was alive, it was well known in educated circles that her ladyship really managed the companies. She may be a woman, and I agree with you that God has set natural limits on a woman's abilities to manage in a world naturally belonging to men, but Lady Macintosh is something of an exception. I do not wish to cast aspersions on your own capabilities Mister White,' McHugh continued politely but forcefully, 'but you are not of Macintosh blood and the shareholders seem to have a peculiar trust in Macintosh blood.'

'Nor is my mother-in-law of Macintosh blood,' Granville reminded. 'She is of the same blood as me. A White by birth.'

'Ah, but Lady Macintosh has intimated that she has someone in mind who *is* of Macintosh blood,' McHugh said quietly, 'to take over from her. And that would bide well with the shareholders.'

Granville reddened and attempted to control his temper in the presence of the smug Scot. 'Lady Macintosh is senile,' he snarled, 'if she thinks there is anyone left alive with her precious Macintosh blood who can replace me, Mister McHugh.'

'I have informed the shareholders that we will accede to her ladyship's wishes for a reasonable time,' McHugh replied mildly. 'She has since informed me that she will disclose her future representative before she sails for England in the next few weeks. So if that is all Mister White,' he rose from his chair, 'I will bid you a good day.'

Granville remained seated, not bothering to display the courtesy of escorting the Scot financier to the door. With a dark and violent anger boiling up in his soul he watched McHugh leave. He had a savage desire to smash anything that was within his reach. It was obvious that his despicable mother-in-law had contacted the Duffys to arrange that the bastard of Fiona and Michael Duffy be groomed as her future replacement. Although unthinkable – considering all she had done in the past to destroy the memory of the boy – Granville realised just how far she would go to destroy him.

But that would not happen. Before sailing, Captain Mort had briefed him of the arrangements to kill the boy and Granville had great faith in Mort's abilities.

As McHugh was leaving the anteroom, where George Hobbs sat poring over his endless books of accounts, he heard a crashing sound. Startled, Hobbs glanced up from his ledgers.

'Och man! I think Mister White's desk just fell over,' McHugh said with a broad grin. 'I think Mister White is having a bad day.'

The burly Max Braun was uncharacteristic of his stoic heritage. He was prone to emotional displays, and it was hard not to be emotional when he gazed at *his* Patrick. The boy was the image of the father Max remembered so vividly. A young man he had taught to fight, drink and chase women.

In those days Bridget had frowned on his influence over Michael. But she had sighed in her resignation when she recollected that the Duffy men were prone to the carnal pleasures of the flesh. Just as they were to a good old Donnybrook. And now she sat in the kitchen of the Erin Hotel, and listened as her son Daniel tried to find excuses for Max not to have time off from his duties at the hotel.

Max listened with an expression of bitter disappointment and a small amount of surliness as young Daniel chided him as if he were nothing more than a servant to the family. 'I haf never got one day off Daniel,' Max replied, 'since I come to work for your father in '55.'

Daniel pulled a pained expression and thrust his hands in the pockets of his waistcoat which was beginning to feel a little tighter each year. 'I would dearly like to give you time off Uncle Max,' the young lawyer said. 'But with the passing of my father, I have come more and more to rely on you to keep the hotel operating. You must understand what I am saying.'

'Colleen can run things,' Bridget said unexpectedly. 'She has a lot of experience with pubs. After all, her father owns one in Bathurst, and she grew up around kegs and taps.'

Daniel glanced at his mother sitting at the table with her hands folded in her lap. He had not expected her to support Max's request for two weeks' leave from the hotel. 'Colleen has the children to look after,' he retorted. 'She cannot run a pub.'

Bridget rolled her eyes and unfolded her hands. 'What do you think I was doing all these years with your father,' she said with a sigh. 'Do you think all the work got done around here by leprechauns? I raised you, Michael and Katie well enough. No, I think Colleen will be able to do her part and I will be able to help her.'

Daniel shrugged his shoulders. He had long learned that his skills in persuasion as one of Sydney's best courtroom lawyers did not extend to arguments with his stubborn mother. 'You can have two weeks off then Uncle Max. But only two weeks. My mother seems to think that she can run things with my wife. As capable as they are, you must remember that a hotel is a man's business, and not for the weaker sex.'

'Your cousin Katie runs one of the biggest businesses in North Queensland,' Bridget gently reminded her son. 'And she is a weak woman like Colleen and myself.' Daniel's face clouded at his mother's unsubtle remark and he stomped from the kitchen.

'Thank you Missus Duffy,' Max said, with a grateful expression on his scarred face. 'This is important to me to haf time off.'

Bridget's sweet smile faded and a look of curiosity spread across her serene face that was marked by soft wrinkles. 'I have known you for many years Max Braun,' she said, staring into his face, 'and I have come to know when something is troubling you. It is young Patrick, isn't it?' He baulked at her question and shuffled his feet unconsciously. 'I have had dreams Mister Braun,' Bridget continued quietly. 'Dreams of muddy water.'

Max looked up and stared directly into the slightly myopic eyes of the woman he greatly respected. He knew about her uncanny dreams. The times she dreamed of muddy water inevitably meant a death in the family. 'Ja. It is my Patrick,' he replied. 'I do not know but I must be free to look after him for a little while, before he goes away from us for a long time.'

Bridget nodded her understanding. 'I have dreamed of Patrick's father,' she said. 'His ghost is with us, and is troubled by something that we do not understand. I know young Patrick and Martin have seen Michael's ghost. Sadly, my own son is too educated to believe in such things. He scoffs at me as if I was a demented old woman. But I know as surely as Saint Patrick chased out the serpents from dear old Ireland that Michael is with us even now. I think that you sense the same things.'

'Ja Missus Duffy,' Max said. 'I think bad things are happening and I think I should keep a vatch out for my Patrick. But I do not vant Daniel to know about vot I haf told you,' he added. 'He vould vorry too much.'

'I can promise you that I will not tell him,' Bridget said, reaching out to pat the big German's hand affectionately. 'The devil took Michael from us but his son has a guardian angel.'

Max was not always prone to demonstrations of emotion. He was forced to turn away so that Missus Duffy could not see the tears welling in his eyes. An evil force had taken Michael from him those many years earlier. But the evil was not going to take Patrick. He would rather die than let that happen. The devil could have his soul for what it was worth so long as Patrick survived the curse.

Somehow Max felt that the evil had a human form – and that he had already met him in the main bar of the Erin Hotel days earlier. He had no rational way of explaining his fear for Patrick's safety, other than he truly believed an ancient Aboriginal curse hung over the family.

TWENTY-FIVE

W hen Luke heard that Kate and Ben were taking supplies to a station located a couple of days south of Cooktown, he immediately insisted on escorting them. Ben was pleased to have the American ride with them. Being bushwhacked by desperate miners down on their luck was becoming a regular occurrence and Luke's rifle and revolver added impressive fire power to the small party.

But Kate appeared indifferent to his offer and bridled at his insistence. She had not needed him in the past, she told herself. And now she did not want to appear as if she had come to rely on him being around.

Despite her protests Luke saddled his horse and announced that he would ride up the track to scout out a camping place for the night. By mid–afternoon he found a suitable location with some shelter afforded by an outcrop of rocks. The location would be ideal as huge, angry thunderheads were boiling up from the west. It promised to be a real downpour and Luke waited with troubled thoughts for the wagons to arrive.

Just before sunset Ben's wagon creaked and groaned its way into the campsite.

'Where's Kate?' Luke asked with a concerned frown.

'She had to stop back down the track,' Ben replied, as he brought his team to a halt. 'Appears one of the beasts might have been bitten by a snake. I said I would wait but she told me I was to go ahead and help set up for the night. Said she would see if her bullock got better. If it didn't she was going to cut it loose and then come on ahead.'

'How far back is she?' Luke asked, swinging himself into the saddle.

'Left her about an hour ago, near a bend in the track.'

Luke did not wait for further directions but kicked his horse into a canter. Maybe he was being over cautious. He knew Ben would not have left Kate down the track alone if he had harboured any doubts as to her safety. Whatever it was, he just knew he had to get back to her.

With a tremendous rolling crash of thunder and vivid flash of lightning the storm broke. Hunched against the driving rain Luke rode into the rapidly gathering darkness. The rain was a continuous roar sweeping across the rocky, twisted landscape as a sharp wind tore flurries in the air. The occasional branch cracked like a rifle shot, and lightning caused the trees to flicker.

Luke dismounted and walked his horse, allowing her to feel her way on the slippery trail. The temperature had dropped and he could feel the chill creep through his bones. He peered into the premature gloom, hoping to sight Kate's wagon on the trail ahead. But it was the lowing of the bullocks that alerted him that she must be close.

'Kate?' he called above the storm. 'Kate?'

'Luke!' Kate's answer drifted as a faint and distressed sound to him. He instinctively knew something was terribly wrong.

'Where are you?'

'Over here,' she called back. Luke thought he could hear pain in her voice. He swore as he brushed at the rain pelting his face. If it were not for the lightning flashes he would have been blind.

'Call again,' he yelled to be heard above the storm. 'Keep calling and I will find you.'

'I'm over here,' she replied. Luke strained his senses to pinpoint her location. A lightning flash illuminated the oxen standing in miserable groups off to his right. He guessed Kate was somewhere between himself and the bullocks. Another flash of lightning lit up a tangle of branches from a tree already downed by a strike.

'God almighty,' Luke swore, as he flung himself from his horse and stumbled to the fallen tree. The wet branches slapped him in the face as he bent to where he guessed she must be. His hands groped amongst the soggy leaves until he felt her flesh. He was touching her face and her hands reached up to grip his. 'Are you hurt?'

'I don't think so,' Kate replied calmly, attempting to dissipate the anguish she knew he was suffering for her. 'I can't move. The tree came down when I was hobbling the bullocks. I think it was hit by lightning because I remember something like an explosion. I tried to get it off, but it's too heavy.'

'I'll get it off Kate,' Luke said, as he felt around her body to determine how she was pinned to the rocky ground. His hands slid along a smooth branch as thick as his thigh. When he ran his hand back along the branch, it came to rest against Kate's stomach.

She reached down to grip his hand. 'Luke . . .' she faltered. She did not know what to say to him. All she knew was that the terrible fear she had harboured before he arrived was gone. The feel of his strong, callused hand in hers made everything right. It was like it had always been in the past when he had been with her. He felt her hand tighten on his.

'Save your strength,' he said gently. 'I'm going to lift the branch. When I do, I want you to get yourself out any way you can. You understand?'

'I'm ready,' she replied, and reluctantly let go of his hand.

Luke squatted on his haunches and took hold of the thick branch. With all the strength he had ever known in his life he hauled upwards. The branch did not seem to budge and he called on a further strength, a strength born of the long years of love he had carried with him, across two continents, for Kate.

It was an uneven contest – man's muscle and sinew pitted against the hardy spirit of a tree which had tenaciously survived years in the earth of one of the harshest continents on the planet. But Luke's love proved stronger than the spirit of the tree. Grudgingly it conceded a mere three inches of clearance. But it was enough for Kate to wriggle free.

Spent from his almost superhuman effort, Luke sank to his knees. Kate's arms were around his neck. He felt her stomach pressed against him and heard her sobs. 'I was so scared,' he tried to say, but his words were lost in the crash of thunder rolling around them. He reached up and drew Kate down to him and stroked her face with his fingers. 'I was so scared that something might have happened to you,' he said, unable to see either her face or the expression in her eyes.

The driving rain, crashing thunder, lightning-torn sky and bitter chill of the night faded from her reality. Nothing mattered anymore except that the years of doubt were being washed away by what was happening between them at this very moment.

His mouth was on her neck and she was aware of the heat of her own desire as he held her and choked her name in a whisper. In the lightning flashes she could see his face and their eyes met as she felt a wave of convulsive sobs rack her body. Luke felt her fear and vulnerability and held her tightly to him. His kiss was at first gentle and reassuring. Kate did not resist. His mouth was as sweet as anything she had ever known and she felt a strange physical weakness which steadily grew into a strong passion of desire. She returned his kiss with her own rising passion and without a word he began to unbutton the man's shirt she wore. She shivered as the last button was undone and his hands cupped her breasts.

He stripped off his shirt and Kate could feel the steel corded muscle of his chest pressed against her breasts. She ran her hands over his back. The hard muscle rippled under her fingers. His face was between her breasts as he breathed her scent deep into his lungs. Her nipples stiffened at the gentle touch of his tongue. Kate threw back her head and closed her eyes. All time became irrelevant except for this precious moment between them. She wondered how his body could have felt so naturally familiar to her – as if it had always belonged to her. She moaned, as he bent her backwards into the wet bed of leaves, and his hand reached down to release the sash about her waist. She was hardly aware of herself helping him pull down her trousers.

His kisses were all over her body and his breathing was heavy and irregular like a man starving for air. She gasped as he entered her and their coupling took on an air of desperation borne of mutual hunger. Joined together, love and lust became one and Kate was barely aware that the screams above the pounding rain were her own expressions of ecstasy as his body was convulsed by his climax and hers.

They lay naked together, oblivious to the stinging cold rain and prickly twigs of the old tree. Kate felt as if he had filled every part of her being with himself and her tears of joy ran in rivulets with the driving rain. For now words were nothing more than unnecessary sounds, and nature was speaking for them both, with its spectacular and savage passion.

With seemingly little effort Luke scooped her in his arms and walked towards the wagon. He attached a canvas sheet to the side, procured a lantern from Kate's supplies and was even able to light a small fire under the big wagon. Propped against a wagon wheel, with a dry blanket wrapped around her, Kate watched Luke bending over the little fire that promised to grow and provide its warmth for them. She was still remembering the steel hard muscles on his lean body as he possessed her. He was like a coiled stockwhip, she thought dreamily.

Luke carefully placed the dry inside sections of bark against the flames to ensure that the blaze grew in strength. He glanced up from his task and smiled at her. 'I am going to have to look and see if that branch did you any injury Kate,' he said. 'Don't see any reason why you might be shy.' She returned the smile and opened the blanket to him. He held up the lantern to examine the bruise across her stomach. 'Looks like you will be all right,' he said, as he touched the bruise gently. 'Just a bad bump.' A little self-consciously he withdrew his hand and Kate wondered how he could be at one moment so assertive with her and yet shy. She reached out and pulled him to her.

'Have I told you that I love you Luke Tracy?' she said, with her head resting on his shoulder. 'That I think I loved you from the very first moment I saw you standing on that wharf in Brisbane. You looked so proud and self-assured standing there with your bed-roll and rifle. I was so intrigued by the tall man with the smile when you looked up at me.'

'I didn't know you noticed,' Luke replied softly. 'You were another man's woman then. I couldn't tell you how much I thought you were the most beautiful woman I ever saw. I . . . ' He felt clumsy expressing a love that he had carried with him for over a decade. A love that had not faltered, as his words did now.

It had seemed a hopeless love. Yet the small but intense fire refused to burn out, despite the odds against winning the beautiful young woman's affections. But now, under the wagon, on an isolated track on Australia's northern frontier, all the years of pain faded to nothing. This strange place was the heaven he had always dreamed of. 'I love you Kate . . . always have,' he stated with simple determination, and the expression in his eyes told Kate just how deep his love was for her. 'I ain't got much to give to a woman. Not a woman as beautiful as you. I . . . '

She placed her fingers on his lips to still his sad recriminations on his lack of worldly possessions. 'Just promise me that you will never leave me again Luke,' she said softly as she closed her eyes. 'I don't think I could ever bear to lose you again. I have lost so many that I have loved.'

Luke did not answer but stared into the flames as

he held her close. She was like a trusting child and he had never felt more miserable – or happy – in the same space of time. He had found something more precious than the River of Gold but there was something he must do before he could give Kate his word that he would never leave her side again. By swearing an old blood oath, when he had been forced to flee Australia for his native America years earlier, he knew he was risking more than his life. He was risking the loss of the love of this woman.

He stroked her hair as one would a child and Kate drifted into a deep and contented sleep. For the first time in many years she was truly happy.

TWENTY-SIX

All was not well aboard the *Osprey*.
    A day's sailing south of Cooktown and Sims seriously pondered the question as to whether he would jump ship and strike out for the Palmer goldfields. He had misgivings about his captain's sanity and his doubts became almost certainties the closer they sailed to the gold port.

At first the captain's ranting in the dark hours of the pre-dawn were ignored by the crew. They were shrugged off as the probable result of secret drinking. But Sims had witnessed the captain wielding his sword as if stabbing a real person and at that time Mort had been dead sober.

'Did you see the nigger?' the captain had cried wildly as he jabbed at a corner of his cabin. Sims had stood dumbstruck, gaping at Mort lathered in sweat.

'What nigger, Cap'n?' he asked in confusion.

Mort ceased his attack on the spectre that only he could see and stared at Sims. 'The myall nigger with the bloody bird feathers all over him.'

It was not the first mate's place to question his captain's sanity and he shook his head as he backed out of the cabin. Not that Mort's antics with his imaginary myall foe worried Sims as much as the captain's instructions to make a search of the Baron von Fellmann's personal possessions in the cargo hold. As he had not been instructed as to what he was looking for, Sims reported back to Mort that he found nothing worthy of note.

'No papers of any kind?' Mort asked, as he stood behind his chart table in the cabin.

'Nothing Cap'n,' Sims replied. 'Jus' clothes an' things. Nothin' more.' Mort dismissed him with an impatient wave of his hand and Sims was relieved to return to deck. He was sure that the captain was stark raving mad. Years earlier he had served under a similar captain whose mind had snapped and had killed three of his crew before he was himself killed. The deaths were reported by the crew as an accident at sea. Their fear of the consequences of the truth outweighed the need to describe their captain's death in terms of self-defence. Sims had been a young sailor then and had conspired with the survivors on a blood oath that he would never speak of the incident.

And now he was seeing it happen all over again: a man in authority who believed he was being haunted by some old myall warrior and had become so suspicious that he was now spying on the Baron for no given reason. The idea of skipping ship at Cooktown was gaining more appeal by the minute.

On deck Sims took in a deep breath of salt air. He gazed at the silvery shimmer on the blue waters and noted with some satisfaction that a formation of dolphins glided gracefully on the bow wake of the barque. Dolphins were the universal tokens of good luck for sailors. He fervently hoped so.

Captain Mort had good reason for his paranoia. He had hoped that his first mate just might find something else of interest to incriminate the Baron. The letter intended for Baron von Fellmann that was intercepted in the port of Brisbane had been enough. But further evidence might have given him the edge in the final, inevitable confrontation.

The damning letter had arrived in Brisbane when the *Osprey* had been laid over for resupply. Mort had secretly opened it as he was a man plagued by suspicions that everyone around him wished to do him harm. What he read gave him justification for his obsessive fear. Lady Macintosh was instructing the German to turn him over to the police upon their return from his expedition. Ah . . . but that would be right, he thought as he read the letter. The Macintoshes had a reputation for never letting personal feelings get in the way of making money. Let him finish his mission for the Germans – and then arrest him!

He guessed the necessary warrants would be in place to arrest him on charges of murder of the numerous young native girls taken aboard the *Osprey* whilst it had been engaged in blackbirding operations in the South Pacific. Someone had talked! But who? He had always been careful to release his crews of islanders back to their homelands and replace them with fresh crews after each trip. It was unlikely that his activities would be reported by the islanders in their faraway home islands.

Mort had racked his mind to think of anyone who had the detailed knowledge of his activities as contained in the letter. The identity of the informant, however, became apparent as he read on. Jack Horton! He also knew why the matriarch of the Macintosh family was determined to see him hang. Just as the damned Duffys did!

But he was wrong! Daniel Duffy had approached Enid for her assistance in bringing Mort to justice for the murder of an almost forgotten girl he had brutally murdered in Sydney. Not the young girls from the islands.

What Mort did not know was that Enid gambled on the possibility the arrested captain – given a choice between the gallows and a life term in prison – might name her nephew in the conspiracy to kill her son. Her considerable influence also spread to the colonial judicial system and in addition she had the young lawyer Daniel Duffy working behind the scenes to secure an arrest in the colony of Queensland.

Mort had considered destroying the letter. On careful consideration he decided that it would be better that the Baron receive it. He had a healthy respect for Lady Enid's deviousness. What was to say she had not somehow contacted the German by alternative means to tell him the same thing.

He had carefully resealed the letter. At least nothing was to happen before the expedition completed its mission, he had consoled himself morosely. It did not make sense to change matters considering the detailed planning for the expedition that he knew had occurred. But a lot could happen between the start and finish of any enterprise. However, he still had his options and gambled that he had the loyalty of his hand-picked crew – men very much like himself – in the event that he may need to use them against the Baron should he make a move to have him arrested.

A disturbing thought occurred to Mort. He remembered from the instructions he had read in Granville White's office that the Baron had recruited some Irish-American mercenary by the name of O'Flynn to his expedition. Even now in the cargo hold, as they sailed north to pick up the man and his small party to work under the command of the Baron, were crates of the new Winchester repeating rifles. Would it be himself and his crew up against the Baron and his men when the time came to dispose of the Prussian? He briefly considered disposing of the German before they reached Cooktown. But dismissed the idea when he considered that O'Flynn might be in league with Lady Enid and the Baron. Should he arrive in Cooktown without von Fellmann then O'Flynn might activate the plan to have him arrested.

No, Mort brooded. He would wait until they sailed away from Cooktown. Experience had long taught him to bide his time and watch for opportunities. He had not lived his often dangerous existence without that vital instinct of knowing when to strike. Very rarely had he ever underestimated any man.

Henry James, his former sergeant, had been one of the few men he had underestimated. It was highly unlikely that their paths would ever cross again. But if they ever did Mort knew he would wreak his revenge on the man who had once made a fool of him.

This man O'Flynn . . . What sort of enemy would he be in the likely event of a confrontation? Irishmen seemed to be the curse of his life, he thought bitterly. Irishmen and the ghost of some old Darambal nigger who came to him every night and stood staring at him with accusing eyes.

It was time to shoot the noonday azimuth with the sextant. Up on deck Mort noticed the Baron chatting with one of his crew. Paranoid suspicion racked the captain's thoughts. What were they discussing?

The German aristocrat also noticed the captain and greeted him warmly. 'Good morning Captain. A beautiful day.'

The Baron was a striking man. A couple of inches short of six foot he seemed to be taller by his very demeanour. Mort had guessed that the Baron was in his late forties even though his handsome, clean-shaven face did not reflect this. His short-cropped hair was a brown colour shot with streaks of grey. His hazel eyes had a depth of intelligence and determination. Everything about the way the Baron deported himself spoke of power. Mort had quickly and grudgingly come to respect his passenger as a man not to be underestimated in any way. He nodded his acknowledgement of the greeting as Manfred continued, 'Your sailor informs me that we are a little over twenty-four hours south of Cooktown. Is this true?'

'Yes. We have been fortunate with the winds and weather Baron,' Mort replied. 'My crewman has sailed these waters before. We spotted the pyramid mountain some time ago, which means we are close to Cooktown.'

The Baron turned to gaze at the coastline off the portside. He saw a vista of beautiful, craggy, jungle-covered mountains topped by lazy puffs of white clouds. The scenery was little different from that he had witnessed in the tropical islands east of the colony.

'This man O'Flynn we are taking aboard in Cooktown,' Mort said, interrupting the Baron's reflections. 'What do you know about him?'

The Baron turned to face the captain. 'An unnecessary question,' he said, with a faint smile on his lips. 'But I will answer it. Mister O'Flynn is an adventurer. Although I have never met the man personally I know of his reputation from others. He is a soldier who has fought many enemies in many places over the last ten years. Although he has lost an eye he is renowned as an expert marksman with rifle and pistol. There is a rumour that at one time he worked for the American government as an agent in South America after the Mexican revolution led by Juarez. I am fortunate that I have been able to acquire his services for our expedition.'

'What would that be?' Mort asked bluntly and Manfred eyed him with a trace of suspicion.

'Establishing outposts for Hamburg traders,' he replied, challenging Mort to further question him. Mort understood the response and let the subject drop. He made an excuse to extract himself from the German's presence and made his way down the deck to the stern.

Manfred watched him go and then turned his attention back to the coastline. His thoughts were troubled. Had he detected a dangerous hostility in the *Osprey's* captain since their departure from Brisbane? He shook his head slowly to console himself that Mort was unaware of the conspiracy against him. For now the mission was far more important than any one person, its ramifications of such a strategic interest against the ever-spreading British imperialism that even the past murders of a few native girls paled into insignificance. He had relayed his concern to Lady Macintosh by telegram that Captain Mort was not to be interfered with in any way whilst he was in the employ of German interests. She had reluctantly agreed in her veiled telegraphic response.

As for Mr O'Flynn . . . Manfred mused about the man as he watched the dolphins glide on the *Osprey's* bow wave in the crystal clear tropic waters. His wife had assured him that O'Flynn was more than he had first expected for the mission. Mister O'Flynn appeared to be a very remarkable man with a mysteriously dark and dangerous past.

TWENTY-SEVEN

Emma James noticed the change in Kate when she returned with Luke from the trip to the out-stations. There was an aura about her of happiness in everything she said and did.

At the first possible moment alone together in the store Emma cornered Kate with a broad smile and exclaimed, 'You're in love Kate O'Keefe!'

Kate smiled shyly and looked away with just the smallest degree of embarrassment. Was her happiness that apparent? Her reputation for hard-headed self-control now a thing of the past? 'It must be Mister Tracy,' Emma babbled on, regardless of Kate's silence. 'Has he proposed?' she added.

'What makes you think I am in love with Luke Tracy?' Kate retorted somewhat feebly, which only caused Emma's smile to broaden into a knowing grin.

'Because it is written all over you Kate,' Emma

replied. 'I have known you for many years now and I have always known that you have carried a torch for him, except you would never admit it to yourself. Something happened on the trip to finally force you to admit what we have all known,' she exclaimed with a woman's intuition on such delicate matters.

Kate finally looked squarely into her friend's eyes. 'You are right,' she said, with a sigh of happy resignation. 'I have finally faced the fact that I have always loved Luke.'

An impulsive and crushing hug from Emma followed her statement. 'I am so happy for you both,' Emma said, with tears in her eyes. 'You truly deserve some happiness in your life. You have always been there for everyone else except yourself and I feel that Mister Tracy is a man who will always love and look after you.'

Suddenly Kate realised that she was crying with her friend. But the tears were a release of bottled happiness which she wanted to share with the world. Henry found them hugging and crying together when he entered the store. Alarmed at the sight of tears he immediately stepped forward and asked what was wrong. Both women looked at him. 'Nothing is wrong,' Emma replied with a gentle laugh. 'Things couldn't be better with the world.'

Confused, Henry frowned and retreated from the store. Better to leave their temporary insanity to themselves, he thought. If they were happy why were they crying? It didn't make sense. But then, Henry was a man ruled by the logic of his gender, and not all that knowledgeable in the mysterious ways of a woman.

'Has he proposed?' Emma asked, as the two women disentangled from the embrace. Kate shook her head and sat down on a wooden keg of molasses.

'Not yet,' she answered wistfully, 'but I know he will . . .' she tapered off, thinking about the conversations on the track back to Cooktown. There was something he was not telling her, she thought, and worry caused her to frown. Like some burden he must unload before he could go further in his life.

Emma saw the frown and took Kate's hand in hers. 'I know he will,' she said. 'I think he is one of those men who are brave in any danger – except facing a preacher.'

Kate glanced up and both women laughed. She had not thought about Luke being a man terrified by the thought of matrimony. Was it that she might have to prompt the tough yet gentle American prospector into asking for her hand in marriage? If she only had her brothers alive to confront Luke and force him to make her an honourable woman, she thought sadly. She remembered how Michael had once fought a terrible fist fight in the backyard of the Erin Hotel with Kevin O'Keefe to force him into a marriage. It was the Irish way, with brothers naturally defending the honour of their beloved and cherished sisters.

'I think Luke will ask me for my hand,' she finally said when they ceased laughing at the thought of a frightened Luke Tracy. 'When he is ready to.' Kate's frown returned. Never before had she felt so happy and yet so frightened. She was sure of her love for him but not sure if he could settle down to marriage. He was truly a man of the limitless horizons. But she also knew that he loved her with his whole being and that everything would be all right in the end. Her frown dissipated along with her brooding thoughts about the future as she realised that only love could bring about so many maddening and conflicting emotions in such a short space of time.

But Kate's hidden fears re-emerged that evening when they both sat together on the verandah of Henry and Emma's house overlooking the river. Emma had insisted that they both dine with them and dinner had passed pleasantly. Over the table the men had discussed the merits of American and English firearms for the Queensland frontier and the price gold was fetching on the Sydney stockmarket. The women had exchanged views on the dear price of groceries and the schooling of their respective children. When the dinner was over Emma dragged her husband aside and insisted that Luke and Kate have some time together sitting on the verandah. Henry grumbled obtusely that he and Luke had much to talk about, but a withering look from his wife quashed any persistence on the subject.

Side by side Kate and Luke sat on the steps to the house and stared out over the river dotted by the lights of the numerous ships and boats at anchor. The warm tropical night was cooling to a pleasant temperature and Luke puffed distractedly on a cheroot. Kate slipped her arm through his and leaned her head on his shoulder. The world was right and the tranquillity complete.

'I love you Kate,' Luke said, and she impulsively

squeezed his arm. 'But I have to do something I don't think you might agree with.'

Kate let go of his arm and faced him. 'What do you mean?' she asked. 'What could you do that I might not agree with?'

He turned to face her and she could see the strain in his rugged features. 'It's just something I have to settle before . . .' he tapered away, and Kate gripped his arm firmly.

'Before what?' she asked. He looked away and stared at the lights on the river. A silence followed and Kate found that she was losing her patience with his taciturn nature. 'Before what?' she again asked, shaking his arm gently.

'Before we can have a life together,' he finally replied.

'Are you asking to wed me?'

Slowly Luke shook his head. 'I cannot ask such a thing,' he replied sadly. 'I have no prospects Kate. I have nothing to give . . . except my love.'

'That is enough,' Kate said softly. 'I have all else that a woman might want.'

'It's not enough for me. I must have something to bring to a marriage,' he said with a fierceness of his convictions. A man was not kept by a woman. A man's job was to look after his woman. 'I need to do something to right a wrong done to me a long time ago.'

The determination in his words frightened Kate. She knew him well enough to know whatever he had to do might prove dangerous. Was he about to embark on another of his lonely, dangerous treks into the wilderness in search of a new Palmer River goldfield?

'I have offered you the means for the expedition back to Rockhampton,' she reminded him.

'It's not that kind of thing I have to do,' he replied evasively. 'It's something personal and I will explain when it's done. You just have to trust me Kate.'

She sighed and let go of his arm. 'I will ask you no questions,' she said quietly, gripping her knees. 'But you will promise me that whatever you have in mind is legal.' Luke ducked his head. 'It's kind of legal,' he replied. 'It's a matter of righting a wrong.'

'I think we should go inside,' Kate said, and Luke noticed the annoyance in her voice. 'I think we are being rude to ignore our hosts.' Luke stood up to follow her. She stopped just before they entered and hissed at him, 'It had better be legal Luke Tracy or you can forget ever seeing me again.'

With a miserable look he averted his eyes from hers and felt as low as he had ever been. How could he explain to the person he loved that there was no turning back from righting the wrong that had taken six years from his life and sent him on a journey far from her. Six years of wandering his native land with her always painfully unobtainable in his memories. More important to him than any El Dorado was Kate's declared love for him. But equally important to a man is his pride. Without that, he was not a man.

TWENTY-EIGHT

The blast of a Colt revolver in a crowded hotel bar is bound to get people's attention. Michael froze – as did John Wong – with his cards in his hands. The Irish mercenary cautiously reached for the pistol in his coat pocket.

'Fellow diggers!' a voice boomed from the main entrance. 'The name's Luke Tracy and I'm one of you.' The silent miners turned to stare at the tall man framed by the doorway. Was he another miner driven out of his mind by the tropical sun or lack of luck on the Palmer? 'I need your help in settling a matter with a low son of a bitch who is drinking here right now,' Luke continued. 'He's not a miner, but a blood-sucking lawyer, who cheats honest hard-working miners out of their rights.'

A low growl of sympathetic voices rose for the man with the gun. Fancy-dressed townsmen living off the sweat of honest miners were not a favourite with them and rheumy eyes cast about for anyone who might be better dressed than themselves. Accusing glares settled on a few merchants, bankers and horse traders. Mumbles of 'I'm not a bloody lawyer!' came from the unfortunate men who fell under the scrutiny of the hostile miners.

Only Hugh Darlington said nothing as he desperately sought a means of escape. His worst nightmare had come true, and he felt that Kate O'Keefe was behind the reappearance of the man whom he had cheated years earlier, then betrayed to the police.

A burly miner who knew and disliked Hugh Darlington grabbed him by the scruff of his expensive coat. 'You mean this fella?' he growled, as he easily held him off the floor. The crowd obligingly parted.

'That's the man himself,' Luke drawled ominously.

'Some of you here might know me,' Henry piped up beside Luke. 'For those who don't I used to be a trap and can tell you from what Mister Tracy has told me it sounds like Mister Darlington here has a case to answer. So I would ask you to listen and pass your judgment after you hear what he has to say.'

The bulk of the patrons nodded and Hugh felt sick with fear. It all smacked of a kangaroo court in the making. *Natural justice,* some called the system!

Luke held up the tattered paper. 'This is a receipt for money I gave Darlington a few years back. The money came from gold I prospected up these ways back in '68. Darlington here took the money for himself and handed me into the traps out of a sense of duty to the gold laws. At least that is what I thought at the time. But I have since learned he swindled me. Sergeant . . . sorry, Mister James here can tell you what I am saying is true and I'm prepared to swear on any Bible you give me to that fact.'

The murmur from the miners grew louder and had a disturbing edge of anger. The big miner who held the Rockhampton lawyer off the floor growled, 'What 'ave yer got to say fer yerself Darlington?'

Hugh knew he would need to be very careful in choosing his words. This was not a jury impressed by the technicalities of the law – only the facts of what had actually occurred. 'If Mister Tracy feels he has a grievance against me,' he replied with all the calmness he could muster, 'then I am prepared to settle with him at my office in Rockhampton any time he should choose.'

'Not good enough,' a voice called from the angry crowd. 'Settle the matter now. Mister Tracy has waited long enough.' The protest was taken up by the patrons in the bar.

'Gentlemen!' Hugh commanded in his best courtroom voice. 'I think Mister Tracy can retrieve the money from Missus O'Keefe as that is who I gave the money to.'

At the mention of his sister's name, Michael half rose from his chair. This was not their fight, John hissed as he pulled him down.

'Mister Darlington here,' Luke said in an icy tone, 'has come to Cooktown with threats of taking the money from Missus O'Keefe which is rightly her own. The rest, which he has, is mine. But threatening a woman is about all you could expect from a man who has never got dirt on his hands, like any honest hard-working digger here.'

'Gentlemen! Gentlemen!' Hugh called desperately above the rising din of angry voices. 'What Mister Tracy is telling you about Missus O'Keefe is a lie. She entered into a business arrangement with me, and the money was to be repaid at a time of my choosing. You can ask her!'

'The money you gave her was not yours to give Darlington,' Luke snarled above the angry voices of the miners. Most of them knew and respected Kate O'Keefe. Although she was a tough business woman, she was fair to them in their dealings, and generous to their families when they were down on their luck. 'You know that fully well. You are the liar Darlington. A no-good lying son of a bitch,' he added savagely.

Hugh paled. He could see the inevitability of where events were taking him. The man was challenging him and he was suddenly very frightened. Even the miners who crowded the hotel bar that late afternoon sensed what was bound to happen.

'You called me a liar Mister Darlington,' Luke retorted calmly, 'and I call you a liar.' The miners in the bar fell into a hushed silence. Luke was smiling grimly and when he continued to speak the miners were left in no doubt as to what the silence had given birth to. 'So how about we settle this outside like gentlemen. Just you and I and Colonel Samuel Colt,' he said, as he let his hand fall to the big revolver tucked in his leather belt.

Hugh could feel the sweat on his hands, and watched with terrible fascination as Henry James limped towards him, with a revolver in his hand. When he reached Hugh, he held up six bullets for the crowd to see. Then he loaded the pistol and passed the gun to Hugh who accepted it as reluctantly as if the man had passed him a venomous snake.

Luke held up one bullet for the crowd to witness, and loaded his gun. The significance of the single round was not lost on the miners: the American had given the lawyer the better odds. A courageous sporting gesture from one of the miners' own. Then Luke turned his back and walked out the front door of the hotel onto the street.

The miners spilled eagerly out to follow the American prospector into the relative privacy of a side street. The momentum of the crowd pushed Hugh before them. Michael and John followed the miners to witness the duel. Curious bystanders realised that a fight was about to occur, not an unusual occurrence, in the tough frontier town.

Many hurried away to avoid getting caught up in what usually ended in a free-for-all brawl. Others remained, when they learned from the patrons of the hotel that the fight with pistols was one to the death. Money changed hands as the two men stood facing each other down the short length of the dusty street. The odds favoured the lawyer – only because he had six shots to the American's single one.

John Wong accepted a wager from a miner that the lawyer would kill the crazy Yankee. He liked the odds of six to one that the miner had given in favour of the lawyer winning the duel. But John did not think he would lose his bet. He had carefully watched the way the American moved and liked what he saw. The man had the deadly grace of a hunting cat, and like the hunting cat, showed no fear. A man who did not fear death was fully in control of his senses.

The mention of his sister's name in the hotel had caught Michael's attention. Just what was this American to his sister? he asked himself with a frown. If the prospector was killed, then he might never know.

The spectators were careful to give both men a wide berth as they squared off for the duel. The destructive power of a stray Colt bullet at close range was impressive.

The American prospector appeared calm but the lawyer was visibly afraid. Hugh had fired pistols before, but only at bottles for fun, and it seemed that the American who faced him cared little whether he lived or died. It was a disconcerting demeanour to confront and Hugh sensed that he was looking death in the face.

This was not like the savage verbal attacks on the opposition's arguments in a courtroom where he had impressed with his legal rhetoric. This was raw justice, more fitting to medieval times, when the man left standing was deemed to be innocent. To his credit, Hugh realised that a plea for an alternative means of settling the matter would have been construed as craven, unfitting for a man of his social standing.

'We won't worry about any fancy rules here, Darlington,' Luke said in a loud, calm voice. 'There will only be one rule and it will be simple. I'll give you the first opportunity to shoot me. If you fail I will shoot you. Do you have any questions?'

Hugh looked about desperately for support and saw none. It was obvious who the miners were backing – on moral grounds, if not financial. 'I just want it known that I am doing this under duress,' he said addressing the spectators. 'And that the death of Mister Tracy will be an act of self-defence forced upon me by the present circumstances.'

He turned to face Luke and raised his pistol. A hush fell on the spectators. Breaths were held frozen by the realisation that a man was about to die. Michael felt admiration for the courage of the American who stood rock still, waiting for certain death. Whoever he was to Kate, he mused, he had guts.

Hugh sighted along the barrel levelled at Luke. But sweat dripped into his eyes and he lowered the heavy gun. As he wiped the sweat from his eyes with a clean handkerchief, a tiny murmur of discontent rose from the crowd. They were angry at the possibility that they might not be able to collect on bets. Hugh put away the handkerchief and raised his pistol.

Once again the hush fell over the spectators. Hugh held the gun for only a second before he squeezed the trigger. Even though the shot was expected, the blast of the revolver caused many amongst the crowd to flinch.

Luke spun and fell sideways as the heavy lead bullet hit him. Blood spurted from his earlobe where the bullet had clipped him. For one terrible second he thought he was going to die. Blood drenched his shoulder as he attempted to struggle to his feet. Darlington was better with a gun than he had anticipated and he still had five shots left! A long moan from the tense spectators tapered away to an expectant hush. Now it was the Yankee's turn.

Hugh levelled his gun at Luke as he was rising to his feet. The rules were forgotten. This was raw survival where reputations meant little if you were dead. He snapped off a second shot. The bullet threw up a puff of dust where Luke had been a split second before.

As he rose from the ground Luke fired his single shot and Hugh felt the bullet strike with a vicious thwack in the centre of his forehead. He crumpled and fell to his knees. He was shot, and he felt the blood trickle from the wound. 'I'm dead,' he moaned pitifully, as he clasped his hands to his forehead.

But death did not come quickly. His head ached as he felt the stickiness of blood between his fingers. To all intents and purposes I'm alive, he thought. He was also vaguely aware that the once-hushed crowd was now laughing uproariously. How could they be so callous towards the plight of a dying man, he thought in confusion.

'Like you I lied Mister Darlington,' Luke said with a broad grin as he stood over the lawyer in the dusty street. 'I loaded with two rounds in my pistol – not one. The first was a kind of special bullet I made,' he continued with his gun pointed at Hugh's head. 'You aren't going to die but you will have a bad headache for a while. Never heard anyone dying from a wax and strawberry jam bullet before. But you might just die from the second round I'm keeping for you unless you transfer the rest of my money to Kate O'Keefe as we originally planned way back in Rockhampton. You've got two days.'

With a roar of hearty approval for the ingenious joke on the crooked lawyer, the crowd surged forward to lift Luke onto their shoulders and chair him back to the hotel. Drinks would flow and the story be retold to those who were unlucky enough to miss the fun. It was a grand joke, that only a man with a steel nerve could pull off. And the elaborate joke would echo in the laughter of miners, teamsters and stockmen around campfires for many a year to come. Such an incident could have adverse ramifications for a man's reputation if he had aspirations to public office in a frontier colony and Darlington knew it. He was now a man hell bent on using the law to his advantage to crush the man who had humiliated him before the crowd of tough miners.

Michael followed the crowd back into the hotel to share in John's win. The miner, who had lost his bet with the big Eurasian, had vainly tried to argue that all bets were off because the lawyer was still alive. But John argued that the American had won by default. Darlington had ignored the rules and fired a second shot out of sequence. The miner pondered on his logic, but still refused to concede he had lost the bet. He only conceded when John grabbed him by the throat, and slammed him against a rickety fence. The coal-black eyes of the young man reminded the frightened miner of a deadly snake. He paid up.

Michael's estimation of the American rose considerably. Here was a man worth having beside you in a tough situation, he thought, as the miners deposited Luke on the bar. And there was the matter of the man's relationship with his sister Kate, he pondered. He had a feeling he should keep the man close, so that he could determine just who – or what – the prospector was in Kate's life.

'The traps are comin'!' a miner called out above the din of celebration. They're acomin' to arrest the Yankee!' A silence descended on the bar. 'Not on his life,' someone roared and the cry went up in support of Luke.

Michael grabbed John by the arm and hissed in his ear, 'We have to get the Yankee out of here before the traps get him.' John agreed, and the two men pushed their way through the crowd, milling protectively around their new-found hero.

'Mister Tracy,' Michael called to Luke who was standing on the bar and holding a rag to his bloody ear. 'We'll get you out of here before you end up in the lockup.'

Above the din Luke heard Michael's suggestion and glanced around. Through a window of the hotel he could see three grim-faced uniformed police officers striding down the street. 'Good idea,' he said as he leapt from the bar. 'But I have to see Kate O'Keefe before we go and explain some things.'

'Not a good idea,' Michael growled, as he helped

make a way through the crowd of back-slapping patrons congratulating Luke on his courageous gesture. 'You might get her involved.'

'If I don't,' Luke protested, 'she will get the wrong idea about what happened here today.'

'No time for that,' Michael replied as they reached a back door to the hotel. 'The traps may take you in. We have to hide you until it's safe to get you on the boat.'

'Goddamn!' Luke swore. 'You don't know what Kate O'Keefe is like Mister O'Flynn. If I don't explain the situation before we leave she is going to think I'm just deserting her.'

Wouldn't make any difference, Michael thought with a grim smile. I know what my sister is like. No, you will be safer with me, going to God knows where.

The police forced their way into the crowded hotel, and called on Luke Tracy to stand in the Queen's name, but were met with derisive laughter and wisely retreated with sheepish grins. The unpopular solicitor had made haste to lay his complaint of attempted murder with them. But independent witnesses had provided an alternative version of the duel. The police recognised the ironically funny side of the confrontation and had better things to do than satisfy the aggrieved Rockhampton lawyer. On the frontier even men sworn to uphold the laws on the illegality of duelling could turn a blind eye.

Hours later, Kate was told of the gunfight by a breathless customer who had witnessed the shoot-out between the two men. She closed her store, and hurried to the hotel, but Luke was gone.

One of the patrons told her that he had left with Michael O'Flynn. He also thought that he was now working for the American. With tears brimming in her eyes, Kate roundly cursed both Luke and Michael O'Flynn, as she walked back to her store. Whoever O'Flynn was, she thought bitterly, he deserved to rot in hell.

Kate had a sick feeling that Luke was about to do something that might place his life in extreme peril. Then and there she swore an oath, that even if he came back alive to her, she would be done with him forever. She was through shedding tears for any man. Especially Luke Tracy! His wild, roving ways had caused her enough heartache for ten lifetimes. The old dog had strayed once too often! Pride was not the domain of men alone, she sniffed, as she walked slowly back to her store. Pride was the stiffness in the spine of the Duffy clan. She, after all, did not need a man.

Luke stood on the banks of the Endeavour River and watched a row boat being steered through a clutter of ships. Beside him stood Michael and five tough-looking bushmen he had recruited to the mysterious expedition. A short distance away Karl Straub stood alone near a pile of expedition supplies.

Michael puffed on an old briar pipe as he watched the *Osprey*'s longboat make its way to the shore. 'Bloody impressive show you put on back there Mister Tracy,' he said as he puffed on the pipe.

'Took a big chance of missing the boat if the traps had got you.'

'Maybe,' Luke drawled, and let the matter drop. Michael sensed that he was in no mood to talk but he was still curious to know why the man would risk his life for Kate.

Luke's thoughts were preoccupied with Kate. In a confusion of events he had been swept away from her. But what had he expected? Challenging a man to a duel was bound to bring him before the law. What did he expect Kate to think of his shoot-out with her former lover? A fit of jealousy? A man who said he loved her and then rashly put their love in jeopardy over a matter of pride? 'Goddamn,' he muttered, 'I'm sorry Kate. I wish you knew why I had to do it.' But his apology wafted away on a sea breeze.

Maybe she would understand when he returned, he thought optimistically. Maybe it would all turn out for the better. His optimism faded. Something told him Kate O'Keefe was not easily swayed by words. She was a woman of action and his actions this day would take a lot of explaining.

The boat nosed ashore amongst the broken stumps of mangroves, and two sailors assisted the party waiting on the shore to clamber aboard. Michael and his bushmen carried little with them: bed-roll swags and few personal weapons. Two bushmen were assigned to remain behind and guard the wooden boxes. They would join the ship when the longboat returned to pick them up with the supplies.

As the boat headed back to the *Osprey* Michael scanned the blackbirding barque. She was not a big ship, but had the sturdy, pugnacious lines of a fighter, and he could see two men standing at the rails watching their approach with some interest.

One of the men at the rail reminded him in a vague way of Karl Straub – but much older. Michael guessed he was probably Baron Manfred von Fellmann: his demeanour and dress certainly fitted that of a Prussian aristocrat. The second man must be the *Osprey*'s captain. If that was so, it had to be Morrison Mort, he thought with a chill. Mort! The man he would kill!

As the longboat neared the barque Michael was able to make a closer examination of the ship's infamous captain and grudgingly admitted to himself that Mort was a striking man.

He was aware that the man was appraising him with just the faintest hint of confusion reflected in his face. Their eyes met and Mort looked away.

Michael was first aboard, and was approached by the man who looked vaguely like Karl Straub. He held out his hand to the Irishman. 'It is a pleasure to make your acquaintance Mister O'Flynn,' he said, gripping Michael's hand firmly in his. 'I am Manfred von Fellmann.'

Michael accepted the extended hand. 'My pleasure Baron,' he replied as the last of his men came aboard. 'I had the honour of meeting your wife whilst I was in Sydney.'

'She told me,' the Baron replied, with just the hint of a smile on his handsome face, 'that you are a man of remarkable skills Mister O'Flynn. Just the man for this mission.' The Irishman flinched inwardly at the German's comment on his 'skills'. Surely Penelope would not have told her husband about their brief affair.

Before the Baron could continue with the uncomfortable line of conversation they were joined by Straub and Mort. The Prussian Baron greeted his fellow countryman cheerfully. 'Herr Straub, I see that you have carried out your orders satisfactorily.'

Straub accepted the handshake. 'Mister O'Flynn has proved to be a good choice to lead our bushmen Baron von Fellmann,' he replied formally. 'The men seem to have accepted his leadership.'

The Baron let the hand drop and turned his attention to Michael. 'I would presume that you have not yet met Captain Mort, Mister O'Flynn.'

'We have not had the pleasure,' Michael said as he stared directly into the dead eyes of Mort. He did not offer to shake the captain's hand – not that Mort made any gesture to do so either.

'Are you sure we have not met Mister O'Flynn?' Mort asked in a puzzled voice, staring at him coldly. 'You seem somewhat familiar to me.'

So you recognise my father, Michael thought with a surge of hatred and angry satisfaction. But you are yet to know me. 'I don't think so Captain Mort,' he replied, calmly disguising his true feelings. 'I have lived all my life in the States.'

'No doubt you have Mister O'Flynn,' Mort replied with a frown. But in his expression Michael could see doubt. 'You just reminded me of an Irishman I had the misfortune to meet some years ago. I was then with the Native Mounted Police in this colony. But I suppose not all Irishmen are criminals.'

The obvious slur on his father's good reputation angered Michael. He was sorely tempted to reveal his true identity to the murderous captain. But it was not the time or place to challenge the man to a duel. He would wait for the opportune moment when the man would die knowing who his executioner was. 'No Captain, not all Irishmen are criminals,' he replied, attempting to defuse the tense situation developing between them. A frightened dog is a dangerous dog, Michael thought. And it was obvious that his uncanny resemblance to his dead father had triggered a fear in the captain.

'You will excuse me gentlemen,' Mort said abruptly. 'I have to get my ship turned around, and ready to sail again.' He turned his back and walked away to issue orders to his crew.

Michael inwardly relaxed when Mort walked away. The tension between himself and Mort was apparently unnoticed by the Baron and Herr Straub.

'We will be sailing midday tomorrow Mister O'Flynn,' the Baron said quietly. 'No-one is to go ashore from now on unless with my explicit agreement.'

'Sounds fair enough,' Michael replied.

'When we are well out to sea I will brief you on your role in our mission,' Manfred continued. 'Until then, rum will be distributed to you and your men. I am sure they will appreciate a drink before the *Osprey* puts to sea. Once at sea some of them will feel less inclined to partake of strong liquor.'

Michael grinned at the Baron's wry observation. 'I think you could be right.'

'I have supper with the captain in an hour,' Manfred said politely. 'You and Herr Straub are invited to join us.' Straub accepted the offer but Michael declined, saying that it was his role to eat and live with the men directly under his command.

'A good soldier always remembers his men first,' Manfred agreed. 'I expected that choice from you Mister O'Flynn and I am not disappointed.'

After a short briefing on the routine of the ship, Michael joined his men below, where the rum ration was issued. They were in good spirits with the unexpected gift and one of them produced a battered harmonica from his bed-roll. Soon the ship's hold echoed to the choruses of popular songs from America and the British Isles.

Michael did not join in the singing. Whilst he sat watching his men enjoy themselves his brooding thoughts were elsewhere. He was thinking morosely about the boxes of supplies the *Osprey*'s longboat had rowed back to the shore to pick up. Even now the bomb was in the supplies being brought to the ship.

On the shore, a portly little man with a silver-topped walking cane watched the last of the bushmen being rowed out to the blackbirding ship. He peered into the gathering dusk and was pleased to see that the box he had Michael include amongst the supplies was in the longboat. Now all the Irishman had to do was complete his mission: to sink the *Osprey* before she could reach New Guinea where Horace was sure his German adversary was bound.

When the longboat was out of sight behind a huge Chinese junk anchored beside the *Osprey*, Horace turned to walk back to his hotel. He had done all that he could. Now the future strategic interest of the British Empire lay in the hands of an Irish mercenary – a man wanted by the police of New South Wales.

Ah, Michael Duffy, Horace thought wistfully. Do not let your wild Irish passion lead you from your primary mission. Captain Mort is of no consequence to the pages of history. But stopping the Kaiser from his ambitions to eventually rule the civilised world is. The Englishman was acutely aware that his plans depended solely on the passion of a man whose loyalty to him was based purely on the powerful personal need for revenge, not on the lofty ideals of patriotism.

The day after the *Osprey* had slipped anchor and sailed out of Cooktown, Kate received a bank draft for a substantial amount of money from Hugh Darlington. It was transferred to her account without explanation, as the lawyer had left Cooktown vowing never to return.

Kate did hear a rumour that the duel had something to do with the transfer of funds to her account. But her bank manager shrugged when she asked him what it all meant. He had long learned to live with strange financial transactions in a town where men paid for drinks – and women – with gold dust and nuggets.

TWENTY-NINE

Charlie Heath hunched against the drizzling rain and peered across the empty paddock. He should have figured that the boys would not be out playing in this kind of weather. For a week he had followed the boy he had confirmed as Patrick Duffy, to and from his school. Charlie had always been alert for a moment when Patrick might be alone in some isolated place. Given that opportune circumstance, he could slit the boy's throat.

But Patrick Duffy had always been in the company of a slightly younger boy who Charlie confirmed as Martin Duffy. He needed to lure them both to some isolated place where he could separate them and get Patrick alone. It did not look promising until Charlie noted that the boys spent a lot of time playing in an area called Fraser's paddock. It had a lot of trees and scrub and, even better still, on some days the boys played long into the twilight before returning home.

He glanced up at the scudding clouds and smiled grimly. The weather was breaking and the next day promised to be fine. Cooped indoors for the last few days, the boys would surely come to the paddock to play tomorrow.

The killer shrugged off his disappointment and trudged down a narrow street. He knew, with the certainty of the hunting animal, that his prey would come to the killing ground the next day. And when he did, he would be waiting in the shadows to pounce.

Max Braun had taken lodgings in a boarding house that was clean, comfortable and relatively expensive. He could afford to do so as he had saved a substantial amount of money over the years whilst working for the Duffy family at the hotel. His landlord was a former Dutch sailor who knew Hamburg well from his seafaring days. Of around the same age as Max, the two found much in common to discuss around the kitchen table of the boarding house and became friends.

The Dutchman had jumped ship in Sydney many years earlier, and had been fortunate to make the acquaintance of a lonely widow, somewhat older than himself. She had owned the boarding house and upon her death bequeathed the place to the Dutchman who had been her lover.

Although the quickly established friendship was based on mutual memories of bad sea captains and good whores, the Dutchman knew it was wise not to ask his German friend of his business. As to where he disappeared between sunrise and sunset was not his concern. It was good enough that his tenant paid promptly and left his room clean.

But on this day Max returned soaked to the skin and shivering from exposure to the heavy rain. He produced a bottle of good schnapps and a frown of mysterious concern. The Dutchman sat with him to share the fiery liquid.

'My friend,' he said, 'the rain is going away you see.' Max took a long swig from the bottle and glanced at the Dutchman.

'Ja,' he scowled. 'I hope so. Time is running out.'

'There's a magpie's nest near the top,' Patrick said, as he stared at the upper branches of a tall gum tree. 'I can climb up and see if there are any eggs in it.'

Martin frowned at Patrick's suggestion. The night was rapidly approaching and Fraser's paddock was falling under its shadow. Patrick was always doing dangerous things – or things that got them both into trouble. Like in the chapel at school where he snitched the altar wine and convinced Martin to try some. They did not hear Father Ignatius approaching with the stealth of a hunting leopard. When he struck it was with the carefully cultured words of a Jesuit priest. 'Turning wine into water Master Patrick Duffy?' he asked with a wry smile. 'For I pray that is what you are attempting to do, as I know you would not commit sacrilege, by imbibing the Lord's wine.'

Terrified, Martin had stood quaking in the shadow of the tall, gaunt priest who was also their Latin teacher. His mouth was too dry with fear to respond. But Patrick did.

'I was showing Martin the Lord's blood,' he replied, showing no fear. 'Martin is going to be a priest one day, just like you Father.'

The Jesuit stifled a smile. 'Then he will be in a position to pray for your soul Master Patrick,' he said, fixing the young man with his dark eyes, as he stood with his hands clasped behind his back. 'When they lead you to the gallows to hang for stealing.' Not that stealing was a hanging offence anymore – but the boys did not know this.

'Our da is a lawyer and he would get me off,' Patrick replied defiantly. Father Ignatius sighed. Young Patrick Duffy was incorrigible and he hoped that an education in England even though it be not of the true faith might reform him. A colonial education seemed to have failed.

'Come gentlemen,' Father Ignatius said 'Father Francis awaits your presence with the reformer.'

Martin had felt his legs turn to jelly at the mention of the reformer. He had never felt the thin cane's stinging touch on his backside as Patrick had. They followed the Jesuit to the dreaded office of Father Francis where Patrick asked if he could speak to Father Francis alone. Father Ignatius was surprised at the boy's forthright request and raised his bushy brows. But he allowed the request and ushered him into the office.

Martin remained outside, wringing his profusely

sweating hands, as he prayed for salvation from the stinging cane. His worst nightmare came true when, after an ominous silence, he heard the swish and crack of the cane.

The door opened and Patrick emerged with a pain-racked face. He was barely able to speak and was forcing himself not to cry. His pride was at stake.

'You are free to leave with your brother, Master Martin,' Father Ignatius said from behind Patrick. Martin gaped at the priest, but quickly recovered his senses as he stumbled down the long corridor. He felt like the condemned man given a last minute reprieve from the gallows.

'What happened?' he questioned out of the corner of his mouth. 'Why didn't I get the cane like you?'

Patrick forced himself to fight the pain as he hobbled beside Martin. 'I told them you really are going to be a priest one day,' he hissed through gritted teeth. 'Said it wouldn't look good if you were punished for stealing altar wine. Father Francis and Father Ignatius agreed. They think you might have a vocation. You bloody well better become one.'

Stunned, Martin fell in step with Patrick, and pondered on the deal Patrick had struck for him. He knew two things then and there. The first was that he loved his tough, courageous brother. And the second was that God had answered his prayers not to face the cane. It was possible that he did have a vocation.

But now, Patrick's suggestion that they climb the tall gum and take birds' eggs from a nest, was one of those things that could get them hurt. He thought about asking God for a miracle to stop Patrick in his foolhardy venture. It was a tall tree with few good branches to grip. The climb was downright dangerous!

He did not want Patrick to think he was scared. He knew that he would climb with him if he went ahead with his foolish venture. Dear God please make something happen so I won't have to climb the tree, Martin prayed. His prayer was answered almost immediately by a voice that came from the lengthening shadows of the late afternoon. 'Master Martin Duffy,' the voice said. 'Your ma told me that she wants you to go home right away.' Both boys turned to watch the man emerge from the shadows.

'Who are you?' Patrick asked suspiciously.

Charlie Heath grinned at him. 'I was up 'avin' a drink in the bar and the big German fella there . . . what's 'is name?' Charlie said, scratching his unshaven chin.

Martin piped in helpfully, 'Uncle Max . . . '

'Yeah, that's 'im,' Charlie continued. 'Your Uncle Max told me to tell you if I see you up this way that your ma wants Master Martin home straightaway. Says you can stay Master Patrick. Seems she's got a job for Master Martin.'

Patrick glanced at Martin. Chores were better than having to follow Patrick up that tree. 'I'll go,' he said.

Patrick sighed with frustration. 'I'll come with you.'

Charlie's grin evaporated. He had not anticipated that the boy would choose to go with Martin when a job was mentioned. 'No need Master Patrick,' he said quickly. 'I see you are tryin' to get up the tree. You after robbin' a nest?' Patrick felt uneasy in the man's presence. He was a stranger – and yet he seemed to know the family. Deception did not really cross his young mind. 'I know where there's a plover's nest with eggs in it not far from here,' Charlie added. 'Be much easier than tryin' to climb this tree at this time of day. I'll show you while yer brother goes home and does his chores.'

Patrick glanced at Martin who shrugged his shoulders before turning to walk back to the hotel. For a brief moment Patrick felt his unease warn him that he should follow. But the stranger was smiling easily, and had turned to walk towards the old creek that had been clear and flowing in the time before the white man came to settle on the sandy lands around the harbour. Plovers' eggs were a prize and Patrick followed the man into the scrubby bushland adjacent to Fraser's paddock.

'What does Ma want me to do Grandma?' Martin asked Bridget as she sat at the kitchen table shelling peas. 'A man said that Ma had some job for me to do here.' Bridget ceased what she was doing and looked up at her grandson. 'What man?' she asked with a puzzled frown.

'The man who Uncle Max talked to in the bar a while ago,' Martin answered. 'He said Uncle Max was told by Ma for me to come back here and do a job for her.'

'Dear God!' Bridget exploded, spilling the peas in her lap as she sprang to her feet. 'Max hasn't been here for days you foolish boy.' Martin's face crimsoned with shame. He had been so intent on finding an excuse to get away from the paddock, and possibly making the dangerous climb, that he had forgotten Uncle Max had been away for the past week.

'Go to the bar and tell your mother to fetch your father immediately,' Bridget said, gripping the stunned boy's shoulders and shaking him in her consternation. 'Tell her that she is to send as many of the men in the bar straight to Fraser's paddock.'

Young Martin reacted quickly and Bridget snatched a shawl from the back of the kitchen door. She did not wait for the patrons to spill out of the main bar before rushing into the darkening shadows.

She stumbled blindly in the night muttering a prayer over and over again. Dear God let Patrick's guardian angel be with him in his moment of dire need. The pools of muddy brown water that had haunted her dreams were quickly turning to crimson pools of blood.

Bridget was the first to reach Patrick. She called his name and he answered from the scrubby land adjoining the paddock. She stumbled through the scrub and saw him standing over the body of a big, evil-looking man who stared with sightless eyes at the tops of the tall gums. Bridget noticed the glint of a knife blade in the dead man's hand.

'Are you all right Patrick me darlin'?' she said, grasping the boy to her in a great hug. Patrick did not respond, but merely stared curiously at the dead man at his feet. Bridget followed his gaze down to the man. 'What happened?' she asked.

Patrick broke his trance-like state to stare at her with wide eyes. 'I don't know,' he answered slowly. He was still attempting to piece together the blur of sights and sounds mere seconds before he heard his name called. 'I was walking along and the man was following me. I was just ahead of him through the bushes there,' he said, pointing towards the old creek. 'And I heard a noise like croaking. When I came back, I saw the man lying here, with his head twisted around strangely. I think he is dead.'

Bridget looked down at the man at their feet. She had seen broken necks before, when the British had hanged rebel Irishmen on the gallows, and the dead man certainly had a broken neck. 'I thought I saw Uncle Max,' Patrick continued hesitantly. 'I thought I saw him running away.'

Before Bridget could reply a party of Erin Hotel patrons stumbled upon them. One of the men swore when he saw the body. 'Charlie Heath,' he said. 'I know him. A bad one from The Rocks.' The man bent to scrutinise the knife still in Charlie's grip. 'Looks like he was up to no good.' The others nodded and the man looked up at Patrick. 'You see what happened?' he asked.

'Patrick did not see anything,' Bridget answered quickly before Patrick could reply. 'He just found the man here.'

'No matter,' he said, wisely dismissing the affair. 'The traps can look after Charlie. Don't think they will be looking too hard for whoever slew him. Charlie's a bad 'un.'

The other patrons from the Erin nodded their agreement and sauntered back to the hotel to recount amongst themselves what they knew about the dead man's evil reputation. Bridget guided Patrick away from the paddock and fell behind the crowd noisily debating who might want to kill the infamous thug.

'Was it Uncle Max?' Patrick asked quietly, as he walked beside Bridget.

'It was your guardian angel,' she replied, and he knew not to ask any further questions.

Later that night Max returned to the hotel via the kitchen. He was startled to see Bridget sitting at the table with her rosary beads in her hands. At this time of night she was normally in bed and it was obvious that she had been waiting for him.

'I would like you to have these Mister Braun,' she said, offering the well-worn rosary beads to him. He did not take them but bowed his scarred head. 'I am not of your faith Missus Duffy,' he replied.

Bridget smiled enigmatically. 'But you are a guardian angel of my faith Mister Braun. I would like you to keep the rosary beads as a gift from an old woman who will not be haunted by dreams of muddy water tonight.'

Max accepted the gift and felt the smoothness of the beads in his hand. 'Danke Frau Duffy,' he said. 'I vill always keep them. Vun day I vill give them to Patrick.'

THIRTY

Wallarie stared in awe at the swirling red eddy of dust twisting and turning in a tortured dance across the plains. He shifted his balance and rattled his spears as the dust devil plucked at the spindly dry trees in the distance. The powerful column of air swirled away, and the Darambal man recommenced his long trek south across the plains.

He trudged with his head down, his left arm hanging by his side, as useless as a dead limb on a coolabah tree. His wound caused each step to be dogged by a fevered vision: the dust devil had spoken to him across the desolate plains, and recounted the story about a spirit woman and a spirit man.

They had met and the spirit woman gave birth to a boy. But the ancient spirits of the Nerambura people had said this was not meant to be. The spirit woman was of the evil tribe who had come as black crows to pick out the eyes of the living, and the spirit woman lost the boy. Now he wandered far, searching for his spirit father who was a great warrior. But the spirit father was at war with the evil spirit of the night, and the time of reckoning was coming.

Shaking his head and muttering at the incomprehensible images in his mind, Wallarie continued to stumble under the sweeping azure skies above. When he looked up at the sun he froze, and began to tremble in his fear. His trembling turned his legs weak and he crumpled into the red earth. For above him the sun had turned black, and he knew it was his time to die.

Although the *Osprey* battled with unseasonable northerlies as she sailed north, Captain Mort was not concerned. That was until he noticed the dramatic drop in atmospheric pressure, indicated by the ship's barometer.

Mort frowned and spread the nautical charts before him on a table in his cabin. He traced a line to the government settlement at Somerset and although it was within a day's sailing, his considerable experience navigating in tropical waters told him that the storm somewhere off the *Osprey*'s bow would be a bad one.

Whilst poring over his charts he felt the ship slow. The wind had dropped ominously and the barque plunged sluggishly into the oily, ominous swell of the tropical sea. The *Osprey* was sailing on a course north to the island of New Guinea and navigating through the treacherous waters of the world's largest coral reef. Mort was many despicable things, but one thing he could be commended for was his skill as a sailor. He had sailed the wild and cold waters of Bass Strait as a young man and had learned his trade under the best skippers who had ever sailed the treacherous southern seas. However, although Bass Strait during its worst storms may have had massive rolling waves and howling winds, it did not have the added peril of deadly coral reefs.

The jagged, mostly uncharted reefs had taken many ships to the bottom; passenger ships, freighters and bêche-de-mer schooners had gone down in the maze of coral shoals over the years. Such had been the toll on shipping and lives that Sir George Bowen, Governor of Queensland, had established the outpost of Somerset on the tip of Cape York Peninsula ten years earlier. The settlement was intended to provide a base from which rescue parties could retrieve shipwrecked sailors. It was established as a rival port to Singapore, strategically located to the Straits of Malacca.

But Sir George Bowen was not to realise his dream of a new Singapore. Within five years of the *Osprey*'s captain contemplating the outpost as possible refuge, it would cease to exist as a settlement. Remote and besieged by both wilderness and hostile tribesmen, Somerset would be abandoned, to be reclaimed in time by nature and the tribesmen of the north.

Mort lay the metal dividers on the chart and pondered the plunge and roll of his ship. He could read the movements of his ship as a horseman understood the moods of his mount. But the approaching storm was not the only problem that he was contemplating.

There was the serious problem of the Baron's men under the command of the American O'Flynn. He had not liked the man from the moment he had set eyes on him. There was something about the big American that disturbed him. It was not just in the man's openly hostile manner but something intangible made him sense that the American was definitely a threat.

'Cap'n?' The first mate stood apprehensively in the open doorway to Mort's cabin.

'What is it Mister Sims?' Mort asked irritably, as he resumed plotting a course for Somerset.

'Mightn't be much,' Sims mumbled. 'But something funny goin' on off the portside bow. Thought you might like to have a look fer yerself.'

Mort abandoned his charts to follow his first mate onto the deck where a peculiar drama was unfolding off the bow of the *Osprey*. Under a purple-black sky, Mort peered across the oily seas, to watch two ships manoeuvring.

'She looks like a Frenchy gun boat out of Noumea,' the first mate speculated, 'in an awful hurry to cut off that Chinee junk over there, off our starboard bow.'

Mort was inclined to agree. The French gun boat was little more than an armed ketch with an auxiliary steam engine. She was using both sail and steam to intercept the lumbering junk which looked as if she had seen a lot of rugged years at sea. Big sailing craft – with their high, raised sterns and peculiar, ribbed sails – were not an uncommon sight in

Queensland waters. They often sailed south with their cargoes of Chinese miners and goods for the Asian workers in Queensland's northern goldfields.

The curious spectators gathered on the *Osprey* could see the crew of the junk frantically rushing about on deck preparing to repel boarders. The match was an uneven one, as the French gun boat had the firepower to sit off at a safe distance and pulverise the Chinese junk into teak splinters.

But behind the French ship, came an even more deadly threat; boiling black clouds and roaring winds lashed the waters into huge, white-crested rolling waves. The storm was moving so fast that it would catch the French before they had time to manoeuvre for action.

Michael Duffy stood at the railing beside Luke Tracy. They had also surmised that the French gun boat was intending to intercept the junk. In the distance, they could see the white-jacketed French sailors man the deck gun with precise drill movements, while other sailors stood ready with carbines and cutlasses.

Mort ignored the unfolding drama and bawled orders to his crew to batten down hatches. As the crew galvanised into action, Michael noticed that the French boarding preparations had radically changed. The French captain was also anticipating a major battle with the Coral Sea's fury. Already his crew had abandoned their stations and Michael too ordered his men below.

~

At first the *Osprey* seemed to be dead in the water. Then her sails flapped and the barque rose with her stern out of the water. The billowing sails cracked as the giant waves rolled under her.

The storm hit with its full fury. The ship rose and lurched violently sideways and as she rose on the crests – and pitched into the deep troughs – the bushmen felt as helpless as prisoners under a sentence of death. It was the beginning of a long and terrifying night for them.

'What do you think that was all about up there?' Luke asked in an attempt to take his mind off the storm. Michael shook his head. It was certainly a puzzling situation. Why would a French naval vessel want to intercept a Chinese junk in Queensland waters?

In the days they had been together on the *Osprey* the two men had formed a friendship based on their common link with America. They had talked about the places and people they had encountered on their travels in the American West.

Michael had hoped to draw out the American prospector's particular interest in his sister Kate, and the opportunity had eventuated the previous evening when both men were alone on the upper deck of the *Osprey*.

'I get the impression,' Michael had said casually, 'that you got yourself into that scrap with that lawyer fellow over a matter concerning the honour of a young lady by the name of Kate O'Keefe.'

Luke did not reply immediately but gazed at the grey-green scrub that bordered white sandy beaches rising and falling off the port. Behind the beaches lay the relatively flat Cape country. 'I suppose you could say that,' he finally drawled, as he puffed on his pipe.

The grey smoke swirled away on the gentle evening sea breeze.

'Must be a pretty special lady for you to risk your life as you did,' Michael noted. 'That Darlington fellow could have killed you with his first shot.'

Luke fell for the carefully set trap. 'She is worth the risk and more,' he answered wistfully. 'Not much else worth dying for in my life anymore.'

'What about working for me,' Michael reminded him. 'You know there is a good chance that you could still get yourself killed. That would not be much good to the lady.'

'The money you are paying makes the risk worthwhile,' Luke replied sadly. 'I figured that after the job is done I could use the money to grubstake me for a prospecting expedition for Kate. And maybe then she would see that I'm serious about settling down in one place when I came back.'

'You fixing to ask the lady to marry you then?' Michael asked carefully.

'Something like that,' he answered. But in his heart Luke felt that something had gone terribly wrong. Events had conspired to separate him from her in a way she would not understand. A man's pride was something a woman did not understand, and the showdown with Darlington had been as inevitable as the sun rising each day.

Michael smiled and slapped Luke on the shoulder. 'The lady could do worse than you Mister Tracy,' he said with a chuckle.

~

On deck Mort fought the storm. No-one and nothing was about to take his ship from him. Chronically seasick bushmen huddled below the decks, where they cursed the ocean and all who sailed on her. The stench of their vomit made Michael feel decidedly queasy. He had travelled the Pacific before but never had he struck a storm of such intensity.

As he sat helplessly with his men he had a nagging thought about the stability of the bomb he had hidden at the ship's stern with the expedition's supplies. Horace had suggested that it be detonated off Somerset so that the *Osprey*'s lifeboats could be launched and rowed the short distance to the settlement.

Michael had formulated a plan to have all his men on the forward deck when the bomb went off. This would then give them the chance to get to the longboats, launch them, and row away from the sinking ship. His excuse to have his men assemble at the forward deck – as well as the barque's crew – would be for a shooting competition. The Winchester rifles would be used to fire at empty barrels they would toss into the sea. He had also planned to have the Baron attend with Karl Straub which would also place them forward of the explosion.

While he had been below decks stowing the bomb, Michael had ferreted through the stores Karl Straub had brought aboard, and found a theodolite in a lined case. A further search revealed charts and tables used by surveyors. He also found engineering manuals on specifications for establishing port facilities and a map of New Guinea with points marked on it, all of which gave credibility to Horace Brown's suspicions of an expedition to annex the southern side of the island.

A day out of Cooktown, the Baron confirmed the expedition's mission, when he summoned Michael to a meeting with himself and Karl Straub. Michael was briefed on his role: to use his men as a security force for Karl Straub and himself when they landed on the New Guinea coast. The Baron did not elaborate any further on the mission. It was not necessary for Michael or his men to know the purpose of the surveying that would be done.

But Michael already knew. The Germans were out to seize New Guinea before the British Foreign Office could react. Once annexed, Bismarck would have a strategic port as a direct threat to one of Britain's colonies – Queensland!

'Any chance of giving notice boss?' one of the bushmen groaned. 'Think I've had enough.' The bushman was the youngest of the men Michael had recruited. He had once served for a short time with the Native Mounted Police before resigning to go in search of gold on the Palmer. He was a pallid green under his tan and tried to make a joke of his request. But as a veteran of many wars Michael knew fear when he saw it.

'Only if I can come with you,' Michael replied with a reassuring grin to the young bushman who tried to return the grin, but suddenly doubled over and was violently sick.

'You think we will get out of this?' Luke asked quietly. Michael did not know how to answer him. The *Osprey* rolled and lunged at unnatural angles with her timbers creaking. It was as if the ship was groaning in protest at the unbearable fury of the storm. With each lurch, cursing bushmen were sent sprawling across the deck into each other. Some prayed quietly. Others simply sat stony faced and prepared themselves for the worst. Never had any of the bushmen felt as helpless as now. At least on land there was somewhere to escape. But at sea, in a ship being callously battered by nature, there was nowhere to run.

Lashed to the helm, Mort fought with the demons of the ocean for possession of his ship, as the great rolling waves of the Coral Sea crashed down on him. He responded with terrible oaths and curses against God. His body ached but he refused to relinquish control of the helm to any of the crew who tried to relieve him. Throughout the night he strained to listen, with fearful anticipation, for the terrible crunching shudder of the ship's keel grinding down on a coral reef. He knew his tough little barque could weather the storm but the reefs were the real threat.

Below decks Michael sat out the night watching over his men. As he thought about his situation he could not help but see the irony of the fact that at this moment his life was in the hands of the man he knew he must soon kill.

~

In and out of his fever, Wallarie occasionally opened his eyes, to stare at the distant horizon. A black beetle was crawling slowly towards him as he lay on his side staring at the thin line between sky and earth. A big, black beetle come to eat his flesh, when he passed into the Dreaming forever.

Soon, the blazing black ball would sink below the earth, and the cool night would come to take away his pain. His only regret was that he had not reached the lands of his ancestors. But had not his brother Tom Duffy died in lands foreign to him? Had he not died far from the green country he had always called his ancestral land?

Wallarie did not have the strength to chant a death song and closed his eyes. He would die quietly and the animals would feast on his flesh. For a brief moment he thought he could feel the earth tremble against his cheek. Then he heard words in a language he did not understand.

'Mein Gott! Was ist passiert?'

THIRTY-ONE

Sydney was enjoying a mild, pleasant day for early autumn. The skies were cloudless. The crisp, still air had only the slightest hint of winter. Granville White stared morosely across the garden to the harbour, wondering why he had been invited to afternoon tea by his distant mother in law. The serene weather had brought ships and boats of all varieties onto the water to sail and steam across its placid blue surface. On the furthermost tree-lined shores he could see smoke rising lazily from cottages and campfires hidden amongst the forests of eucalypts. Although the day had been pleasantly warm, the night promised to be chilly.

Granville ignored the frantic prattle of his two daughters pleading with their mother for a cream bun. She in turn chided the girls while they eyed the cakes with undisguised desire: they would have to wait until their grandmother joined them. Despite their innermost desires to cause havoc to the sweets, both girls were very well behaved, as would be expected of young ladies in a prim and proper society. Nevertheless, they exploded with childish delight when they saw their aunt Penny arrive. She was their favourite adult, because she spoilt them rotten with gifts whenever she returned from one of her many trips away from Sydney.

Granville frowned at the unexpected appearance of his sister. Penelope in turn was as equally surprised to see her brother. To receive an invitation to Enid's house was totally unexpected by all three.

Penelope greeted her brother coldly but spoke to Fiona with warmth as she fended off her two excited nieces. 'Betsy told me Enid will be arriving very soon. I wasn't informed that anyone else would be attending afternoon tea.'

Granville's face reflected his own puzzlement. 'All I was told at my office last week,' he said, 'was that it was extremely important that I should bring Fiona and the girls here today to have afternoon tea with her. She said that she wanted to discuss some important business matters before she left for England next month.'

The invitations were the first in years from Enid, who lived an almost hermit-like life in the rambling Macintosh mansion. Granville did see his mother-in-law from time to time at business meetings, held at the Macintosh offices in Sydney, but never at her home.

At first Fiona had refused to accompany

Granville to her mother's house. He had in turn pleaded with her to at least attend for appearance's sake – if nothing else. He also pointed out that their attendance was important from another point of consideration; Enid had seen very little of her granddaughters, and it was important that she have contact with them if they were to some day inherit the Macintosh estate.

Fiona had relented, yet was as confused as Granville and Penelope as to why her mother had suddenly decided to have them all share afternoon tea at her place. It was very odd indeed!

Granville had come to the conclusion that whatever she wanted to see them about had something to do with her rather mysterious forthcoming trip to England. He had seen the invoices pass through the company's office, with regard to closing down the house, and transferring her key staff to England. It was obvious that she was planning to be away for years. He was mystified as to why she should do this, when she had been so active in the management of the companies after the death of her husband.

As the chill of the early evening crept with the lengthening shadows across the lawns they waited patiently in silence. There was a tension about the affair that Penelope decided was intolerable. She did not wait for Enid to arrive before she ordered Betsy to fetch tea and coffee for them and started tucking into the sandwiches.

Her precedent was quickly followed by her nieces who were unleashed onto the sweet cakes with a long sigh of disapproval from their mother.

That's what the two little girls liked about Aunt Penny; she didn't worry about being polite all the time. She did what she wanted. They knew that Aunt Penny was somehow rather naughty for a grown-up, and they had both secretly agreed they were going to be just like her when they were young ladies.

'I'm rather glad you didn't wait for me,' Enid said as she swept into the garden. 'I must apologise for not being here to greet you when you arrived. But my carriage was held up in the traffic in George Street. There was rather a nasty collision between two wagons. I fear a man was killed in the accident.'

Dorothy and Helen stared at the boy who stood shyly beside their grandmother. He was tall and his clothes were plain. He was like no boy they had ever seen before.

Fiona also stared at the boy. He was remarkably good looking, with his thick and dark curly hair. She surmised the boy was a little older than her daughters, and wondered who he was and why he was with her mother. It was unlikely for her mother to have one of the servant's children accompany her to a family . . .

Fiona gasped with shock. 'Oh my God!' she said in a strangled voice. There was no mistaking the good looks of the boy and the way he proudly stood staring back at her. With the exception of the startling green eyes he was a younger Michael Duffy in every way.

Patrick saw the stricken expression on Fiona's face and wondered why the woman looked as if she had seen something terrible. He realised that his presence was causing the pretty lady some distress. But he was perplexed as to why this should be as he had never met her before.

He glanced sideways at Lady Enid who had a strange, fixed expression of savage satisfaction on her face. When he glanced at the faces of the other adults he noticed that they *all* had similar expressions of shock, except the two girls who stared at him with a mixture of curiosity and hostility. Boys were horrid creatures, and this one looked extra horrid, the girls silently agreed with each other.

It was fortunate for Fiona that she had been sitting down, otherwise she may have collapsed with the shock. Even now she was fighting to refrain from fainting. 'Michael!' The name escaped her lips with a soft hiss, breaking the stunned silence that had followed Enid's casual apology for her late attendance.

'No, not Michael,' Enid said quietly. 'I would like to introduce Master Patrick Duffy to you all. Patrick, meet your aunt Penelope, uncle Granville, your cousins Dorothy and Helen . . . and their mother, your aunt Fiona.'

Patrick smiled awkwardly at the family he had never known before. It was all very confusing, he thought. No-one had taken the time to explain just how all these people could be related to him.

'Dorothy, Helen, take Patrick,' Enid said quietly to the two little girls who stared at the tall young boy, 'and show him the garden. Don't go down to the water. And wipe the cream off your faces,' she added sternly.

The girls immediately obeyed and wiped away

the cream with linen napkins. Their interest was in the boy who was horrid – but interesting. If they took him away from the adults, he might be able to tell them about himself, and why his presence had caused the grown-ups to react as they had.

Patrick was reluctant to accompany the girls. The confusion around him had triggered his curiosity, especially as to why his presence seemed to cause grief to the beautiful woman with the eyes like his own. He felt a great pity for her seemingly limitless depth of grief. He could not bear to see it as it seemed to touch him in a way he could not understand. He wanted to ask questions but did not know where to start. Instead, he looked away and grudgingly let Helen take his hand to lead him away as she fired questions at him, without waiting for his answers.

'I cannot believe this!' Granville finally exploded when the three children were gone. 'I cannot believe you could be as evil as to do this to your own daughter!' His outrage was prompted less by any concern for his wife's feelings, as for the consequences to his own position in the Macintosh business empire. His devious mind had already extrapolated what the sudden appearance of the boy meant. Oh, he knew Enid too well and he knew what she was playing at! 'How could you bring the boy into Fiona's life after all these years? How could you when she had reconciled herself to his absence from her life?'

Fiona listened to her husband's words. She was not fooled by his feigned concern for *her* feelings.

A mother never reconciled herself with the loss of a baby – especially if she blamed herself for its possible death. Seeing her son for the first time in eleven years brought both extreme joy and sorrow. A joy that he was alive and a sorrow that she had lost all those years of being with him. A handsome young man, he was so very much like Michael as she imagined he would have been as a young boy. She felt Penelope's hands resting reassuringly on her shoulders. It only seemed natural that she would console her rather than Granville.

Enid took a seat, and listened patiently to Granville feign his righteous indignation. Now that the secret was out, Enid knew she was again in full control of all that would transpire in the Macintosh dynasty. She experienced some sympathy for her daughter's pain. But the sympathy was short lived when Enid remembered that her own daughter had taken sides with the man she knew beyond a doubt had organised to have David so vilely murdered. 'No matter what you think of my motives, Granville,' Enid replied when he had finished his tirade of sanctimonious outrage, 'Patrick is the rightful heir to the Macintosh estates unless Fiona produces you a son which I think is highly unlikely under the present circumstances.' She glared at her daughter and Penelope. 'God has yet to devise a way for two women to create life between them in ways that He has deemed natural between a man and a woman.'

Penelope's nails dug into Fiona's shoulders. The old bitch knew! Penelope was acutely aware that her aunt was staring accusingly at her.

'I have known for a long time,' Enid said with both bitterness and sadness. 'Oh, don't look so shocked. I think I could truly understand how such a thing could eventuate, knowing what I know of your husband Fiona. *And* knowing Penelope as I do.'

'You only *think* you know Aunt Enid,' Penelope retorted. 'I love Fiona, I always have. And I don't care if you think what happens between us is unnatural. Love has many forms. But I doubt that you would know *any* of the human forms of love, dear Aunt Enid.'

Enid smiled smugly at her niece's attempt to upset her. No, she was not about to allow any of them to upset her in her moment of victory. She had yet to complete the divisive thrust between the two women. 'I know you think Fiona loves you, as you say Penelope,' she replied bitterly. 'But I think the situation might change between you when my daughter hears what I have to propose.' Enid looked directly at her daughter. 'If you are prepared to give up this unnatural relationship you have with your cousin and also leave your husband to move back into my house, I will let you have Patrick.'

Fiona stared in horror at her mother. How dare she think that she could manipulate people's lives for the sake of her own twisted interests!

'You can think about what I have proposed Fiona,' Enid continued calmly. 'But I expect your answer very soon. At least before I take Patrick with me to England.'

'I think we should leave,' Granville said quietly. 'I think you have said enough Enid.' He turned to call

438

to his daughters but Penelope checked him with a raised hand. His sister had something important to announce.

Penelope did have something important to say. She realised that she could easily lose the one person she truly loved, as she differentiated her love for Fiona from the passing physical pleasure men provided her. 'I don't think Patrick is yours to have Aunt Enid,' she said with a quiet conviction. 'I think his *father* might have something to say about his son's future.'

'Michael Duffy is dead,' Granville sniffed contemptuously. But suddenly he felt a cold chill of fear. Michael Duffy was dead! He tried to console himself. Was not his death confirmed so many years past by the newspaper report?

Penelope turned to her brother. Ignorance was a blessing, and Granville's blissful ignorance was about to be shattered. 'Mister Duffy is far from dead,' she said quietly. 'As a matter of fact, he is alive, and working for my husband. He is currently in Cooktown and is not aware that he has a son . . . unless I have reason to tell him.'

Granville felt the chill turn to icy terror. If the Irishman was still alive, then he was in mortal danger. Duffy might come looking for him. 'You said Duffy is working for the Baron?' he queried his sister. 'From this, I presume you mean he is part of the *Osprey* expedition?' She nodded. By her acknowledgement she had sealed Duffy's fate, as far as he was concerned. Thank God for the telegraph! And thank the devil for the loyal services of Morrison Mort.

Granville was already mentally drafting the coded orders for the Irishman's demise.

'It *was* him!' Fiona said so softly that only Penelope caught her words. She answered with a gentle squeeze of Fiona's shoulder as she bent to whisper in her ear, 'We will talk of the matter later. This is not the place or time.' It was then that Fiona intuitively knew that her cousin had slept with Michael. How could she betray what they had between them?

It was Enid's turn to be shocked. In her carefully plotted plans she had not considered Patrick's father as a factor to be reckoned with. She had been sure he was dead – as had Granville. She had no doubt that if Michael Duffy knew he had a son, he would fight to keep him. Everything was crumbling around her. But she fought back desperately like a boxer with one good punch left. 'I daresay that the Baron would be horrified to learn that his wife is engaged in an unnatural relationship,' she said smugly.

'Oh, Manfred not only knows about Fiona and I, Aunt Enid,' Penelope smiled sweetly, 'he actually enjoys watching Fiona and I make love.' Her smile became a triumphant smirk as she witnessed the shock on her aunt's face.

Had her daughter sunk so far into the depths of depravity! Enid thought as her grand-daughters returned from the shoreline with Patrick in tow, both girls having decided that Patrick was not such a horrid boy after all.

When Granville scowled at him Patrick felt again the tension his presence seemed to cause. He was confused, and pretended not to notice the obvious expression of hate for him. Why would Uncle Granville hate him when they had only just met? He glanced across to Lady Enid for support and could see that she was upset. Patrick felt very protective towards the grand lady and sensed that Granville had upset her. He also knew that if the man did anything to hurt Lady Enid, he would use his fists to teach the surly man a lesson.

He instinctively moved to Lady Enid's side, and she felt a rush of love for the same boy she had once schemed to have disposed of. She had thought of him as nothing more than a social embarrassment to the Macintosh name. Now he was the only person present prepared to stand up for her.

She reached out to take Patrick's hand. He liked the soft touch of her hand, but wondered at the impulsive gesture of the woman who, up until now, he had thought was so aloof.

Fiona saw her mother's gesture and the way her son reacted to the woman's touch. I have lost you my son, she realised with unbearable pain and despair. Her son belonged to her mother, and nothing could ever change that so long as her mother had him with her in England.

Even if she conceded to her mother's wishes – to leave her husband and also Penelope – her mother was too strong for her. Just as she had dominated her life when she was young, she would dominate Patrick. Fiona did not need time to consider her mother's proposal. Penelope loved her. Nothing could change that and she would not give up that love. She would need precious time to win back her son. Now was not the time, nor the place, to show her hand.

Granville sat in his library through the silent hours of the night. He listened to the lazy ticking of the grandfather clock in the hallway and stared bleakly at the walls of the library festooned with Aboriginal artefacts. The wooden weapons had been a present from Sir Donald after a dispersal on Glen View in '62. His gaze settled on a long Aboriginal spear fixed above a narrow wooden hand shield.

Was there really a curse? he brooded. Whatever the answer, Granville knew one certainty: that his attempt to have the son of Michael Duffy eliminated had failed. That was a curse in its own right.

The following day, Granville carefully worded a telegram in a code. He would alert Mort that aboard his ship was a man who must be killed, no matter what it took.

Granville's veiled murderous words travelled over the long line of wires, and through relay stations to Cooktown, where the telegraph operator read the transcribed morse words of the telegram. The operator sighed and stared out his window at the driving rain. A check with the port authorities had confirmed that the *Osprey* had sailed days earlier. To all intents and purposes it was somewhere north in the heart of the storm that presently raged in the Coral Sea.

He folded the telegram and filed it before plumping himself at his desk, and pouring black coffee from a big pot that sat permanently on the little pot-bellied stove in the corner. He raised his mug in an ironic toast. 'To you lads,' he muttered, 'wherever you are on this godforsaken day. I hope you make it.' His words were swept away by the howling of the wind, and the pounding of the rain on the tin roof of his office. His only option was to transmit back down the line that delivery of the telegram was impossible.

THIRTY-TWO

Towards dawn the storm eased. From below decks the bushmen – weak from lack of sleep and stomachs emptied by vomiting – crept up onto the deck of the storm-battered barque.

They were stunned at the scene that met them. The *Osprey* had lost one of her masts and her decks looked as if a major battle had been fought over them, with the *Osprey* the loser. But despite her appearance, the *Osprey* was a winner. She was still afloat and had lost none of her crew. Even Michael gave tacit, grudging credit to the courageous efforts of the captain.

The Chinese junk had not fared as well. She was stuck firmly on the coral with her bottom torn away. Her decks were awash and as the observers on the *Osprey* watched, she keeled over as a big swell washed her from the reef. In a desperate search for anything loose to cling to, panicked survivors thrashed around in the water fighting each other.

'Not many going to make it,' Michael said without emotion. 'She hasn't launched any boats and there isn't enough debris in the water for them all to float on. Guess the sharks will have a feed soon enough.'

'You're wrong Mister O'Flynn,' Luke said, pointing towards the sinking junk. 'There's some kind of boat being launched now.' Michael stared across the oily waters. The occupants of a lifeboat appeared to be beating off the survivors in the water.

'Bastards!' the young bushman snarled as he joined the two men at the rail. 'Ought to give the yellow bastards a taste of their own medicine when they get here.'

Michael did not comment on the young man's expression of indignation. In his years of soldiering he had seen worse acts committed by Europeans. He merely shook his head and turned his attention to the French gun boat afloat in the distance. He could make out that she had fared badly in the storm. Missing a mast and her sails in tatters, she still had her auxiliary engine for power and as he watched, he could see a wispy streak of smoke rising from her single funnel. The French seemed to be turning about to navigate towards the junk.

Mort ignored the boat being rowed across from the stricken junk. In his opinion the survivors were Chinese and, as such, rated on a par with niggers.

His only concern was to make his ship seaworthy again. He barked orders to his crew, who reluctantly broke off watching the junk sink below the tropical waters to go about their duties.

Michael directed his men to help the crew. Sims accepted their offer and put the bushmen to work below decks baling sea water that had washed in through the hatches during the night. Michael was about to go below decks with his men when the Baron joined him.

'Mister O'Flynn, I have been discussing our position with the captain,' he said as he gripped the railing and watched the Chinese lifeboat drawing nearer. 'He feels – and I agree – that we must return to Cooktown for repairs. I want to assure you that you and your men will be paid out in full once we berth. It is not your fault that we are unable to continue with our mission. I am sure that after last night, your men will welcome your news.'

'You are very generous Baron,' Michael replied courteously. 'I will tell the men when they have completed their work for Captain Mort.'

'You will of course not divulge the destination of the *Osprey* to anyone Mister O'Flynn,' von Fellmann said, quietly fixing him with his piercing blue eyes.

'I have not told my men anything Baron. As you instructed at our first briefing.'

'Good!' von Fellmann replied. 'I had a friend once, Gustavus von Tempsky, who told me that there were men of honour, even amongst the Englishers he knew. Ach! But you would not know the Von, as the Englishers called him, would you Mister O'Flynn?'

Michael thought he saw the trace of a mocking smile. Was it coincidence that he should use von Tempsky's name in the conversation? 'No. I'm afraid I only knew of the man from what I have read of his exploits Baron,' he lied, boldly returning the piercing stare. 'But he sounded like a good commander.'

Von Fellmann nodded, and walked away leaving Michael elated that he did not have to sink the *Osprey*. Unhappily, however, the return to Cooktown would make it more difficult to kill Mort. He would need to re-evaluate his chances of killing Mort on land. At least then he might get the opportunity to personally confront the devil himself, and have the satisfaction of informing him why he was being executed.

He turned to gaze out to the reef where the Chinese junk had foundered. She was gone now. Her passing marked by a huddle of the tiny bobbing heads of survivors treading water, or clinging to floating debris. When the sharks found them they would be gone, unless they simply drowned as their strength gave out. The lifeboat was drawing closer. Michael could count five people. They all appeared to be Chinese and three of the men were armed with old-style muskets.

Mort was also watching their approach, but he had no interest in taking aboard the Chinese survivors. He turned his attention to the horizon off the starboard bow and noticed that the French ship was steaming towards them. Whatever had motivated the French to try and intercept the junk in the first place had not been lessened by the storm. They were coming at full steam towards the lifeboat, which, however, reached the *Osprey* before the French could reach them.

From their lifeboat, rising and falling on the swell beside the barque, the Chinese survivors pleaded to be taken aboard. Mort ignored their wails and pleas and prepared to issue orders for the Chinese to be fired on by his crew. He despatched two men below to break out the rifles in his armoury.

Michael immediately realised what the murderous captain was about to do. Luke had also realised what was about to occur and looked to Michael for direction. Their eyes met and in an instant the decision was made. Michael reached for the small Colt revolver in his jacket. Although the opportunity for a confrontation had come unexpectedly, he had the excuse to kill Mort – and he sensed that he had the loyalty of his bushmen to back him. But the reaction from Mort's crew was an unknown factor. They might stand and fight. Some of his bushmen might be killed, along with the Baron and Herr Straub. Was it worth their lives?

Michael felt his first rush of savage elation dissipate into an angry frustration. Above all else, the lives of the men he had recruited were entrusted into his hands. With a scowl he shook his head to warn Luke not to get involved. The murderous captain would have his way and there was nothing they could do for the moment. Luke turned away and spat his disgust at the feet of a sailor who had levelled his rifle on the terrified survivors. The bushmen, who had gathered on the deck, muttered angrily about bloody murder. Despite their dislike of Asians, they recognised the fellowship of helpless humans.

It was the Baron who unexpectedly stepped forward to intercede. Although he acknowledged the captain's right to make decisions concerning the sailing of the ship and the welfare of those aboard, he argued that the taking aboard of survivors was Mort's duty as captain. *Some rule of the sea . . .* he reminded Mort, who reluctantly conceded to the Prussian's arguments.

It did not pay to put the German offside at this stage, Mort brooded as von Fellmann walked away. He had not yet thought out a scheme to neutralise Lady Macintosh's plans to have him arrested when the expedition was officially over.

The *Osprey* crewmen reluctantly helped the Chinese clamber aboard the barque, surprised to see that one of the survivors was a beautiful young Chinese girl dressed in pants and a jacket in the same manner as the Chinese sailors. Her flawless skin was a perfect cream colour, in stark contrast to her jet black and waist-length hair. Her eyes were so dark that they were like black liquid pools, Michael thought. Although she was obviously frightened by the leering stares and comments of the sailors assisting her aboard, she refused to cower to them.

The crew quickly disarmed the Chinese and forced them to sit in a huddle on the deck. But the girl refused to join the huddled survivors cowering under the baleful stares of the sailors. She stood defiantly while the others squatted obediently. The tough *Osprey* crewmen were impressed with the young woman's dignity, and her choice to stand, rather than join the frightened survivors. Michael noticed that the girl did not have bound feet as was fashionable for Chinese women. She acted as if she were born to royalty, he thought, not with the servility of a peasant fresh out of a rice paddy. She was not only very beautiful but an interesting young woman.

'Anyone here speakee English?' Mort demanded as he glared at the frightened survivors. A squat, evil-looking man with a scarred face rose uncertainly from the group. 'I speakee English. Me captain of *White Lotus*. Me likee talk you captain boss. Me likee talk you away here,' the man said, as he took uncertain steps towards Mort.

'I will talk to you alone,' Mort growled to the Chinese captain. 'We will go below to my cabin.'

The Baron stood back with a smouldering cheroot between his lips. His attention was not on the Chinese captain but on the rapidly approaching French gun boat. What concern was the Chinese junk to the French that they should send one of their gun boats after her? He suspected that they were about to find out. As the French boat manoeuvred to draw alongside, he observed with a military man's eye, that the French were at action stations. This had not been the first time he had watched Frenchmen go to action stations – except that the last time, less than four years ago in Sedan, he had been a colonel in command of an elite Regiment of Uhlans, and it had been on land. 'I do not think you will have time to converse with the man Captain Mort,' von

Fellmann said quietly. The French ship was within a hundred yards of the *Osprey* with her deck gun manned and pointed directly at them. 'It appears that the French have business with us. Of an urgent nature.'

'Captain of the *Osprey*. I am Captain Dumas of the Imperial French Navy.' The heavily accented voice drifted across the water between the two ships. 'I am sending a boarding party over.'

The white-jacketed French sailors looked tired and worn from the effects of the storm. But despite their dishevelled appearance, they also appeared grim-faced, and determined to fight.

'I deny permission for you to board my ship,' Mort called through a conical loud hailer. 'I am a British ship and you have no authority to board.' His defiant reply seemed to cause a stir on the French gun boat. Her officers huddled on the bridge in an animated conversation.

Both the Baron and Mort had quickly reached a consensus. The French were to be denied whatever they were seeking. For the captain of the *Osprey*, his pride was at stake. No arrogant Froggie was about to board *his* ship. For the Baron, his Teutonic blood arrogantly detested the French whom he viewed as effeminate weaklings.

'You have aboard your ship, captain of the *Osprey*,' the voice came back from the French gun boat, 'property belonging to France. And if you do not allow me to take that property I will be forced to board you regardless of your wishes.'

The Baron turned to Michael and quickly issued

orders. Michael had his men hurriedly armed with the Winchester rifles broken out of the armoury below decks. He ordered his men into line and gave the order to present arms for action. Although the crews on both ships were dangerously exposed on the open decks, Michael fully realised that the French still outgunned the *Osprey.*

Captain Dumas of the French gun boat was impressed that the *Osprey* was not about to be boarded without a fight. He also fully realised that both sides were bound to take casualties in such an event. The bearded bushmen lining the British ship's deck appeared as if they were prepared to sell their lives to keep his sailors off British property. Bluff or no bluff, Dumas knew that the situation was at a stalemate. It was up to him to break it as he had thrown down the gauntlet.

Mort watched with rising apprehension as the crew on the French ship adjusted their deck gun to bear directly at the centre of his ship. He had a sick feeling that his bluff already had been called. But the *Osprey* flew the Union Jack, he thought desperately. And any attempt to seize her by force of arms could be construed as an act of war against Britain. He had calculated that the French captain was not about to risk a confrontation that could escalate into a war between the empires, especially when the French had taken a beating at the hands of the Germans only short years earlier.

It seemed that neither side intended to back down. The pride of two mighty nations was at stake in an obscure corner of the world. Michael stood beside his men who held their rifles levelled on the French sailors. 'When the shooting starts,' he said quietly, 'aim for the crew of the deck gun first.'

Michael had armed himself with a Colt revolver and bowie knife, both useful weapons for the close-quarter fighting of men in hand-to-hand combat on a deck. He glanced across at the Chinese girl, who was glaring defiantly at the French. He had a strong feeling that all this was about her.

After what seemed an eternity, a voice finally floated over the short space between the two ships. 'Captain of the *Osprey*. We will follow you to your nearest port. We will lodge a strong protest with your government as to your deliberate obstruction in the internal affairs of the French government. I am sure we will receive a sympathetic hearing from the Queensland government and you will bitterly regret your foolish actions here.' The French gun boat raised steam and drew away from the *Osprey*.

All on the barque waited tensely as the French pulled away. Was she pulling back – out of rifle range – to shell them? The thought was in all their minds. But the French took up a position off their stern and waited. The captain indeed intended to follow them, as he said he would.

When Mort was satisfied that the French weren't going to shell his ship, he gave the order for his crew to continue repairing the *Osprey*, while the Baron gave the order for Michael to stand down his men. Satisfied that his crew were carrying out their tasks, Mort took the Chinese captain below, with von Fellmann following them. They were no sooner out of sight when Michael was startled to hear the Chinese girl speak French. Although he did not understand the language, Luke Tracy did. He had spent a short time in New Orleans where he had discovered that he had a natural gift for acquiring languages. Although he was not fluent, and his knowledge rudimentary, he did have enough grasp of the language to understand her impassioned plea for help. And even as the girl pleaded for sanctuary – from both the French and the Chinese – Mort was learning from the captain of the junk just why the French had brought the two ships to the brink of a near international incident.

The Chinese captain, as Mort had guessed correctly, was a pirate who had been operating in the South China Sea. Mort took his sword from the wall of the cabin and held it at the Chinese captain's throat. The terrified man knew he was looking into the eyes of death. He quickly realised that lying was not an option with such a man and told them how he had captured the girl in a night raid against one of the small fishing villages on the Cochinese coast. The men who had formed her bodyguard had fought to the death defending her and their valiant but futile defence had aroused the pirate captain's suspicions concerning her status – a status confirmed by one of the badly wounded bodyguards who the pirates had slowly tortured by disembowelling. Hearing his agonised screams gave as much sadistic pleasure as the information he gave them in return for a quick and merciful death.

The pirate captain realised the monetary worth

of his prisoner, if she was to be returned to her aristocratic family. But first he had a mission to complete: to continue sailing south and eventually meet ashore with his tong leader currently somewhere on the Palmer goldfields. He had been sailing south when the French came after him. They had learned of the girl's kidnapping.

The Chinese captain revealed the identity of the girl he had brought aboard the *Osprey*. She was Dang Thi Hue, a member of a Chinese mandarin family from Cochin China. She had been very effective in organising armed resistance to the French colonial government in her region of the country. Mort and von Fellmann exchanged grim expressions. They had certainly got themselves tangled in French politics!

As the Chinese captain related in his broken English the story behind the French interest in the Cochinese girl, Mort was already formulating a plan towards his own ends. There was a deal to be struck with the pirate captain – but definitely not in the presence of the Baron. The pirate captain and the girl were the key to his future plans to destroy all those aboard who plotted to have him hanged.

'She has no value to us,' von Fellmann commented when the pirate captain finished talking. 'Better we let the French have her and avoid any embarrassing questions in Cooktown.'

'As captain of the *Osprey* I must remind you sir,' Mort replied stiffly, 'that I have final say in what happens to people aboard my ship.'

Von Fellmann was surprised at Mort's sudden and seemingly humane reaction. After all, he had not even wanted to have the junk survivors aboard in the first place. 'I will not argue with you Captain Mort,' he said, conceding to the captain's rights. 'This ship is under your command and I have always respected that. But I cannot see any purpose in keeping the girl.'

Mort did not have a plausible excuse for keeping the girl, but he would have to convince the Baron. 'I think we should take the survivors back to Cooktown,' he said. 'I feel the matter is best handled by the proper authorities there.' The Baron was puzzled but merely nodded.

Michael stared with some awe at the slight figure of the girl.

'It's hard to believe,' Luke grinned.

'From the actions of the Frenchies,' Michael replied, 'I think we have to believe her story. So that means you and I are addressing royalty, in a manner of speaking. None less than the daughter of a mandarin. And if what she promises is true, worth a mandarin's ransom. That's got to be the same as a king's ransom.'

'The trouble is I can't understand everything she is telling me,' Luke frowned. 'My French isn't as good as hers. It also seems she's not exactly Chinese.'

Michael was surprised at his statement. She looked Chinese enough to him and he glanced warily at the crew and his bushmen who gave no sign of having understood her French either. But the pirate captain was talking to Mort, and Michael was in no doubt that Mort was learning what they on the deck already knew.

The girl pleaded for sanctuary with the British government but Luke's French was not good enough to understand why she was in the village where she said she had been captured by the pirates. He did, however, get the impression that she was involved in some kind of resistance to the French.

Michael extrapolated from what Luke had learned that the French possibly wanted her as some kind of political prisoner, and that she must be more than just any kind of resistance fighter for the French to send a gun boat after her! The politics of far-off Cochin China were as remote to him as his knowledge of the moon. He was not exactly sure what the girl meant to his future plans. Horace Brown would know what to do, he thought, as he stared at the distant, monotonous grey scrub-line of the Cape. 'Tell the princess or whatever she is called in Cochin China that we will ensure she gets handed over to the British authorities as soon as we land,' he finally said.

Luke translated as best as he could and the girl seemed to understand. Tears of gratitude welled in her eyes. She spoke passionately, in her own language. Michael guessed she was thanking him and shrugged off her gratitude. The Chinese pirates huddled on the deck exchanged surly looks with each other. They also guessed what she had been saying to the barbarians.

Hue told Luke that they would be well rewarded for helping her return to her family. She could see honesty in the face of the big man with the eye patch. Surely this man was a leader of warriors!

Mort and the pirate captain returned to the deck. Woo addressed his crew huddled on the deck and their faces lit up with broad smiles of relief. But the girl was not smiling. She cast a desperate glance in Michael's direction before being segregated from the men on Mort's orders and hustled below decks by the first mate.

Michael guessed that she was being taken to Mort's cabin. There was little he could do for the moment for the girl. His priority still remained settling with Mort when they returned to Cooktown. The reward for the return of the Cochinese girl was another matter.

The *Osprey* sailed her way slowly south, at all times shadowed by the French warship. But Mort did not intend to return to Cooktown. He had struck a deal with the pirate captain, and had at his fingertips an unexpected but welcome present. The bomb that Michael had brought aboard had been found by the first mate whilst he had been carrying out a routine check of the stores below deck. The wooden crate containing it had split during the storm, exposing a large tin the size of a small suitcase.

Sims was puzzled at first when he had found the device. Then he noticed the uncoiled fuse trailing away and quickly realised what he was looking at. But how had it come to be on board – and why? Maybe the captain would know.

Mort discreetly followed Sims below, paling

considerably when he saw the bomb. He immediately assumed it had been planted on the Prussian Baron's orders. So, Lady Macintosh was capable of killing him if all else failed. If he had remained calm enough to consider the logical possibilities of the bomb being planted by the Baron however, he would have also rationalised that such an idea would have been counterproductive to the German's plans.

The acutely paranoid captain was not in any state of mind to make rational decisions. All he knew was that the Baron was under an obligation to Lady Macintosh. No doubt he planned to blow up the ship when they reached Cooktown. Lady Macintosh's hate was so great that she preferred his death rather than risk the vagaries of a jury. Ah, but the Baron was going to get a taste of his own medicine, Mort thought savagely. And so would the rest of the men who worked for him.

When night fell over the Coral Sea Mort changed course, skilfully navigating his ship dangerously close to the Queensland coast. The French captain was puzzled by the actions of his counterpart on the *Osprey*. To sail during a cloudy night inside the treacherous reefs were the actions of a madman. Was the captain attempting to shake him off? Well, it would not work.

He issued orders and the French gun boat altered course to dog the blackbirding barque. Both ships came so close to the shore that the sailors on the gun boat could smell the sulphur-smelling gases of the mangrove swamps, and sometimes hear the splashes of the big saltwater crocodiles taking to the water, disturbed by the presence of the two ships.

Captain Dumas decided to remain on his bridge during the night. On more than a few occasions he had questioned the sanity of steaming so close to this perilous shore and had seriously considered breaking off the escort. The crazy captain of the *Osprey* could sink his own ship! At least he would take the Cochinese girl down with him, and release him from his mission of neutralising her subversive activities against French interests in Cochin China.

He was about to give the order to steer a course away from the shore when the inky darkness of the tropical night was lit by a brilliant sheet of flame. Like a subject illuminated by the magnesium flash of a photographer's camera the *Osprey* and a nearby stretch of white beach stood in stark relief for just a second. Then the blast wave hit the French ship, like a giant door slamming, as the stern of the blackbirding barque disintegrated. The French sailors did not need to be ordered to action stations.

They tumbled from their hammocks, and were hardly on deck when they witnessed the once proud Macintosh ship roll over and sink. The feared predator of the South Seas had died a violent death befitting her infamous role.

When daylight came Captain Dumas and his crew were only able to find three exhausted survivors clinging to pieces of the ship's wreckage. The three men were hauled aboard the gun boat where they lay on the deck more dead than alive.

THIRTY-THREE

The toughest situation Daniel Duffy ever had to face did not involve the defence of acquitting some hopeless case facing the threat of the gallows. It involved his own nephew when he told him the truth concerning his parentage.

Patrick's face was expressionless as Daniel sat with him in the kitchen of the Erin Hotel, and explained the true relationship of each person he had met at Lady Enid's house. The only flicker of emotion occurred when Daniel explained who his real mother was. The boy had paled. He had opened his mouth as if to ask a question, but changed his mind and remained silent.

Daniel felt a sense of unease. It was as if the boy were bottling up a volcanic explosion of emotion. Patrick was very much like his father in so many ways.

'Is that all?' Patrick finally said when Daniel came

461

to the end of his narrative on the Macintosh and Duffy family lineages.

'Only if you do not have any questions Patrick,' Daniel said gently. 'And as far as we are concerned, the situation does not change how Colleen and I feel about you as our son.'

'Should I call you Uncle Daniel?' Patrick asked with a coldness that was clearly discernible in his voice.

Daniel felt his unease growing. 'If you wish,' he replied. 'If that will make you feel comfortable.'

'It will,' Patrick said, in a voice of a man much older than his years.

He is tough, Daniel thought, as he gazed at his nephew. He was standing defiantly alone against the world and its intrigues. Too tough for a boy his age.

'If that is all, Uncle Daniel,' Patrick said with finality, 'I would like to go outside on my own for a while.'

Daniel nodded and sensed that the boy had left his childhood behind. He was now a young man whether he liked it or not.

Max found Patrick sitting on a crate in the backyard of the hotel. He was staring with unseeing eyes at the rickety wooden fence. The big German sought a sturdy crate and sat down beside Patrick.

'Your father fought with your aunt Kate's husband right here in this backyard,' he said quietly in German. 'Your father beat Kevin O'Keefe in a fight that many men would have paid a lot of money to see.'

Patrick's knowledge of the language was good enough for him to understand what Max had said. But he did not reply, and continued to stare straight ahead with his chin in his hands, as if contemplating the structure of the wooden fence.

'Your uncle Kevin O'Keefe was always tipped as the better fighter, still your father beat him. But you are already a fighter as good as your father. Now you have to fight a different kind of fight. You have to fight with the pain of learning Martin is not your brother, Charmaine is not your sister, and your aunt Colleen is not your mother. Amongst you Irish I don't think that matters anyway. You are all Duffys and that counts for everything.'

Patrick turned to stare at Max. He struggled for the words. 'Why did my mother leave me?' he asked, the first crack in his resolute defence not to display unmanly emotion. Max saw the tears well in the corners of the boy's emerald-green eyes.

'I don't know,' he shrugged. 'Maybe she had her reasons.' He hesitated, then reached out impulsively to hold the boy in his bear-like arms. 'They would have to be damned good reasons,' he added, as he crushed the boy to his chest and felt his silent, racking sobs. He held Patrick until the sobbing ceased.

The boy sat silently, recovering from his unintended display of feelings. He felt foolish at revealing his weakness in front of the man he loved and admired. A tension crept between the two. 'What was my father like?' Patrick finally asked, and Max felt the tension dissipate. This was a question he could easily answer.

'Your father was a real man,' he said. 'All men respected him and he was kind to everyone. He would stand up for the family and his friends. And would have been a great painter if . . . ' Max trailed away as he remembered another young man, and another time when he had sat in the evenings, discussing the world, women and everything else.

For a moment Max felt overwhelmed by the realisation of his importance to the lives of Michael and now Patrick. The tough former sailor sniffed and turned away. He was embarrassed that Patrick might see his tears, the first in a long, long time.

When he was sufficiently recovered Max sighed and turned to face the young man. 'Michael Duffy,' Max continued, 'your father, would have been very proud of you, young Patrick. So you must remember always that you have his blood. You must never forget who you really are when Lady Macintosh takes you away to make you into a fine young English gentleman. Remember that you have the blood of your grandfather who fought at the Eureka Stockade, the man who saved my life when the redcoats tried to bayonet me.'

For a fleeting moment, Patrick remembered the shadow that had loomed out of the darkness in Fraser's paddock to snap the neck of the man who he now knew had intended to kill him. Having Uncle Max beside him now, he knew that the shadow which had killed so easily could not belong to him. But to want his arms reassuringly around him was something that only women craved. Now he was an adult such feelings were unmanly. Patrick rose from the crate. 'I think I should go inside now Uncle Max,' he said. 'Dinner is on the table.'

Max did not look at Patrick as he stood over him. 'Ja, you should,' he replied in English. 'They vill be expecting you.'

Max remained sitting in the yard as the sun fell below the tops of the tenement houses surrounding the hotel. Once Patrick was gone to England, would he have anything left to live for? He shrugged, and rose stiffly from the crate. Maybe one day Patrick's children . . .

The next day Patrick did not go to school – nor did he return home to the Erin. For two days he was missing. Daniel alerted the police to be on the look-out for him, whilst Bridget sat in her room wringing her hands and praying. When questioned young Martin mumbled that he did not know where Patrick was. Charmaine simply moped around the hotel. She missed the boy, who she still considered her brother, as no-one had explained Patrick's actual relationship to her. Not that it would have mattered anyway to the little girl who idolised her 'big brother'.

Having trouble coming to grips with all that he had learned about himself, Patrick had set out to walk across the city to seek answers from a woman he trusted. Red-eyed and grimy from sleeping in the streets, he stood before the gates of Lady Macintosh's grand house, and now wondered why he had come seeking answers. Was it that he sensed that she cared for him in some special way? That she had sought him out when his mother had ignored his existence all these years? But the most important question lying so heavily upon his eleven-year-old shoulders was why his mother rid herself of him.

Betsy the maid noticed the boy standing so forlornly at the gate. She informed Lady Macintosh who issued orders for him to be fetched to the house. Patrick watched suspiciously as a smiling man strolled down the long driveway. During these turbulent days intrigue and suspicion seemed to be all around him.

'Lady Enid is expecting you Master Duffy,' the manservant said kindly, and Patrick cautiously followed him to the house.

Enid had buttermilk and cakes sent up to the sombre library. For herself she had tea. Patrick sat silently in one of the big leather chairs, while Enid poured him a glass of buttermilk. 'I have been expecting you Patrick,' she said, passing him the rich milk drink. 'I suppose by now your uncle Daniel has told you the truth about who you are.'

Patrick did not answer but sipped at the milk. Except for a pie he had purchased he had eaten very little in the last forty-eight hours. Not that it mattered much. He had lost his normally healthy appetite in the past few days. Even so, he appreciated the milk.

'I think I understand your reluctance to speak,' Enid continued, sitting down beside him. 'And I believe you have come here to ask me questions that are of great importance to you. So do not be afraid to ask.'

Patrick stared at her and noticed how green her eyes were. It was a strange, comforting realisation that he had the same eyes as the woman who sat beside him. In her eyes he thought he saw a genuine warmth. 'Why did my mother . . . ?' he blurted, without being able to stop the most important question of his young life. But he was unable to think of the appropriate word to describe the terrible betrayal he felt.

'Why did your mother desert you?' Enid sighed. 'Because she did not want you,' she answered. 'I know that is a terrible thing for you to learn Patrick. But I must be honest with you if you are to learn to trust me. And I know this truth will cause you even greater pain.'

For just a brief moment, when she saw the agony in his face, she was tempted to tell the real story of his birth and subsequent adoption, albeit by Molly O'Rourke's machinations, rather than her original desire to have him disposed of at one of the infamous baby farms. But to tell him the truth would mean alienating him from her forever, and so this thought was quickly dismissed. Enid lived in a world of no compromises, and there would be no compromise in her struggle to bring down the men who had killed her beloved son David. She waited every day of her life for the news that Captain Mort was in chains. She knew that this would be the first step to exposing her son-in-law's complicity.

Even the boy who sat in the library with her was part of her grand plan to wrest power from Granville. But her determination was tempered by an unintentional and unforeseen element – she was genuinely learning to love Patrick. In accepting her feelings for the boy, she knew that it would tear her apart if he grew to hate her as the others of her family did. By accepting this, she knew the facts of eleven years earlier must be buried in a lie. 'Before you were born your mother met a man . . . ' Enid said.

'My father,' Patrick interjected quietly, and Enid realised by the tone of his voice that the young man must have strong feelings for him. Probably an admiration encouraged by the papist Irish Duffys, she thought, shrewdly realising that she should not appear to denigrate his memory.

'Yes, your father,' she continued. 'But your mother realised that she loved her cousin Granville even more. To marry him, she knew she could not have you in her life. So when you were born she had you sent away. She wanted to send you to an evil place where babies are killed. But I secretly issued orders to your mother's nanny to have you taken to your father's family.'

The expression of anguish on Patrick's face unsettled Enid. It was like some terrible force boiling up. At eleven years of age he was verging on manhood and such a force unleashed was almost too terrible to contemplate. Or was it? Was not the boy a Macintosh as much as a Duffy? Molly O'Rourke was long gone, Enid consoled herself, and was not in a position to contradict her untruthful version of events. The sooner they left New South Wales for England the better. 'I am sorry you had to learn at such a tender age,' Enid continued sympathetically, 'about how your mother felt about you when you were born. She was but a young and confused girl, madly in love with her cousin.'

'I hate her,' Patrick growled. His eyes burned with a fire that Enid had seen in her own daughter. It was the inherent Macintosh ruthlessness. 'I will go to her and tell her so to her face.'

'I think if you did,' Enid moved quickly, 'she would tell you that she had not really wanted to dispose of you. That you were always in her thoughts. She would even probably say that she still loves you. No . . . it would only hurt you even more to see your mother Patrick. Your uncle Daniel can tell you how years ago I sought you out when your mother did not care enough to do so. I think my actions speak stronger than any words she may utter.'

Patrick turned to his grandmother and stared into her face. He was too young to detect duplicity. The eyes that he looked into spoke only of concern for him. There was a plea for trust and he looked away.

'Would you like to stay with me until we sail?' Enid asked gently. 'I could have my carriage go to your uncle's hotel and my driver tell him that you are safe. He could arrange to pick up anything that you may require.'

Patrick turned to her. 'I would rather go home,' he said. 'They will be worried about me. I suppose I will be in trouble,' he sighed, and a slight twinkle came to his eyes as he added, 'but I don't think I will be in great trouble.'

Enid smiled. He had the intelligence to understand the nature of those who loved him, obviously a trait he had inherited from his father, a natural charm.

She suddenly remembered that the boy's father was still alive. It made her feel uneasy, with good reason. Should Michael Duffy ever learn that he had a son . . . She felt an involuntary shudder. That must never happen. The journey to England could not come fast enough for her. Patrick must be removed from Australia to sever any chance of that occurring. 'I will have my carriage return you to your uncle's place,' she said. 'But first, you must have something to eat with me, and we will talk about how exciting your life will be in England. You will have a rare opportunity to see all the great places of London. We will visit museums; I know you like museums. And you will attend one of the best schools in the empire.'

Patrick appeared to be listening to his grandmother's cheerful monologue. But he was not listening to her actual words. He was thinking about his mother. He hated her more than any person on earth and one day he would punish her for what he perceived as the greatest betrayal possible. But Lady Enid cared. And somehow she would be his means of punishing his mother in the future.

Enid watched from the window of the library as her carriage departed with Patrick. Her intuition told her that the boy was now hers. They were bound in a duplicitous betrayal. He, for a mother he believed had desired to dispose of him. And she, for the fact that her daughter had sided with the man who had conspired to have her beloved David murdered.

She turned away from the window and, staring at the spears and boomerangs mounted on the library wall, felt a touch of dread for all that had occurred in the library with the boy. She knew that her lies would compound in the years ahead. But her dread was also prompted by the irrational thought that somehow she and the Duffys were victims of an Aboriginal curse.

Dorothy was finally alone with her aunt Penelope. Penelope had planned it to be so, and towards that end had suggested to Fiona that the girls be brought over to her house by their nanny while she went on a shopping trip into Sydney. Later she could join them for afternoon tea.

Fiona had liked the idea. She always felt a strange kind of freedom when Granville was away on one of his many trips out of Sydney. And when she experienced that freedom inevitably she was in the mood to go shopping. The suggestion also meant a pleasant interlude for afternoon tea at Penelope's house at the end of her shopping spree.

Dorothy stood before her aunt and sensed by the grave expression on Penelope's face that she wanted to talk to her about something grown-up. 'Sit down on the couch beside me,' Penelope said, gently indicating the big sofa in her drawing room. 'You and I can have a little talk about some things.'

'Do you want to talk to Helen too?' Dorothy asked as she sat down beside her aunt.

'No darling,' Penelope said, and impulsively reached out to stroke her niece's long hair. 'Your sister can join us after we have talked together.'

Dorothy gazed up at her aunt with big grave eyes and wished that her younger sister was with her. But Penelope had organised for Helen to help the cook prepare scones for the afternoon tea. Prompted by her terrible nagging suspicion she had then lured Dorothy into the drawing room for a talk. Ever since she had first noticed the subtle changes in her favourite niece, Penelope had desperately tried to convince herself that it was not happening all over again. Dorothy was so like herself at the same age.

Dorothy sat patiently with her hands in her lap waiting for her aunt to speak. 'Darling,' Penelope said gently, 'does Papa do things with you that frighten you?'

The sudden, stricken expression that came over Dorothy's face caused Penelope to feel as if she had been stabbed in the stomach with a hot knife. 'No Aunt Penny,' Dorothy replied in a tight, frightened voice, 'Papa doesn't play . . . ' she hesitated, and fell into a frightened silence. She had almost told someone what Papa had said she must not.

'Doesn't play what?' Penelope asked quietly. 'Doesn't play games with you that frighten you very much?' The little girl stared wide-eyed at her aunt. Her bottom lip trembled, forewarning a flood of tears to come. Penelope felt the hot knife in her stomach twist and turn to a smouldering rage. So, her brother had found another victim for his nefarious evil.

'I cannot tell you any more Aunt Penny,' Dorothy said in a tiny voice. She stared down at her hands folded in her lap. 'Papa said I would be punished if I told anyone about . . .' The tears rolled in great wet droplets down her face and the sobbing came in great waves racking her little body. ' . . . He said he would send me away if I told anyone. And I would never see Helen or Mama ever again.'

Penelope drew her niece to her and held her against her breast. 'Hush darling,' she crooned as Dorothy sobbed uncontrollably. 'Aunt Penny won't tell anyone about what Papa does. Aunt Penny knows your pain and I promise you that your papa will not play his games with you ever again.'

Dorothy felt the soothing words wrap around her like a protective cloak. She could not have told anyone else in the whole wide world about Papa's secret – except Aunt Penny. Not even Mama. But Aunt Penny was kind and gentle. She was different.

For a long time Penelope held her niece. And as she held her, Penelope felt her rage boil to a point where even the hardest steel would melt and turn to vapour. He would pay, she thought, with a quiet and savage fury. Not only for what he had done to his own daughter, but for the continuing pain she still felt for her own lost childhood. Taking Fiona from her brother was not enough. There had to be more she could do to punish his insidious evil. A lot more – before he died and went to hell.

When Dorothy had cried until she could cry no more Penelope took her to her room and laid her down on her bed. She sat stroking her hair gently until the little girl fell asleep. Satisfied that Dorothy was resting, Penelope rose from the bed to go down to the kitchen. She had the conviction that there was one other who must know of her brother's evil – one whose silence had contributed to the terrible anguish in the life of the little girl.

Penelope found the cook, Helen and Miss Pitcher kneading the dough for the scones. They were sitting at the kitchen table laughing and young Helen had flour streaks on her face.

'Miss Pitcher,' Penelope said, 'may I have a word with you? In private?'

Gertrude Pitcher glanced up at Penelope and frowned. 'Certainly ma'am,' she replied apprehensively and rose to follow Penelope to the drawing room.

Penelope closed the door behind them and turned to face the stern nanny. Gertrude immediately felt her unexplainable apprehension turn to fear as she noticed the strangely dark expression on the Baroness's face.

'There is a grave matter I wish to speak to you about,' Penelope said, with the hint of a cold fire in her blue eyes. 'Concerning my niece Dorothy.'

'I'm sure I do not know what you mean,' the

nanny replied coldly, attempting to disguise her own rising fear. Had the damned girl talked, despite her father's threats?

'Dorothy has told me everything, including that you know what has been happening,' Penelope bluffed. She watched carefully for the flicker of guilt in the other woman's eyes. Miss Pitcher caught her breath and a trapped look flashed in her eyes. Penelope knew she was right. The woman had known of her brother's evil and yet had done nothing to stop it. She could guess just what means her brother had used to coerce the nanny into his conspiracy. 'How much did he pay you Miss Pitcher?' she asked, without giving the woman time to gather her thoughts. 'I said how much?'

'It wasn't the money,' Miss Pitcher whispered, as she stared down at the parquet floor.

'Threats then,' Penelope proposed harshly. 'Did my brother threaten violence against you?' Miss Pitcher nodded. She opened her mouth as if to say something but no words came. Instead, she stood and stared bleakly at the floor. Penelope realised that she would achieve more by adopting a sympathetic attitude. 'Sit down Miss Pitcher,' Penelope said gently. Gertrude reacted with a puzzled expression as she took a seat on one of the imported French chairs. 'I am not going to tell anyone of your part in my brother's evil,' Penelope continued. 'And for my silence on the matter you will do exactly as I tell you.'

'I fear that Mister White will find out that I have talked to you ma'am,' Miss Pitcher said, trembling. 'He is a dreadful man I greatly fear.'

'He is,' Penelope agreed. 'But you have more reason to fear me if you do not do what I command, Miss Pitcher. Believe me when I say that,' she added, fixing the frightened woman with her icy blue eyes.

'What is it that you require of me?' the nanny asked wearily. She was resigned to dealing with the Baroness who she sensed may indeed be more dangerous and devious than her depraved brother. The stern nanny had little respect for men, and was almost glad that she would no longer have to cooperate in the depraved activities of her employer. She had tried to pretend that nothing was happening. But the reality of the traumatised little girl after her visits to the library had worn her down. She knew herself that she would not be able to stay much longer under the Whites' roof.

'You will provide me with a full written account of all you know,' Penelope said. 'That account will be held by me. Also, you will give notice to Missus White without notifying her why, other than that you have better prospects elsewhere. She is not to know what her husband has been doing to her daughter. Do you understand what I am saying so far?'

Miss Pitcher nodded her head slightly. 'Good!' Penelope said. 'When you have done all I have requested you will go to a place for employment where I will be able to contact you should I need your corroboration on the account of my brother's evil activities. Oh, do not look startled Miss Pitcher. You will be safe. My brother will never know of your whereabouts. It just happens that I know a family in need of a nanny. I suspect that other than this lapse in your duties as regards the well-being of my nieces, you have provided an excellent service to them.'

Penelope could see tears welling in the stern woman's eyes. As she ducked her head and sniffed loudly, Penelope felt just a touch of pity for the woman's obvious distress. She knew that Granville would have coerced her with a combination of greed and fear.

'Baroness von Fellmann, I . . . ' Miss Pitcher was lost for words of gratitude for her apparently lenient treatment, considering the gravity of what had occurred whilst Dorothy had been in her care.

Disgusted, Penelope turned her back on the woman and walked to a window with a view of the lawns. It was still raining outside. Afternoon tea would be taken in this very same room with Fiona. It was strange how one place could suffer within its walls so many diverse emotions, Penelope thought, as she gazed out at the grey sleeting rain. When Fiona arrived she must feign cheerfulness. She did not want to alert her cousin to anything of what had transpired during the day.

She turned from the window to see the nanny standing forlornly. 'You may leave me now Miss Pitcher,' Penelope said tersely. 'I will expect your account to be clearly written and in my hand before you leave with Missus White this evening. You can go to my husband's library to carry out your task. You will find pen and paper on his desk. That is all.'

Miss Pitcher mumbled her gratitude and left the

room with her back bowed under the weight of her conscience. Penelope remained staring out at the rain. She was trembling. It was easy to make a threat, she realised grimly. But it was another thing to carry it out.

THIRTY-FOUR

Pastor Otto Werner and his wife Caroline were lost in the wilderness. It was to them as desolate as any place Moses had crossed in the great exodus from Egypt. Otto Werner was a man in his late thirties. Stolid, with a strong face graced by a bushy black beard to his chest, he wore a black suit and his once white shirt was stained by sweat to a dirty red colour. His wife was a contrast to her husband: fair and dainty. They were an odd couple, but shared a burning zeal to bring God's word not only to the impressive numbers of German settlers and miners in North Queensland, but also to the Children of Ham.

Off the ship from Hamburg they had purchased a horse and sulky, packed supplies and a crate of Bibles in both English and German, and set out from Cooktown to visit a devout German Lutheran grazier who they had been informed was considering setting aside land for a mission station.

But, being Europeans, they had presumed in their ignorance that the vast, semi-arid continent had landmarks which would show them the way. Furthermore, the sketchy map they had purchased in Cooktown did not indicate distances between the vaguely marked creeks and hills. This they discovered, as their supplies dwindled and the landmarks ran out. Soon enough they faced a flat, endless horizon and realised that they had passed the point of no return on their lonely trek south west. But despair was not an emotion Otto entertained. All adversity was merely a test from God, of the strength of his faith.

The discovery of the wounded Aboriginal who spoke a rough form of English was perceived by the Lutheran minister as a sign from God. His wife was not so sure. A request for tobacco from the wild-looking heathen were the first words he uttered in their meeting in the wilderness, a request far from Godly, in her opinion.

With his big, battered leather-bound Bible in his hand, Otto knelt beside Wallarie. 'God of my fathers,' he intoned in a booming voice, 'thank You for sending us Your messenger to guide us out of the wilderness.'

Caroline glanced at her husband from the corner of her eye. She was more practical than he in the ways of life and wondered how this badly-wounded native could help them find the Schmidt farm. 'And now Lord guide my hand so that I may heal this poor heathen's body and save his soul from eternal damnation.'

Wallarie listened to the strangely guttural words being said over him. He wondered if this man were some kind of magic man. As weak as he was Wallarie still checked for any sign of a weapon, and when he could not detect a pistol or rifle, felt a little more reassured that the strange man in black meant him no harm.

'Wife,' Otto commanded, 'fetch me the medicine chest from the sulky.' Caroline did so as the missionary examined the badly infected bullet wound. It had swelled into an ugly dark lump, hot to touch.

She returned with a small wooden box and knelt beside her husband. 'Be careful my husband,' she said quietly. 'He has weapons with him.'

Otto gave the spears and war clubs beside Wallarie a scornful look. 'He will be dead if I don't help him,' he replied. 'I think the bullet is lodged in the muscle and I will have to get it out to relieve the pressure.' He riffled through his medicine chest to produce a scalpel and a pair of forceps. A year at Heidelberg University medical school had not been entirely wasted. 'This vill hurt my friend,' he said in English. 'But I vill not hurt you more than I must. Do you understand?'

'Yeah boss,' Wallarie croaked, and tried to grin. He knew just what the man was going to do. He had once helped Tom remove a spray of shotgun pellets from his back when a squatter had resisted their attempts to steal his horse. The evil magic of the bullets was greater the longer they were in the body. 'You cut 'im this blackfella good.'

Otto nodded and proceeded to cut into the flesh.

A steady stream of yellow-green pus burst from the lump, followed by a stream of dark blood. For Wallarie the pain was beyond even the initial impact of the Snider bullet. He tried to spring to his feet, but a powerful blow from the man of God's fist laid him out, and for the rest of the operation Wallarie was blissfully unconscious.

Grunting and sweating, Otto probed for the bullet while his wife hovered nearby with the forceps, blanching at the sight of the open wound. Wallarie was coming around as Otto clamped the lead projectile with the forceps. He paused and steadied himself for the final tug at the bullet which was stubbornly clamped in the muscle. Wallarie came out of his unconscious state as the bullet came out of him, vaguely aware of the bearded face grinning at him. Otto held the misshapen projectile before his eyes. 'I think he will live,' Otto said to his wife. 'I have read that these people have an unusually strong constitution in such matters.'

Caroline frowned. She could not understand why they should have stopped their journey to assist an Aboriginal heathen when they were so desperately close to death themselves. Another day and their water would run out.

The missionaries set up camp a short distance from where Wallarie lay under the shade of a small bush. Otto had bandaged the wound with a liberal application of stinging antiseptics. Wallarie had flinched but accepted the doctoring. He sensed that the strange man in black had a magic not unlike that of the big Irishman Patrick Duffy who had helped save his life so many years earlier when Mort had shot him during the Glen View dispersal. Otto's gruff words had the same soothing effect as those of the Irish bullocky.

'I will take him water,' Otto said to his wife who was unharnessing their horse from the shafts of the sulky. 'He will need it if he is to last the night.'

Caroline bit her lip. She wanted to point out that the water was the last of their supply, but fought her natural response in favour of her husband's decision. He was a good man, whose faith in the Lord was very rarely disappointed, and she prayed silently that he was right this time. If not, then they would most probably be dead within days.

Otto bent to Wallarie and helped him so he could sip the water from the canteen. When he had finished drinking, Wallarie lay back and fell into a deep sleep. The loss of blood had drained him of strength and left him feverish.

When Otto was satisfied that his patient was resting, he rose and returned to the campsite, where a blackened pot of coffee steamed over a small fire. Caroline poured a cup and passed it to her husband. 'We only have enough water for one more pot,' she said quietly. 'Not even enough for our horse tomorrow.'

Otto squatted by the fire and gazed out at the sun sinking below the flat horizon. 'Have you noticed how beautiful the sunsets are in this country?' he said, as if ignoring his wife's slightly accusing statement. 'It must have been like this when God created the earth.' Caroline did not comment, but continued to busy herself around the fire preparing the evening meal. 'In Berlin,' he continued, 'we would be shivering with the cold and praying for the warmth of summer.'

'Instead we die of the terrible heat out here,' Caroline replied bitterly. 'And the dreadful scourge of flies.'

'I thought that you must have lost your tongue wife,' Otto said with a touch of mirth. 'I thought that it had dried up and fallen out.'

Caroline looked up from her work and into the dark eyes of her husband. She saw the humour, and a slow smile spread across her face. 'I am sorry my husband,' she said. 'I fear my faith is not as strong as yours. I fear that . . . ' her words faltered as she touched the edge of a great concern.

'Fear what my wife?' he asked gently.

'It is nothing,' she said, and continued with preparing the meal.

'Fear that we may die out here in God's wilderness,' he said. She glanced up at him with just the hint of tears. He saw her fear and placed his arms around her. She wanted to cry, but knew that if she did, she would only cause her husband to feel despair. Her quiet strength had always supported her idealistic husband in his ventures since he had joined the Lutheran ministry. To cry now would strip him of confidence in his faith. 'God will find His way to provide for us,' he said tenderly as he held his wife. 'Just as He did for the Chosen People on the Exodus. Just as He does when He brings us the cool evenings out

484

here to take away the terrible heat of the day from our lives. And now He has sent us the Aboriginal man as our dark angel to guide us to the Schmidt farm. I know that the Lord will always be with us in our mission to bring light to this new country.'

Caroline gently pushed her husband at arm's length. 'You are right Otto,' she said with the faintest of smiles. 'God has not forsaken us.'

'You will see,' he said, beaming her the brightest of smiles. 'His will be done.'

Caroline disengaged herself from her husband's arms and went about serving the meal.

That night, Caroline lay on her back and gazed at the spectacular canopy of shimmering southern stars. Beside her, Otto snored loudly, blissfully confident in the Lord's providence. She could not sleep. Her faith was weak and she wondered at God's cruel sense of humour in sending them a badly wounded heathen whose only concern was for tobacco and who drank the last of their reserve of water.

She longed for white fields of snow and the pungent smell of the dark pine trees of Germany. This land was so alien with its harsh, ugly landscapes of grey scrub and dry red earth. But, as she gazed up at the Milky Way, she noticed the constellation of the Southern Cross and felt a strange peace, as if she were seeing for the very first time God's sign of hope. Now, if only the black heathen lived, and Otto's faith in Him was rewarded, they would live to carry out her husband's ministry.

A short distance away Wallarie stirred in his fevered sleep. A voice was calling to him from a place beyond the living world. It was Tom Duffy! He needed Wallarie to return to the dark forests of the dreaded northern warriors.

Wallarie groaned his protest. It was not possible, he responded. He did not have the strength to do so. And besides, the journey was fraught with danger from the armed prospectors. Had he not already felt the sting of their bullets? But Tom was calling to him with the voice of the White Warrior spirit. He must leave as soon as he could and travel north. For there a great event would take place. An event that would still the Nerambura's cry for vengeance.

When the morning came to the plains Wallarie still lay in his fevered world. Otto tended to him, as the sun rose to a pinpoint of biting heat, scorching the earth below. He changed the bandages whilst Caroline looked on with a worried frown. 'I think the Lord has willed that the heathen depart this world,' she said over her husband's shoulder. 'He does not appear to be recovering.'

'He sleeps,' her husband grunted. 'It is a good sign. These people have a reputation for being able to suffer wounds that might kill a European.'

Caroline turned and walked back to their horse. Its head lolled and it did not appear to notice her presence. 'I do not think our horse will last the day without water,' she said when Otto joined her. 'We are down to our last cup, and unless we are found very soon, we will be joining the heathen.'

Otto gazed at the sweeping panorama of flat plains dotted with clumps of spindly trees that seemed to dance in the heat haze above the earth, and knew that his faith was being tested by the God of the Old Testament. 'God has sent us the black man,' he said simply. 'He will save us.'

'God helps those who help themselves,' his wife retorted, with an edge of frustration for her idealistic husband's optimism. 'I think we should attempt to travel further west. Surely we must find a river or a stream soon.'

'We cannot,' Otto replied quietly. 'To travel with no reserve of water would certainly kill the horse and most probably us as well.'

Caroline shook her head angrily. Inactivity was not something she perceived as an option. 'So we stay and wait for providence to save us,' she said with a bitter smile. 'But I will accept God's will my husband,' she added, 'so long as you do.'

Otto glanced at his wife and realised why he had grown to love the once flighty golden-haired girl from Brandenburg. She had been an unlikely catch for a man devoted to his ministry, a young woman who had given up a whirl of parties and balls to join him in a life devoid of luxury. But she had and now they faced possible death in a harsh land thousands of miles from their home. The flighty girl had matured, possessing a courage greater than his own, he admitted to himself. 'Have faith my beautiful wife,' he said gently, as he reached for her hand. 'God loves us and I love you.'

Caroline felt the tears well up in her eyes. Otto was not a man to express his love very often. He was a taciturn man, except when he preached to his congregations. He had been so different from other men she had known: quiet, strong and intelligent, a man whose charisma she often felt should have been turned to politics or business. 'I have faith in you Otto,' she said as she took his hand. She did not mention God.

They spent the day in the shade of the sulky. Otto read silently from his Bible whilst Caroline occupied herself sewing. The day droned with a silence broken only by the screech of an eagle and the distant cawing of crows.

At sunset the horse lay down and refused to rise. Death was near. Otto gazed sadly across at Wallarie who had not moved all day. Was it that God had deserted them? Was it that he was a hopeless dreamer as Caroline's father had once accused him?

The night once again came to blanket them with its crystalline spread of tiny white lights. Otto held his wife in his arms and realised with savage self-recrimination that he had brought her to the point of a slow and terrible death from thirst. She was weak, and her skin felt hot and dry, but she had not complained. He knew that water was all she now craved. She had retreated to an imaginary world of icy waterfalls and clear-running streams of abundant water. He too felt the thirst but had to remain strong for his wife. As a last resort, he would put the horse out of its misery and they could drink its blood. It was not an option he wanted to consider, but it was all they had left.

Sleep came fitfully to Otto. When he woke in the morning, he gazed through rheumy eyes, to where the black man was lying under the bush. He was gone! Otto jerked fully awake and cast about the plain for a sign of the Aboriginal warrior.

Beside him Caroline stirred. 'What is it Otto?' she asked, rubbing her eyes. 'You seem agitated.'

'He has gone,' Otto replied in a surprised voice. 'He must have gone during the night.'

Caroline sat up and attempted to brush down her long skirt, a feminine gesture strangely out of place considering their situation. 'It was God's will,' she said in a hollow voice. 'He is a child of this land and we could not have expected him to understand our need.'

Otto nodded and stared blankly at the rising ball of fire on the eastern horizon. In the long days they had travelled south west, they had not sighted a fellow European. How long would it be before their bones would be found for a Christian burial?

He staggered to his feet, and started walking uncertainly towards the horse which was breathing in ragged snorts as it lay on its side. He paused. Something was moving like a dot across the plain. He shaded his eyes and peered at the object which slowly took on a human shape. 'Caroline!' he shouted. 'He returns!'

Within minutes, Wallarie stood grinning before the missionaries, with canteens full of water dangling from his shoulder. 'I get water,' he said simply. 'You drink.'

It took only half a day for Wallarie and the Werners to reach the tiny bark hut Otto had referred to as Schmidt's farm. Ironically the missionaries had only been a half a day from the creek that held the muddy pools of precious water. Wallarie had picked up the signs of whitefella habitation – the fading prints of cattle, horses and boots – when he had gone with the Werners' canteens.

The sulky jangled into the dusty clearing that served as a front yard. Adjacent to the single-room bark hut, were the termite-infested rails of the stockyards, long fallen into disrepair. The place was eerily silent and the front door banged on its hinges when a gentle breeze stirred the gritty air. The Werners sat on the seat of the sulky and gazed around the deserted yard.

'This could not be the place,' Caroline said. 'It does not look like anyone has lived here for a long time.'

Otto leapt down from the sulky and strode across to the hut. Wallarie hung back. He had an uneasy feeling about the place and fingered his spears nervously. It was a place of ghosts.

The German missionary disappeared inside the hut and in a brief moment reappeared holding a book in his hand. 'It is Herr Schmidt's Bible,' he said, holding up the book. 'But it appears that he has not been here for some time.'

'Do you think something has happened to Herr Schmidt?' Caroline asked, as her husband helped her down from the sulky.

'That is a possibility,' he replied with a frown. 'Or he may have just gone somewhere else.'

'He would not have left his Bible,' Caroline said quietly.

'You are right my wife,' Otto nodded.

Wallarie watched the two conversing in the language he did not understand. His keen eyes surveyed the area looking for signs. But whatever signs might have existed were long gone. All he sensed was that death owned the place they had come to. He could see the deep worry written in the missionaries' faces. 'Whitefella go away,' he said.

The Werners turned to him. 'Vot do you mean?' Otto asked. 'Vot you mean go avay?'

Wallarie shrugged and squatted. His explanation was all the reassurance the white man and his woman needed. It was the way of the land. Walkabout, the whitefellas called it. 'Go away,' he repeated, and waited to see what would happen next.

'I do not know your name,' Otto said to Wallarie. 'You have saved our lives and yet I do not know your name.'

Wallarie looked up at the big German standing over him. 'Danny Boy,' he replied. 'Whitefella call me Danny Boy.'

Otto smiled. 'Thank you *Herr* Danny Boy,' he said. 'We owe you a great debt. I think the Lord sent you to us and I hope you vill remain to be the first of our flock.'

491

Wallarie stared at the missionary. He had lied about his name. He knew that the Native Mounted Police had posted a reward for his capture. He had learned much about the European way from Tom Duffy and the name Danny Boy came easily to him.

He thought the offer to remain with the kindly whitefella and his missus had great merit. He was in lands where few would know of Wallarie the Nerambura warrior, and so he could stay legitimately in the care of this powerful spirit man. The bullet wound had not yet healed and the pain was still with him. He would stay and help the white man until he was better, then he would make his trek north for the sake of the spirit warrior. 'I not stay,' he finally answered.

A frown clouded Otto's face. He reached out with his hand to assist the warrior to his feet, and Wallarie had a vague recollection of another time, when another white man had clasped his hand in the same manner. How could he tell the spirit man that the voices called to him to return to the dark forests of the dreaded northern warriors. The white man could not understand that the voices had become stronger as his body healed.

'Mebbe I come back one day,' Wallarie said, letting go Otto's hand. 'Mebbe help you and the white missus.'

'Mein friend you vill alvays be velcome,' Otto said sadly. 'It might be that you have a mission from God to be elsevhere.'

Wallarie did not know if he had a mission from God. All he knew was that he must travel as fast as he could to the humid and wet forests of the north. For there he was needed for a purpose, one that would be revealed by the spirits of his ancestors, when they deemed so.

The Werners watched the tall Aboriginal walk away, trailing his long spears. Wallarie broke into a loping trot. He felt the pain of his wound but the need to return overcame all physical sensation. Before sunset he would be well north of the Schmidt farm.

They watched until the heat haze swallowed him from their sight. With a long, drawn-out sigh Otto turned to gaze at the desolate, silent lands that seemed to go on forever. 'This is where we will establish our mission,' he said softly. He could see Caroline's troubled thoughts etched in the lines of her face. 'God gave us one of His lost souls to guide us here. I am sure that He will not desert us now.'

THIRTY-FIVE

The arrangements had been made and Patrick was taken to Lady Enid Macintosh's house. Duly prepared in a new set of clothes, he found himself beside his grandmother in a carriage driving into the city for a meeting.

Enid had noticed the young man's silence. She said little herself except for perfunctory words about his health and how manly he looked in his tailored suit and his replies in turn were short but polite.

When they reached the head office of the Macintosh enterprises in the city Patrick followed his grandmother inside. He was suitably impressed by the sombre building of granite facings and heavy timber doors. Even at eleven years of age he was aware of the power of money. People obeyed his grandmother when she told them to do something and she owned everything desirable in the world, like all the books in the library.

'We are going to meet some important men,' Enid said quietly, as they were escorted by a smartly dressed doorman up a broad flight of marble stairs. 'You will not say anything unless I tell you to do so. If you are asked questions by any of the men, I will expect you to conduct yourself as the young gentleman you are.'

Patrick listened carefully to his grandmother's orders and nodded. She smiled quickly at his response as they arrived at an important-looking door on which the doorman knocked before opening. Enid stepped inside. Patrick followed, filled with curiosity. He was assailed by the heavy scent of cigar smoke mixed with leather, and sensed something very important was happening – and that he was very much a part of it.

'Gentlemen,' McHugh said in a commanding voice. There was a rustling scrape of chairs in the softly lit room as ten men pushed back their chairs from a huge table. 'Lady Macintosh,' he formally announced.

The men nodded and Enid accepted McHugh's hand. Patrick only recognised one man in the room and shuddered when he felt the eyes of Granville White glaring at him with undisguised hatred.

'Lady Macintosh,' McHugh said warmly as he ushered her to a chair at the table. 'The directors are all here as you requested.' Enid smiled, and Patrick followed to stand behind her chair once she was seated.

'With all due respect Lady Macintosh,' Granville said, with undisguised animosity in his voice, 'this is no place for *that* boy to be.'

'It is if he is to one day run the Macintosh companies, Mister White,' she said. 'Gentlemen,' she continued, as the men took their places at the table, 'I would like to introduce to you my grandson, Master Patrick Duffy.'

Not a word was said. The stunned silence said it all. Without a word of apology for withdrawing, Granville stormed from the room.

McHugh smiled. The young man standing behind Lady Enid Macintosh reminded him of a young prince in waiting at a royal court. He certainly was impressive, with his fine, aristocratic bearing and dark good looks. A man born to rule the Macintosh financial empire.

For a moment their eyes locked and McHugh saw an open frankness in the boy's expression. There was nothing servile about him and yes, a sense of willingness to help those in need. As for which side of the blanket the boy was born, that mattered little. All that counted in inheritance was the right blood line. 'I would personally like to extend my good wishes to yourself and your grandson Lady Macintosh,' McHugh said with a genuine smile. A mutter of 'hear, hear' rolled around the room.

Granville was suffering an impotence he had not experienced since the night all those years earlier he found his wife in bed with his sister Penelope.

He stood in the foyer of the Macintosh building shaking with rage. The boy was still alive, as was his father. Now all hope of inheriting the sprawling

Macintosh enterprises was wrenched from him forever – unless something unfortunate occurred to Fiona's bastard son. He thrust his trembling hands in his trouser pockets. No, he was not beaten. Death can come in many forms.

'Would you be wanting your carriage Mister White?'

Granville did not hear his question. Only the sound of his voice. 'What!' he snapped irritably.

'I said would you be wanting me to fetch your carriage Mister White?'

'Yes,' Granville snarled. 'Immediately.'

The doorman hurried away leaving Granville alone to smoulder. Slowly he brought his feelings under control and focused his thoughts on giving himself time to consider the future. What he needed was a physical release – and he knew just how he would achieve that. Money was power and power was the ability to indulge in any depravity he desired. He knew exactly what he would do. Already he was experiencing the thrill of lashing the young girl's buttocks with a leather strap. She would cry for mercy and beg him to ravish her.

Granville had his carriage take him to his Glebe tenements where a former Rocks thug greeted his boss with deferential respect. He listened attentively as Granville issued his order for Mary to be brought to him and sauntered away to find the young girl.

Granville went to the room set aside for his private pleasures. He took off his coat and sat down on the bed. Inflicting pain on the innocent felt good, he reflected as he waited for the girl to join him. But his reverie was disrupted by the sound of raised voices outside the room and he was stunned to hear his sister's voice raised in anger.

The door crashed open and Penelope appeared in the doorway, the thug hovering uncertainly behind her. 'I tried to explain to the Baroness,' he mumbled apologetically, 'that she shouldn't disturb you Mister White. But she insisted.'

Granville stared at his sister. 'What are you doing here?' he asked as Penelope stepped inside the room.

'I chose to see you here, dear brother,' she replied icily, 'because I wanted you to know that I know everything you think I don't. Including this place.'

Granville glanced across her shoulder and waved the doorman away. Whatever the reason his sister had chosen to visit him in Glebe, it was not for general knowledge. 'My day has not gone well,' he said wearily as he slumped back on the bed. 'So state your business and leave.'

'I suspect that before I leave,' Penelope said, staring down at her brother, 'your day will be even worse.'

Granville looked sharply at her. 'What do you mean?'

With a touch of menace he rose from the bed. Not intimidated, Penelope stood her ground. 'I know what you have been doing to your daughter,' she stated bluntly. 'And I have come to tell you that you will never touch her again so long as I am alive or so help me God I will destroy you. You will never receive that knighthood you so much desire. Nor will the government submit your name for the honour should they learn of this place here and your ownership of it.'

For a moment Granville's eyes glazed and his face reddened. With a raised hand he took a couple of steps towards his sister. Penelope did not flinch. 'I will thrash you to within an inch of your life,' he raged, 'for the lie you bring to me.'

'I would not do that Granville,' Penelope replied calmly, fixing him with her blue eyes. 'Or my husband will kill you as easily as he has killed many men in war.' Granville checked himself and stumbled backwards to the bed. He knew his sister meant every word. 'I have a witness in Miss Pitcher,' Penelope continued. 'She is prepared to swear that you have been making improper advances towards Dorothy during Fiona's absences.'

'Miss Pitcher,' Granville blinked. 'Miss Pitcher has left my employ.'

'I know,' Penelope said with a faint smile. 'I told her to. And don't even consider trying to find her. She is under my protection. You see dear brother, you are not the only one who can frighten people. It seems you still continue to underestimate the power of a woman. Just as you underestimated Lady Enid.'

'You were at the office today?' Granville asked suspiciously.

'Yes,' Penelope answered. 'And Hobbs informed me that you left a meeting when Aunt Enid introduced young Patrick to the board members of the company. It appears that his acceptance is inevitable and I can sympathise that under the circumstances you have not had a good day.'

'Only if the bastard lives long enough to turn twenty-one,' Granville snarled.

'You will not even consider anything untoward happening to Fiona's son,' Penelope responded with savage determination. 'I may not be able to prove your complicity in David's death but I do remember your link with Jack Horton who you sent to kill Michael Duffy. And now that we both know Michael is still alive, I am sure that it would not be difficult to relay what I know to him. Somehow, I doubt that you would want that. From what I know of Michael Duffy, he is an extremely dangerous man who, inadvertently, you helped to create. In a sense, you created the very rod for your own back dear brother, and now must live with it. I will bid you a good day Granville,' Penelope concluded, as she turned to leave the room. 'I feel that enough has been said.'

Granville glared at his sister with undisguised hatred. It was a sorry history repeating itself, he thought. Like some ancient Aboriginal curse . . .

Penelope settled back in her carriage and reflected on her impulsive gesture to protect the son of Fiona Macintosh and Michael Duffy. No, it was not an impulsive gesture, she reflected as the carriage pulled away from the tenements of Glebe. It was the natural reaction of any mother protecting her young . . . or the young of one she loved.

THIRTY-SIX

'They took us by surprise,' Michael said as he slumped into a cane chair on the hotel verandah. Horace Brown sat with his fingers entwined on his ample stomach listening attentively to the Irishman relate the events that had led to the sinking of the *Osprey*. 'I was asleep,' Michael continued, 'when the first mate woke me to say that Mort wanted to see me in his cabin. I didn't think much of it. I wasn't even surprised to see the Baron with Mort. But what came next took me by complete surprise. Mort started accusing von Fellmann of trying to kill him with the bomb that I had planted. The bastard was out of his mind with rage and I thought he was going to kill us then and there. If he suspects the Baron then why has he got me here, I thought. Then he turned on me, and started to rant that he and I had met somewhere before, and

501

wanted to know where. The bastard was out of his mind.'

So Mort was truly mad, Horace thought. And in his scrambled mind was being haunted by the ghost of the Irish teamster, Patrick Duffy. Michael must look a lot like his dead father, he reflected, as he gazed at the battered, bruised man who had lapsed into a brooding silence. Michael tried to remember the faces of the men he had recruited. They were still living and laughing men in his mind. 'What happened?' Horace prompted gently.

'I told him we had never met before,' Michael answered quietly, recalling the madness he had seen in Mort's eyes. 'He didn't appear very convinced, and had us seized and bound by a couple of his crewmen, who left us tied up on the floor of his cabin. It never occurred to me he was going to blow up his own ship. I just thought he was going to toss von Fellmann and myself over the side. I knew there was no way he was going to let us live.'

'How did Mister Tracy get involved?' Horace asked, knowing that the American prospector had been the key in saving Michael and the Baron from certain death.

'Luke just happened to be on deck taking in the night air when he noticed the ship's longboat being launched and the Chinese boarding with Mort and some of his crew armed with our Winchesters. He kept out of sight, it didn't take much to see something was up. When they had cast off Luke went below. He heard the Baron and myself thumping about in Mort's cabin trying to get loose. He came

502

and set us free. I had a suspicion that if Mort knew about the bomb, he had probably set the fuse. So I tried to get to my men . . . '

Michael ceased talking and stared across the verandah at the sunlight sparkling on the river. He was alive but the five men who had trusted in his leadership were dead – as was Karl Straub. Michael had lost men in the past in battle. But they had died with at least a slight chance of fighting back. The Irish mercenary took a deep breath before continuing to relate the bloody events that followed.

'The murdering bastard had locked the door to the hold where my men were. I could hear them banging on the door trying to get out. They knew what was going to happen because when Mort had them locked in, the bastard he had taunted them about the bomb. We were in the process of ripping off the hatch when the bomb exploded and blew us into the water. I found the Baron half-dead, floating. Luke was all right, but the Baron was pretty badly stunned. So I kept him afloat until he could gather his senses, and we swam around all night calling for help. The captain of the Frenchie gun boat told us later that he dared not come in to pick us up, at least not until he had enough daylight to navigate the shallows. I suppose I can't blame him for that. Captain Dumas treated us well enough. He allowed me to go ashore with a party of his men to search for any sign of Mort. We searched for three days along the shore and found his longboat but no sign of him or his men. Looks as if they struck inland just after they landed. The rest is history, as they say. The Frenchies brought us to Cooktown.'

Horace eased himself from his chair and walked over to the wrought iron railing of the verandah. The heat of the midday sun had driven most people to seek the shelter of the many verandahs along the main street. Under the shady awnings men sat against the walls to gossip about the latest happenings on the Palmer. The mysterious blast that sent the *Osprey* to the bottom was also an item of speculation. As far as it was known there were only three survivors. A few miners who knew the men recruited for the mysterious prospecting expedition blamed the ship's captain for his carelessness in stowing the blasting powder.

'So Captain Mort took the girl and the Chinese pirates ashore with him,' Horace surmised. 'And from what you say he also took some of his own men. No doubt the cut-throats he needed.'

'The bastards went well armed,' Michael replied bitterly, thinking of the loss of the Winchesters. 'It looks like they were preparing for an expedition of their own.'

'You are probably right,' Horace agreed. 'None of my sources have seen them around Cooktown.'

By his sources, the English agent meant the small army of Chinese, who worked for Soo Yin. The tong leader had strategically placed eyes and ears in the market gardens the Chinese diligently tended, as well as in the laundries, brothels, gambling dens and opium houses often frequented by white miners. Although Mort and his party had not been seen in

Cooktown itself, there was a rumour that a rival tong with its headquarters just off the Palmer goldfields was expecting an important 'guest'. An escort of armed Chinese from a rival tong of Soo Yin's had suddenly departed Cooktown a day after the Macintosh ship had gone to the bottom.

At the time that Horace had received this information, it had no connection to anything he considered relevant to his preoccupation with the sabotage of the German expedition to New Guinea. But, when Michael arrived on his doorstep with the story of the Cochinese girl, the astute British agent had immediately conferred with the captain of the French gun boat. He smelt a connection between these events, and with French involvement he knew he must investigate.

Horace had introduced himself as a representative of the Foreign Office, and had inquired as to where the *Osprey* had sunk. A careful study of charts indicated to him that Mort had carefully plotted his course to put him very close to Cooktown before he scuttled his ship. Via a Chinese messenger travelling overland, it was then possible for the man to have made contact with Soo Yin's rivals and arranged for them to meet him north of Cooktown, with an escort, for a journey overland to the rival tong's fortified head-quarters on the Palmer.

Horace wondered how much Michael knew about the political importance of the sixteen-year-old girl to the emerging resistance movements against French interests in the Indo-Chinese province of Cochin. Already, Horace had calculated, any assistance to the French to secure the Cochinese girl for them, would be looked upon favourably by his masters in the Foreign Office. Britain was moving towards reconciliation with their closest European neighbour after centuries of suspicion and war.

'The French want that girl,' Horace said, 'and so does the Tiger Tong.'

'The Tiger Tong?' Michael queried.

'Soo Yin's rivals. They are Macau men. Soo Yin is a Cantonese. The rivalry is a bit like that between the Irish and the British,' he said with a grim smile.

'So they kill each other,' Michael commented. 'Some things never change.'

'Something like that,' Horace said, as he eased himself back into his cane chair. 'But we have the problem of getting the girl out of the Tiger Tong's hands and back to the French.'

'Why should you want to help the French?' Michael asked.

'Not my personal choice, old chap. A strategic political decision. At the moment the Froggies are preoccupied with colonising Cochin China, Annam and Tonkin. And from what we know of the people there they are a particularly stubborn race with a fierce sense of national identity. It looks like the place has the potential to tie up a rather large proportion of French colonial forces attempting to subdue them. It is a matter of letting the French bog themselves down there, while Britain gets on with bringing enlightenment to the rest of Asia, Africa and the Pacific. By helping them get back the girl, who it seems is some kind of rallying point for the Cochinese, we appear to be interested in helping our European neighbours further their colonial interests. A goodwill gesture you could say.' Horace paused and pursed his lips in contemplation of his other peculiar interest. 'The Germans are the ones who worry me the most,' he continued. 'They are emerging as the real power to be reckoned with in Europe and I suspect that very soon we will have to face them on the battlefield as the French have done so recently. But alas, I don't seem to be able to convince my colleagues in London of this fact. They keep pointing the finger at France as the major threat to Britain's interests.'

'And you don't agree?' Michael said.

'No. All Germany needs now is a navy,' Horace replied, 'and they will be in a position to challenge the rest of Europe. I can see the day when we will be at war with Germany and her empire. And when this war inevitably comes, the Germans will have established bases across the globe. That is why your mission was of such importance although you may not have appreciated that at the time. But I fear we only bought time, as I doubt that the Germans will give up on New Guinea easily.' No, Horace thought, the short-sighted fools in London were not students of history. If they were they would have remembered the lessons the Romans learned the hard way. It was from the dark forests of northern Europe that the barbarians had come to sack the empire that seemed invincible. And so too, would be the fate of the British Empire, if the German Kaiser had a chance to expand his.

Horace Brown was an unlikely looking crusader. Middle-aged and plump, he commanded an army of only one man, Michael Duffy, and an intelligence system of Oriental people traditionally loathed by the Europeans. 'The job I am offering you to retrieve the Cochinese girl pays well,' Horace said, as he leaned forward in his chair. 'And I presume you still have a matter to be settled with Captain Mort. If you go after the girl I am sure Mort will not be very far away.'

'You were too quick with your offer to pay, Horace,' Michael replied with a wry smile. 'I was planning to go after Mort regardless. I will track him to the gates of hell and beyond if I have to.'

'Then I think you will accept some help.'

Michael nodded. He was aware of the magnitude of the task before him but had no intention of confiding to the English Foreign Office agent that he and Luke Tracy had already plotted to keep her for a reward. It had nothing to do with Horace's gesture of goodwill.

'Good. I know of a man who might prove to be of use to you,' Horace said. 'His name is Christie Palmerston. Have you met him?'

'Christie Palmerston?' Michael shook his head. 'No. But there are few people up this way who haven't heard his name. I tried to recruit him for the Baron's expedition. Lucky for Mister Palmerston that I failed to find him.'

'Mister Palmerston has been out prospecting

with Venture Mulligan,' Horace explained. 'He was speared last year by the natives when they attacked Mulligan's party west of here. But that hasn't deterred him from going bush again. The only problem that we are going to have with getting Mister Palmerston to act as a guide is that he doesn't like Chinamen much.'

'I would have thought that was an advantage,' Michael commented with a grin, 'considering who I am going after. There will be a good chance I might have to deal with some armed and angry Chinee.'

'Ah yes, that it might be,' the Englishman said casually. 'But you are going to need John Wong to identify the location of the Tiger Tong stockade.'

'Stockade!' Michael said with a note of alarm. 'You mean the bastards have some kind of fort?'

'Yes, I am afraid so,' Horace replied awkwardly. 'It was built to keep out their fellow countrymen. At least Soo's tong.'

'I don't think Mister Palmerston will object to Mister Wong going along,' Michael commented. 'After all, John informs me that he is half Irish, on his mother's side.'

'That he may be,' Horace said with a chuckle, 'but I'm not sure about Mister Palmerston's feelings towards the Irish either. He might object violently to both halves of Mister Wong along on the trip.'

Michael smiled ruefully at Horace's joke. The actual planning of the expedition had lifted his spirits. Here was a second chance for him to settle scores for a lot of dead people.

Horace produced a map which he unfolded and

placed on the verandah at their feet. He had sketched the map from information he was able to glean from various experienced bushmen and after consultation with government surveyors. Regretfully it had little information apart from major landmarks as the rugged and often near impenetrable country in the far north of Queensland had not been explored. 'This should help you work out how you will go after Captain Mort.' He pointed with his unlit cigar at the map between them. Michael stared down with his one good eye. Distances were vague, as were actual locations. 'From my calculations,' Horace said, still stabbing with his cigar, 'Mort is probably going to use this track to escort the girl to the Tiger Tong stockade on the Palmer. The track is not often used now I've been told, and my guess is that he will be about here . . . ' he said, tapping the end of the cigar on the sketch at a point on one of the tracks. 'From what I know Mort and his party are on foot.'

Michael stared at the sketch and estimated time and space calculations with the eye of a military man while Horace continued his briefing. 'Soo Yin has volunteered some of his men if you need them. In fact, he insists you take them with you.'

Michael frowned. He had planned going after Mort on horseback. As far as he knew not many Chinese knew how to ride. If on foot, they would never catch Mort, who had a lead on them. 'Tell Soo Yin thank you. But the four of us will do the job.'

'Four?'

'I'm taking Luke Tracy with me. He's a bushman I trust.'

Horace slumped back into his chair with a sigh. 'I think you are being over ambitious. I think you will need more than four. You don't know the numbers you might come up against.'

The Irishman smiled at his caution and answered confidently. 'From what I have heard of Christie Palmerston and what I know of John and Luke I think they are equal to an army of Chinese. Besides, the four of us on horseback can move further and faster than men on foot.'

Horace raised his bushy eyebrows. 'It will be your plan that will ultimately determine how you get the girl out. But always keep her rescue in mind. Your dealings with Mort are your affair alone and I will deny any knowledge in that matter. I hope you understand.'

'I understand,' Michael replied grimly. 'You get me Christie Palmerston and John Wong and I will do the rest. I promise you, on my mother's grave, that the rescue of that Chinese girl will be my primary purpose in going down the track. What happens between Mort and myself will involve no-one else.'

'I believe you Michael,' the Englishman replied with a heavy sigh. 'But be assured, I will put in place means to ensure that you stick to your primary mission.'

'So who is it going to be? John or Mister Palmerston?' Michael said with a cold smile. He knew the way the Horace Browns of the world worked. He was utterly ruthless, and one of the two men accompanying him would be under instructions to remove him, should he deviate from his contract. And 'remove' probably meant a bullet in the back of the head.

'It could be both,' Horace replied with an equally cold smile. 'But you will never know unless you do not stick to the mission you have been given.'

Michael shrugged nonchalantly at the implied threat. 'Well, if there is nothing else, then I think you and I should retire to the bar for a drink to seal the bargain.'

Michael heaved himself from the cane chair. His body ached in places he had not ached before. Although he was only thirty-two his battle wounds made him feel old.

As Horace followed Michael along the verandah his thoughts were on the Prussian baron. Although the German had been foiled in his first attempt to annex New Guinea for the Kaiser, he would certainly try again. Horace had learned that he had booked a passage to Sydney. The loss of Herr Straub in the sinking of the *Osprey* had been a personal blow to von Fellmann, more than just the loss of a colleague, as Horace had discovered in his discreet inquiries. He felt some sympathy for his opponent, but he also knew that they would inevitably find themselves pitted against each other in the years ahead. The little English agent hoped he would have the services of Michael Duffy in the next confrontation.

The forced march was gruelling in the oppressive heat of the day. Captain Mort pushed the Chinese pirates and his own European sailors mercilessly as they trekked south west. At their present rate he calculated that they would strike the main trail within hours.

'We stop for a rest soon Cap'n?' Sims said puffing as he struggled up to Mort striding at the head of the column. 'Men all done in if'n we don't.'

Mort slowed his pace. 'Call a stop Mister Sims,' he said grudgingly. 'I'll use the time to take a bearing.'

Sims straggled back down the column strung out through the tall rainforest. He gestured to the men to take a rest. When he came to the sweating Cochinese girl she slumped to the ground and hardly looked up at him as he passed.

Hue felt her body ache in every joint from the almost continuous twenty-four-hour forced march. She took deep breaths and gazed at the surrounding thick forest. So this was the land of the barbarians, she thought. It was lacking in character compared to her own lush forests of Cochin China.

She pulled herself to a tree, and rested with her back against the great forest giant while one of the Chinese armed with an ancient flint lock musket, squatted a few feet away, staring at her with barely concealed lust. She was not afraid of him. The cruel European barbarian with the piercing blue eyes and hair like the dried grass had quickly established his authority over the pirate captain, and the Chinese who had been fetched from Cooktown to join them.

The barbarian captain's name was Mort. In French it meant *death*. An apt name, she thought. He had so casually killed one of the Chinese escort who had attempted to fondle her when they had stopped early in the morning. He had walked up to the Chinese pirate and simply run his sword through the man's chest as smoothly as he had drawn it from its sheath. With the man dead at his feet, he had turned to Hue and, just as casually, wiped the bloody sword across her shoulders. Although she did not understand the words he had muttered, she did feel the chill in the tone of his voice.

Captain Woo had been outraged by the slaying of one of his men without his permission and had moved to intercept Mort. But the barbarian had been backed by his European sailors, who had brought their rapid-firing Winchesters to cover him, and the matter of who was in command was quickly established by force of arms.

So now Hue knew she was safe from the unwanted attentions of all the men – except perhaps for Mort. As the leader would he have her for himself? She shuddered, remembering those pale blue eyes examining her just after he had so casually killed the Chinese sailor.

Hue tried not to think about the future. The little hope she had felt since her capture, had been swept away by the blast that had ripped apart the barbarian's ship four days earlier. Up until then she had entertained a single ray of hope. When she had looked into the face of the big barbarian with the eye patch, she had almost felt safe.

But he was gone now, and so was any hope of her return to Cochin China and her family. All that lay ahead was a fate she knew would inevitably bring her to a French prison. What would happen before her captors handed her over to the French worried her more so.

Hue closed her mind to the future and any chance of salvation. All she could do for the moment was, with the stoic patience of her people, endure the nightmare of her captivity.

Mort slipped the small brass compass back into his pocket. Although he had lashed his column with scathing words for their tardy behaviour on the march, he was secretly pleased with their progress. All had gone to plan, from the very first moment he had formulated his scheme in the cabin of the *Osprey*.

He had set his ship on a course that had practically brought him into Cooktown. When he scuttled her he was able to run the lifeboat ashore with his small complement of crew and Chinese pirates. They had enough supplies to survive until one of Woo's men was able to get a message through to Cooktown's Chinese quarter.

Reinforcements had duly arrived, and the matter of command been settled, with the help of the Winchesters. All he had to do, was get the girl to the Tiger Tong stronghold just off the Palmer River goldfields, and there collect his ransom from the tong leader.

Mort did not fear a doublecross, as the rapidfiring rifles gave him a distinctive edge over the ancient muskets of the tong men. Once he had the ransom in his hands, it would only be a matter of returning to Cooktown, and taking a passage on a ship sailing for the Americas.

The thought of a ship brought a deep sadness to him. He had destroyed the only thing in his troubled life that had brought him close to happiness. And yet, he reflected, he had been forced to kill his own mother when she had betrayed him to her gin-sodden customers. Such was the way life was meant to be, he philosophised. One must sometimes destroy that which is loved in order to survive. His brooding thoughts caused him a melancholy that he knew could distract him from his present mission. He forced himself to concentrate, and gazed beyond the rainforest before him where he could see the vegetation thin to the drier eucalypts of the country below the Great Divide.

He turned and snarled to his mixed command to get to their feet. They did so reluctantly, although none dared show any aversion. The sword that hung at their leader's waist was more than a symbol of his rank.

Only Captain Woo displayed any defiance. He shouted to his men that they would obey the blue-eyed barbarian only until the time they reached the Tiger Tong in the mountains of the land of gold. Then he, Captain Woo, would personally assist in slowly and agonisingly sending the barbarian to meet his ancestors. Woo was not afraid that his boast was heard by Mort and his European accomplices. He spoke in Chinese, which he knew they could not understand.

But Hue could understand and she shuddered involuntarily. She had personally witnessed the bestial cruelty of the Chinese pirates. Not even a demon deserved such a fate, she thought sympathetically. But Hue did not know Captain Morrison Mort as other young girls had in their last agonised moments of life. If she had, then she might not have wasted her sympathy.

THIRTY-SEVEN

The misshapen, dried sea creatures piled in heaps along the wooden plank counter always made John Wong shudder. Although he knew that they were delicacies highly prized by his Oriental relations, for most of his twenty years he had lived with the smell of corned beef and cabbage.

In Soo Yin's store he felt uneasy for an unfathomable reason. Was it that the dreaded leader of the Cooktown-based tong had commanded his presence? Or was it simply his feelings of trepidation for the arduous and very dangerous mission that lay before them? Whatever it was, he was about to find out.

One of Soo Yin's bodyguards, a thin, surly Chinese man around John's age, beckoned him to follow him into the back room. John ducked his head as he passed through the tiny doorway built low to resist an onrush of would-be assassins, and entered a world divorced from the antiseptic scent of euca-lyptus. The pungent but sweet aroma of the East wafted from burning incense sticks and opium pipes.

The bodyguard moved to a corner of the room and stared vacantly into thin air. John was not fooled by the man's seeming indifference to his presence. He knew the man was one of the tong leader's best killers, and could move with the speed of the deadly cobra if required to defend Soo Yin's life.

Soo Yin reclined on a low bed in the dimly lit room, staring menacingly at the tall young Eurasian who he did not like for his mixed blood. He blamed John's seeming arrogance on the fact that he had been denied the venerable teachings of Confucius in his youth. John did not cower in the face of the tong leader's barely concealed hostility. To do so would be a loss of face.

A small hessian sack in the centre of the room attracted John's curiosity. It seemed to have been placed there especially.

'You are satisfied with the supplies,' Soo Yin said rather than asked.

'Yes,' John answered in Soo Yin's dialect. 'I think Mister Brown will be satisfied with what you have supplied.'

'You are now alone,' Soo continued. 'Brown has told me that this man of his, the Irishman, does not wish to take a contingent of the Lotus Tong with him. It will be up to you to bring the girl back to me at any cost.' John nodded and Soo Yin's deceptively soft voice continued. 'The barbarians do not recog-nise you as one of them . . . they never will . . . so you must decide to whom you swear your loyalty.'

'You employ me,' John answered simply. 'As my boss I recognise you alone.'

Soo did not acknowledge John's reply, but gestured to the surly young bodyguard standing in the shadows. He stepped forward and picked up the small sack from the floor and with a twisted grin held it up to John. John felt the weight of the hessian bag and sensed the sticky slime of its contents. Every instinct told him what the bag contained and he fought the desire to let the bag fall from his grasp. He stared back at the tong leader and was careful to conceal any feelings of fear. 'Dispose of that,' Soo Yin said. 'Now go and remember where your allegiance must always be.'

Turning on his heel, John left knowing, with a vicious triumph, that he had remained seemingly impassive to Soo Yin's gesture.

The tong leader made a slight nod of his head to his bodyguard, who discreetly followed John from the Chinese quarter to the river. He would report back later to Soo Yin that the Eurasian had opened the bag to look inside, before hurling it into the crocodile-infested waters of the Endeavour River.

A faint smile creased the tong leader's face. Then the Eurasian would have seen the hands, tongue, genitals and head of the coolie who had betrayed him, he thought with some satisfaction. Such a lesson was not easily forgotten. Fear would ensure that the young man did not deviate from his task, should the Irishman succeed against all the odds, and rescue the Cochinese girl. From the little that Soo Yin knew of Captain Mort's reputation, he did not hold out much hope he would ever see the Eurasian again. But that was of no consequence as John Wong was, after all, a barbarian, as far as the Chinese tong leader was concerned.

Soo Yin sighed and beckoned to one of the beautiful doll-like girls who ministered to his every need. Head bowed, she shuffled forward from behind a silk curtain and knelt before her master, who reached out to fondle her naked flesh.

Horace's meticulous preparations for the expedition gave Michael a chance to stand down and enjoy a night on the town. Having planned that his party would set out first thing in the morning, Michael went in search of a poker game. Win or lose at cards – it did not matter – when he knew he was faced with the daunting mission of going after the man he must kill. They would be in unfamiliar country, as hostile as the dreaded tribesmen who haunted the forests and hills west of Cooktown. Michael was in luck when he found John Wong and Luke Tracy at the Golden Nugget. But he was surprised to see Henry James sitting with them.

Although Henry sat at the card table, he declined to play poker as they were playing by the American rules of the game, and Henry was unfamiliar with that style. The hotel was crowded and the secretive conversation between the three men was ignored by the drunken miners, crushing the bar with shouts for drinks while arguments over the merits of the various means of taking gold from the Palmer raged around them.

'I want in on any expedition Mister O'Flynn,' Henry growled as he gripped his tumbler of rum. 'Don't let my gammy leg worry you, because I know you are going after Mort on horseback, and I can outride any man in the north.'

Michael scowled at Luke who shuffled the deck of cards ignoring his anger. 'You can get your backer to include Henry on the payroll,' Luke said quietly without looking up. 'After all, you got me on your expedition to go north with von Fellmann.'

'Different paymaster,' Michael snapped tersely. He was not pleased that Henry James wanted to join them, even though he respected the man's experience. He was secretly concerned that he might get him killed, and he understood from his conversations with Luke that the former trooper sergeant had a wife and son. He did not want the big Englishman's death on his conscience.

But he also understood the importance of friendship between men. Mateship was a bond as strong as any, even as strong as that between men and women in marriage. He stared at the cards in his hand and chewed over the reasons why he should either include, or exclude, Henry James. When he glanced up at Henry, he could see a smouldering fire in his eyes, one that he recognised in himself. 'What's Captain Mort to you Mister James?' he asked quietly.

Henry tossed back his rum and wiped his mouth

with the sleeve of his shirt. 'He killed a good friend of mine once,' he growled. 'A darkie trooper who was as good as any white man including present company. I let Mort get away with it. Maybe you could say that if I'd done my job back then and reported the murdering bastard, your men might still be alive today Mister O'Flynn. Is that good enough reason for you?'

He stared at Michael, daring him to rebut his reasons for inclusion. The Irishman stared right back into the smouldering eyes and understood the terrible torment within the man's soul for revenge. 'That's good enough reason for me Mister James,' Michael finally replied, and extended his hand to seal his inclusion in the small but growing force of bushmen. 'Your shout on this round Mister James,' Michael added with a slow grin, as Henry took the extended hand.

'Sounds fair,' Henry replied. 'But my friends call me Henry.'

Michael nodded and Luke slapped him on the back. 'Good decision partner,' he said. 'Henry knows the bush and he's pretty handy around horses.'

Although Henry breathed a sigh of relief for being included in the expedition, he dreaded having to face Emma. He knew that she would take his leaving hard. How could he explain his reasons to her when they were not all that clear to himself? He knew that the bravest thing he could do was lie to his wife. He would tell her that he was going with Luke on a short trip to poke around some places he suspected might be likely places for gold. It was a thin story, but he hoped it would hold up.

'You seen Kate O'Keefe since you got back?' Michael asked Luke conversationally when Henry went to the bar to buy a round of drinks.

Luke winced and shifted uncomfortably. 'Not exactly,' he replied. 'Henry tells me that Kate told Emma that she never wanted to see me again, when she heard I'd survived the sinking of the *Osprey*.'

'I wouldn't take much notice of that if I were you,' Michael replied as he glanced at the cards Luke had dealt him. It was not a good hand but he was still ahead.

'Yeah, well you don't know Kate,' Luke replied, looking down at the hand he had dealt to himself. It was not a good hand either.

Michael smiled to himself. If only you knew . . .

It was Ben Rosenblum who inadvertently told Kate of the expedition, when she had gone to the paddock behind her house, to talk to him about purchasing a new yoke of bullocks for her wagons. And no sooner had he told her that Henry was with Luke Tracy and the American O'Flynn, than her eyes flashed with anger. He had cursed himself for not thinking. Now Henry would have to face Kate's full wrath.

'Why is Henry with them?' she had asked in the quiet way that Ben had long come to recognise as a precursor to an explosion of anger.

'I'm not sure Kate,' he mumbled. 'Just gone for a drink I suppose.'

She fixed him with her eyes and Ben wished he

could tell her all that Henry had confided in him. But he had sworn to keep silent on the matter, and even regretted that he had not been able to go himself. It was rumoured that the American had paid well to the men he had recruited for the ill-fated expedition on the *Osprey*. No doubt he would pay well to those who went with him on this expedition too.

Kate sensed that she had stumbled onto something she was not supposed to know about. But any further questioning of Ben would force him to break the code of mateship. That she would not do, as she realised its sacred importance to men on the frontier. 'I would like to see Henry,' she said casually, still holding Ben's gaze. 'Where might I find him this time of day?'

'He's gone to the Golden Nugget,' Ben answered. 'But I didn't tell you that Kate.'

'You have my word on that,' she answered with a grateful nod.

'Stupid bastard,' Ben muttered miserably to himself as she turned to leave him alone with the big beasts. He could tell from her purposeful strides that she was looking for trouble. Whoever it was with, he felt sorry for them.

Kate knew exactly who she would confront and why. That damned American O'Flynn! How dare he even consider recruiting Henry to one of his nefarious schemes. She did not stop to consider that it could be Henry who was making all the overtures for enlistment. All she knew was that whenever the man she had come to know as Mister Michael

O'Flynn was around those she cherished, they were placed in jeopardy.

She slowed her pace and checked her emotions. Why was she so upset? Was she actually thinking about Luke's welfare rather than Henry's? Had she not vowed to forget Luke? A tiny voice told her she could not so easily forget him, and she quickened her pace, as if to walk away from the guilt. No, she thought with her chin set, Luke was well and truly out of her life forever. He would never come and go again, as he pleased. Her concern was for Henry and the danger involvement with the American mercenary posed to him. She had Emma and young Gordon to consider.

Kate reached the hotel just after dark. Already the sprawling frontier town was awakening to a night of riotous, sordid living. Rollicking and drunken miners who did not know Kate made lewd suggestions, whilst those who did know her tipped their hats respectfully. She ignored the former and acknowledged the latter with a forced smile.

Kate paused outside the hotel. She wanted to bring her anger under control before entering the bastion of men. She was about to enter when Henry appeared unexpectedly through the door.

'Kate! What are you doing here?' he asked.

'I came to see you,' she replied, stepping up to him. 'And this Mister O'Flynn whom I have heard so much about.'

Henry took her by the elbow and steered her

away from the front of the hotel. 'Did Ben tell you?' he asked as he walked with her in the direction of her store.

'He didn't mean to,' Kate answered protectively of her trusted employee. 'It kind of slipped out that you were here to see O'Flynn.'

'I won't lie to you Kate,' Henry answered. 'I came to see if I could get a job with Mister O'Flynn but I cannot tell you anymore than that I'm afraid so please don't ask me.'

'What are you going to tell Emma?' Kate flared.

Henry did not answer immediately. 'Well?' Kate asked again. 'Are you going to tell Emma what you are doing with that damned American soldier of fortune?'

'No,' Henry answered quietly. 'I'm going to lie to her and I want your sworn promise that you will not tell her of my meeting with Mister O'Flynn either.' He could see the determined set of her chin and sensed that the fiery Kate O'Keefe had a confrontation in mind with the American mercenary.

She stopped and turned to face him. 'You are asking more than I should say yes to, Henry,' she pleaded. 'I suspect that you will be in great danger with that man, from all that I have heard of him. It seems he walks with death and I care too much for you and Emma to see you hurt.'

'I have been riding with death for many years now Kate,' he smiled sadly. 'What I am about to do I must do, for reasons I do not fully understand myself. It's not even the money, but something in my life that goes back a long time to when I was with the

Native Mounted Police. That's about all I can tell you. Please promise me you will not go back and attempt to change Mister O'Flynn's mind.'

Kate frowned. She could see the deep torment in his eyes, and had no answer to what she saw. She turned away bitterly. Henry was a man of the frontier and physical danger a way of life for him, she thought with resignation. She would keep his secret. 'I will respect your wishes. But half my mind tells me I should go back and confront this man so callous that he would possibly deprive a woman of her husband, a son of his father.'

Henry grinned down at her. 'He is no match for you Kate O'Keefe. He is only used to staying alive on battlefields, not confronting the likes of you.'

Kate felt the mirth in his opinion. 'A pity,' she sighed as she started off towards the store. 'I was looking forward to meeting this man who, it seems, has the whole town speculating on your mysterious mission out west. But Emma has dinner waiting for us and you have things to tell her, as only you can.'

Henry nodded gratefully and fell into step beside her. They walked in the balmy evening with the raucous sounds of the town around them. Kate found the sounds comforting, unlike the silence of the bush which always held an ominous hush for the dreaded screech of the black cockatoo, the war cry of the fierce northern tribesmen.

When Horace's late evening meeting with Soo was concluded and money had been exchanged for the horses, rations and guns procured through the tong leader's contacts he walked to French Charley's to meet Captain Dumas. The meeting had been arranged as part of the English agent's extension of British hospitality to the Frenchman, although Horace assured him that, as a simple civil servant with the British Foreign Office, he abhorred talk of politics and intelligence intrigue. Anything that the captain might tell him concerning his country's affairs was not of any great interest.

Both men knew that was a lie. But Captain Dumas was suitably impressed by his fellow countryman's famed establishment. French Charley's did indeed rival the best colonial restaurants that the French gun boat captain had dined in. The food and wines were excellent, and the girls who worked for Monsieur Boeul were beautiful, although he had to smile at their attempts to imitate his national accent.

Captain Dumas had attracted the admiring glances of the ladies of French Charley's as he dined in his smart dress uniform and his host for the evening had promised him that the ladies were well and truly available to entertain lonely sailors. Captain Dumas had his eye on a little redhead with a saucy disposition. She smiled coyly at him whenever he fixed her with a champagne-induced leer. Although the female entertainment offered by the famed establishment was not to Horace's tastes, in all other respects he could not fault the restaurant as a venue to loosen the Frenchman's tongue.

Already Captain Dumas had told him much concerning his mission and Hue's importance to

French intelligence. The girl was already being likened by Cochinese bandits, who saw themselves as nationalist patriots, to Trieu Au, a third-century girl who herself could be compared to France's own Joan of Arc. Hue's historical predecessor had fought the Chinese invaders and, when defeated at the age of twenty-three, had chosen suicide before capture.

Through various subtle and less than subtle means French intelligence agencies were hoping to extract from Hue the names of those persons in the royal court of the Cochinese emperor who were plotting against French interests. But the captain himself was strictly a naval man who kept out of politics and was not particularly interested in what his intelligence counterparts did with her.

'I must congratulate you on your excellent grasp of the English language, Captain Dumas,' Horace said. 'I myself have great difficulties with learning languages,' he lied, 'and only wish I had spent time visiting all the exotic places you have in your time with the French navy . . . ' Horace's voice trailed away as his eye caught a tall, commanding man entering the restaurant with a pretty young brunette on his arm. *Manfred von Fellmann!*

Captain Dumas had also noticed the Baron enter the crowded room, and lurched to his feet full of bonhomie for the Prussian he had fished out of the sea. 'Ah Baron von Fellmann, please to join us,' he called above the din of voices. The Baron turned, and said something to his pretty escort, who pursed her lips with feigned disappointment as he left her alone, to stride over to their table.

Horace watched him approach with mixed feelings. So, he was about to meet the man whom he had recognised from afar in Samoa, but had never formally met for professional reasons.

'May I introduce Monsieur Brown to you Baron von Fellmann,' the Frenchman slurred. He had trouble remaining on his feet as he waved vaguely at Horace, sitting very still at the table. Horace watched the dawning recognition on the Baron's face, as he clicked his heels in the Prussian style, with his hands at his side.

'It is good to meet you Mister Brown,' Manfred said. 'I have never had the honour of meeting a man with such a formidable reputation as yours.'

The flattering insinuation was lost on the inebriated French naval man who gestured for the Prussian aristocrat to sit with them.

'It is an honour to meet you *Oberst von Fellmann*,' Horace replied with a nod of his head.

'I am no longer a colonel Mister Brown. But I am sure, as two old soldiers, we could discuss the campaigns we have seen. Yours in the Crimea and mine against the army colleagues of my French *ami* at the Sedan. No my friend, I am a man only with commercial interests these days.'

Horace slipped the spectacles from his nose to wipe them. 'And sadly,' he sighed, 'I am but a simple servant in Her Majesty's colonial outposts.'

Manfred's laughter rolled around the room at the little Englishman's description of himself. They both knew who and what they were: two very professional – and dangerous – men fighting in an undeclared war for the interests of their respective nations. 'I think we should toast this occasion Mister Brown,' Manfred said when he stopped laughing. 'Here we are as friends from Germany, France and England, enjoying the night in a neutral French restaurant, in a British colony far from our homes and loved ones.'

The French captain slopped champagne into their glasses which they raised to each other in toast.

The pretty brunette appeared at the Baron's elbow, petulantly whining in a poor imitation of a French accent that he was ignoring her. Manfred patted her on her bottom and leaned forward to the Frenchman. 'A little gift from Germany to France, Captain,' he said with a conspiratorial wink. 'The young lady has informed me that she would like to take French lessons – in privacy.'

Before the girl could protest the Frenchman lurched to his feet, and gallantly took her hand, which he swept with a kiss. The gesture stilled her protests. She was impressed by the Frenchman's manner and colourful uniform. He was a rather interesting look-ing captain, she thought, for a foreigner.

'Gentlemen, you must excuse me if I leave you to give a lesson in the true language of love.'

As he was led away by the young lady who was to learn what the Frenchman meant by *l'amour*, Horace refilled the crystal goblets. 'To Herr Straub,' he said solemnly. 'Or should I say, *Kapitan* Karl von Fellmann.'

Manfred did not raise his glass but stared at the Englishman. 'I am not surprised that you know Karl was my brother, Mister Brown,' he said menacingly.

'Just as I suspect that the bomb that Captain Mort found on his ship was put there by you.'

'I am truly sorry that you lost your brother Baron,' Horace said, placing his glass on the table. 'But it was never intended to kill anyone. Just, shall we say, slow down your ambitions to go sightseeing around New Guinea.'

The German agent stared hard at his English counterpart but could not detect cupidity in him. Given similar circumstances he would have used similar tactics. The Englishman had not tried to deny the bomb was his. 'My brother was a good soldier,' Manfred replied. 'He died for his Kaiser as surely as if he had died on a battlefield. So I accept your toast to a courageous man. And now, I would like to propose a toast to the success of your man in his mission, to kill the murderer of my brother. Mister Michael Duffy.'

It was Horace's turn to look stunned. How could the Prussian know Michael's identity and that he worked for him? He sat staring at his glass of champagne. 'My wife tells me everything Mister Brown,' Manfred smiled grimly, as if answering Horace's unspoken question. 'And it was not hard to confirm my suspicions that Mister Duffy was the man who had brought the bomb aboard. And who would detonate it at the appropriate time. Your actions just now confirmed my suspicions.'

Horace blinked and cursed himself. He had fallen for the German's bluff so easily. His adversary was damned good at his job! 'But do not concern yourself my friend,' Manfred continued. 'Because Mister

Duffy's proposed act of seeking out and killing the murderer of my brother and saving my life when we were in the sea more than exonerates his betrayal of my trust, for the moment at least. My wife tells me he is an excellent lover. Such a man as your Irishman is exceptional. I will regret having to kill him some day. That is, if he remains working for you. But we both know how unreliable mercenaries are.' Manfred raised his glass. 'To *Herr* Duffy, an exceptional man.'

Horace raised his glass. 'Her Majesty,' he muttered. 'God bless her.' His thoughts drifted briefly to the Irishman. Would he ever see him again? Or would Mort claim yet another Duffy life?

THIRTY-EIGHT

Max Braun did not try to hide his tears. He embraced Patrick in a powerful bear hug as they stood on the wharf amongst the throng of passengers who had come to farewell the voyagers to Mother England. They were an incongruous pair; the burly scarred man with a nose flattened across his tear-streaked face, and the tall boy with the fine patrician features promising a handsomeness that few women would be able to resist in the short years to come.

Max lifted Patrick from his feet and hugged him tenderly. 'Travel safely my little fighter,' he whispered in words choked with emotion. 'Never forget that your uncle Max loves you.' The tough former Hamburg sailor wiped self-consciously at the tears streaking his face, and turned away, so that Daniel and his family would not see his grief. He might never see the boy again, he thought in his sorrow. Michael had been taken from him years earlier and yet had given him his son. Now Patrick would be sailing from his life for many years – if not forever.

Fiona watched the scene from her carriage and would have given her very life to be in the place of the man who held her son. She ached to hold Patrick and tell him of so many things. But the graceful clipper that rocked at her mooring by the wharf, strained impatiently against the ropes like a champion racehorse, ready to take him from her life.

Men in top hats and ladies in long dresses cried and hugged those who had come to farewell them on their passage to England. Porters and dockside workers sweated in the warm sun of the Sydney autumn day as they worked quickly to bring on board the last of the cargo for the trip that would take the clipper halfway around the world. An authoritative voice cried out above the din of laughter and tears for all to board and a bell clanged, warning of the imminent sailing.

Fiona sat alone in her thoughts but not alone in the carriage. Penelope sat beside her, watching the pinched expression on her cousin's pale and beautiful face. Penelope had seen pain before, but not the kind of pain she was now witnessing.

She reached over to gently cover Fiona's hand reassuringly. How could one reassure a mother who was losing a son she had only just found after years of silent mourning? How could she tell the woman she loved that she had the barest inkling of the pain she was suffering?

Fiona turned momentarily to flash a weak smile of gratitude for her cousin's tender gesture. 'I have lost him forever. My mother has taken him from me twice in a lifetime. Once was almost more than I could bear.'

Penelope followed Fiona's gaze to the crowded wharf. She could see Daniel Duffy, stiff and formal in his suit and top hat, waving gravely to Patrick who was following his grandmother up the gangway. Standing beside the tall lawyer was a pretty red-headed woman, weeping as she held the hand of a little girl very much a miniature of herself. A young boy about Patrick's age waved to him and Patrick paused on the gangway to return the wave. An older woman stood beside Daniel. She had snow-white hair and reminded Penelope of the eternal grand-mother of quiet and gentle ways.

The crowd of well-wishing farewellers milling on the wharf pushed forward to reach out to the passengers lining the clipper's deck, and the Duffy family was obscured. The crowd now gave three *hurrahs*, to speed the passengers safely to England.

The dockside gangs cast off the ropes that held the ship captive to Sydney's shores, and a brass band played a medley of popular tunes, before breaking into the traditional Scottish tune *Auld Lang Syne*. Penelope scanned the ship's railing and saw Patrick and Enid standing side by side at the bow. She could see Enid saying something to Patrick whose smile was sad as he waved to his family on the dock.

A steam tug strained to pull the graceful clipper into the main channel where she would be set on her voyage across the Great Southern Ocean and around the Cape of Africa to England.

Fiona did not wait for the ship to be towed to the main channel. She did not want to remember her son as a tiny blur amongst strangers lining the deck. She wanted to keep the picture of the boy's face clear in her mind, as he stood at the railing, rather than remember the clipper taking him away from her. She had no doubt that she had seen Michael's spirit in the boy's eyes and no matter what her mother tried to mould him into he would always hold a part of his father's rebellious spirit.

Fiona knew that her son would be groomed to oppose Granville directly, and herself indirectly. Her sin was not that she had lusted for Michael Duffy. Her sin was that she had taken a side against her mother who was punishing her now by using the fruit of her liaison to hurt her in the cruellest possible way.

The bumping of the carriage on the packed earthen road along the route to South Head made Penelope feel ill. It was a warm day, one that gave promise of fires that would burn uncontrollably in the eucalyptus forests around the city, choking the town with the brown haze of cinders.

But such sickness was not uncommon to a pregnant woman. Penelope knew that Manfred was the father of her unborn child as she had been careful in her affairs with other men. Apart from her doctor, only she knew of the pregnancy now into its third month, and she wanted Fiona to be the third person to know. It was her pregnancy that made her especially empathetic to her cousin's grief. She realised how precious the life within her was. How would she react to her baby being wrenched from her arms, from her life? The answer was clear. She knew she would be capable of killing any person who tried to take her baby from her.

Fiona stared out at the passing drays, wagons and carriages as they rattled past. The tall gums appeared weary from the industrial pollution that had come with Sydney's growth as a city. Fetid smelling tanneries and factories spilled out noxious fumes, while sewage fouled the sandy earth. Once clean and clear swamps were now cesspools of poisonous waste. Sydney had an ugly face for Fiona. With its magnificent harbour, she had once thought the city to be the prettiest in the world. But Sydney was the home of the Macintoshes, a name she had grown to detest for all its implications in her life.

'We still have Michael,' Penelope said gently as the coach rattled and bumped along the dusty road. 'So long as Michael is alive, you have an ally to win Patrick back one day.'

Fiona gave her cousin a bitter smile. 'I think it is too late for Michael to help me,' she replied sadly. 'He is God knows where, and could even be dead, for all we know. No, I doubt that he could do much,' she added bitterly.

Although Penelope respected her cousin's opinion,

it was not one that she shared. Michael was a born survivor and his scars a testament to his ability to withstand the worst that could happen to him. She was certain, however illogical it seemed, that one day he would return to help Fiona in her quest to regain her son.

'You slept with Michael when he was in Sydney.' Fiona's unexpected accusation was stated with such casual aplomb that Penelope was taken unawares. Fiona had not even bothered to face her when she spoke.

Penelope remained in a stunned silence for a brief moment, considering how she should reply to her cousin's accusation. 'I slept with the man you knew as Michael O'Flynn not Michael Duffy,' she finally answered.

Fiona turned on her with a cold fire in her eyes. 'You and I both know Michael O'Flynn *is* Michael Duffy,' she flared.

Penelope smiled sadly at her cousin's bitterness. 'We have shared the same body,' she replied quietly, 'but not the same man. Michael is not the young man you once knew. Michael Duffy has become Michael O'Flynn. A man whose soul is as scarred as his body. The young man who once had dreams of creating beauty in his paintings is now a man who will never know peace. Oh Fiona my love, I have seen into his soul, and I have seen the pain for what he can never go back to. No. I did not sleep with *your* Michael. I slept with an Irish soldier of fortune. I doubt that the man I knew intimately would even know your Michael. They have little in common.'

Fiona's bitterness dissolved. Penelope was right, she thought. The man she had briefly met at

Penelope's house was so different from the gentle and carefree Michael she had once loved with her body. The man who had then stood before her on the lawn had the air of one who had seen far too much violence in his life. Yes, they had shared the same body, but not the same man!

Fiona took her cousin's hand in hers. 'I know what you mean Penny,' she said with a wan smile. 'I think we have both been fortunate to have known Michael in our lifetime. It is something we will always have in common, you and I.'

Penelope slipped her arms around Fiona and held her to her breast. It was then that she told her the wonderful news concerning her pregnancy. There were joyous squeals of delight as the coach drove into the driveway of Penelope's house.

Their lovemaking that afternoon was both passionate and tender. But when it was over, and Penelope slept in Fiona's embrace, Fiona found her thoughts drifting to both her son and his father. The thoughts wandered the empty places in her life. There was laughter in the memories of a beach at sunset, and the face of a tall, broad shouldered young man, who talked impulsively of taking her to America. And sorrow in the thoughts for the milk that once swelled her breasts for the son she had never had suckle her. 'Where are you Michael Duffy?' she whispered softly, as she stroked away a wisp of Penelope's golden hair from her sleeping face. 'Will we ever meet again? And how would you react to the knowledge we have a son?'

TO A PLACE OF RECKONING

THIRTY-NINE

With his rifle across his chest Michael Duffy lay on his back and gazed up at an eagle circling the dry valley. As graceful as it was lethal in its intent, the majestic bird dived earthwards. Michael tugged the broad brim of his hat down over his eyes and prepared to take a short nap.

A short distance away, using his rifle as a support, Luke Tracy crouched in the long grass, peering eastwards. Vigilant and alert he scanned the surrounding scrubby bush. They were deep within the territory of hostile tribesmen and such vigilance was essential to ensure that the shadows cast by a shimmering tropical sun did not suddenly move with the flash of a warrior releasing a deadly spear. Luke eased himself into a sitting position to take the strain off his legs.

'No sign?' Michael inquired lazily from under the shade of his hat.

'Nothing yet,' Luke answered as he reached for his water canteen.

A horse whinnied from a stand of scrub behind them. The sound instantly awoke Henry James who had been dozing under a spindly tree in the scrub. The horse was answered with a distant whinny, and the three men scanned the eastern horizon of low, scrub-covered hills.

'It's them,' Luke said, as he rose and waved his rifle above his head.

In the distance one of the two shimmering mounted figures acknowledged them by waving his rifle above his head. After a short time the shapes took on more distinct outlines, as the two outriders rode towards them across the sun-baked plain.

Christie Palmerston and John Wong rode side by side with their rifles resting on their hips. They reined in at the edge of the tree line and Michael stepped forward to greet the two men. He gazed up at Christie Palmerston whose reputation as a superb bushman was well known to the people on the frontier.

Michael knew very little about the bushman's past, except that it was rumoured that he was the illegitimate son of the famous opera singer Madame Carandini and Viscount Palmerston, an English lord. He was not really interested in the young man's parentage but rather his considerable experience and skills as a bushman. He was a man in his mid-twenties and sported a long, dark beard down to his chest. Michael felt a kind of empathy with the young man whose left arm had been withered from birth.

Michael's own lost eye made him aware of how frustrating a physical disability could be.

'They're about three hours aback and coming this way,' Christie said without being asked the crucial question.

'How many?' Michael asked.

'Counted twenty-nine all up. Mostly Chinee. But saw four white men with them. Travelling single file and, as far as I knowed, not expecting a lot of trouble. Got a lot of arms for a Chinee coolie party though.'

'You see a girl with them?' Michael queried. He was fairly certain from the young bushman's brief description of the approaching column that it was Mort's party. Confirmation of the girl's presence would be a bonus.

'Too far away to see,' Christie answered, as he wiped sweat from his brow with the sleeve of his shirt. 'Anyway, all Chinee look the same to me . . . man or woman.'

'Doesn't matter,' Michael muttered. 'It's got to be them.'

Once Michael had scouted the valley with Henry and Luke, Christie and John had ridden away to locate Mort's party. Christie had used his skills to skirt the track he knew the Chinese would most probably use, and the trail he had chosen had taken them up onto the ridges overlooking the narrow valleys and shimmering plains below. From their vantage point on the ridge they had observed small parties of prospectors winding like ants along the track. Eventually they had spotted the Chinese column snaking its way south west along the track towards the Palmer.

Michael turned and walked to the stand of scrub where their mounts grazed. Very little needed to be said. The five men, four days out of Cooktown, knew the next stage in his plan. Now it was only a matter of waiting for Mort to come to them.

The men watched with some curiosity from astride their horses as Michael walked the ground he had selected for his ambush site. He was a master tactician in ambushing and the site was carefully chosen for maximum advantage to compensate for their smaller number over Mort's party.

Henry had more of an appreciation for what the Irish mercenary was doing, when Michael occasionally stopped, and crouched to scan the surrounding terrain. As a veteran of the Crimean War, he understood the importance of ambush; a small party of men had the odds on their side when they utilised surprise, concealment and cover, to catch an enemy in ground not advantageous to him.

Mort's party was most likely to enter the killing ground that he had chosen because of the way the terrain naturally channelled them; a steep hill covered in forest to one side, and a sharp drop from the edge of the plateau on the other side left little choice.

An all out assault on a tong stockade was out of the question. In the open, and without the reinforcements of the Tiger Tong located somewhere along the track, Mort was most vulnerable. Satisfied at his choice of ground, Michael briefed his men and they dismounted to carry out the tasks he had assigned them.

The ambushers sweated under the tropical sun as they hastily erected log defences from the fallen timber they carried from the nearby hill. The trees, brought down by termites or storm, were made to appear as a natural part of the plain. Only those experienced in the tactics of ambush might notice the potential danger of the area. And Michael was gambling that Mort was not one of them.

When everything had been prepared the four men stood in a semicircle around Michael's plan scratched in the earth. The ambush layout resembled an L with Henry and Luke to be positioned at the bottom. Michael and John would form the stem, while Christie would be positioned at the top, ready to cut off any attempt to retreat as well as to give early warning of the approach of the column. The only way out of the carefully laid ambush was over the steep edge of the plateau.

Michael used the tip of his bowie knife as a pointer. 'That gully behind us will be our way out,' he said waving to the cut in the hill behind them with his knife. The gully was a dry watercourse that had carved out the rock and provided a convenient cover for the withdrawal. 'When we withdraw we will do so in short stages. One group on the ground providing covering fire while the other group moves. Are there any questions?' They tugged at beards and scratched at the insect bites that covered their bodies. The plan appeared simple and effective and no-one spoke. 'Good!' Michael grunted as he stood and stretched. Each man knew his job and all had at one time or another in their lives known what to expect when the shooting started.

'We ought to get the horses up there now,' Henry said as he shaded his eyes against the glare of sun reflecting off the rocks.

'Good idea,' Michael said, sliding the bowie down the side of his boot. 'We'll hobble them on the other side. I don't think we have much time.'

And he was right. They had hardly taken the horses over the hill, when Christie came running back from his vantage point. Sweat streamed down his face and into his beard. 'They're coming!' he gasped breathlessly.

The ambushers melted into the ground behind their improvised timber defences and waited – but not for very long.

FORTY

From his concealed position Michael could see the lead man of the approaching column. He was one of the Chinese tong men and carried an ancient flintlock musket carelessly across his shoulder.

Michael set the rear sight of his Snider to two hundred yards, the distance he estimated the lead man was from him. Beside him, John did the same. Both men held their breaths as the man passed them and was followed by others.

No flanking scouts! Michael thought and breathed a little easier. He had gambled and won. He adjusted his rifle sights to one hundred yards. The centre of the column came into sight opposite them. Michael could see that they were bunched two abreast. It appeared that they had no intentions of falling behind their comrades, to be picked off by tribesmen, who might be lurking in the silent grey scrub. He could see that the Chinese were armed but that their weapons were a motley collection of ancient flintlocks with even a blunderbuss or two. At the centre of the column a handful of Europeans were clustered together carrying Winchester rifles.

'There!' John hissed. 'There she is.' Although John had never seen Hue before, she was as he had expected a member of a Chinese mandarin family to be. She carried herself with a regal dignity and was as beautiful as Michael has described her. John found that he could not take his eyes from the slender young girl.

'Get ready!' Michael hissed, and John reluctantly tore his eyes away. Michael scanned the line of men and found his target. 'Tell 'em now,' he said softly to John as he focused the former *Osprey* captain along the sights of his rifle.

'Brothers! Throw down your weapons,' John called out in Chinese. 'Or you will die as you stand!' Immediately the escort party milled uncertainly, peering in the direction from which the strange voice had come. But they had not dropped their muskets, and he could see Mort saying something to Woo, the pirate captain. Michael centred the fore-sight blade of his Snider on Mort's chest.

'Throw down your weapons brothers. There are many of us,' John called out. 'We can pick you off before you know death has come to you.'

One of the more daring Chinese raised his musket. Michael saw the man's movements and immediately shifted his sights from Mort to the Chinese musketeer. Michael fired and the shot echoed off the hill behind them. The big slug of the Snider took the musketeer through the chest. He cried out and threw up his arms as he crumpled to the ground. A flight of sulphur-crested cockatoos rose as a screeching white cloud into the azure sky, the sound unhinging the Chinese who panicked and began firing wildly. It had been a split-second decision that had reprieved Mort from certain death.

The return fire from the ambushing men proved deadly accurate. Three out of four shots found targets. The escort party was now reduced by four and none of the panicked return fire caused any casualties to the ambushers. Michael's party brought down four more Chinese as they remained standing to reload the cumbersome muskets, before wisely following the *Osprey* crewmen's example and dropping to the ground.

Only the return rapid fire of the Winchesters had any real effect on the ambushers. It forced Michael and his men to keep their heads low, and some of the Winchester rounds flew uncomfortably close to pluck at the grass and whine off into the distance.

'Who in hell is out there?' Sims croaked with fear. 'They'll pick us all off.'

'Must be another one of those murdering tong,' Mort growled as he scrabbled in the pocket of his trousers for a box of cartridges. When he reloaded a thought nagged him. The ambush was too professional for what he had seen of the tongs. Whoever was out there, had laid a textbook ambush on them. He knew that they were trapped.

'I'm hit!' The strangled cry came from one of the crew members who had foolishly exposed himself to gain a better view of the plain. The sailor toppled on his back clutching his stomach, and dark blood oozed from the wound, staining the man's dirty white shirt a dark coffee red. 'Jesus it hurts,' he groaned, as he writhed in agony. 'Help me! For God's sake help me Cap'n Mort.'

Mort chambered a round and levelled his rifle at the sailor. He fired and the bullet smashed into the sailor's skull, killing him instantly. Sims gave his boss a frightened and shocked look. 'Had to be done,' Mort grunted. 'The man was gut shot. He would have taken a long time to die.'

The firing tapered off as neither side presented themselves as targets. Mort cautiously raised himself on his elbows for a better view of their situation. He knew that they were boxed in, with just the drop of the plateau behind them. He considered the options; if he and his party remained in their present position the ambushers would be hard pressed to leave their own positions without exposing themselves to his guns. To opt for withdrawal, using the cliff behind them, invited the ambushers to advance, and pick them off when he and his men were exposed on the cliff face.

Mort knew full well the effective range of the Snider to be five hundred yards. Not reassuring knowledge, he thought dismally. In the hands of marksmen, the Snider rifle could pin them down for-ever. The men who had ambushed him were good.

'Captain Woo!' he bellowed. The pirate captain slithered through the long grass. Mort could clearly see fear etched in the man's sweating, pockmarked face. 'Do you know who might be out there?' he asked.

Woo shook his head.

'Man who call to us,' he replied shaking his head, 'he no speakee Chinee velly good. Me tink he maybe white man.'

Mort was puzzled. If what Woo said was correct, then he was lost for who might have reason to ambush them.

'Mort! If you are still alive I suggest that you listen carefully.'

'O'Flynn!' Mort hissed. He should have been killed when the *Osprey* went down!

'If you want to live, send the girl unharmed forward of where you are. If you do this we will let you all live . . . for now.'

For now . . . The last words were not lost on Mort. So, O'Flynn was out for revenge. He was not really interested in wiping out the rest of the party, just him. 'I'm here O'Flynn. And I hear what you are saying,' he called back. 'But as I see the situation, we are at a checkmate. You cannot advance. And we cannot retreat without losses on both sides.'

An ominous silence followed but was soon shattered by a single shot. A Chinese screamed as the Snider round took him through the head. Christie Palmerston had wriggled forward with the stealth of an Aboriginal warrior to pick off a Chinese musketeer who had foolishly moved. There was a murmur of frightened confusion amongst the Chinese.

'As you can see Captain Mort,' Michael called, when the sing-song voices had settled into a low moan of fear, 'we can pick you off one at a time until we get to you.'

'Captain Mort. You givee white man the woman,' Woo said, plucking fearfully at Mort's sleeve. 'He will kill us all.'

The pirate captain's plea was cut short by a voice calling to them across the plain. The words were in Chinese and its effect was to make him even more urgent in his entreaty to allow the girl to go.

'What was said?' Mort asked the terrified pirate. Aboard his junk Woo was afraid of no man. But in the heat and dust of this terrible land, death came randomly to pluck life away, and there appeared to be no answer to this kind of fighting.

'He say you be killed by us if you no let girl go,' Woo replied, staring wide-eyed at Mort. 'He say all Chinaman go . . . not kill Chinaman you let girl go.'

Mort glanced around at the Chinese and noticed that one of the tong members was watching him with a dangerous and calculating look. He contemplated the rapidly deteriorating situation. There was a good chance his own men might turn on him. 'We will give them the girl,' he said quietly. But although he was giving her up, he had no intention of allowing the Irish-American to win. Two could play at ambushing! Already his murderous mind had formulated a plan. 'Tell your men to let the girl go,' he said to Woo, who nodded vigorously, and crawled back to Hue.

He ordered her to stand and she did so cautiously. She had also heard the strangely accented

Chinese voice. As far as she could tell she was only going from one band of brigands to another.

Michael and John peered across the open plain as the slender young girl rose uncertainly. 'Hue, do not be afraid,' John called to her in Chinese. 'Do as I say. Walk forward of where you are now standing. Walk towards the place on the hill where the big rocks are and wait. Be assured, we are friends come to save you, and return you unharmed to your home.'

They could see the girl's chin tilt with hopeful expectation as the voice calling to her did not sound threatening. She walked slowly towards the rock-lined gully behind the ambushers while Michael and John slithered away from their position behind the log. As Michael crawled with his rifle cradled in his arms he bitterly regretted not killing Mort when he had the chance. But he had been true to the promise he had made to Horace Brown; the rescue of the Cochinese girl came first. Besides, the man he had vowed to kill would come after them, because he had no other choice. Without the girl, Mort's sinking of the *Osprey* would have been a senseless and wasted act.

Hue walked uncertainly past John and Michael. If all was going according to plan Christie, Henry and Luke would now be snaking their way through the sea of long grass towards the gully. Michael would wait in his present position to give covering fire if necessary.

But Mort also waited patiently. He was in no hurry to expose himself to the guns of the ambushers as he had a healthy respect for his opponent's military skills. While he waited he issued orders down the line of Chinese, using Woo as his interpreter. They knew they must obey. Tong leaders were murderously unforgiving. They must get the girl back or suffer the lethal consequences of failure.

'I am John Wong. And the men with me are here to help you,' John told Hue as she stood in the gully surrounded by the ring of tough-looking men. Although she was frightened, the young, clean-shaven giant who spoke to her had a gentle voice belying his tough appearance.

She recognised both the man with the eye patch, and the tall man who spoke bad French. But Hue was most intrigued by the tall young man who towered over her. She could see that he was part Chinese and part European. Never before had she met an Oriental man of his size. His dark eyes seemed to have a cold, deadly smoulder – except when he smiled. Then she felt the warmth that was at the core of the man who called himself John Wong. 'I believe you John Wong,' she replied in Chinese.

Michael kept an uneasy eye on the plain. When the rest of his party had scrambled into the safety of the rocks he flashed them a smile of relief. 'C'mon,' he snapped. 'We have to get to the horses and out of here before Mort can close in on us.' He had no doubts that even now the murderous former sea captain was probably redeploying his men to intercept them and cut off their retreat.

The scramble along the rock-littered gully,

towards the dense rainforest on the summit above them, was made with few words. Michael noticed that Henry was lagging behind. He gritted his teeth and pushed on, despite the searing agony in his leg. He had insisted on joining this rescue party and had given his word that he would keep up with the others.

Breathing in ragged gasps from lungs tortured by the gruelling climb, they reached the top of the hill where Michael gave the order to take a short rest. Sweat soaked, they collapsed amongst the shadows of the majestic rainforest. All they had to do now was descend into the tiny valley below, where their horses were hobbled. From there Christie would guide them over the top of the range, and out onto a trail that led to the main track back to Cooktown. Mounted, they could easily outpace any attempt Mort made on foot to outflank or circle them for an ambush. So far it had been so easy, Michael thought as he surveyed his weary party.

Christie was first to pick up the ominous sounds that drifted on the humid, still air of the rainforest. Then Michael heard the distant whinnying and immediately recognised the sound as the pitiful cry of horses in distress. 'Mort?' he hissed his question.

Christie shook his head. 'Bloody myalls!' he spat, leaping to his feet. The others scrambled down the hill after him. When they finally reached the bottom of the narrow valley Michael groaned in despair at what they found.

Riddled with spears, the horses lay dead or dying, among them Henry's chestnut. Blood-specked foam covered his muzzle as he made a feeble attempt to regain his feet. Henry raised his rifle and the big horse's body quivered briefly in death from the single shot. As Henry reloaded there were tears of rage in his eyes for the men who had forced him to kill his gentle mare.

Without the horses they would have to elude any pursuers on foot across some of the most rugged country on the island continent. Their saddle bags had been riffled too and anything of value taken. The only remaining items were those which they carried. They were at least well armed and ammunition was not a problem. But they were without food and had lost a critical advantage over Mort. And they now had the additional problem of whoever had speared the horses.

'Probably Merkin,' Christie muttered as he threw aside one of the thin reed spears. 'Killed the horses so they get a better chance to pick us off later in the bush.'

Hue stared fearfully at the dead horses and unconsciously shifted closer to John.

'We will be safe,' he said to her when he saw the expression of fear in her face. 'The big man with the one eye is a great warrior.' He shrugged nonchalantly as if to dismiss the situation as a minor setback to their plans. 'He has seen worse.'

She understood his quietly spoken words. The men gathered around her indeed had the unmistakable look of tough warriors. In her own country she might have called them bandits.

Christie hefted his rifle and walked away from the horses. Sunset was almost upon them and he wanted to get to high ground before the sun sank in the deep valleys. Once the sun was gone they would be plunged into the total darkness of the rainforest night. The others followed as he led them out of the small and narrow valley.

Mort gazed up at the rainforest-covered hill. The Irishman was somewhere up there but finding O'Flynn without an Aboriginal tracker was going to be extremely difficult. Nevertheless it was imperative that they should keep close on his heels.

He had debated with himself whether he should split his party and send on one half to try and set up a cordon near Cooktown. But he dismissed the idea, thinking of how easy it would be to slip past a few men in the dark near the town. This left him with one option. 'Mister Sims. We are going up the hill.'

Sims groaned and passed on the message to the pirate captain. Woo stared with disbelief up at the range of hills covered in a tangle of rainforest and realised that the search for the men who had ambushed them would not only be physically arduous, but also downright dangerous. The ambushers had a ruthless efficiency in the way they had hit and run.

Woo's fears were echoed silently by Sims. He too had no desire to plunge into the ominous rainforest above them in the pursuit of O'Flynn. But his fear of Mort was greater than his fear of the Irish mercenary, and he now bitterly regretted that he had changed his mind about jumping ship in Cooktown when they had initially sailed into port.

Mort's men advanced with great caution up the hill. Within the hour they stumbled onto the dead horses in the small valley below. The discovery sent a chill through every man. With frightened looks they glanced around the valley, as if expecting to see the painted warriors suddenly emerge, ululating blood-chilling war cries of the black cockatoo and falling on them with stone axes and spears. They were more than eager to leave the oppressive valley and return to the more open plains of the Palmer track.

But Mort was forced to make camp for the night. Already the deep gloom of the valley descended into an inky blackness and he knew it was hopeless to try and find the Irishman in the dark. Besides, he figured, with a sense of savage satisfaction, O'Flynn would also have to make camp for the night.

Mort stared at the dead horses realising that their discovery had been a gift from the devil. The Irish bastard no longer had horses to get himself and his party clear of the mountains. Now he would be on even terms to hunt down O'Flynn and kill him.

FORTY-ONE

Wallarie had been gone two days when the Werners received their first visitors at the Schmidt farm. Caroline first noticed the tiny cloud of dust on the horizon and the faint outline of a small column of horsemen. 'Husband,' she called from the brackish, reed-covered waterhole about a hundred yards from the shanty, 'men are coming.'

Otto pulled on his black coat over his shirt and braces and hurried down to join his wife. 'They are mounted policemen,' he observed, shading his eyes against the rising sun hanging low behind the men. 'I count five of them.'

They stood together waiting for the patrol. A young officer rode ahead of the troop which came to a halt a short distance away. The man was hardly in his twenties. His uniform was covered in dust and his eyes a rheumy red from too many hours of scanning the plains. Behind him were three rough-looking white troopers and an Aboriginal trooper dressed in the uniform of his colleagues. The young officer reined in before the missionaries.

'I am Inspector Garland sir. Who may you be?' he asked somewhat brusquely.

From his manner Otto deduced that the young man was not used to polite niceties. 'I am Pastor Werner and this is my vife Frau Werner,' Otto formally replied.

The young officer glanced at Caroline with unbridled desire and she instinctively moved closer to her husband. Otto had seen his look and bridled at the boorish manner of the young policeman sitting haughtily in the saddle looking down upon them.

'You must be the godbotherer the old German mentioned in his letter,' Garland said, rustling in the saddlebag behind him. He produced a large leather wallet crammed with papers and a letter which he passed down to Otto. 'We found the old German yesterday on our patrol.'

Sadly Otto glanced up from the letter. 'Herr Schmidt is dead. Ja?' Both Caroline and the policeman expressed looks of surprise. 'I know this Inspector. This is Herr Schmidt's final vishes.'

'Thought it might be,' the inspector grunted. 'Don't read German but I did recognise your name written in there.'

Otto turned to his wife and spoke in German, not feeling obliged to be polite to the young man. 'Herr Schmidt has left us this place to be used as a mission station. He has said that the only friends he had out here were the wandering Aboriginal people who were very kind to him. He has begged us to look after them, my wife.'

Caroline nodded and tears came to her eyes, remembering the man who, despite being obviously wounded by a European bullet, had saved their lives when he could have just as easily let them die. 'We have found God's will,' she replied simply, 'and it is to give our lives to the true people of this land.'

Otto felt a burst of love for this beautiful woman who had followed him into hell. He knew that it would be she who would provide the true strength he would need to go on.

'Sorry to interrupt you Reverend,' Garland said somewhat irritably at being ignored. 'But how did you get here?'

Otto turned his attention back to the officer.

'An Aborigine person guided us here when we were out of vater.'

'His name wasn't Wallarie by any chance?' Garland asked as he leaned forward in the saddle. Otto frowned at the question.

'Who is this Vallarie you talk about?' he asked.

'A murderin' charcoal we have been tracking since a body was found a few days from here with his spear in 'im. At least that's who my tracker tells me got the prospector. Trooper Jimmy used to be with the Native Mounted Police a few years back down in Rockhampton. That's where he said he's seen the spear before. This Wallarie speaks a bit of English.'

Otto stared into the eyes of the officer. 'The

Aboriginal who helped meine vife and I could not speak German or English, Inspector.' The officer returned the stare for a brief moment. It was a contest, as they both knew.

'Then my tracker must be wrong,' Garland finally said. 'He says that the blackfella we are tracking is the legendary Darambal man of central Queensland and well-known killer of Europeans, good, God-fearing Christians.'

'The man who helped us was very old,' Otto lied without hesitation. 'Maybe in his seventies. How old is this Vallarie person you are hunting?'

The Inspector straightened in his saddle and glared at the missionary. 'From what I have heard about him, he would not be that old.'

'Ach, then the man who helped us could not be this Vallarie you are hunting. The man who helped us is probably just a vild blackman from the bush around here.'

'Well, we will not bother you any longer Reverend,' Garland said as he reined his horse away. 'I am sure a man of the cloth would not lie to Her Majesty's constabulary,' he added sarcastically. Trooper Jimmy was the most experienced tracker on the frontier and was never wrong about anything to do with charcoals. If he said they had tracked the notorious killer blackfella to Schmidt's farm – then that was it. It was obvious that the German missionaries had been helped by the blackfella in some way and were protecting him. But it did not bide well to harass a member of the clergy. The authorities frowned very strongly on such matters. From what he had heard of Wallarie's reputation the hunt would not be easy. Legend had it that the warrior had been the companion of the equally notorious bushranger Tom Duffy and that the Darambal man had a great knowledge of European ways and weapons. Coupled with his inherent skills in the bush he was indeed a formidable foe to pursue. But Trooper Jimmy was an equal match.

As he rode to rejoin his troop waiting in their saddles a short distance away he noticed a strange expression on Trooper Jimmy's face. If he did not know any better he would have thought he saw a terrible fear in the Aboriginal police tracker's dark eyes.

'You still have his tracks?' Garland asked when he reined in beside his tracker. Jimmy ducked his head. Garland could see that his man was extremely nervous. He had never seen Trooper Jimmy behave like this before. 'Can you still see Wallarie's tracks?' he asked again irritably.

'No boss,' Jimmy answered furtively. 'Track all gone . . . track all blown away . . . Wallarie gone.'

'You lyin' to me?' Garland hissed menacingly. 'You've had him all the way to Schmidt's farm. So how could he disappear? I know you Jimmy. You could track a fart in a crowded pub on pay day.'

'Sorry boss,' Trooper Jimmy mumbled. 'Track all gone.'

Garland shook his head in resignation and sighed. He knew from his long experience with his tracker that nothing would budge him when he set his mind to it. At least now he had an excuse to turn around and return to the camp a hundred miles back. There was enough to do around the goldfields without setting out on an expedition in pursuit of just one blackfella suspected of killing a prospector. At least back in the police camp he could get a drink, a wash and a woman. As it was he had been warned by the older troopers back at the barracks that hunting Wallarie was a waste of time. There was an almost grudging respect for the man from both Aboriginal and European troopers who had attempted to hunt him years earlier. He remembered something an Aboriginal trooper once said to him. Garland turned to his trooper. 'He has used magic, hasn't he?'

Jimmy did not answer but glanced away guiltily. How could the whitefellas know about blackfella magic? How could they read the signs that he could when their eyes were closed. Jimmy glanced at the eagle feathers scattered across the track. They were the signs put there by Wallarie to warn him off. Jimmy sensed the power of the magic and feared its deadly strength. Working for the white man for tucker and tobacco was not worth his life.

Garland did not expect an answer from his tracker. He had the answer in the stricken expression on the man's face. He glanced back at the tall missionary standing beside his pretty wife by the dwindling waterhole. If a man of the Bible was prepared to lie for a myall killer then there could be something in the magic bit that protected the Darambal warrior. The police inspector was starting to feel that he had worked amongst the Aboriginal

568

people for too long. He was starting to believe in their ways.

Otto watched the horsemen disappear in the direction from whence they had come. He knew that for some reason they were no longer interested in continuing the pursuit of the man who had saved their lives.

'You did not tell the policeman the truth,' Caroline said quietly as she watched the patrol fade into the dust. But it was not an accusation.

'No my wife. I lied. Just as Danny Boy lied to us,' he answered ruefully. 'But I understand why he had to lie to us.'

'Do you not think that it was our duty to tell the policeman that Danny Boy might have been the man they sought?'

Otto glanced at his wife from the corner of his eye. 'God sent us an angel to save and guide us to our new home, not a devil as the police think this Wallarie person to be. The black man who helped us had a good soul. I could sense it as strongly as I can smell the red earth of this land.'

Caroline touched her husband's elbow. It was her way of letting him know that she accepted what he said to be true.

'Well, Herr Schmidt has left us all his land to build a mission station,' Otto said as he turned to walk back to the rough bush hut. According to his letter it seems he knew that he was dying and set out for help. When he realised that he would not make it he set out his last will and testament leaving all that he owned to us and the Aboriginal people. It has been witnessed and formally notarised. This land is legally ours . . . and the Aboriginal people we must help in the years ahead.'

'Do you think Wallarie will ever return to us?' Caroline asked quietly as they walked towards the hut.

'I think Danny Boy will,' he replied with an enigmatic smile. 'After he has done what ever mission God has sent him on.'

FORTY-TWO

'No use going on. We could walk off a cliff,' Christie advised as he and Michael stood on a ridge gazing across the magnificent vista. The night was rapidly descending and as spectacular as the view was, Michael saw the valleys and ridges not for their natural beauty, but for the lung-tearing, strength-sapping obstacles they presented to their retreat from Mort.

'We move out before first light,' Michael said wearily. 'We set up a sentry roster for the night. No fires and we keep close together.'

The others listened and nodded their exhausted agreement. With glazed eyes they stared at the soft purple shadows covering the mountain in front of them while a scatter of mauve-edged clouds drifted like a delicately stained blanket hiding the tree-lined ridge. If that mountain was to be climbed the next day they held out little hope of getting back to Cooktown.

But Christie had no intention of tackling the mountain. His keen eyes were already plotting a course through the valley below. He could distinguish a creek line in the thicket of rainforest as the shadows pointed out the changes in the valley's topography to him. It would not be easy in the dense scrub, he surmised. But they did have jungle knives to hack a way through the tangle of vines.

Hue followed John to the base of a giant tree, the buttress roots of which provided a cosy nook for the night. She sat beside him and he passed her something to eat. 'It's dried meat,' he said when he saw her puzzled expression. 'Like the way your people dry fish.'

With a delicate bite she gnawed at the meat stick which had the consistency of leather. Finally, she was able to bite a piece off. It tasted salty but good.

John smiled at the girl's suspicious reaction to her first taste of jerky. 'You will have to make it last because that is all I have,' he said with a sigh.

'You speak Chinese well for a white man,' she said as she savoured the strong flavour. 'But then, you also have Chinese blood.'

'You speak Chinese well for a Chinese,' he replied with a grin. Hue looked away shyly. He was surprised to see her unexpected reaction. She was, after all, the daughter of a mandarin, and he had not expected to see her act as a young girl might. His smile continued as his eyes roamed over her. She was tiny in comparison to him, and under her blue trousers and jacket, he could see that she was slim in a boyish way.

Hue found his frank appraisal refreshing. He was not intimidated by her simply because she was the daughter of a mandarin. She guessed that his brashness was part of his European blood.

'I also speak French,' she said proudly, and anger suddenly clouded her beautiful face. 'It is the language of my enemy,' she frowned. Although John was only vaguely aware of the place called Cochin China, he was less aware of the French insidiously colonising the land of the Viets.

'Tell me about you,' John said disarmingly, and Hue's thoughts of politics waned under his friendly and frank gaze. She smiled, and talked softly about her life until Henry came late in the night to tell him it was John's turn to stand guard.

When Henry and the girl made their way back to the makeshift camp, John sat with his back against a tree, while the others snatched some welcome sleep. He sighed. Of all the girls to be interested in, he mused as he watched and listened in the night, it had to be one who just happened to be the daughter of nobility and a rebel against the French.

Possums rustled in the trees and their sound was vaguely reassuring. But John tensed when he heard the rustle behind him. Very slowly, he raised his rifle, and Hue's pale face suddenly loomed in front of him. He relaxed, and lowered the gun.

'I was frightened and could not sleep,' she

whispered in a small voice as she sat beside him. 'I feel safer with you.' For the first time since she had been taken prisoner by the Chinese pirates, Hue felt an overwhelming need to trust in another human – and a need for emotional comfort. Her life as a rebel against the French and many of her own people who had collaborated with the European colonisers had kept her in a perpetual state of tension and suspicion. But deep in the forests of the land so alien and far from her own she felt that she was no longer the young woman who had once stood against the French invaders. Here she was a woman who depended on the courage and determination of others to save her. Her fate had passed from her hands.

Within minutes she was asleep, her head resting against John's broad chest. Very gently he slipped his muscled arm around her shoulders and holding her he experienced a tenderness that he had never known before. He felt awkward. It was as if he were holding some ethereal creature, something so fragile that the mere movement of his arm might crush her. Her breath was warm and moist against his throat. But his moment of tenderness was short lived when he remembered Soo Yin's instructions. To betray Soo Yin was to invite death in an obscenely slow manner. Inevitably, he would have to betray the men he depended on to survive the flight across the jungle-covered range, and that would not be easy. But he knew his sworn duty to the tong leader in Cooktown.

FORTY-THREE

Within the walls of her tiny room at the top of the stairs Miss Gertrude Pitcher sat at the edge of her bed and stared at the flicker of the lamp wick. Her position as governess that Missus Penelope had secured for her was everything she could have dreamed of. The children were a delight and the master and mistress of the house were wonderfully generous. The Baroness certainly had a considerable amount of influence in Sydney social circles.

But Gertrude hated being alone when the night came and her busy duties caring for the children were at a temporary standstill. For it was in the dark hours of the night that the memory of a great betrayal crept into her room to sit at the end of the bed and torment her with overpowering guilt. Now she was exposed to a truly close family, the torment seemed to be greater, and she often cried alone in the privacy of her tiny room. Mister Granville White's threat – to do her a terrible mischief – should she tell Missus White of what had occurred in the library with Dorothy was rapidly fading in its ability to terrify her anymore. But the guilt she lived with every time she looked into the innocent faces of her young charges in this new household was far worse than anything Mister White could do to her.

Gertrude turned down the wick on the lamp by her bed and undressed in the dark. She slipped into a long nightdress and crawled between the crisp sheets of her single bed. She lay staring in the dark. Weeks had passed and still Dorothy's screams of despair and pain echoed in her mind. Gertrude twisted and turned as she vainly attempted to stop the screams in her head. The anguished, pain-stricken face of the little girl floated near the ceiling and Gertrude clenched her eyes shut to make it go away. But the tormented face remained in her head and she cried out in her despair.

Was not the desertion of a soldier in the Queen's army an aberrant crime punishable by death, she thought, as she threw back the bed sheets and placed her feet on the cold floor. Nigh on thirty years she had devoted her life to children. She had no other family other than a brother in England. She had always been alone in the colonies, except for the children she had raised for other people – children who had grown to adults and loved her for the maternal concern she had lavished on them.

Gertrude reached for the lamp and lit the wick. The room was filled with a soft light and the demons dissolved. The time had come to stop fearing Mister White. She would leave this place and go to one where he could no longer hurt her with his threats. Before she did, however, she would expose the man feted to become a knight of the realm for what he was — a truly evil man with no soul.

For a long time the governess had known this time would come. She had prepared herself carefully, and had all that she needed hidden in the room.

Calmly Gertrude changed from her night wear into the best dress she owned. She pinned back her hair into a bun and sat down at the table in her room. From a drawer under the table she took writing paper and by the light of her lamp she wrote a short letter.

When the letter was written she placed it in an envelope and wrote across the front 'Missus Fiona White'.

FORTY-FOUR

By mid-morning Michael and his party found the going harder. The rainforest closed against them with a tangle of vines and brush as they descended from the ridge and into the narrow valley below. Under the canopy of the close-packed trees, they sweltered in the still, humid air.

The stagnation in the valley brought back terrible memories to Luke. He vividly remembered similar conditions years earlier when he had trekked across the mountains west of Port Douglas to the dry plains and broad valleys, south of the Palmer River.

In the late afternoon Michael called a halt at the edge of a mountain stream and their battle with the undergrowth and scrub of the valley was temporarily set aside while water canteens were refilled from the stream that gurgled crystal clear over a rock and pebble bed. With sweet notes it swept along fallen leaves from the forest giants and swirled around rocks where tiny shrimp-like creatures scuttled out of sight of predators.

Hue modestly excused herself to go into the bushes while the men stripped to wallow in the shallow stream and wash the cuts and leech bites that covered their sweat-grimed bodies. The water soothed their tired bodies, lulling the bushmen into a lethargy. But Hue's agonised screams galvanised the men into action. They tumbled from the stream snatching their clothes and rifles as they ran to her.

John had been standing guard whilst the other three bushmen had been bathing and was the first to reach Hue. She stood with her pants around her ankles and clawed frantically at her arms and legs.

'Jesus!' Henry gasped. 'She's brushed up against a stinging tree.' The nettle-like leaves were covered in tiny glass-like spikes and Christie shouted a warning to the others to be careful not to go near.

The pain inflicted by the leaves was excruciating. The young woman's delicate skin was particularly vulnerable, and such was the extent of the searing pain, that she was not even aware that her pants were still around her ankles as John gripped her wrists to stop her scratching any further. He pulled her away from the tree and sat her down in a small clearing. 'It will sting and hurt but it will not kill you,' he said, as tears of pain and confusion welled in her eyes. 'You have been stung by the leaves of a tree.' Hue responded positively to his soothing words and fought to control her panic while the men averted their eyes to her nakedness, a reflex action to years of learned respect for the sanctity of a woman's body.

'We're going to have to rest up here,' Michael said flatly, 'until the girl gets over the worst of the stinging.'

'How long?' Luke asked, as he gazed through the gloom of green foliage. He was half-expecting to see Mort and his men close behind them.

'Not long. Maybe half an hour,' Michael replied. 'Means we will have to send somebody back the way we came to stand guard.'

'I'll go,' Luke volunteered.

John had quickly stripped Hue of her clothes and explained that they would need scrubbing in the stream to wash away any nettle barbs. She whimpered, and her face was contorted with pain as she gripped his big hand, as a child would an adult. Her dark eyes held his as if she were imploring him to take away the agony. But he felt helpless. There was very little he could do but empathise – and wish he could take on her pain himself.

He sat Hue gently on the bank of the mountain stream and placed his shirt around her slim body. Although the coarse shirt helped keep her warm she still shivered uncontrollably from the effects of both the stinging tree and her acute embarrassment at being seen naked in front of the bushmen.

Michael knew they should have a fire to help warm the girl. But he also knew that the smoke would mark their position to anyone who might be on the ridges above them. Nor did John request a fire for her. He also appreciated the deadly position that they were in. It was not only Mort they had to fear but possible detection by the Aboriginal warriors who had slaughtered their horses.

While John tended to Hue's stings, Henry very cautiously scrubbed Hue's clothes, using sand to remove the tiny poisonous barbs. Even Christie who disliked the Chinese felt sorry for the young woman. He watched as the girl whimpered and John stroked her long ebony hair while crooning soothing words as one would to a child in distress. Christie yanked a blood-bloated leech from under his shirt and flicked it into the bush. He tugged thoughtfully at his beard as he scanned the crest of a hill that rose to one side of the trail. He had earlier seen the faint wisp of smoke rising from the hill and guessed it was an Aboriginal fire. According to his calculations it would have been impossible for Mort to have been on the steep ridge. 'Mister O'Flynn,' he called softly, as he squatted on his haunches gazing up at the ridges. 'I think I've got an idea that might help us.' He did not wait for Michael to respond. 'I'm going to talk to the darkies. Might be our only chance if Mort is after us.'

Michael gave him a look as if to say he was mad, but he remembered that the bushman spoke some of the Aboriginal dialects of the north and nodded. They were both aware of how grim their current situation was. Henry was having trouble keeping up and now the girl was temporarily incapacitated. 'You talk the lingo here Mister Palmerston?' Michael asked.

'I hope so,' Christie answered with a grim smile, and rose to his feet.

John left Hue while he attended the impromptu briefing Michael had called. She was much calmer and had steeled herself against the stinging pain that continued to plague her. He glanced back at her sitting at the edge of the creek and smiled when he caught her eye. Hue returned a weak smile of reassurance. She thought about his gentle and caring manner and tried to dismiss the disturbing thoughts that she was attracted to a man who was neither European nor Chinese. In her culture such people were non-people.

The men gathered around Michael in a small clearing by the creek. 'Mister Palmerston is going to try and make contact with the local blackfellas,' Michael said, turning to Christie who crouched sketching a map in a patch of earth he had cleared.

'I will get food,' Christie explained. 'And maybe they can help us with this Mort fellow if he is still following us. Best you stay put until I get back.'

'For how long?' Henry asked quietly.

'Until tomorrow morning,' he replied. 'If I'm not back by then you carry on. Take this valley until you come to where the creek strikes a river. When you are across the river you'll come to some hills. When you get to the hills strike north. That'll take you into Cooktown – a day's walk.' When he had finished his briefing, he snapped the twig he had used as a pointer for his crude map and tossed it aside. He rose, slung his rifle on his shoulder, and was swallowed by the thick scrub as he strode away.

When he was gone Michael organised the camp for the night. Luke attempted to catch the tiny crustaceans that hid around the rocks in the calmer waters of the stream. He was only partly successful, however, and the few he did catch were eaten raw.

During the night they shivered and slept only in snatches between sentry duty. It was going to be a long and uncomfortable night, Michael realised, and felt the gloomy darkness of indecision. Should he have pushed on regardless of Hue's injuries? Had he decided wisely in letting Christie go in search of the tribesmen?

Just after midnight Michael inched his way into the scrub. It was his turn to relieve Henry of sentry duty. Vigilance was an utmost priority as the trail they had left when they hacked their way through the dense scrub was like a finger pointing in their direction. But at least the night concealed them so utterly that even Michael had to move by feel, using landmarks he had memorised before nightfall.

'It's me Henry,' he hissed when he was close to a tree with a massive trunk.

'Over here Mister O'Flynn,' came the soft reply from the inky darkness. Michael adjusted his course to grope towards the disembodied voice and found Henry sitting with his back against the rainforest giant. He plumped himself down beside the Englishman. 'How is your leg?'

'It's not good,' Henry sighed, and instinctively rubbed the old injury. 'But I think it will keep me going for one more day. Then I don't know.'

'If it gets so bad that you can't go on,' Michael

said softly, 'I will stay with you. Luke can keep going and send help back to us when he gets to Cooktown.' Henry attempted to protest but was cut short. 'You don't have any say in the matter Henry,' Michael said roughly. 'You are in my command for the duration of this expedition. As such, I am responsible for making the decisions as to what happens to my men.'

'Thank you for the offer Mister O'Flynn,' Henry replied quietly. 'But it's not necessary. Some things are ordained in life that we cannot change. Tomorrow, I either keep going or I die, one way or the other.'

'Nothing's *ordained* in this life,' Michael snapped angrily. Henry was talking like a man who was already dead and he had heard men talk that way before. It was usually the night before a battle when the agonising wait released the demons of despair that plagued men's imaginations. 'If life ordains whether we live or die then let life tell us to our faces. No. If that was so then I should have been dead a long, long time ago. *We*, Mister James, ordain by the choices we make whether we live or die.'

'My fate has been told to me in a way I do not expect you to understand,' Henry sighed sadly. 'From the day I followed that murdering son of the devil on the dispersals, he and I have been under a death sentence. The *how* I do not know. But I think I know the *when* of my death.'

Michael felt a spark of anger. 'No-one can know when they will die. That's foolish talk.'

'Foolish it may be to you Mister O'Flynn,' Henry replied sadly, 'but there are things about this land and its people we will never truly understand no matter how many years we are here.' He paused and stared into the night. Yes, Emma would miss him and grieve for a time. Gordon would some day grow to know of his father as a memory. 'I have known many men in my lifetime,' he continued. 'Men I have whored with in the brothels. Young men who I saw dead before they grew a week older. Strange, when I think about them. Young men who will be forever young. And I have known the men of this land. Fine men as you could know anywhere. One of the finest men I ever knew was a bushranger I once hunted the length and breadth of the colony. I think you know who I am talking about. Don't you Michael?'

Michael felt a stillness descend on him like an icy cloak. The disembodied voice in the dark was not that of the crippled former sergeant of the Native Mounted Police but the intimate voice of his dead brother Tom. He felt a hush descend on the bush as if all nocturnal life had stopped to listen to his reply. 'How did you . . . ?' he whispered hoarsely as his throat was suddenly dry. 'How did you know?'

'I wasn't completely sure until now,' he replied gently. 'You gave yourself away when you answered me.'

'But you thought you knew. How?' Michael asked. 'Did someone tip you off?'

'No. But I was a trap long enough to see things others missed,' he answered. 'And your sister Kate told me enough about you to make you as real to me as your brother Tom was. The way you talked. The way you were . . . are. Do you know that you look so much like your brother Tom you could have

585

passed for him? Maybe it was a good thing you weren't in Queensland when we were hunting him or someone might have got you two mixed up. But it was something else about you. It took the blindness that night gives our eyes for me to see you clearly. I cannot explain what I do not understand myself. Except to say that when you called to me a little while ago, I thought I was hearing Tom. It was like he was calling to me in the dark. But I know he's dead. I know because I watched him die out there in Burkesland. So when you called, something told me that Tom was also alive in you. The nights out here in the bush can do strange things to a man's soul. That's all I can tell you though I know it doesn't make sense.'

A silence fell between them and the soft sounds of the night returned: the rustle in the treetops of tiny glider possums seeking the branches of trees on which to land, the distant gurgle of the stream and the monotonous whirr of crickets. Finally Michael spoke. 'Tomorrow we go on and my order still stands. If you cannot go any further with your leg, we stick together until Luke sends back help.'

Henry rose stiffly to his feet and Michael felt his hand on his shoulder. 'We will see,' he said simply. 'We will see.' How could he tell Michael that an old Aboriginal elder had come to him in his dreams, night after night, to stand in the dark corners of his mind. Logical and learned men could explain the visits as nightmares brought on by his guilt for his participation in the murderous dispersals under Mort's command. But no, Henry thought, the old

Aboriginal was real. As real as Michael Duffy who now sat vigil in the night.

The mist–covered mountains felt the first touch of the rising sun as the damp fogs retreated to the cool safety of the valleys. Mists settled on the placid stream and by the time the warm sun had swallowed the last of the night fogs on the creek, Christie Palmerston had not returned.

Michael had half–expected the worst. Still days from Cooktown they were missing the man with the most experience to guide them out of the rain-forests. The previous day had sapped precious energy reserves and left them hungry and tired. He gave the order to move out and, as exhausted as they were, they obeyed. It was just after midday when they stumbled into a broad, flat valley under a sea of waving grasses. Tattered clothes streaked with dried blood marked their battle with the cruel-hooked barbs of jungle vines. Sweat–soaked shirts clung to their backs which were wet and clammy, and salty moisture dripped incessantly from their foreheads to sting their eyes. Exhausted, they paused to gaze down the valley. To be out of the cloying forest was a welcome relief.

Michael scanned the valley of waving grasses high as a man's waist and his eye followed the line of ridges either side of the valley. His military instinct told him to use the high ground to traverse the valley. But when he glanced back at his straggling file he noticed Henry rubbing his leg and knew that an attempt to climb another ridge could possibly lame him for life.

Hue's condition was little better than Henry's. Her sandals had finally given out and her feet were cut and swollen. John had been forced to carry her piggyback fashion for the last four hours of the trek. The Irish mercenary made his decision. They would traverse the valley floor and gain precious time.

When Mort emerged from the rainforest and onto the plain of the grass-covered valley he brought his party to a halt. The Chinese squatted and produced small round bowls and chopsticks and quickly devoured a cold meal of gluey rice and dried fish.

Mort chewed on a stick of jerky as he scanned the way ahead. He had a good view of the broad valley with its flat open spaces and his gaze settled on the two low hills either side under a heavy growth of rainforest. If he could get up there he could command a panoramic view of the valley below, he mused. He may have lost the Irishman's trail but he was determined to keep on his present course; he had calculated that his enemy would have had to traverse the valley if they were still travelling north to Cooktown. 'Mister Sims. Get the men on their feet. We have a climb ahead of us.'

Suddenly something caught Mort's eye. He could not believe his good fortune when he looked down on a tiny file of figures winding their way across the valley floor below. The Devil was on the side of those who cursed God! He spat in triumph.

He was now going to use O'Flynn's tactics against him!

Quickly seizing the initiative, he doubled his men into an ambush site at the end of the valley, where it was only a matter of waiting. With muskets and rifles ready Mort's men waited for the tiny party to file into *his* killing ground.

FORTY-FIVE

The clipper creaked and groaned as she sailed into the rolling seas of the Great Australian Bight. Having departed the port of Melbourne the sleek ship was now on a westerly course and well on her way to England.

Patrick Duffy spent most of his time above decks where the salt-laden sea winds crusted his hair, much to the despair of his fastidious grandmother. She had hoped that he might spend more time with her and in the company of the first-class passenger clique. But he seemed more at home sharing the companionship and conversation of the working-class crew who had taken a liking to the confident but not brash young man. He displayed an interest in their work without being intrusive and the sailors wondered at how Patrick failed to notice the small party of young girls around his own age who unabashedly followed him everywhere he went aboard ship. Their shy giggles and flirtatious behaviour had no impact on Patrick. They weren't to know he was absorbed in deep thoughts about his turbulent past and his uncertain future.

He stood at the starboard side of the clipper and gazed across the rolling waves at a grey horizon. He knew that somewhere below the horizon was the colony of South Australia and soon enough they would round the southern tip of the colony of Western Australia. At that point he would have left the land of his birth for the land of his grandmother's birth.

'Patrick,' the voice called gently to him, 'do you not feel that it is time to go below and join the captain? He has invited us to dine with him tonight.'

Patrick did not need to turn to see who had spoken to him.

'I will,' he replied quietly, 'as soon as the sun is just off the bow five degrees.'

Enid raised her eyebrows in surprise. The boy was a quick learner. He was even absorbing the language of the mariner.

'You will catch your cold if you remain too long above deck,' she said, and startled herself by placing her hand on his shoulder in a maternal manner. She wondered at the gesture as she had very rarely done the same to her own children. Emotional displays were something of an indulgence for the working classes. Patrick, however, did not seem to notice her touch and continued to stare at the distant horizon. 'Are you frightened

Patrick?' she asked, and his gaze dropped to the hissing seas kissing the hull of the ship.

'No Lady Enid,' he answered without looking at her. 'I was just thinking that a lot of things have happened.'

'Of what things were you thinking?' she asked, and he finally turned to face her.

'I was thinking of how things might have been different if my father were alive.'

Enid suddenly stiffened and felt a stab both of guilt and fear. She knew Michael was somewhere on the northern frontier of Queensland. But she had her reasons for concealing from Patrick her knowledge of his father's existence. Patrick was hers to use in her ongoing war with her evil son-in-law Granville White. And from what she had gleaned from Penelope, it did not seem that Michael Duffy was a man likely to survive Baron von Fellmann's expedition. Her guilt, however, was less for concealing from her grandson the fact that his father lived, than for the fact that she hoped that Michael would die, since he was the only person who truly posed a threat to her keeping Patrick.

'As we all know,' she replied a little tensely, 'your father was killed in New Zealand about the time you were born.'

Patrick's expression reflected his belief in her lie and she relaxed. 'I am going to be a soldier like my father,' Patrick said suddenly. 'I know he would have wanted that.'

Now Enid felt a rising horror for her grandson's aspiration to don the Queen's uniform. All her plans were centred on him receiving the finest education the English system could offer and then going on to rule the family fortunes.

'I think you will change your mind as you grow older,' she said quickly. 'You are young and I am sure that once you attend Eton you will see how much more there is to life than that of the soldier. So much more responsibility in managing the family's financial affairs. It is upon your shoulders to take us into the next century.'

Patrick stared into her eyes and she sensed a will as strong as her own in the boy. 'Uncle Max told me how my father died a hero in the Maori wars,' he said stubbornly. 'It is my duty to be like him.'

'Your father never wanted to be a soldier,' Enid countered. 'He was forced into that war because the evilness of your uncle Granville forced him there by circumstances none could foresee. Your father had always wanted to be a famous painter . . . not a soldier.'

Patrick frowned. 'Uncle Max told me that too,' he said, and Enid sensed a slight confusion in his reply. The irony of explaining the gentle nature of a man who she had always hated for his involvement with her daughter did not escape her. For a moment she felt confusion as she gazed at her grandson and noticed the very different physical appearance of him from the men of her own bloodline. He was in so many ways a true Duffy man. And yet he shared her blood through her daughter. He must therefore be part Macintosh. This thought consoled her and she decided to let him live in his dreams of aspiring to be like his father. 'Should you wish to be a soldier when you have completed your studies,' she sighed, 'I promise you that I will use my influence to purchase you a commission with a fine Scots regiment. My late husband's family ... your family now ... have commanded Scots regiments in the past for the crown. I am sure you would make a fine officer of the Queen.'

'You truly promise,' Patrick grinned, 'that you will allow me to be a soldier?'

'I do,' Enid replied with a smile, 'but only if you return the promise to do well at Eton and not display crude colonial behaviour at any time. Your uncle David won academic prizes when he was a student at Eton,' she added wistfully, thinking of her long-lost beloved son. 'But I know you will do so too as you have a fine tradition of nobility in your heritage.'

For a moment Patrick tried to think of any Irish royalty in the Duffy family. He could not, and knew that Lady Enid was referring to her ancestors. He also knew that he must start thinking about his Macintosh blood even though his uncle Daniel had sworn him to a sacred oath not to forget his Irish roots or religion.

'I promise Lady Enid,' he replied with a disarming smile.

'Good,' she said with a gentle squeeze of his shoulder. 'Then we shall go below and join the captain, young man. And there you shall display all the charm and manners of your aristocratic heritage.'

Patrick glanced up the deck at two young girls watching him from behind giggles, their mouths covered to contain their girlish secrets. He pulled a face at them and turned to accompany his grandmother. Girls were a confusing species, he thought. They were a bit of a pest. But even so, lately he had experienced strange and confusing thoughts about them. It was something in the way they smelt different and in the compulsion to touch their soft skin. And an even greater mystery was what they seemed to want from him.

FORTY-SIX

Michael's normally astute judgment was dulled. Exhaustion had taken its toll and he had no real indication that Mort was pursuing them, and was even now beginning to believe that he had either given up, or lost their trail. According to Christie Palmerston's last instructions they should be close to Cooktown and it seemed to Michael that the young bushman had sacrificed himself for nothing.

With the dark forests at their backs they now faced a broad, grassy plain that tapered to a rocky defile which led up and over a low saddle between two hills. It would be an arduous climb, but not as difficult as the steep hills either side of the valley, Michael estimated, hoping that they would be able to see the river from the crest of the saddle. To do so would raise morale and, although weak and hungry, his party still had reserves of strength to struggle on.

He glanced over his shoulder at his tiny command trudging behind him. At the rear of the file trudged Luke while John still carried Hue in front of Henry who limped with his rifle slung over his shoulder. Henry's twisted expression reflected his pain but was able to flash Michael a reassuring smile. Michael acknowledged his courage with a nod as he turned to resume the march. He flicked open the lid of a small brass compass to check their bearings. They were on a northerly course. Satisfied that the bearing put them close enough to Cooktown, he was in the process of closing the lid of the compass, when a sudden crackling volley of shots shattered the serenity of the valley.

Henry grunted as a Winchester bullet ripped through his chest. He died without a chance to fight back and Mort smiled with savage satisfaction to see the former sergeant hit by his well-aimed shot. Fate had dealt him an ace. His first round had been meant for O'Flynn, but the sight of his former sergeant limping behind O'Flynn allowed him an unexpected opportunity to kill the man whose actions many years earlier had indirectly brought him to his current predicament.

Michael pitched forward in the tall grass, hit by a bullet that seared a long furrow across the back of his shoulder. But his fall saved his life as a second volley of gunfire filled the air around him. Even as he had hit the ground he instinctively crawled away to take up another position, denying the ambushers an exact fix on where he lay.

Luke only knew that he had been hit. He could

feel a stickiness at the back of his leg and was not surprised to see his fingers covered in blood when he reached down to feel the source of the wetness. The bullet had hit him low across the thigh and shock had acted as a temporary anaesthetic. But the effect was rapidly wearing off to be replaced by a very painful stinging sensation.

'If you are still alive Mister O'Flynn,' Mort's voice taunted across the fifty yards or so that separated them, 'I suggest that you surrender. I promise you that I only want the girl. You have one minute before I send my men in after you.'

Michael slipped the Colt from its holster and pulled back the hammer. Between the rifle and the pistol, he had seven shots of rapid fire. Although the waist-high grass of the valley concealed him from view it did not provide cover from probing bullets. Mort had set his ambush with the professionalism of a trained soldier. They were spread in a skirmish line along the plain, and Michael's small party had walked right past the men crouching in the long grass. Michael's error of judgment had rendered his party virtually ineffective when the first volley had ripped through their ranks. Only John and Hue had been spared as Mort had given strict orders that they were not to be fired on.

Michael did not know whether he was the only one left alive. He dared not cry out to the others lest he give his new position away to the ambushers. He well knew that Mort had every intention of killing him, and cursed himself for not keeping to the high ground as his military instinct told him he should.

He felt sorrow, not for himself, but for the others whom he had led into the ambush. One minute was not a long time to reflect on thirty-two years of life, he thought sadly, as he lay on his stomach waiting for Mort's men to advance on him.

Although he was wounded, Luke was not out of action, and like Michael did not know who was left alive. He was at least sure Henry James was dead. The situation was looking hopeless. The long grass waved gently as a gust of wind funnelled down from the saddle of the ridge. Luke's face was pressed into the dry earth and the brittle grass felt harsh against his face.

The grass!

He suddenly remembered a time when he had been attacked in Burkesland years earlier. The tribesmen had fired the grass to force him away from his camp and into a line of spear-wielding warriors. Luke slid his knife from its sheath and sliced a handful of dry grass in front of him. He fumbled with a tin of wax matches and struck one of them. The match flared, and he thrust it into the improvised firebrand, which ignited with a soft crackle.

He shoved the firebrand into the grass and the dry grass hissed into life. The wind was still blowing in Mort's direction, he noted with grim satisfaction, and within seconds the fire had raced away from him, consuming all in its path. Without waiting he crawled dragging the firebrand behind him.

Mort was peering cautiously above the tall grass when he saw the first wisps of smoke. The wisps rapidly turned into a crackling black billow that spread along his front as a wall of flame rushed towards him and his men. How in hell?

As Luke crawled through the grass he came upon the body of Henry James lying on his back staring with blank eyes at the sky. Luke did not spend time mourning his friend but crawled on until he came across John and Hue huddled together, John keeping himself between the terrified girl and the direction from which the firing had come. 'Henry's dead,' Luke hissed as he passed them, and continued crawling towards Michael's last-known position.

The grass fire was now well alight and the rising gusts of wind swirled burning embers into the clear blue sky. The crackle turned into a roar and the sheets of flame rose in the smoke as a wall of orange and black.

'Get back to the hill!' Mort screamed as he rose from the grass. The hill had less grass to provide combustible material to feed the greedy flames. The Chinese did not have to understand English to know remaining meant being roasted alive. As one, they rose and fled with the European sailors towards the relative safety of the hills behind them.

Michael crawled through the grass until he almost collided with Luke. 'Henry's dead,' Luke said, 'but John and Hue are all right.'

'He knew he was going to die,' Michael said softly with a frown.

'What?' Luke asked. He had not caught Michael's words as they were drowned in the roar of the fire.

'Nothing important,' Michael muttered.

The wind was pushing the wall of fire away from

them. Burning cinders fluttered down, as the valley was seared by the fire, causing it to twist on itself like a tortured animal being scorched. Michael glanced up to see John running towards them. He was dragging Hue after him and when they reached Luke and Michael, the four survivors ran towards the saddle between the hills.

Mort saw them make their desperate dash for the hill and turned to snap a rapid fire at the retreating figures. He cared little if he hit the girl, such was his rage at having the tables turned on him. But the rounds fell short as the wall of flames roared towards him, and Mort turned and fled with his men to the hills.

The enraged captain could see the tiny enemy figures climbing the rise of the saddle between the hills. But all was not lost, he thought bitterly. He could still catch them. He still had Sims and two of his former crew with him as well as seven armed Chinese. They still outnumbered and outgunned O'Flynn's party. The grass fire was burning itself out and was only a temporary setback. Ultimately he would kill them all and take the girl.

'Goddamn! It hurts like blazes,' Luke said gritting his teeth. 'But I can still walk.' The wound was painful but not severe, and John bandaged Luke's leg with a sleeve he had torn from the American's shirt.

Hue attended to Michael's wound. It was an ugly, puckered, bleeding mark across his back leaving Michael with a stiff and painful shoulder. He stood stripped to the waist as Hue poured water from a canteen over the wound and marvelled at the scars that covered the big man's body. He was surely a warrior who had seen much combat in his lifetime she thought, and winced at the pain she knew she must be causing him.

Michael ignored his pain to stare across the valley at the forested hills where he could see Mort gathering his forces. He estimated that he was less than half a mile away and considered his options. His choices were dangerously limited. They could stand and fight from a defendable position. But Mort could lay siege and wear them down. Or push onto Cooktown thus exposing their backs to Mort's guns. Or choose an option that combined elements of the first two choices. 'We have to keep going,' Michael said, gritting his teeth as he stretched his arm to test its flexibility. 'I'm going to keep Mort busy while you get Hue to Cooktown.'

Neither Luke nor John made any comment. Michael was making the only possible decision under the circumstances. It was not a matter of heroics, but a tactical decision, one that gave the best chance of the majority surviving. If the river was close they would then be most vulnerable to Mort's guns while they were trying to cross. Someone would have to stay and hold Mort off when the time came to cross.

Hue was puzzled by the strange expressions on John's and Luke's faces. There was a resigned sadness she did not understand as the two men turned to walk away from the warrior with the one eye.

'Luke?' Michael called softly to the American who was about to join John with Hue. 'I want you to give my share of whatever we get for Hue's reward to my sister,' he said quietly as he stared across at the hills where Mort's party had disappeared into the trees.

'I'll do that,' Luke replied. 'Just tell me where I can find her and I'll make sure she gets it.'

'You won't have any trouble finding her,' Michael said with an enigmatic chuckle. 'You already know the lady. Kate O'Keefe is my sister.' Luke gaped at him in a stunned silence. Michael grinned at his friend's utter surprise. 'She and the rest of my family think I was killed in New Zealand back in '63. It's a long story and we haven't got time to chat about things right now.'

Luke suddenly felt guilty that it was Michael, and not he, who had volunteered for certain death. He reached out and placed his hand on Michael's shoulder. 'You go with them,' he said grimly. 'I can hold Mort off.'

'Better I stay behind,' Michael said gently. 'As far as my family is concerned I have been dead for many years now. And that is how I want it to stay. Besides, I've got nothing to leave behind. I always figured this is how I would go anyway. Been a lot of men in the past who have tried to do what Mort's men will probably do. But at least I will get a good chance to settle with him before they take me out. Kind of fitting that he and I go together.'

'You aren't dead yet,' Luke said roughly, although he knew that Michael had little chance of beating off any determined attack.

'Go now,' Michael said, as he thrust out his hand to his friend. Luke accepted the gesture as a bond between them. 'Be careful with John Wong when you get near Cooktown,' Michael added softly. 'Just keep up your guard at all times.'

Luke did not understand Michael's warning, but nodded and walked away without looking back.

As Luke walked away with his rifle over his shoulder, Michael turned his attention to the tree-covered hills to his front and pondered the threat John Wong posed. Christie would not have left them if Horace Brown had given him secret orders to ensure that they got the girl back to the French, he considered, as he checked his supply of Snider rounds. So it had to be the Eurasian who was under orders to keep the mission on track. But Michael Duffy had made the mistake of considering only one possibility. Soo Yin had not entered into his calculation.

'What was said to you when I was with the girl?' John asked suspiciously as they made their way down the reverse slope into the scrub below.

'Nothing much of interest,' Luke replied, parrying his question. 'Just that I have to buy him the first round of drinks when he gets back to Cooktown.'

'You know he is Kate O'Keefe's brother,' John said unexpectedly as the three cautiously picked their way down the slope.

'I do now,' Luke replied sadly, gazing at the thick tropical scrub below. He could hear the steady, low roaring sound of water over rocks and guessed it had to be the river that Christie had told them about. If so, then Cooktown was very close.

FORTY-SEVEN

'Sims,' Mort said as he watched the tiny figures disappear behind the rise, 'get the men together and follow me.' Sims, who stood a short distance away leaning on his rifle, turned and bellowed his orders in English. Although the first mate's orders were in a foreign language his belligerent tone translated into Chinese. Somewhat reluctantly, the Chinese looked to Captain Woo who snarled at his men to follow the white devil.

Grass burned to a fine powder swirled in the eddies of the valley's breezes around the pursuers as they trudged across the valley towards the saddle. Weapons were primed and senses alert as they filed past Henry's body. Mort spat contemptuously at the dead man. James was dead and O'Flynn was next!

Hawks and kites gathered in a swirling brown-feathered cloud to circle and swoop on the unexpected feast that the fire had left in its wake, while Mort and his men struggled up to the crest of the saddle. Despite his assurances that the survivors they hunted had fled from the high ground, they approached the summit warily. But without a shot being fired at them as they advanced up the scope they relaxed on the crest to gaze down the open landscape of the other side.

Sims saw the blood spattered on the rocks and a fragment of blood-stained shirt. Mort looked pleased when the grinning first mate held up the bloody scrap of cloth. The survivors had not come out unscathed from the ambush, he mused. And maybe their injuries would slow them down even more! With any luck their injuries might even prove fatal, but hopefully O'Flynn would be alive when they caught up with him. The man had troubled him in the same way that his nightmares did, and to hear the Irish bastard scream for mercy would exorcise the ghosts that haunted his sleeping hours. With a wave of his arm, Mort signalled to his men to descend, following the blood trail into the rainforest below.

The hunters were less cautious as they trailed down the slope. It seemed obvious that the party they hunted were in full, panicked flight. They were halfway down when their complacency was shattered by the explosive crack of a Snider rifle. Before the sound had time to roll away as an echo in the midday heat haze, one of the European crew men grunted, and fell with a bullet through his chest.

The pursuers momentarily froze in terror before

scattering to seek the meagre cover of rocks up on the saddle. A second well-aimed shot took Sims in the stomach before he could retreat. He dropped his rifle to clutch at his belly and with confused, terror-filled eyes stared at Mort standing on the slope. Mort swore viciously as he flung himself behind the rise. The sniper's ruse of ambushing had caught him like an amateur!

Michael flipped the breech of the Snider and slipped a cartridge in the chamber. With the systematic removal of Mort's former European crew members, the final fight was brought down to just the two of them. He did not consider the Chinese pirates to be an immediate threat; as he had noticed that they responded with surly reluctance to the murderous captain's directions when he had issued his orders. And the systematic killing of the two Europeans would demoralise them, he calculated.

He slithered from his cover behind an earth bank at the edge of the rise content in the knowledge that his ambush was buying precious time for the three survivors. It was not his intention to be located, pinned down and outflanked, and he already had selected a second position from which to fire on the pursuers. He tucked the rifle into his shoulder and searched for another target.

Mort lay on his stomach on the rise and was mysti-fied as to why the unidentified sniper had not shot him when he had the opportunity. It was as if the unseen man was taunting him, he thought, and killing the first mate who had stood beside him a contemptuous gesture that his life was the unknown sniper's personal property.

The thought caused Mort to shudder with superstitious fear, but he did not let his fear cripple his thinking. His fertile mind was already planning to out-manoeuvre the sniper. He would send half the Chinese under the command of the pirate captain to bypass the sniper and go after the rest of the survivors, while he and the remainder kept the sniper busy pinned down on the slope.

He called for the pirate captain who crawled up to where Mort lay peering cautiously over the edge of the crest and quickly issued his orders to him. Woo understood the tactics and slithered down the reverse slope to pick six of his best men who now had the task of cutting off the fleeing survivors. Woo preferred this task to remaining on the hill; the tangle of the thick rainforest would provide cover.

When the pirate captain was gone Mort took careful aim and casually shot Sims through the head. The first mate had tried to plead for his life, but fell silent when he realised that there was no pity in Mort's cold eyes. The Chinese on the summit stared sullenly at the white devil and pondered if following him could be any worse than returning to the tong and confessing the loss of the girl.

~

Michael had a fleeting glimpse as the pirate captain and his team plunged into the jungle. They were fifty yards out and only exposed for a second. He snapped off a shot and was rewarded with one of the Chinese pitching forward with a short, strangled scream of despair.

His shot was answered with a volley of musket fire from the ridge above him. He swore as dirt spattered his face from one of the musket balls that had ricocheted away across the slope. Mort had outguessed him, he thought bitterly, and was now attempting to pin him down. If nothing else, he consoled himself, he had forced his adversary to split his forces giving Luke and John a better chance in any armed confrontation in the rainforest.

He rolled away and reloaded the Snider. He had not seen Mort with the Chinese who had disappeared into the rainforest, and guessed he was still amongst the scattered rocks of the saddle with the remainder of his men. He could not expose himself for a second as the shots had come from positions closer than when he had first fired on Mort's party. In addition, he was now effectively pinned down until the night came to provide him concealment. By that time, either John and Luke would have escaped Mort's men or they would be dead and the girl once again Mort's prisoner.

Michael lay under the hot sun waiting for Mort to make his next move. At least he had a near-full water canteen and starvation was not going to be a problem, he thought with bitter irony. Before he had any chance of starving to death, he would be long dead from a bullet.

Mort had a fleeting glimpse of the man who had fired on the pirate captain's party. So it was Michael O'Flynn they were up against! He turned and indicated to the remaining Chinese that they were to recover the discarded Winchesters lying beside the dead Europeans on the forward slope.

The Chinese slithered forward to retrieve the rifles and gather ammunition from the pockets of the dead men. No shot challenged them, and they dragged the rifles back up the slope where they quickly figured out the weapons' mechanisms.

Michael's sniping battle could be heard from the river. It drifted on the air as a faint popping sound and seemed distant and unreal to Hue. She had asked John why the big barbarian with the eye patch had not come with them and he briefly explained the plan they had formulated back on the saddle. Hue wondered why the man should sacrifice himself for her. For whatever reason he had stayed behind, she knew she would never forget his sacrifice.

The river flowed between the thick tangle of rainforest with a strong steady current. Luke calculated that it was about twenty yards wide. They had been unfortunate to have stumbled on a particularly wide stretch of the stream. But they did not have the luxury of time to search for a narrower stretch, and he sought timber that they could use in their crossing. All he could find were fallen pieces of timber long decayed to an earth-like consistency.

Both men conferred and decided to dump their guns. They would keep only their knives as the weight of the guns could easily drag them down when they swam the river. The only consolation of leaving their guns behind was that Mort's men too would be seriously hampered by attempting to cross the fast-flowing river with their weapons.

Hue could not swim and shrank from the dreaded thought of having to plunge into the murky waters. The two men, however, were both strong swimmers and John promised the frightened girl that he would get her safely across.

She trusted him and tentatively waded into the river. The water demons snatched at her legs and she clung desperately to John's neck. He was forced to gently prise her vice-like grip from around his neck and he calmly explained to her how they would swim across. He would swim side-stroke and tow her with one arm. But she must remain calm and not resist him. If she did not panic she would not be a burden.

John kicked out strongly with the terrified girl in tow. The powerful flow of the river immediately swirled them downstream. Slowly but strongly he swam towards the middle while behind him Luke fought the swirling current with all his strength. They were halfway across when the shots and shouts erupted in the jungle behind them.

Luke had a sick feeling of despair. Caught in the water they could be easily picked off by marksmen on the shore. They were still a long way from the opposite bank which beckoned with a promise of safety and the shouting and musket fire from the jungle spurred him on.

Then the noise of terrified men fighting for their lives confused them. Within a very short time, however, the desperate shouting ceased. By then they had reached the far river bank and scrambled ashore, waterlogged but alive.

The brief skirmish was still a mystery. They knew it could not have been Michael Duffy who they had last heard firing his Snider half a mile or so away. He could not have reached the river in such a short space of time. But both John and Hue had recognised that the terrified voices were shouting in Chinese. Although neither could understand the other strange yells that blurred with the panicked Chinese voices, Luke could.

They were the war cries of the fierce Merkin warriors. From what he could discern, they had caught the Chinese unawares. The tribesmen must have always been close by, he thought with a shudder. But why had they not attempted to strike at them when they had reached the river?

Both Michael and Mort had also heard the distant sounds of the skirmish and the ominous sound of an armed clash caused Michael's hopes to sink. Had the Chinese reached the three before they could cross the river and killed them?

On the saddle above Mort smiled grimly. The distant sounds could only mean one thing: that Woo had been successful. He expected to see the pirate captain return with the girl before sunset. O'Flynn was now isolated from all immediate help, he thought with savage satisfaction, and it would only be a matter of deciding whether to leave him to his fate, or risk the lives of a few of the Chinks to finish him off.

It was a decision that could wait for the moment. There was still a chance that the Chinese he had deployed on the slope might get into a position to flush O'Flynn out before nightfall, when the damned Irishman could escape under cover of darkness. He glanced at the sun hovering low over a mountainous horizon and knew that the night's cloaking darkness was only a few brief hours away.

Running, stumbling and beating their way through the dense undergrowth, Luke, John and Hue put as much distance between themselves and the river as they could. Finally Luke gave the order to rest, and they slumped to the ground where the fecund scent of the forest floor rose up to tell them that they were still alive.

'Hear anything?' Luke gasped. John shook his head, too exhausted to provide a verbal reply. 'I think we are safe,' Luke added, with the semblance of a weak and tortured grin. 'I think whoever was after us has met with foul play back at the river.'

'Sounded like myalls,' John finally said as he lay back against the roots of a forest giant. 'Think they got the better of my relatives.'

'Think yer right,' Luke said, plucking at a thin

613

leech preparing to attach itself to his arm. 'So I don't think it's wise to hang around here too long.'

John nodded and glanced at Hue who sat with her eyes closed and her head back. The decaying forest floor litter had stuck to the bloody soles of her feet like a pair of Chinese slippers, and the exquisite paleness of her skin was accentuated by the mottled shadows. He felt a surge of pride for her courage. In the gut-wrenching retreat from the river crossing she had kept up without complaint, despite the obvious pain her badly cut feet had caused her. She turned her head in John's direction and her obsidian eyes gazed directly into his. No, it was more than pride he felt. It was love. The enigmatic young woman was the most beautiful creature ever created on earth. Or in heaven for that matter. 'Do you think you can go just a little further?' he asked her.

'I can with you beside me John Wong,' she replied softly and John felt the wave of emotion crash down around him, pummelling him with its violence. The woman fully trusted him, he thought bitterly.

Hue saw the agony in his expression as he glanced away and wondered at its meaning. 'Is something wrong?' she asked.

John shook his head savagely and lurched from the ground. 'Nothing is wrong,' he said. 'We have to get going.'

Puzzled at the sudden change in his expression, she took his outstretched hand as he roughly helped her to her feet. Then he turned his back on her and stepped out as if attempting to leave her behind. Hue followed. How was it that he could be so gentle one moment and then so cruel the next? She whimpered like a kitten when a sharp stick bit into her feet and John heard her pain, slowing his pace. He dared not turn to face her lest she see the agony in his face. She trusted him and he loved her. Yet he was leading her to certain death, on the strength of a blood oath more binding than the love a man could feel for a woman. Loyalty to the tong was not something he expected her to understand.

As he strode through the forest he tried to walk away from his torment. But she grimly hobbled behind him like a child frightened of being left alone. He knew his duty and Soo Yin would get his prize. But soon the night would fall, and he would be alone in his thoughts of who he was in his confused world, a world somewhere between Asia and Europe. John was hardly aware of the bitter, salty tears streaming down his face.

FORTY-EIGHT

Four items lay side by side on the desktop: a letter, a half-empty glass of gin, a loaded revolver, and its cleaning kit of rods and oily rags.

Fiona sat behind the desk in her husband's library and stared at the gun. It was her father's Tranter which, after his death at the end of a Darambal spear, had been returned to the family in Sydney by the new station manager.

It was a deadly weapon in the hands of an enraged person and it was the letter from a woman who now lay in a morgue that had fired Fiona's deadly rage. Gertrude Pitcher had described the events that had occurred in the very library where Fiona now sat waiting for her husband to return from his club. The letter had concluded with a heart-rending plea for forgiveness for the terrible betrayal of trust. She could forgive the former nanny but the same could not be said for her husband's abominable crimes against their daughter.

But Fiona also experienced the same guilt and despair that had driven the nanny to suicide. Why had not she seen the signs? Why had not she been alert to her daughter's suffering? She now realised why the nanny had submitted her completely unexpected notice to terminate her employment and understood Penelope's insistence on placing the former employee in a new house. It was not that the woman had been bad – just another victim of her husband's innate evil. Just another life sacrificed to satisfy his absolute disregard for human decency. Somehow Penelope must have learned of Dorothy's plight and coerced the nanny into resigning. Penelope had not told her as a means of protecting her from her own dangerous rage. Well, her cousin's good intentions had come to nought, Fiona thought bitterly. Not for her cousin's need to protect her, but because as a mother she had failed to protect her own flesh and blood.

Fiona's rage was tinged with an icy-cold reasoning. Hers was not the despair of a guilt-driven woman pushed to the point of suicide. She had been born a Macintosh and the inner strength of her illustrious warrior ancestors came to the fore. She had turned her guilt and initial despair into a rage for vengeance.

Fiona lifted the pistol from the desk and curled her fingers around the butt. Her older brother Angus had many years earlier shown her how to load and fire the gun. It was a cap and ball revolver where each of the chambers required loading with gun-powder, a wad and a lead ball. She could see the lead balls at the open ends of the chambers and knew it was ready to fire. All she had to do was point it at her target and pull the trigger.

She placed the gun on the desktop and raised the half-empty tumbler of gin. It tasted bitter. She would kill her husband and tell the police that he had accidentally shot himself whilst cleaning the gun. Why should the police suspect her; they were the perfect couple when they appeared together in public.

She realised, however, that the story of accidental death was fraught with danger; she must shoot him at close range. She had once read that powder burns were essential to prove the proximity of the shot and, coupled with the close range of discharge, understood that he must die from one shot only. Any more than one shot would destroy her feigned, grief-stricken story of finding him dead by his own hand. That she was alone in the house with the servants out on errands at least meant that no-one else would be involved to witness for the police. She would simply play the distraught wife and wear black.

The lazy tick-tock of the big clock in the hall-way outside the library came to her like the booming of ocean breakers; but the distant sounds of horse hooves on the street was a soft clop-clop that was strangely reassuring. It was as if the world was completely unaware of what was about to happen.

Fiona heard the clattering noise of Granville's coach on the gravel driveway. She reached for the pistol, surprised at how calm she was feeling considering that she was about to slay her husband. In her mind his claim to being her husband and his daughters' father had been forfeited the moment he had abused Dorothy. She was resolved in her mission when she remembered the words in Gertrude Pitcher's letter. They helped keep her nerve as she listened intently for the coach to rattle away, vaguely conscious of everything around her, including little things she had once taken for granted. Even the click of the front door being opened seemed to drift to her at the top of the stairs as something unique.

There was a brief moment of silence when she could feel her heart pounding in her breast. The ominous silence was broken by the sound of Granville's footsteps on the stairway. Her hand trembled as she levelled the gun at the doorway and she was forced to grip the revolver in both hands to steady it as the library door was opened and Granville stepped inside.

His eyes took time to adjust to the dimly-lit interior of the library. 'Fiona!' he gasped when he became aware of his wife's presence – and of the gun pointed at his chest. 'What in damnation are you doing woman?'

'I am going to kill you Granville,' she hissed, watching as he blanched in terror. Their eyes locked and he saw the absolute determination in her eyes. He was struck speechless and stood frozen in the open doorway. 'I am going to kill you for what you have done to my daughter and probably for all the death and misery I know you have caused throughout your evil life,' she added in an icy tone, her hands no longer trembling.

'Why? What have I done to deserve this?' he finally croaked as Fiona stood up and walked around the edge of the big desk to plant herself before him. Not once had the barrel of the gun wavered.

'At first I was only going to kill you for the shame that you brought on my daughter,' she said calmly. 'But I think I am doing this just as much for my beautiful brother David . . . and God knows how many other innocent people's lives you have destroyed over the years.'

'What are you talking about?' Granville pleaded. 'What do you mean about David?'

'I know in my heart that you had him murdered,' she replied with an edge of sadness. 'I had always tried to tell myself that you were not involved despite my mother's insistence that you gave orders to Captain Mort for my brother's death. But my time with you has confirmed beyond any doubt in my mind that my mother was right.'

'Your mother is a mad woman,' Granville spat. 'She is out to do you harm.'

'Not I,' Fiona answered. 'I can see that now. My mother is a woman not unlike myself. And like my mother I know that I am capable of killing you here and now.'

Granville had a fleeting thought of another time and place. Many years before he had wondered if his wife had any of the characteristics of her mother. He had always feared Enid and now knew that his fears were justified. Fiona indeed had all the characteristics of her ruthless mother. All these years he had been living with another Enid Macintosh. But his terror was rapidly being replaced with an animal cunning to survive. 'If you kill me,' he said licking his lips, 'you will surely hang for murder and that will be a shame your daughters will have to live with. No, dear wife, you will not shoot me. Your sense of family honour is too strong.'

'You will go to the desk and sit down,' Fiona said, ignoring his attempt to appeal to her fears. 'There is a letter on the desk I want you to read.' If he was sitting at the desk when she shot him, her story of his accidental death would be more believable when the police arrived.

Granville glanced suspiciously at the desk then back at his wife. 'Reading a letter has little relevance to my life if you intend to kill me,' he replied. For a brief moment he found his attention drawn to the revolver in her hand. He had not wanted to even look at the deadly weapon but something had clicked in his mind when his eyes roamed over the Tranter. 'But I do not think you are going to do that.'

The sudden change in his attitude alarmed Fiona. Here was a man who knew a secret unknown to her. A dangerous secret, one which would threaten her safety. 'If you give me the gun of your own free will, I might not thrash you to within an inch of your life.'

They faced each other a pace apart and Granville stepped towards her. Fiona raised the loaded revolver uncertainly and levelled it at his chest. She had not wanted to kill him in the doorway; that would be harder to explain later. But his sudden threatening movement forced her to pull the trigger.

Just an empty click as the firing pin connected with the chamber!

Fiona felt a stinging pain as the back of her husband's hand caught her savagely across the face. The force of the blow sent her reeling across the room and she slammed against the wall displaying the Aboriginal weapons taken after the dispersal. With a clatter, the spears, shields and fighting sticks fell around her as she sat on the floor stunned by the blow. Her head was awash with red sparks, and she was vaguely aware that Granville was standing over her with the Tranter pointed at her head. 'Before you can fire this pistol you require percussion caps over the chambers, dear wife,' he said with a cold fury. 'For a moment I could not believe that you would even dare pull the trigger. You were truly going to kill me.'

Fiona could taste blood in her mouth and the red stars were fading. She realised that in his cold fury her husband was now capable of killing her. Her hand rested on something hard – a short spear with ornate barbs intended to rip its prey and lodge inside. It was now or never. If she did not kill him he would certainly kill her. With all the strength she could muster she gripped the spear and thrust it upwards at her husband. Startled, Granville yelped and leapt aside to avoid the point from taking him under the chin, the gun in his hand now as useless to him as it had been to Fiona.

Fiona was on her feet but still too groggy to continue a determined assault. However, she did have the consolation of seeing the fear return to her husband's eyes as he backed towards the door. 'You will never see my daughters again,' she spat between tears of frustration as she advanced on him with the spear. 'I may not be able to kill you now but so long as I am alive I swear you will never go near Dorothy and Helen again. I am taking them with me to Germany to live near Penelope and Manfred while you will continue to provide us with the means to live in the style befitting the daughter and grand-daughters of Sir Donald Macintosh.'

As he continued to back to the doorway, Granville nodded his agreement to her terms. He had once been told that some Aboriginal spears were tipped in a deadly poison that could bring a slow and agonising death. Even a nick from one of the barbs could be fatal and he was taking no chances of a mistake occurring. His wife had the upper hand – at least until he could find a way to disarm her.

The click of the front door drew them both to their senses. The housemaid had returned with a parcel of groceries. 'Are you there Missus White?' she cheerfully called from the foyer. Granville pocketed the pistol and Fiona lowered the spear. 'I am here,' Fiona answered in a tired voice. The confrontation had emotionally drained her. How close she had come to murdering her husband. He scowled as he turned to walk away and she could hear his angry voice from the foyer, telling the maid that he would be moving into his club. Confused, the maid glanced up to see her mistress standing at the head of the stairs. With a shock she could see that there was a large swelling around her mistress's left eye and blood smeared across her face. But more of a shock was seeing the Aboriginal spear still gripped in her hands. It did not take a policeman to figure out what had happened, the maid thought. Mister White had savagely attacked her mistress. She clucked her sympathy and dropping the groceries, rushed to Fiona's side.

FORTY-NINE

Michael placed the remaining rounds for the Snider within easy reach and scanned the bush around him carefully for any signs of movement. He was rewarded for his alertness. The grass was moving in an odd way on the forward slope of the saddle. He pushed his rifle forward. One hundred yards he calculated, and set the rear sight for the range.

Someone was crawling towards a low jumble of rocks on the slope, he guessed grimly. With fire support from the saddle he would be in a position to catch him in a cross-fire. Michael squeezed off a shot and the rifle butt bit reassuringly into his shoulder. Although the bullet missed, it did pass close enough to the crawling man to cause him to leap to his feet and dash for the rocks.

Michael expertly flipped the breech and reloaded. His sights were set and he had the range.

He aimed at a point slightly in front of the running man and fired. The terrified Chinese had almost reached the safety of the rocks when his ribs were smashed by the lead bullet. His forward momentum propelled him into the rocks where he crumpled like a rag doll. With the expertise of an experienced soldier, Michael had reloaded, even before the man had crashed into the rocks.

Michael hugged the earth and the expected return fire from the saddle above splattered around him. The concave shape of the slope provided extra protection against direct fire, and the Irish mercenary knew that he was safe in his position, so long as he kept them at bay. He also knew that he could meet any rash assault with the Colt that lay reassuringly beside his hand. Mort might have him pinned down, but they were again at a stalemate. For the next four hours neither side made a move.

Mort had watched the drama with professional interest. O'Flynn was deadly with the Snider, he admitted. He had to admire his adversary's skill. The former police officer reassessed the situation. Maybe the night would provide him with the chance to turn the tables on O'Flynn. It would also provide an opportunity to use stealth in an attack under the cover of darkness when Woo returned with the Cochinese girl and his extra men.

It was just before sunset when one of the Chinese sentries found the pirate captain crawling towards him. Half his face had been sliced away by some kind of axe and he was losing a lot of blood. Although his injury was horrific, Mort figured that the man would probably live, albeit remaining horribly disfigured for the rest of his life. 'You say the girl got away! You incompetent bastard,' Mort spat savagely, and the pirate glared at him with hate-filled eyes.

'Black man, many black man attack,' the pirate captain babbled through waves of pain from his terrible wound. 'White man with them, boss man to black man. Kill all Chinee man . . . kill me.'

Mort shook his head and sighed bitterly. It was all over! He knew the survivors of O'Flynn's party would be just about at Cooktown by the time they went after them. And besides, with O'Flynn still alive and on the slope with his deadly Snider, he still posed a threat to them. He was certain that O'Flynn had already resigned himself to die – and seemed determined to take as many of them as possible to hell with him.

Well, if that is what you want, Mister O'Flynn, Mort brooded as he watched the pirate captain bind his wound with his jacket, that's what you will get. Woo was tough and Mort was glad that the pirate captain had lived through the Aboriginal attack. He needed every man who could fire a rifle to grant O'Flynn's death wish.

Mort slid the infantry sword from its scabbard and placed it by his side. He gazed westward at the slowly sinking orange ball of light. The approaching night came as a gentle pink glow in the west as the long shadows crept across the grassy slope. Then the gentle breeze dropped and the glow was gone, replaced by deeper and softer shadows. And finally the shadows were gone, absorbed by the darkness that came with stars filling the sky with sparkling crystalline light and shining down on the lone sniper lying out on the slope.

Michael's shoulder throbbed from the wound. When he tried to crawl to another position he felt his shirt sticking to his back where the blood had congealed from his wound. He felt a strange and beautiful peace descend on him. So, he was slowly bleeding to death, he thought idly, and made a feeble attempt to reach for his water canteen to quench his raging thirst. Dying was not as bad as he thought it would be, and with all the strength he could muster, he brought the canteen to his lips.

'O'Flynn!' Mort's voice cut across the calm of the tropical night. 'If you can hear me I would like you to know that I will kill you myself. O'Flynn . . . ?'

So the murdering bastard wants to know if I'm still out here, Michael thought dreamily as the waves of euphoria washed over him.

'O'Flynn?' Mort called again. Had the Irishman slipped away in the dark? He raised his head cautiously to peer over the edge of the saddle. There was nothing out there except the foreboding silence and the sinister night. 'Woo,' Mort whispered softly to the pirate captain who sat holding a shirt to the side of his badly injured face. 'Get a couple of your men to go down and see if our friend is still there.'

Woo hesitated, but was acutely aware that the

devil had his rifle pointed at him. Now that the girl was well out of their grasp, he had no reason to follow the orders of the barbarian demon, except that he had an evil aura that made even the tough Chinese pirate think twice about killing him. Maybe later, he mused, and hissed orders to two of his men. They slithered over the rim of the rise, crawling cautiously towards where they suspected the leader of the men who had caused them so much trouble to be. These men had crept upon the fishing villages of their helpless victims in the dark, and night fighting was a form of warfare that suited their tastes.

A rustling in the grass . . . a snake . . . or a small marsupial hunter in search of prey? Lying on his back, Michael fought the urge to keep his eyes closed. He knew he must be ready, no matter how seductive the world beyond the darkness that beckoned to him with promises of eternal sleep. The chirping of the crickets had ceased. With the Colt in one hand, and the rifle in the other, Michael rolled very slowly onto his stomach, the painful effort causing his vision to twirl and blur.

They loomed simultaneously as silhouettes against the night sky. The two men were so close that Michael thrust the barrel of his rifle into one of the men's chest when he pulled the trigger. Both Chinese had moved too soon and their fatal miscalculation cost them their lives. Michael emptied his Colt into the second man who had fired wildly in the dark.

Mort heard the shots and the unnerving, strangled death screams. At least he was certain that the Irishman was still out there. But why had he not used the night to escape? Because he could not! The Irishman must be badly wounded. Even so, he had to presume that the two men sent out to stalk O'Flynn had joined their ancestors in the next world. All he could do now was wait for the first light of morning. O'Flynn would be dead – or at least in no shape to resist a final assault on his position.

Mort rolled on his back. A few hours sleep was important if he was to have the vital edge for the final confrontation in the morning. And before he drifted into sleep, he had the satisfaction of knowing that the Irishman could not afford to close his eyes if he were to stay alive to see another dawn.

Michael closed his eyes. On a grassy slope of an unnamed hill, he entered a twilight world where he hovered between life and death. The dreams that came to his fevered mind were as real to him as the two dead Chinese only a few feet away staring with sightless eyes up at the Southern Cross. His night was filled with the ghostly faces of comrades long dead. He spoke to them, his fevered words drifting across the dark void.

The pistol slipped from his fingers.

Mort woke and shuddered with superstitious fear as he listened to the litany for the dead. It was as if his adversary was calling on a phantom army. 'Shut up you Irish bastard!' he screamed down the slope.

For a fleeting moment he entertained the idea that he could go down the slope and finish O'Flynn off with a thrust from his sword. But he cautioned himself that O'Flynn might be playing an elaborate ruse to lure him. No, he would wait until the morning; he would not allow the ranting of the man to keep him awake!

In his world of ghosts Michael walked the corridors of his life. Or was it that his life was a parade that passed before him? Sometimes he would choose to linger: to stop and watch Aunt Bridget stoking the kitchen fire at the Erin Hotel, or climb a tree in Fraser's paddock with Daniel, when they were boys. Now he was teasing Katie, who scowled at him for his mischief; and now he was on a beach where seagulls cried with human voices. Fiona was holding his hand, and he held the hand of a little boy with green eyes.

'Patrick!'

The name screamed in the night snapped Mort from his fitful sleep. He sat bolt upright staring with mad eyes into the dark. But there was nothing out there, except the ramblings of the Irishman, and the great canopy of stars shimmering overhead. The Irishman had screamed the name of the teamster he had slain so long ago.

Asleep in her bed in Cooktown, Kate was catapulted into consciousness by a scream. She sat up and could hear her own laboured breathing and the thump of her heart. But she sensed that she was not being threatened, and that the scream had no physical substance. A nightmare, she decided, as she pulled a shawl around her shoulders, and slipped from the bed to check on the sleeping children.

Reassured that they were safe in their beds, Kate returned to her bedroom where she sat in a chair with the lantern on a sideboard, lighting the tiny space that she shared with no man.

The silent scream still haunted her as the room seemed to resound with its echo. It had been so real. As real as had the experience eleven years earlier, when the old Aboriginal had come to her on the brigalow plains of central Queensland. He had been daubed in ochre and covered with colourful feathers. Kate still had vivid memories of his surreal visit in the night. He had come to her on the wings of an eagle and revealed in her dreams the destruction of his people. He had spoken to her of a spirit person – a white warrior – whose destiny was bound in blood and revenge. The images had been vague, however, and the time of destiny too far in the future for the seventeen-year-old girl to comprehend.

As she sat staring, her present dreams returned as frightening whispers; a vision of a muddy pool of water and an evil-eyed crow. The shadow of death stalked a member of her family. In despair Kate realised that there was nothing she could do to prevent the imminent tragedy.

But whose death – or dying – had reached out to her?

Tears welled in her eyes and she reached for a pen and paper. It was time to write to her family in faraway Sydney. She suspected that, in due course, she would receive a letter informing her of a death in the family.

As Kate poised with the pen over the blank page she had the oddest of thoughts. For a moment an image of her long-dead brother Michael came to her. She shook her head, dismissing the strange recollection of him. But the thoughts of her brother persisted.

She placed the pen in the inkwell and attempted to rationalise her thoughts. Was it because she had been so close to Michael in life that his spirit should naturally come to her thoughts when she had a premonition of a death in the family? That her ancient Celtic blood turned her brother into a bearer of tragic news in her life? Whatever the answer was, she knew that soon she would learn of a death in the family, and it would not surprise her.

She lifted the pen from the inkwell once more. She could hear the calls of the distant curlews in the night, a high keening moan which caused her to shudder.

FIFTY

Michael woke with the sun in his face and a raging thirst. His shoulder felt as if it was on fire and his body was covered in a sticky sheen of sweat. *The fevered dreams had been so real!* And there was something important in the dreams. *Something that he must remember . . .*

He rolled painfully onto his stomach and reached for the canteen and swallowed the water until there was none left. He felt better for drinking but he was still very feverish and his shoulder throbbed even more than the day before.

A shadow fell across him. Michael rolled on his back and snatched desperately for his pistol, with the despairing recollection that he had not reloaded.

The boot came down on his wrist with a jarring crunch and a voice above him snarled. 'I was hoping you weren't dead yet.' The sharp point of a sword nicked at his throat.

'Captain Mort,' he replied hoarsely as he struggled to sit up. 'Good of you to be concerned about my health. Did you bring your friends with you?'

'I'm afraid you scared the worthless bastards off,' Mort said with an evil smile. 'Woke up this morning and they were gone. Except for these two,' he said, indicating the two dead Chinese beside Michael with the revolver in his other hand. 'Just you and I left out in God knows where to chat for a while before I kill you.'

'Thought you would have by now, you murdering bastard.'

Mort ignored the slur. 'You are right about me being a murdering bastard Mister O'Flynn,' he replied calmly 'But I'm no worse than you. From what I can gather you have always killed for money. For me, killing has always been for the pleasure. Now, I think my motives are far purer than yours. Don't you?'

He expected no answer from the badly wounded man at his feet. But what kept the man alive, he wondered as he stared at the dark splash of blood that stained Michael's shirt. Most men would have been long dead by now from the same wound.

When Mort shifted his gaze to the wounded man's single grey eye in which he saw a smouldering fire. Immediately he sensed that at this place, and at this time, he was fated to learn of something that had haunted him for years. In the dark hours of his deepest dreams the old Aboriginal had visited him. He had stood daubed in feathers and ochre and watched him malevolently with ancient, accusing eyes, causing him to wake screaming in the night. Nightmares, he consoled himself. But the spectre of the Aboriginal had come to him the previous night and had remained even though he had been wide awake.

'I have a question for you, Mister O'Flynn,' Mort said in a deceptively polite tone, as if they were simply two men chatting under a warm sun on another magnificent day. 'Did you ever know an Irishman by the name of Patrick Duffy?'

Michael did not reply. The sword was still at his throat and he could hear the sweet warble of the magpies calling. Tiny insects rose with a soft whirr. The situation seemed hopeless as Mort kept the point of the blade firmly at his throat. The same blade that had killed my father, Michael thought as he glared up at Mort.

Michael's attention shifted to an image straight out of the pits of hell. He shuddered and smiled grimly at Mort. 'Well you might kill me Captain Mort,' he said calmly, 'but I doubt that you will ever get out of here alive.'

A puzzled expression clouded Mort's face.

'As a matter of fact,' Michael continued, 'whether it is you who kills me or that party of myalls behind you it doesn't matter. We are both dead men it seems. At least I hope so, because I hear the myalls around here like to roast their prisoners for a meal.'

Mort shook his head slowly and smiled with feigned sadness for the desperate man's feeble attempt to distract him. But the slight whisper of grass underfoot caused him to feel a dread he had never known before. With the blade firmly at Michael's throat, he slowly turned his head, and was transfixed with terror.

Twenty or so yellow- and white-painted warriors stood ominously silent a mere ten paces away, watching them. They were naked except for the lethal weapons they carried. Screeching the blood-chilling cry of the black cockatoo, they exploded into action and rushed Mort before he could raise his pistol.

A wooden club came crashing down on his head with a sickening crunch. Stunned, Mort's legs crumpled under him as he was seized. The warriors gave a triumphant whoop as they hoisted him on their shoulders. Now he knew what the old Aboriginal had told him which he did not want to hear!

The painted warriors ignored Michael and carried Mort to the rocks where Michael had killed the Chinese pirate the day before. Puzzled as to why the warriors had left him alone, but still fearing their unwanted attention, he cautiously reached for the revolver Mort had dropped when he had been seized by the tribesmen.

'You won't be needing that,' a familiar voice called to him across the slope. Michael glanced up to see Christie Palmerston striding towards him from the rainforest.

'I thought they got you Mister Palmerston,' Michael said, as Christie helped him to his feet.

'No. I was lucky enough to run into a few old friends,' he replied grimly, casting a wary glance in the direction of the tribesmen who were holding Mort down on the rocks. 'They said they were sorry for killing the horses. But I said that would be all right. I promised them a good feed of Chinese which they got yesterday down on the river and they told me about your hold up hereabouts. I waited until this morning to come after you. Had no choice. They were a bit busy last night . . . feasting.'

A tribesmen swung his stone axe and smashed Mort's kneecaps. The stone axe had travelled north along the Aboriginal trade routes from a small, ancient quarry on a hill sacred to the Nerambura clan of the Darambal people of central Queensland. But Christie's narrative tapered away as Mort's drawn-out scream of agony filled the early morning air. He babbled for mercy, and soon would be granted it in the same manner that he had given it to the young girls who had begged him to stop their unbearable pain when he had tortured them for his bestial pleasure.

'I think you and I should leave Mister O'Flynn,' Christie said, quietly fingering his revolver nervously. 'Doesn't pay to be around these boys for too long when they get up a hunger.'

'Before we go, I just want to tell Mort something,' Michael said, taking a few tentative steps to test his legs. He was extremely weak and walking caused a giddiness that threatened to lay him out. But he knew he must speak to the murderer who had brought death to so many. He tottered over to where Mort lay helplessly on his back, spread-eagled across the rock in a semi-conscious state. He was whimpering like a child while the warriors argued over who should get his sword. They took little notice of the white man standing over their helpless prisoner.

Mort's pale blue eyes fixed on the man standing over him and Michael steeled himself against the unspoken plea for mercy. He stared directly into the doomed man's eyes. He wanted his full attention for what he was about to tell him.

'My name's not O'Flynn – it's Duffy,' Michael said softly. 'You met my father once, on the track to Tambo. Back in '62 I believe.'

Mort stared wide-eyed at the Irishman standing over him. *It was surely Patrick Duffy come back to punish him!* He opened his mouth to plead for mercy but only a long, piercing scream escaped his lips. And he screamed again, not for the agonising pain he was experiencing from the smashed knees but for what he knew was to be his fate at the hands of the dreaded tribesmen. He screamed. And screamed again until he could scream no more.

Christie gathered up Michael's rifle and revolver. Supporting Michael on his shoulder, he led the way down the slope as the two men headed north towards the river in an attempt to put distance between themselves and the fickle tribesmen. Mort's agonised screams followed them for a distance, until at last the noise was absorbed by the dense rainforest on the river bank, where they stopped to rest.

Michael felt light-headed and knew the fever was

on him again. He knew death would follow. Whatever had kept him alive long enough to know that Mort was facing his Maker seemed to have deserted him now.

But it no longer mattered as he had so little to lose. He had realised his old oath to avenge his family – an oath sworn in the beer cellar of the Erin Hotel eleven years earlier.

He stared at a kingfisher flying towards a log jutting into the river. The morning sun caused the bird's azure feathers to shimmer with a light so brilliant that it hurt his eye. Suddenly the hues of the kingfisher's feathers exploded into a thousand colours of the universe, and Michael slumped forward with a groan onto the carpet of rotting leaves, rich with the scent of decay. A voice called to him. *Remember, you must remember!*

Remember what? the dying Irishman asked the kaleidoscopic spirals of exploding light.

Christie was forced to strike a camp to watch over Michael for the night. He had seen death before and knew it was waiting to snatch away the Irishman's spirit. As he watched over the man toss and turn in his fever, he sensed that the dying man would need a stronger reason than his own love for life to fight the debilitating effects of the wound. If Duffy had nothing to live for, Christie thought morosely, then he was surely a dead man. The situation seemed hopeless. To get Duffy to Cooktown and medical help he would need at least one other to assist him. But they were alone in a vast land and in a region hardly explored. The odds of being found by a white man in the wilderness were next to nothing.

The soft crackle of a dying fire and a strange chanting sound brought Christie out of his sleep. An initial gripping fear paralysed him as he became more aware of what had happened while he slept. With his eyes closed he continued to feign sleep and very carefully wrapped his hand around the butt of the revolver beside him.

He knew the sound well as so often he had heard the tribesmen singing their songs at their corroborees. He slowly turned his head before cautiously opening his eyes to focus on the fearful sight of a wild-looking Aboriginal warrior squatting beside Michael.

With his eyes closed, the man was crooning softly. The dying flames of the fire flickered shadows on his black gleaming face. Despite his fear Christie found himself transfixed by the man's chanting, and any thoughts of shooting him seemed to be lost.

The Aboriginal stopped chanting and opened his eyes. Christie was acutely aware that he was looking directly at him and the gripping fear returned to break the spell.

'You got any baccy?' the warrior asked with a broad grin spread across his face.

'Yeah, I've got tobacco,' Christie replied, sitting up and blinking away the tension of the moment. 'You want some?'

Wallarie nodded and Christie rustled through his pocket for a twist. When he found a stick he tossed it across the fire to Wallarie.

'You got paper?' Wallarie asked patiently.

'Sorry, no paper,' Christie replied. 'Lost it a few days back when your cousins speared our horses.'

'Not my mob,' Wallarie grunted as he slipped the precious tobacco into a small dilly bag at his waist. Later he would find a leaf and wrap the whitefella weed for smoking. 'Blackfella mob from around here speared your horses.'

Christie peered at Wallarie and his experienced bushman's eye confirmed that the man was not a local tribesman. 'Where you from?' he asked.

'Down south,' Wallarie replied. 'Bin walkin' north to find Tom Duffy's spirit.'

'God almighty!' Christie swore, as realisation dawned on him. 'You must be that blackfella Wallarie I heard about a few years back. Thought you were dead!'

'Most whitefella think that,' he chuckled. 'Whitefellas think Wallarie a spirit man who come an' get them in the night.'

Christie felt the hair bristle on the back of his neck. Was he dreaming? Was the man squatting over Michael Duffy an apparition?

'But Wallarie come to get Tom Duffy's spirit and take him to his totem woman in the big whitefella camp.'

'Cooktown?' Christie queried, and Wallarie nodded. 'This whitefella not Tom Duffy,' Christie added. 'This fella Michael O'Flynn.'

'This whitefella got Tom Duffy spirit in 'im,' Wallarie simply stated. 'Don't know about this other whitefella. This fella got Tom Duffy spirit.'

Christie sighed in resignation. What use was it to try and explain that the man asleep in his fever was an American by the name of Michael O'Flynn. If the intention of the myall was to take O'Flynn to Cooktown to meet his totem woman then he had come along at the right time. Without medical help Michael was sure to die out in the bush. Between the two of them they would be able to get him to Cooktown. The town couldn't be that far away. 'Yeah, well you and I can get Tom Duffy's spirit to Cooktown when the sun comes up – that is if O'Flynn doesn't become a spirit tonight.'

Wallarie looked down at Michael tossing and turning in his fever, his face a sheen of sweat and deathly pale. He wondered at the wisdom of the cave spirits of his ancestral lands. The man who had Tom Duffy's spirit looked as close to death as any man he had ever seen before.

FIFTY-ONE

The bullocky bellowed his incomprehensible instructions to his ox team. The ponderous wagon, loaded with precious supplies for the Palmer goldfields creaked and groaned under the weight of stores, as the powerful beasts strained against the weight. He kept a wary eye on the track ahead while his young Aboriginal woman walked behind him, scanning the monotonous scrub that bordered the dusty, wheel-rutted track for any subtle signs of those who might attempt them harm – white or black.

The teamster, trudging beside his wagon and trailing a long stockwhip, stared curiously at the three people ahead of him on the dusty track. From their wild appearance he guessed that they were down on their luck. They were a sorry sight and the bullocky shook his head. When would they learn the Palmer was not a River of Gold?

'How far to Cooktown?' the tall man with the bandage around his leg called as he approached.

''Bout two hours. Probably three from the look of youse,' the teamster replied loudly so as to be heard over the creak and rattle of his wagon. 'Jus' keep goin' from where I came from.'

Luke thanked him and the three hobbled off the track to collapse amongst the shade of the tall eucalypt trees as his wagon rumbled past. The days of being hunted like animals were mercifully near an end. Exhausted as they were, they knew the next two hours would bring them into contact with the simple things in life: food, sleep and a hot bath!

John's thoughts, however, went beyond the immediate pleasures they could look forward to. His were dark and troubled for what he must now do. He had sworn an oath to complete a mission regardless of his personal feelings. But now his feelings were in turmoil.

He slipped his long-bladed knife from inside his boot and hacked idly at the ground between his legs. 'You know I'm supposed to kill you,' he said as casually as if he were discussing the weather and not the elimination of a man.

Luke was an experienced knife fighter but he knew that the younger man was in better physical condition than himself. 'Michael kind of warned me,' he answered, as he slid a knife from his own boot, 'that you and I might have some troubles when we got back to Cooktown. Fair of you to give me a chance, warning me first,' he said, tightening the grip on the handle of his knife.

John raised his knife and, with a flick of his wrist, hurled the knife at a tree on the other side of the track where, with a dull thud, it buried itself in the trunk. 'I'm not going to do it Luke,' John said, gazing out into the scrub. 'But I'm going to ask for your help.'

'Before you go any further,' Luke said, slipping his knife inside his boot, 'maybe you should tell me why you changed your mind?'

John's gaze shifted to Hue who was oblivious of the potentially deadly situation that had flared – and died – in the split second it took for the knife to leave his hand. Her eyes were closed and she slept in a world of jade and incense dreams. 'For her. For Michael Duffy and yourself. For Henry and even for Christie Palmerston,' he answered haltingly. 'I was given orders to take Hue away from you when we got back. And I knew I would have to kill you and Duffy to do that. But things have got a bit personal over the last few days. Duffy's staying behind meant he had little chance of coming out alive. I think I knew then that I owed you and him more than I owed Soo. And Hue . . . well she kind of messed up my plans to hand her over to him.'

'Pretty obvious you like the girl,' Luke prompted gently.

'Yeah, I do,' John replied wistfully. 'You know, Soo was doublecrossing Horace Brown. He was going to make a deal with the French himself.'

'Who's Horace Brown?' Luke asked. It was the first time he had heard the name of the shadowy agent.

'Brown was Duffy's boss,' John replied. 'He's the

man we were working for. And I doubt that he'd be very happy about what I'm going to ask you to do.'

'You want me to help you get away with the girl,' Luke answered quietly, and glanced across at the exhausted young woman deep in a blissful sleep. 'I suppose your boss isn't going to think too kindly of you doublecrossing him either. I hear your tongs can be a bit unforgiving about that sort of thing.'

John nodded. Soo would be more than unhappy. He would be murderously furious as he also had to answer to those above him. Failure was not tolerated. 'I want to get Hue back to her home,' he said.

'You know she is worth a lot of money,' Luke reminded, 'to whoever hands her over. To either the French or her own people. Michael and I had the same idea. If her folks back in Cochin China pay up you will be a rich man. Bit unfair on myself and Michael, wouldn't you say?' he scowled.

'I was never considering any ransom,' John retorted with a frown. 'Just getting her back safely to her family.'

From the young bushman's reaction Luke felt that he was probably telling the truth. Either that or he was the most accomplished liar he had ever met. He stared hard at him, but the Eurasian's dark eyes were absent of any signs of deceit. 'I'll try and help,' Luke finally answered.

John broke into a broad smile of gratitude. 'If her family insists on giving me anything,' he answered with visible relief, 'then I will split the proceeds fifty fifty.'

'Any split is three ways,' Luke replied quietly. 'Michael might be dead or he might not be. Either way he gets his share, or his share goes to Kate O'Keefe. It was what he made me promise when we last saw him.'

'Three ways,' John echoed, and thrust out his big hand to seal the deal.

'I have a gut feeling,' the American said pessimistically, 'that your boss Mister Soo will get to know that you have doublecrossed him when we get back to Cooktown.' The running battle with Mort and his men might be over but he knew the tong leader had eyes and ears everywhere in Cooktown. It would not be long before Soo was informed that the girl was now with him. The second running battle to get Hue out of Cooktown and eventually the colony of Queensland was inevitable.

Luke stood and tentatively tested his wounded leg. Against all the odds the wound had not turned septic. He limped across to John and placed his hand on his shoulder. 'I think I know someone who can help us,' Luke said reassuringly. 'But I don't think she is going to be very pleased to make my acquaintance again.'

'Missus O'Keefe?' John guessed.

'I'm afraid so,' Luke sighed. 'Think I'd rather go back and face Mort. At least we stood a chance against him. He only wanted to kill us.'

John smiled. Bloody women, he thought wistfully. More trouble than Horace Brown, Soo Yin and the French put together.

Kate sat with her hands in her lap. She was pale and her eyes were puffy from crying. Luke felt awkward now that silence had descended between them.

Both Emma and Kate had been in the store when the wounded American had hobbled back into Kate's life. Her first reaction was an overwhelming joy to see him alive, albeit in a pitiful state, but she resisted the urge to tell him so. Although he now returned wounded and weary from God knows where, she thought, he had forfeited any future chance of her wanting him in her life again. So it had been Emma who had tended to Luke's wounded leg and made him a mug of sweet black coffee. Kate's seemingly cool indifference hurt him more than his wound. He knew she would be angry but her silence was worse than he could have ever imagined.

When Luke broke the news of Henry's death as gently as he could Kate had passionately damned Michael O'Flynn to hell for allowing Henry to go with him. Luke did not tell the grieving women the real purpose of the trip except to say that they had been prospecting for gold with Mister O'Flynn when Henry had been killed by myalls. But neither woman was fooled by his thin story. Kate had noticed how uncomfortable he was in telling the lie. And Emma did not query him on details of Henry's death. For her the past was the past and any account he provided would not bring the big bear of a man back into her life. She wiped away her tears and waved off Kate's insistence that she fetch the buggy to take her home, saying that she preferred to be alone.

Henry had once said that grief was a personal thing and now Emma understood what he had meant. She left the store with her head down to avoid the curious stares of people on the street. Many had heard the rumours that her husband had last been seen in company of the notorious Irish–American adventurer, Michael O'Flynn, a man reputed to have been a soldier of fortune. It was obvious from Emma James's distraught appearance that something had gone badly wrong for her husband on the mysterious expedition west of Cooktown.

When they were alone Luke cleared his throat. 'I am going to have to ask you a big favour Kate,' he said self-consciously, still feeling guilty for having had to lie to the woman he had always loved more than his own life. How had things gone so terribly wrong, he wondered sadly.

Kate stared stonily at him. 'I will help you if it is within my power,' she answered coldly. 'If it is money you want . . . I can arrange that.' She saw his crushed expression and regretted appearing so hard. But building a wall between them was her only means to protect her own vulnerability.

'Not money Kate,' Luke said softly. 'I need your help to get some folk out of Cooktown. Without help they are as good as dead.'

'Then you will need money,' she replied less coldly, and Luke was grateful for the change in her tone. He felt miserable enough that he had to remain silent on the true identity of Michael O'Flynn. To tell her now, that the man she had cursed to hell was her brother, would have only caused her a grief greater than he knew she could bear. It had been bad enough breaking the news to Emma of her husband's death.

'Thank you Kate,' he replied gratefully. 'Some day I will make sure you get the money back.'

'I would rather have had Henry back,' Kate retorted bitterly. 'Nothing can help Emma's grief. Nothing can give a life for one that has been taken.' He had no answer to her bitter recrimination and sat awkwardly staring at the floor of the depot. 'These people you spoke of, who are they?' she added. 'Do I know them?'

Luke frowned and debated whether he should tell her. To do so might place her life in jeopardy. But he also knew that Kate O'Keefe wielded considerable power in the town. Maybe more power than Soo Yin, he considered. 'One of the folks is John Wong,' he answered. 'The other is a Chinese girl you do not know. But it wouldn't be wise for you to get mixed up in what I'm doing. Not right to risk yourself in this business.'

'Are Mister Wong and this Chinese girl in fear of their lives?' she asked. 'If so, I shall give Mister Wong all the help that I can.' Luke attempted to protest but she held up her hand to cut him short. 'It was not that long ago that Mister Wong saved not only me but also Ben, young Jennifer and her son Willie. Had he not risked his own life against the spears of the myalls then I may not be here now. It is only right that I am as gracious to him as he was to us in our time of need. I feel that you should fetch Mister Wong and the girl here until I can arrange passage for them out of Cooktown.'

Luke conceded to her argument but felt a gnawing fear. The last person on Earth he wanted to put in danger was Kate. As if reading his doubt Kate added, 'You forget that I have faced all the dangers of this place as a man would. As do all the women of the north who travel with their men. Except I have had to do those things without a man beside me.'

As Luke listened to her speak he could not help but reflect on the tough Irish mercenary whom he had befriended on the *Osprey*. He had followed Michael Duffy without question on the hellish flight from the murderous captain of that ship. And that same man had chosen certain death in defence of those he commanded. In Kate's words he felt the strength that was the Duffy spirit. 'I will go and get them Kate,' he answered. 'But I will need to borrow some things.'

'Take what you need,' Kate said as she walked to the door of her shop. She paused for a moment with her hand on the door frame. 'It seems from what you have told me Mister O'Flynn has shared the same tragic fate as Henry.' Luke nodded. 'I cannot say that I feel any sympathy for a man who,' she continued bitterly, 'would allow Henry to accompany you on your expedition whatever it *really* was. Mister O'Flynn should burn in hell for allowing Henry to go with him.'

'Kate, I . . . ' he swallowed his words as their eyes met. How could he tell her that it had been his suggestion that had secured the former police sergeant a place on the expedition? For that alone, he would carry the terrible guilt to his grave. He shook his head and looked away.

Kate closed the door behind her. Despite her protests of wanting to be alone Emma needed a friend. Or was it that she needed Emma in the confusion of her own feelings?

~

Kate found Emma sitting alone on the back verandah of her house. She was staring vacantly over the town below towards the ships anchored in the estuary. Kate sat down beside her and took her hand.

'I don't know what to say to young Gordon,' Emma said in a flat voice. 'I don't know if he will understand that he will never see his father again. Not even his body for a proper funeral.' She trembled and tears welled in her eyes already swollen red from crying.

Kate held her. There was nothing else she could do. 'Kate, don't be hard on Luke,' Emma said softly. 'He loves you. And I know you love him. Don't let that love be lost. You can't make Luke into something he isn't, you can only love him for what he is. Just accept that men like Luke and Henry are not like all those others who choose to live safely in their towns and cities. We love men like Luke and Henry because of what they are – not what they should be. Tell him you love him or you will lose something that might never come into your life again.'

As she rocked Emma gently in her arms Kate listened to her words. In her grief Emma was trying to give life: to see something bloom that she knew from her short time with Henry was worth the risk. 'Henry is gone Emma, because of what he was,' she said softly. 'Don't you resent him for leaving you and Gordon when he could easily have been with you now?'

'Oh, I'm as mad as hell that he is gone,' Emma retorted bitterly. 'And I even feel guilty for being angry at him for leaving us alone. But I married Henry knowing that some day I might have to give him up to the life he loved so much . . . give him up to this harsh land. And knowing all that I still married him. And I would marry him all over again knowing what has been.'

Kate looked away. She would never make the same mistake as Emma. There were too many men who were prepared to live lives as real husbands. Men who came home every night and were always there for their wives and families. Luke Tracy was not one of them!

As Kate sat consoling Emma, Luke went out to the bush to fetch John and Hue. Soo Yin's intelligence network would already have informed the tong leader that it appeared Michael Duffy's expedition had been successful in snatching the Cochinese girl from Captain Mort.

Indeed the information came to Soo Yin from the brothel of his rival tong. John Wong's greatest fear was about to be realised. He had been marked for a slow, agonising death for his betrayal of a sacred oath. Soo sent a message to his best assassin.

FIFTY-TWO

Christie Palmerston leaned on the table, staring with seemingly vacant eyes at Horace Brown. Around them in the crowded hotel bar, men swapped stories of good fortune and bad luck. The sun was going down and the bar was filling quickly with thirsty gold seekers.

'I got Mister O'Flynn back to the miner's camp outside town,' Christie said in a weary voice. 'The doc says I may as well get him a coffin.'

Horace sighed and tap-tapped the point of his walking cane on the floor. He had listened with interest to Christie Palmerston's unfolding story of the past few days. Henry James was dead, as was Captain Mort. Luke Tracy, John Wong and the girl's whereabouts were unknown and Michael Duffy appeared to be on the verge of joining James and Mort. He listened with interest to the strange tale about a wild blackfella who had seemingly appeared from nowhere to help the young bushman get Duffy back to Cooktown. As mysteriously as the Aboriginal had appeared he also disappeared. Although Christie had not mentioned the man's name Horace had an eerie feeling. 'The blackfella's name wasn't Wallarie by any chance?' he asked quietly, and Christie shot him a startled look.

'How did you know?'

Horace smiled enigmatically. How could he tell the man on the other side of the table? How could he explain the mysteries of life that occurred from time to time with rational explanation? He was aware of the name Wallarie from his discreet inquiries into the history of the Duffy clan. It was a name with a vague and almost supernatural overtone in their family history. A name to inspire both awe and fear. 'Dear boy, if I even tried to explain how I know of the name of your dusky Samaritan I think you would consider me quite mad. So let us move on to matters pressing the moment. You have no idea where Hue might be?' he asked, as Christie downed a shot of rum.

Christie shook his head and stared seemingly into thin air. 'No idea,' he replied. 'Could be any-where in Cooktown, if they got back all right.'

But Horace had an idea where he might find out the missing trio's location. Did he not have the services of the tong leader whose intelligence net-work in Cooktown was better than his own? 'I would like to see Mister O'Flynn,' Horace said gently. 'I owe him a debt for his courage.'

'I can take you to him tonight,' Christie replied, rising like an old man from his chair. 'He's not far away.'

'I will, in time,' Horace said. 'But I have an urgent appointment first.'

Christie nodded and bade his good night to the little Englishman. Horace watched him leave and brooded on the situation. The Eurasian and the American had Hue somewhere and he had an obligation to get her back and into the hands of the French for the sake of Anglo–French relations. Michael Duffy had kept his word and completed his mission. It was a pity that it seemed it would also cost him his life as he was undoubtedly a courageous and resourceful man. Horace rose from the table and made his way to the door.

Soo Yin eyed the Englishman from under hooded eyes as Horace stood in the small room where from time to time they shared their opium dreams. There was one other in the room with them, a solidly-built Chinese with a toad-like face and many ugly scars covering his body. Horace was surprised to see the third man in the room as he had heard from his Chinese contacts that the man was none other than the dreaded enforcer of the tong. A man very rarely seen unless someone's demise was imminent.

'I do not know where John Wong is,' Soo lied. 'He will no doubt report to me in due course.'

'That surprises me,' Horace replied in Chinese. 'I thought you knew all that occurred in this town.

I thought you would have known John Wong is somewhere in Cooktown.'

Soo's expression altered slightly and Horace thought he recognised the trace of a dangerous scowl on the man's face. His statement was a contemptuous challenge to Soo Yin's competency. Any other man would be dead for such an expression of contempt. But Soo was a businessman above all else and knew that he needed the Englishman's European contacts in the colonial service. Both men stared at each other across the short distance of the small incense-filled room. Soo Yin did not fear the barbarian who was, after all, an effeminate man who had a taste for both willing Asian boys and opium. Such a man was no threat, he dismissed contemptuously. From the corner of his eye Horace glanced at the Chinese assassin and noticed that the man was sneering at him. Horace could tolerate much in life, except contempt, and felt his anger rising. Neither the tong leader nor his killer noticed the flash of anger from behind the Englishman's spectacles.

'If you cannot help me find John Wong,' Horace said, 'then I shall bid you goodnight and return to my hotel.'

Soo did not rise but remained reclining on his pillows as Horace left the room. When he was gone Soo nodded to his assassin.

But Horace did not return to his hotel. Instead, he walked a short distance from the Chinese quarter and took up a position in the shadows opposite Kate O'Keefe's merchandise depot. Very soon his suspicions were confirmed. The Chinese assassin was in the street, mingling with the busy traffic of miners out for a good time. Horace had guessed that if Hue was with either John Wong or Luke Tracy, the American would have naturally sought Kate O'Keefe for help. Now it was obvious that Soo Yin was also interested in the Cochinese girl. Horace had long lost faith in trust. Trust was not a characteristic of intelligence work and he had guessed that the sudden appearance of the Chinese killer was too coincidental. The man had been fetched to kill John Wong and anyone else who might oppose him taking the girl back to Soo. Still smarting from Soo's contempt, Horace watched the assassin disappear down a dark lane behind the depot.

He is going around the back to seek a way in, Horace realised.

From a bale of cotton cloth Hue watched John Wong move about the small store room. He was like one of the great and feared tigers of her homeland as he paced, acutely alert and ready to pounce, she thought. And his dark eyes reflected the tension he was experiencing as they waited for the American to come and fetch them. 'You must rest,' she said softly and John ceased pacing, 'or you will tire yourself out.'

His warm smile seemed to fill the room and he sat down on the bale beside her. 'Everything will work out,' he said with a gentle sigh. 'Luke Tracy can be trusted.'

'I know,' Hue replied. 'He has done much for me

already, as you have.' John felt the brush of her small hand on his arm and he turned to look into her eyes.

'Hue,' he said, and paused. It was hard to find words delicate enough for the moment. They did not come and he looked away.

'You want to tell me that you love me,' Hue prompted gently, and he looked at her with an expression of great surprise. She was smiling sadly and he felt as if his heart would burst.

'I think so,' he choked, and in halting words continued, 'I think I loved you from the moment I first saw you with Mort's party back on the track. I . . . ' His words trailed away when he saw the expression of pain in the beautiful young woman's face.

'I wish it could be so,' she said looking away. It was not the way of her people to keep eye contact as it was considered impolite, even though Europeans misinterpreted the gesture as evasiveness. 'But I can never marry any man not promised to me by my family. I must return to my country and continue the war against the French invaders. Just as my ancestors have resisted the Chinese and Huns before me. And who knows . . . after we have defeated the French.'

'I love you Hue,' John said. 'I always will and want to help you in your fight against your enemies.'

Surprised, Hue turned wide-eyed to stare into the face of the man she had grown to respect – and even love – in the short time they had been together. 'You would journey with me even though I cannot return your feelings?' she asked. 'You would risk your life in a war that is not of your own?'

'For you I would,' John said simply. 'And maybe,

with time, you might get to like me enough to reconsider your family's wishes.'

Hue frowned. 'I cannot promise you that might happen,' she said. 'And I would pray that you remain in this country which is really your own. You are more of this land than of Asia. You don't even speak Chinese very well,' she added teasingly, and John laughed. Impulsively he gripped her shoulders and kissed her on the lips. Startled, Hue did not resist, and felt his kiss as warm as the breeze in the tropical gardens of her father's palace.

He drew back and gazed at her. 'Then maybe I might do a better job of learning your language,' he said, still laughing softly. 'I always found Chinese a hard language to master.'

Hue smiled. She so badly wanted to let this big barbarian possess her. She realised the great depth of her desire to always be by his side, but she must conceal her anguish from the man she most wanted. They were both in a time and place not of their choosing and she still had a mission to free her land of the European invaders. 'If it is in our destinies,' she said softly, 'we will be as one.'

That is all John wanted to hear. He knew then that he would follow his princess to hell and back if their destiny determined it. Hope was a tiny but intense flame that defied any attempt to put it out. Such was the strength of his love for the beautiful Cochinese girl. And, he suspected, such was her love for him.

~

Hah! Only the girl and the Eurasian! The tong assassin peered through a window in Kate's store. It would be easy when the big Eurasian went to sleep. He would pry open the window, slip in, and cut his throat. But he would have some hours to wait. It seemed the girl and the Eurasian were deep in conversation. They almost looked like lovers from the way they conversed, he thought with some amusement. And it would be a long time before they decided to sleep.

The toad-like killer felt reassured that the unlit yard would conceal him. All he must do was stay awake and then carry out his task. He had no fear; the victim was not expecting him, and he had killed many times before in Hong Kong, without any real fuss. He settled down with his back against a wooden fence and waited.

'Ah, my good man,' Horace said, suddenly looming out of the night in the backyard. 'I thought I might ask you a question.' Startled, the assassin stood up, knocking over an empty wooden crate.

How had the contemptuous barbarian moved on him so easily? Before he could answer his own question he felt a searing pain in his chest. Confused, he remembered vaguely the flash of light on a sword blade. The Englishman was only a face away and smiling at him as the pain radiated through his chest. How . . . what had happened . . . how could the effeminate barbarian kill him? He was, after all, Soo Yin's best enforcer.

Groaning with pain the assassin slumped to the ground, his fingers wrapped around the long thin blade of the sword cane. His grip soon relaxed, however, and he died with a surprised expression contorting his face. Horace placed his foot on the dead man's chest and yanked the blade free. It had been a clean kill, he congratulated himself. The razor-like tip had pierced the man's heart without him getting a chance to react to the killing thrust.

When the blade came free Horace casually wiped it on the assassin's jacket before sliding it into the hollow shaft of the silver-knobbed cane. He riffled through the dead man's clothes and found a large, finely honed knife. No doubt the weapon that would have been used to kill John Wong, he thought idly. And it would do to complete the task he had in mind. Softly whistling an old tune he remembered from his days soldiering in the Crimea, Horace carried out his task with the professional efficiency of a master butcher.

Soo Yin's ghastly expression gave Horace great pleasure. The tong leader had actually recoiled from the thing that had rolled with an obscene splattering of blood right up to the pillows where he reclined. He looked up at Horace who had casually removed his spectacles to wipe them, annoyed that some of the assassin's blood had smeared his spectacles when he had cut off the man's head. When he was satisfied that the spectacles were clean, he replaced them on the tip of his nose, and spoke. 'I have no doubt that you are somewhat upset that I killed your man,' he said casually. 'But I do not like being doublecrossed.

Or lied to. Both you and I know that the Cochinese girl is staying in Kate O'Keefe's depot. And as far as I am concerned, she will remain there under your protection, in the company of John Wong.'

'Why should I listen to you?' Soo Yin hissed. The head lay inches away, staring with sightless opaque eyes at him. It was acutely unnerving that the man who he had dismissed as an effeminate barbarian had killed his best assassin. When he looked up from the head to the portly little man standing before him he saw only an expression of mild amusement; there was absolutely no sign of fear at all from Brown, considering that he had dared make such a gesture. Only feet away were men that he could call on to kill the barbarian here and now without question. But Brown seemed oblivious to the threat. 'I could have you killed Mister Brown,' he continued. 'You were a stupid man to think you could come here in an attempt to make me lose face.'

'That is not my intention Soo,' Horace replied. 'You are a businessman, and as such I knew I could not come to see you unless I had something of importance to offer.'

'What might that be?' Soo queried. His expression reflected an interest in the statement Horace had made and he could see that the tong leader was even now forgetting the presence of the head at his feet.

'For your compliance with my wishes to leave the Eurasian and the Cochinese girl alone,' Horace said calmly, 'I will pledge assistance in you expediting the remains of your dead countrymen back to the land of their ancestors.'

'You have contacts in the customs service?' Soo asked with rising interest. 'Who will assist me?' How had the Englishman learned of his means of smuggling gold in the bodies of dead coolies being sent home to Hong Kong? He should not have wondered. Horace Brown was a remarkable man for a barbarian. Not only did he speak his language with fluency but he was also a spy.

'I have,' Horace replied, and Soo smiled for the first time in Horace's memory of the man.

'Then I will comply with your wish Mister Brown,' he replied. 'Wong and the girl are under my protection. But you must realise that Wong can never return to Cooktown whilst I am here. It is a matter of face, as you know from our ways.'

'I understand,' Horace answered gravely. 'I doubt that you will see Mister Wong after tonight – and your honour will remain intact. What has transpired is between you and me only. You can tell your men to retrieve your assassin's body from behind Kate O'Keefe's depot in Charlotte Street. Other than a missing head and a wound to the chest it's in remarkably good condition for transporting back to Hong Kong. Now I will bid you a good evening as I have a lot to do tonight. People to visit, old friends and all that.'

Soo watched the Englishman turn on his heel and give a little wave with his walking cane. He had always wondered why Horace Brown had required a cane when he had always appeared quite mobile without one.

FIFTY-THREE

Kate's money purchased John and Hue a passage south on a chartered ketch. The captain was more than pleased at the generous fee paid to sail south to Townsville with just two passengers and in return he asked no questions.

Luke shook hands with John late at night on the jetty and John's grip was firm with his gratitude. Both knew that their handshake symbolised a bond that could be called on at any time – and in blood – if necessary.

When John and Hue boarded the ketch tears of gratitude flowed down the Cochinese girl's cheeks. She choked back the words, '*Merci, Monsieur Luke.*' As she stood beside John on the deck she thought of many things that had passed in her life in the land of the barbarians. She thought about the big, scarred warrior with the one eye who had sacrificed his life fighting a rearguard action so that they could escape the clutches of the tongs. And the tall American, who stood in the shadows of the jetty, was risking his life even now by smuggling them out of Cooktown. And there were the others: The big Englishman with the limp who lay dead in a dry, burned out valley in the mountains to the west. And even the bearded young bushman with the withered arm who made it plain he did not like those of Chinese blood. She owed them all a debt for her life. Big, generous and warm-hearted barbarians, with the courage of the jungle tigers of her homeland.

Hue did not attempt to wipe away the tears and swore a silent oath on the spirits of her ancestors that some day she would repay her debt to the men who had fought so stubbornly to return her to her home. Hers was a silent oath, sworn under the constellation of the Southern Cross on the lives of her yet unborn children.

Luke watched with a heavy heart the schooner glide gracefully between the ships at anchor on the river until it was swallowed by the night. They were all gone now – leaving him with his solitary life, and little else. John might never return with the ransom. But at least they were out of the immediate clutches of Soo Yin, he thought, as he turned and slowly walked along the jetty to the town alive with sound and light. It was just another night of drunken celebration for the successful miners returning from the Palmer with billycan and pockets full of gold. Another night of whores, gamblers, pickpockets and confidence men relieving the drunken miners of hard-earned wealth.

It was during the long nights that he felt the loneliness most. The exciting and garish life of the gold town was so much a pulse of his own life. An eventful life that had stretched back to his youth on the Californian goldfields of '49 and then to the Victorian goldfields of Ballarat in '54 and now, to the port town of the Palmer, twenty years later.

His was a life without roots. He was forever searching for a dream as elusive as the opium dreams in the smoke-filled dens behind Charlotte Street. He was somewhere at the beginning of the fourth decade of his life and he had nothing to show except the scars on his body, his callused hands and sad memories of a dead wife and child long buried under the earth of his adopted country.

But he also had memories of a young, beautiful Irish woman whom he had grown to love. Memories and scars, he thought despondently. He felt that his life lived out on the frontiers of the harsh and some-times savage land had left him with little to offer the future.

Somewhat despairingly, he unconsciously walked towards the hotel where only days before he had shared drinks with Michael Duffy and Henry James. Now it all seemed a lifetime ago. So many friends lost in such a short time. He knew he was going to get drunk . . . falling-down drunk.

'I think I should buy you a drink Mister Tracy,' the voice said at his elbow. 'You look like you need one.' Luke turned to the speaker who had joined him in front of the hotel noisy with music from a fiddle and the laughter of miners at play. 'My name is Horace Brown,' the portly man said as he politely offered his hand to the startled American. 'We have never met before,' he continued, 'but we have mutual friends I would like to join you in toasting.'

Luke blinked. This was the man behind the ill-fated expedition to seize Hue from Mort, he thought. 'Were you following me?' he challenged Brown, ignoring the outstretched hand.

'Yes and no, old chap,' Horace replied. 'You see, I ran into a mutual acquaintance of ours at my hotel this afternoon and he told me that you and Mister Wong got clear away with the girl, as far as he knew. Except that my other old friend, Soo Yin, hasn't seen his trusted employee since he seconded him to Mister Duffy's expedition. One could only believe that Mister Wong was avoiding Soo for one reason or another. I suspect that Mister Wong was under orders to seize the girl for Mister Soo to ransom to the French for certain favourable business opportunities he has planned in Saigon.'

'You suspected John Wong and yet you allowed him to come with us Mister Brown?' Luke queried, as he eyed the little man with the spectacles. 'It don't make a lot of sense to me.'

Horace coughed and cleared his throat. 'Well, it didn't really matter who got the girl back to the French,' he replied. 'The main thing was that the British government was seen to be assisting them, in whatever way we could. The means justify the end as they say.'

'You know the French aren't about to get their hands on her, don't you Mister Brown?' Luke said quietly, watching closely to gauge the Englishman's reaction.

'Yes, I know that. I saw you put them on a boat sailing for God knows where,' he replied.

Luke gaped in surprise and Horace was pleased to see that he had unsettled the American. 'Oh do not concern yourself,' he continued. 'I think, considering what the expedition cost in lives lost, we have impressed the French intelligence service with our efforts to assist them. I'm sure they will learn about the events through their own agents here and will be still grateful for the assistance Her Majesty's government has granted them. In a very discreet way, of course. As for any ransom . . . well I know nothing of that,' he said, with a conspiratorial wink which was not lost on Luke who fully realised that the Englishman could have easily prevented Hue from leaving the town. He held out his hand to the Englishman and Horace accepted the gesture of reconciliation.

'I think we will have that drink. If you're payin',' Luke drawled.

'It will only be one drink, Mister Tracy,' Horace replied. 'Because I think you will want to see Michael O'Flynn tonight, He's . . . '

'Michael. He's alive!' Luke exploded and grabbed the smaller man by the shoulders.

'Yes. Christie brought him in. More dead than alive,' he sighed. 'Seems his wound went bad on him and he's barely with us . . . '

'Where? Where in hell is he now?'

'He's with Mister Palmerston at the miners' camp outside town. But he could be dead by now. I'm afraid only a miracle will save him.'

It did not matter who had the girl, Horace reflected. And it was even fitting that the Cochinese girl was the property of the adventurers who had earned the bloody right to her.

With a casual shrug of his shoulders he reckoned on it being time to pack his meagre kit and go elsewhere. His mission in Queensland's far north was accomplished, and although the Germans had suffered a temporary setback in their efforts to annex the mysterious great island to the north of the Queensland colony, Horace knew that they would try again in the future. It would be his mission to thwart their attempts.

FIFTY-FOUR

The night was pleasantly mild and the children were tucked in bed when Luke came for Kate. She was writing a letter to her aunt Bridget in Sydney about events in her life when she heard the urgent rapping on the front door. She pulled a shawl over her shoulders and unlatched the lock when she heard Luke calling to her.

Luke's expression was grim as he stood in the doorway and his determined look did not invite questions. He ordered her to dress for a journey while he prepared the buggy for a short trip out of town. Kate hurried away and changed out of her nightdress. 'Where are you taking me?' she called from the verandah.

'The miners' camp out of town,' he replied, as he led the buggy horse from the stable.

Kate knew the camp well. It was a transitional place where miners stayed after returning from the Palmer down on their luck – or on their way up the track, to try their luck. It was a noisy place filled with the sounds of drunken singing, children bawling and the high pitched voices of women complaining about their spouse's drunkenness. As part of her charitable works Kate would visit the camp, to meet with the women, and ensure that their children had enough food and medicine. The beautiful Irishwoman was well liked and respected by the transient population of miners.

'Don't ask me why,' he added tersely, then, more softly, without taking his eyes from the track, 'I can't bring Henry back Kate but maybe I can bring back another life for you.'

His answer intrigued Kate. She had absolutely no idea what he meant. As they drew near the tent city, many who recognised Kate called to her cheerful greetings, which she acknowledged with a smile and a nod.

Luke hitched the buggy and led Kate to a canvas tent at the edge of the camp where they were met by the legendary bushman she had heard so many colourful stories about but never encountered. She was surprised to see that Christie Palmerston was not ten feet tall with the eyes of a fire breathing dragon. In fact, he was very ordinary looking, and his eyes reflected a deep and sensitive intelligence she found attractive in a man.

Christie pulled back the flap of the tent and Kate adjusted her eyes to the weak glow of a kerosene lantern on an old packing crate. She saw a big man stripped to the waist on a camp stretcher with a clean gauze bandage around his chest. He wore a leather eye patch and on his body Kate could see the outline of many old scars.

The man was sweating profusely and Kate guessed that he was in the grip of a bad fever, exacerbated by the wound he had obviously recently received. She looked at his face again. There was something vaguely and hauntingly familiar about it.

'Hello Kate,' Michael said hoarsely, before she fainted.

Brother and sister were left alone in the tent while outside Luke spoke quietly to Christie. They had mutually agreed that what had happened in the last week of their lives would never be spoken of and both swore an oath to that effect. Christie was especially happy to do so. It was bad enough that the traps were always after him for one thing or another. Accusations concerning stolen horses and abuses of Chinamen – but the killing of Europeans! No, the events never happened as far as the bushman was concerned. He knew that there was much he must do in his life, and the embarrassing questions that might be raised about the dead sailors from the *Osprey* could make life difficult for him with the authorities.

Holding his hand Kate knelt by her brother's side. She found herself laughing and crying as she stroked his thick, curly hair matted with dirt. She prayed that there would be time to talk as there were so many questions to ask and so much to catch up on. For now, she could see that her beloved brother was very weak. He drifted in and out of consciousness and this was not the time for such talk. His grey eye glittered with the fever and his forehead was hot to the touch. But he gripped his sister's hand as strongly as she gripped his.

'Luke brought you here, didn't he?' he asked in a hoarse whisper and Kate nodded. Michael shook his head slowly. 'Told him to keep his bloody mouth shut.' He struggled to sit up and Kate held a water canteen to his lips. When he had sipped the water he turned to his sister. 'Kate, I'm dying,' he said. 'I know it.' Kate's face crumpled. And the tears were no longer happy tears. 'Don't cry old girl,' he continued weakly. 'I've used up a lot of lives over the years. But at least I got to see you one last time . . . before I take that walk to the other side.'

'You aren't going to die Michael,' she said between her tears as she tried to wipe them away. 'You are going to get well and join me in the business.' Her tears splashed her brother's face as he slumped back on the stretcher.

Michael gave his sister a sad smile. 'Luke will look after you when I'm gone Katie,' he said softly, exhausting his last reserves of strength. 'He's a good man and I think he has always loved you. He must have loved you a lot, to get that slimy lawyer to pass on to you all the money he had in the world a few years back. And love you enough to risk his life facing him down before we left Cooktown on the *Osprey.*'

Michael's eye was closed when he spoke and he was not aware of the shocked expression on Kate's face. A lot of things were suddenly making sense. Things that had bothered her for a long time. Things like the donation Hugh Darlington had supposedly made to her. She remembered now that it was about the same time Luke disappeared from her life. 'Luke gave me that money?' she gasped. 'Not Hugh?'

'Never belonged to Darlington,' Michael sighed. 'The money was always Luke's. He was too proud to tell you and the bastard robbed him blind. Luke had too much pride to let you know he was always with you Katie . . . ' His voice trailed away as he drifted gently towards the abyss of death.

Kate knew that she was listening to his last words. Her brother was giving into the peace that waited for him on the other side. He had always been a fighter, but now he was being seduced by the sirens who called from the rocks of the abyss. She buried her head on his chest and wept as she sensed the life force ebbing from his exhausted body.

Remember! Remember and you will live! The distant voice of a child called to Michael in the darkness.

Remember what? He heard his own voice call as an echo in the night. The whispers came to him from all sides . . .

Remember the woman with the green eyes . . .

'Michael!' Kate threw herself across her dying brother and her anguished cry brought Luke rushing into the tent. 'Michael's dying,' she sobbed as she knelt by her brother, holding him, 'and there is nothing I can do.'

Luke felt as if his heart would break for her pain and very tenderly took her in his arms. 'A man has to have a good reason to fight on Kate,' he said gently. 'A reason stronger than his own life.'

She pushed herself away from Luke, her face set with a fierce expression of determination. 'Michael has a reason to fight!' she said as she knelt again by the camp stretcher where her brother lay listening to the whispers in the dark. 'Michael. You must fight to live,' she said firmly. 'You must fight, so that you live to see your son grow to be a man. Yes, Michael.' Kate's sternly delivered words were those of a chiding mother rather than a despairing sister and she noticed a slight response to her voice. 'Your son will need you more than any other person on earth when he too becomes a man like his father . . . '

I remember! The boy with the green eyes! Yes, the boy with the green eyes was not Daniel's son! That is what I had known the night on the slope. Michael could hear the voice calling to him from far away. *A boy's voice!*

'Father!'

'Patrick . . . my son!' Michael's whispered words seemed to echo in the tent. The barely uttered words assured Kate that her brother would not die. How he could know his son's name she could not guess. But she did know with all her body and soul that her brother would live.

She turned to Luke with an expression of serene victory. 'Michael will live,' she said triumphantly. 'He has much to do in his life. And I love you Luke

. . . I always have.' She rose to go to the arms of the American. 'And I'm afraid you will have to marry me Mister Tracy,' she continued with a wicked smile. 'Because if you don't . . . then the child that I carry will not have a proper father.'

EPILOGUE

On a clipper in the southern oceans west of South Africa, a young boy stood at the railing of the sailing ship and watched the big seas rolling off the graceful bow. The clipper rose and plunged into the wave troughs, and the night wind ruffled Patrick Duffy's thick curly hair. He felt the sting of the waves lash his face with hissing salt spray and felt so alone in the dark.

He did not understand the irresistible urge to go above decks in the stormy night. All he knew was that a woman's voice had called to him, like a soft whisper in his mind, from across the ocean. It was not a voice others could hear – and it was not a voice that he had heard before. He stood and stared into the howling wind that strained at the mass of canvas above his head, and moaned through the rigging with the voices of the lonely and desolate places of the spirit.

Lady Enid woke with alarm to find Patrick gone from the cabin. In her concern she collared a member of the crew to locate the young boy and the surly crewman reluctantly went in search of Patrick. He had a fair idea where the boy might be. He had seen a tall and handsome young fellow make his way above decks a short time earlier, and reassured the distressed woman that he would go and bring him safely below. It was not a good night to be above decks, he grumbled as he left Enid alone in her cabin.

He found Patrick standing at the bow of the clipper, deeply immersed in his thoughts. The young man could not know that the sailing ship was in the exact same waters where many years before his birth, Elizabeth Duffy, his paternal grandmother, had been buried at sea. Above the tortured creaking of the ship's timbers, and in the wailing of the winds of the southern ocean, he heard his name called. 'Father!' he answered without thinking. But when he turned, he saw only a crewman who had come to fetch him below, on Lady Enid's instructions.

Why had he used the word 'father', Patrick pondered, as he followed the crewman below. It was just a word that came naturally to his lips. At least he knew who his real father was. Uncle Daniel and Max had told him all about the legendary Michael Duffy. And Lady Enid had told him of how his father had died bravely fighting the Maori warriors in the Land of the Long White Cloud. She had also told him to forget the past. It was a place of ghosts, she had said.

Patrick paused at the hatchway leading down to

the lower decks and cast a last look at the storm raging in the night. He shuddered, not from the cold, but from a strange feeling that the ghosts of his past were all around him in the dark.

'C'mon boy,' the crewman growled. 'Get below before her ladyship has my hide.' Patrick turned away from the storm and followed. Before him was a life of unimaginable power and wealth. He had been assured of that by his Uncle Daniel and Lady Enid. But right at that moment he would rather have known his mother and father.

AUTHOR'S
NOTE

Little known to many Australians, the Palmer River goldfields of our northern frontier were the setting for some of the bloodiest scenes in Australian history. We will never really know how many people died as a result of murder, fever, hunger, heat stroke, hostile native actions and just sheer exhaustion. Every form of death stalked those who went in search of the elusive fortune.

But probably the people who suffered the most were the Aboriginal tribes of the region. Courageous defenders of their traditional lands, they gave their lives in a hopeless guerilla war over many years as their fighting technology was no match for that of the European invaders.

If the legendary Wentworth D'Arcy Uhr could be likened to the famous lawmen of the American Wild West, then the adventurer Christie Palmerston must have things in common with America's own Kit Carson. Christie's involvement with Michael Duffy is purely a fiction in this novel but his subsequent life as an explorer of the far northern rainforests is well entrenched in the Kit Carson tradition. A colourful and enigmatic man whose real life played like a Hollywood epic, the most comprehensive coverage of his life I came across in my research can be found in Paul Savage's work *Christie Palmerston – Explorer.*

But to mention Christie also warrants a mention of another real character mentioned in passing in the novel. In September 1873 James Venture Mulligan posted his famous notice in the little North Queensland frontier town of Georgetown . . . *J. V. Mulligan reports discovery of payable gold on the Palmer River. Those interested may inspect at this office the 102 ozs. he has brought back.* The rest is history.

It is interesting to note that in a skirmish at Round Mountain some months earlier, Palmerston and Mulligan, whilst prospecting with others, were speared in a furious fight with the northern tribesmen. Mulligan's life and times are no less colourful than Palmerston's.

And on the subject of gold, Kate's hunch about Ironstone Mountain would prove to be beyond anyone's expectation. It was later renamed Mount Morgan and turned out to be one of the richest gold and silver mines of the 1880s anywhere in the world.

Sadly, French Charley's, which was a real establishment in the days of the Palmer goldfields, is long gone. But Cooktown remains and is well worth a visit from the intrepid tourist.

The German attempts to annex the giant island of Papua New Guinea are a work of fiction in this novel. However, a well-planned and executed covert operation a few years later based out of Sydney, succeeded in an annexation of the northern sections of the island and its surrounding island groups. The subject has provided a real canvas for the third book in this trilogy. *Flight of the Eagle* is set against the years 1884/5 when the Germans succeeded in hoisting the Imperial eagle on New Guinean soil.

As for the rest of the historical backdrop, I again pay tribute and acknowledge the works of Glenville Pike and Hector Holthouse, whose considerable and colourful works provided the paint for the story told in this novel.

Peter Watt
Flight of the Eagle

No-one is left untouched by the dreadful curse which haunts two families, inextricably linking them together in love, death and revenge.

Captain Patrick Duffy is a man divided between the family of his father, Irish Catholic soldier of fortune Michael Duffy and his adoring, scheming maternal grandmother, Enid Macintosh. Visiting the village of his Irish forbears on a quest to uncover the secrets surrounding his birth, he is beguiled by the beautiful, mysterious Catherine Fitzgerald.

On the rugged Queensland frontier Native Mounted Police trooper Peter Duffy is torn between his duty, the blood of his mother's people – the Nerambura tribe – and a predestined deadly duel with Gordon James, the love of his sister Sarah.

From the battlefields of the Sudan, to colonial Sydney and the Queensland outback, *Flight of the Eagle* is the stunning concluding novel to the trilogy featuring the bestselling *Cry of the Curlew* and *Shadow of the Osprey*, with master storyteller Peter Watt at the height of his powers.

MORE BESTSELLING FICTION FROM PAN MACMILLAN

Peter Watt
Cry of the Curlew

I will tell you a story about two whitefella families who believed in the ancestor spirits. One family was called Macintosh and the other family was called Duffy...

Squatter Donald Macintosh little realises what chain of events he is setting in motion when he orders the violent dispersal of the Nerambura tribe on his property, Glen View. Unwitting witnesses to the barbaric exercise are bullock teamsters Patrick Duffy and his son Tom.

Meanwhile, in thriving Sydney Town, Michael Duffy and Fiona Macintosh are completely unaware of the cataclysmic events overtaking their fathers in the colony of Queensland. They have caught each other's eye during an outing to Manly Village. A storm during the ferry trip home is but a small portent of what is to follow... From this day forward, the Duffys and the Macintoshes are inextricably linked. Their paths cross in love, death and revenge as both families fight to tame the wild frontier of Australia's north country.

Spanning the middle years of the nineteenth century, *Cry of the Curlew* is a groundbreaking novel of Australian history. Confronting, erotic, graphic, but above all, a compelling adventure, Peter Watt is an exceptional talent.

Beverley Harper
The Forgotten Sea

*Not a pretty sight. Certainly not one the authorities
on Mauritius, that gem of a tourist destination in a
trio of idyllic islands once known as the Mascarenes,
would like to become public knowledge. Their
carefully nurtured image was of sparkling blue sea,
emerald green palm fringes haphazardly angled
along pure white beaches…This was ugly, messy.*

When Australian journalist Holly Jones flies to
Mauritius to cover playboy adventurer Connor
Maguire's search for buried ancestral treasure, it
promises to be a relaxing two weeks in an exotic
island paradise. What she hasn't planned on is an
infuriating, reluctant subject with a hidden agenda. Or
one who stirs the fires in a heart grown cold. But can
she trust him…

After the body of a young woman is washed up on a
beach, Holly finds herself caught in a deadly murder
investigation and the island's darkest secrets.

A compelling, passionate tale from Beverley Harper,
author of the bestselling *People of Heaven, Echo of
an Angry God, Edge of the Rain* and *Storms Over
Africa.*

'We have our own Wilbur Smith in the making here in
Australia'
SUN-HERALD

Matthew Reilly
Ice Station

At a remote ice station in Antarctica, a team of US scientists has made an amazing discovery. They have found something buried deep within a 100-million-year-old layer of ice. Something made of METAL.

Led by the enigmatic Lieutenant Shane Schofield, a team of crack United States Marines is sent to the station to secure this discovery for their country. They are a tight unit, tough and fearless. They would follow their leader into hell. They just did…

'The pace is frantic, the writing snappy, the research thorough. Unputdownable…'
WEEKEND AUSTRALIAN

'It never slows down…it is unlike any other new Australian novel'
DAILY TELEGRAPH

'There is enough technological wizardry, military know-how, plot convolution and sheer non-stop mayhem to place it in the premier league of international bestsellers'
THE WEST AUSTRALIAN

'His publisher compares him to Grisham and Crichton, but I reckon the 23-year-old is a cut above'
RALPH

'This is Indiana Jones goes to Antarctica'
NW

Juliet Marillier
Child of the Prophecy

BOOK THREE OF THE SEVENWATERS TRILOGY

A freezing terror ran through me. It was not just that I had done the unforgivable. It was something far worse. Had not I just proved my grandmother right? She had told me I bore the blood of a cursed line, a line of sorcerers and outcasts. It seemed I could not fight that; it would manifest itself as it chose. Were not my steps set inevitably towards darkness? I turned and fled in silence.

Raised in an isolated cove in Kerry, the young sorceress Fainne has been sent to live at Sevenwaters and burdened with a terrible task. She must use whatever powers she can to prevent the Fair Folk winning back the Islands, no matter what the cost. Even if it means denying herself the one she loves.

But can Fainne turn her back on the family for whom she has come to care? And, more importantly, can she bring herself to rid the world of the chosen one ... the child of the prophecy?

'Juliet Marillier is among the most skilled of fantasy writers – she is far better than Marion Zimmer Bradley. The Sevenwaters Trilogy is so beautiful, and so magically woven, that it deserves to become a fantasy classic. This trilogy should be a "must have" for any fantasy reader'
SARA DOUGLASS

Cecilia Dart-Thornton
The Ill-Made Mute

The Stormriders land their splendid winged stallions on the airy battlements of Isse Tower. Far below, the superstitious servants who dwell in the fortress's depths tell ghastly tales of evil creatures inhabiting the world outside, a world they have only glimpsed. Yet it is the least of the lowly – a mute, scarred, and utterly despised foundling – who dares scale the Tower, sneak aboard a Windship, and then dive from the sky.

The fugitive is rescued by a kindhearted adventurer who gives it a name, the gift of communicating by handspeak, and an amazing truth it had never guessed. Now Imrhien begins a journey to distant Caermelor, to seek a wise woman whose skills may change the foundling's life.

Along the way, Imrhien must survive a wilderness of endless danger. And as the challenges grow more deadly, Imrhien discovers something more terrifying than all the evil eldritch wights combined: the shunned outsider with an angel's soul and a gargoyle's face is falling in love…

In a thrilling debut combining storytelling mastery with a treasure trove of folklore, Cecilia Dart-Thornton creates an exceptional epic adventure.

'Not since Tolkien's *The Fellowship of the Ring*…have I been so impressed by a beautifully spun fantasy' ANDRE NORTON, author of *Brother to Shadows*

California
Contractors License Law
& Reference Book

2008 Edition

With Rules and Regulations

Contractors State License Board
STATE OF CALIFORNIA
Arnold Schwarzenegger, *Governor*

This book is an official publication of the State of California. It may not be reproduced in whole or in part without the express permission of the California Contractors State License Board.

The *California Contractors License Law and Reference Book with CD-ROM (2008 Edition)* is available from Matthew Bender & Company, Inc. Copies may be purchased by calling 1-800-533-1637 or faxing 518-462-3788; or by writing to Matthew Bender & Company, Attn. Customer Service, 1275 Broadway, Albany, NY 12204-2694; or through the Internet Website at http://www.lexisnexis.com. The price is $ 17.00, plus $5.35 Shipping & Handling and is available as follows:

> Mail order:
> Send a check or money order, payable to Matthew Bender & Company, Inc., and include a street address and the recipient's name. *All orders are shipped by carrier and cannot be delivered to a post office box.*

The *California Contractors License Law and Reference Book* is not sold at any office of the Contractors State License Board. Copies may be available from specialty bookstores—check your local telephone directory.

ISBN: 978-1-4224-4751-2

© 2007 California Contractors State License Board

© 2007 Matthew Bender & Company, Inc., a member of the LexisNexis Group.

All rights reserved.

LexisNexis, the knowledge burst logo, and Michie are trademarks of Reed Elsevier Properties Inc., used under license. Matthew Bender is a registered trademark of Matthew Bender Properties Inc.

The California regulations appearing in this publication have been extracted from Barclays Official California Code of Regulations, copyright © 2007, State of California.

This material may not be commercially reproduced or sold in printed or electronic form without written permission of Thomson/West, and is subject to the following disclaimer:

THOMSON/WEST MAKES NO WARRANTY OR REPRESENTATION WHATSOEVER, EXPRESS OR IMPLIED, WITH RESPECT TO THE MERCHANTABILITY OR FITNESS FOR ANY PARTICULAR PURPOSE WITH RESPECT TO THE INFORMATION CONTAINED IN THIS PUBLICATION; AND

THOMSON/WEST ASSUMES NO LIABILITY WHATSOEVER WITH RESPECT TO ANY USE OF THIS PUBLICATION OR ANY PORTION THEREOF OR WITH RESPECT TO ANY DAMAGES WHICH MAY RESULT FROM SUCH USE.

® LexisNexis®

Matthew Bender & Company, Inc.
Editorial Offices
P.O. Box 7587
Charlottesville, VA 22906-7587
800-446-3410
www.lexisnexis.com

Product Number 2970014

(Pub. 29700)

ABOUT THIS BOOK

The California License Law & Reference Book begins with several narrative chapters that describe many of the legal requirements affecting contractors. These narrative chapters contain references to the laws, rules, and regulations included in the later chapters. The laws and regulations contained in this book are those in effect on January 1, 2008, unless otherwise noted.

———

DEDICATION

This edition of the law book is dedicated to the more than 315,000 licensed California contractors who abide by the laws and guidelines set forth in this publication and whose hard work and professionalism help fuel our state's economy.